17 NOV 2010

Tom & Mary,

Thanks for being proud
U.S. Citizens and people
of faith. Keep on Pressing On!

HOSEA 6:3

Charles M. Causey

IN DANGER EVERY HOUR

- A CIVIL WAR NOVEL -

CHARLES CAUSEY

WAR MAPS BY KYLE CARROLL

WESTBOW
PRESS
A DIVISION OF THOMAS NELSON

Cover art by Dan Nance
www.dannance.com

WestBow Press books may be ordered through booksellers or by contacting:

WestBow Press
A Division of Thomas Nelson
1663 Liberty Drive
Bloomington, IN 47403
www.westbowpress.com
1-(866) 928-1240

ISBN: 978-1-4497-0436-0 (sc)
ISBN: 978-1-4497-0437-7 (dj)
ISBN: 978-1-4497-0583-1 (e)

Library of Congress Control Number: 2010933996

Printed in the United States of America

WestBow Press rev. date: 10/25/2010

CONTENTS

LIST OF MAPS AND PICTURES

Dedicated With Gratitude,

To the American Infantry foot soldier. Despite the worst of circumstances he does his duty. Fighting each battle through to the end, he gives people he will never meet their freedom.

President Abraham Lincoln's Cabinet in 1862

Hannibal Hamlin	Vice President
William H. Seward	Secretary of State
Salmon P. Chase	Secretary of the Treasury
Edwin M. Stanton	Secretary of War
Edward Bates	Attorney General
Montgomery Blair	Postmaster General
Gideon Welles	Secretary of the Navy
Caleb Blood Smith	Secretary of the Interior

PROLOGUE

The more war changes, the less people change. The prisoner thought about that quote from one of his college professors when he looked up at the man who just kicked him. It was dark and damp in the punishment room where the usual meeting took place. The man there was named Muldoon, and he glared back at the pitiful soul. The prisoner had been in confinement for weeks with little to eat and a beating nearly every day. The food deprivation was probably the worst punishment. He could feel the inside of himself starving. He could sense his muscles and other tissues wasting away trying to nourish him with each movement he made. His bruises never turned yellow and faded. There were always new wounds to set back any healing his body tried to create. This day he felt another rib crack when the boot struck him hard in the chest. When he was brought back to the other prisoners and chained to the floor, he wept.

The men with him were part of the government's "special" prisoners. They were the prisoners who knew important enemy information, the traitors who used to fight for the right side, or the stubborn prisoners who escaped confinement and were later caught. They were also the ones who would not reveal secrets about their government. When the usual torture techniques (performed in prisoner-of-war facilities sprinkled around Washington and Baltimore) didn't work, the prisoners were brought offshore. Now there would be no hope for escape. Even if they were told which direction to swim to find land, none of the prisoners would be strong enough to make any progress in the ocean current. As far as the eye could see in every direction from the torture ship there was endless roaring water. But the prisoners were never allowed to go on deck and take a look. Once a day the hatch would open for a moment and a tiny bit of fresh air would drift down when the guards did their interrogations. The crew living on the main deck of the vessel would quickly shut the hatch because the odor drifting up from below was unbearable.

The man continued to weep. It was his usual habit after a beating. He routinely thought it would be his last day to live, but the next morning the sun would appear, shining through the narrow cracks in the boards above them, and he would wake up to the same hellish nightmare. He began weeping two weeks prior. The pain and grief made the tears mostly involuntary. He hated being reduced to an emotional weakling.

"It would be much easier if you would repent of your ways and pledge your loyalty to us. Then you could die in honor instead of in rebellion," Muldoon said to the prisoners as a matter of fact.

"All right," croaked an older man sitting in a shadow in the corner of their quarters. "I will repent."

The guard laughed but then asked, "Are you serious, old man? Or are you merely wanting some fresh air like the last confessor?"

"I am serious," the man said.

The younger prisoner with the newly broken rib choked out, "Don't do it, Joseph."

"I will die today if I say nothing," the older warrior mumbled as the guard began to unshackle him. "I would then be tossed into the water for my burial."

"We died the day we were captured, and now you are burying the shred of glory you had left," said the younger inmate.

As the newly released prisoner crawled past the younger soldier he whispered very softly in his ear in the form of clearing his throat, "I'll let them know you're here."

PART I

INNOCENCE

The innocent and the beautiful have no enemy but time.
WILLIAM BUTLER YEATS

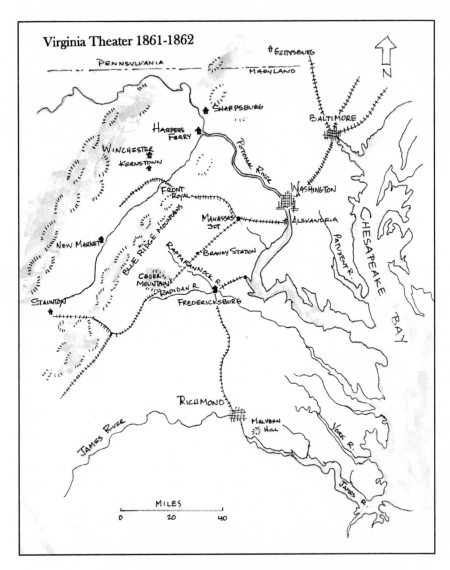

Virginia Theater 1861-1862

1.

Winchester, 1849

It was a beautiful, peaceful day—one of those warm and lazy Saturday afternoons during the summer when little boys play cowboys and Indians for hours and forget about suppertime.

Bruce and Moss Crawford, Riley McNair, and Henry Gallagher all sat by the stream on their newly constructed stone wall. They were daydreaming, listening to an assortment of birds singing high in the massive oak trees whose branches hung over the water. Big Brian "Jonesy" Jones was also there, stretched out across the fertile ground on his back. While chewing on a long blade of grass, Jonesy watched the slow-moving clouds without a thought in his mind.

The eight-year-old boys were resting after assembling a wall made with field stones from the pasture and smooth rocks from the creek bed. They had placed each rock carefully, one over the other, to make the two-foot-high wall.

Both ends of the semi-circle stone wall stopped at the creek, and along the inside of the wall was a nice patch of long, green grass and seven large weeping willow trees. The project took several Saturdays to construct, but the boys worked hard as a team and felt satisfied each afternoon when they left for supper. In fact, they had never worked on a task with as much diligence as they had on that wall.

The only problem with their project was that it was on the edge of the property owned by Kathryn Montgomery's family. Eight-year-old Kathryn caught them working one Saturday a couple of weeks before and told them she appreciated the nice picnic area they were making for her and her girlfriends. The boys were not happy about this new development and today they hoped she would not show up so they could enjoy their success. They were not at all lucky in this hope. Kathryn came by, and she was accompanied by Molly Harrington, Molly's older brother Ned, and Julia Bridgeman.

"Looks pretty good, boys." It was Kathryn, her blonde hair blowing in the breeze. She and her friends approached the outer rim of the wall where the trail ended. Ned hopped onto the wall and looked around. He was a little older than the other boys but not any bigger. His most distinguishing feature, besides his red hair, was his long neck. Ned Harrington rarely came out to play with the other boys.

Bruce Crawford usually assumed leadership of the group. Bruce had led the boys in many episodes of Americans fighting Mexicans, with himself being Winfield Scott or Zachary Taylor. One of his favorite pastimes was pretending to be guarding the Alamo or storming into Chapultepec. His little brother, Moss, was usually Jefferson Davis leading the mounted Mississippi riflemen.

Bruce didn't like these intruders climbing his wall. He immediately stood up on the wall and shouted at the trespassers, "This is our fort, and girls aren't allowed."

Molly, a spirited, bright-eyed, brown-haired seven-year-old, jumped over the wall and ran between the willow trees toward Bruce.

"Listen here, Bruce Crawford, this is not your property," Molly huffed.

"We built this fort with our own hands. We didn't ever see *you* helping us out," Bruce rebuked. The other boys all stood up with anger on their faces, tubby Jonesy being the last one up.

Lanky and freckled Ned, who was always a little ornery, tried to run on top of the wall around its curve and slipped off, knocking a stone or two out of position.

"Now look what you did, Ned," piped up Moss Crawford as he went to repair the damage. Bruce and Moss were brothers, born eleven months apart. Moss had just turned eight, and Bruce would turn nine in a few weeks.

Bruce jumped off the wall, took a step toward Molly and gave her a little shove so she would get the message not to come so close.

With fire in her eyes, Molly put both her arms out in front of her and charged her opponent. Bruce quickly attempted to dodge out of the way, but he wasn't quite fast enough. Molly connected with one arm, and it was just enough to knock Bruce off balance and fall backwards. Molly tumbled forward as well, hitting the grass with both hands and bouncing right back up. Bruce's pride was shattered. He looked up at her from the ground with real fire in his eyes and suddenly all the boys sprang into action chasing the girls.

Bruce jumped up and ran after Molly, who was already being chased by Henry. Kathryn and Julia didn't need any more inspiration to flee; the other boys, yelling like wild Indians, were pouring over their stone wall and heading right for them. The girls shrieked, turned, lifted up their dresses, and headed back down the trail.

"Don't you come near me, Henry Gallagher, or I'll blast you like I blasted Bruce," Molly yelled. With her arms out she made her hands into small but intimidating fists.

Henry stopped abruptly, and Bruce almost ran right into his back. Both boys glared at Molly as she turned around to leave. Bruce decided to mend his wounded pride of being bettered by a girl and charged at her back, pushing her with all his might. Molly was caught off guard, and her head and arms snapped back while her body plunged forward. She landed on her face, luckily on some old ferns. It was a mighty hard fall for a little girl in a dainty dress.

Jonesy and Riley had just turned around from chasing Kathryn and Julia and saw Bruce push Molly from behind.

"Hey, don't ya know you're not supposed to hit girls?" Jonesy bellowed out.

Riley walked up to Molly and tried to help her up. "Are you okay, Molly?"

Molly was more humiliated than in any real pain. Her face had some black dirt on it and one of her wrists hurt.

Bruce was scared now and felt sheepish. He meant to push her hard, but not *that* hard. He was sure when she turned around she would have tears in her eyes.

But not Molly. Her big, brown eyes were softer now as she got to her knees and said calmly, "That really hurt, Bruce." With her assailant speechless, Molly stood up—taking no help from Riley—dusted off her dress, and ran down the trail after her friends.

"I'm telling my parents that you hit Molly," Ned screeched, coming up from behind. "What'd ya do it fer, anyway?"

"You saw her push me first with your own eyes," Bruce mumbled.

"You better come over and apologize, or my ma is going to go over and yell at your ma, and you're going to get into trouble. That was Molly's new dress you just messed up."

"I'm not coming over to your house, Ned. Come on, Moss, let's go home," Bruce said to his brother as he turned to leave.

The boys all walked down the path toward Kathryn's house, and Ned followed behind, annoying the boys and wheedling Bruce about picking on a girl. Before they got to the large Montgomery farmhouse, the boys cut off the path and ran across the pasture to a dirt road which would take them back into town. They all said goodbye and congratulated each other once more on finally completing their new fort.

Later on that evening, during supper, young Moss couldn't keep the day's events to himself. He told his parents about completing the stone wall and about the visit by the girls. He then told about Bruce pushing Molly twice and knocking her down into the ground.

Lawrence Crawford looked up from his plate of corn on the cob, black-eyed peas, coleslaw, ham, and corn bread. "Bruce, is this true?"

"Yes, sir."

"Did you hurt her?" his mother Sarah asked with concern.

"I don't think so," Bruce mumbled. He really didn't like where this was heading and wanted to wallop Moss for being such a chatterbox that night.

"Yes you did, Bruce." Moss turned back to his parents. "He knocked her face into the ground and ruined her new dress," Moss added.

"Bruce?"

"She didn't cry!" Bruce pleaded hopelessly.

"Bruce, you know you're not supposed to hit a young lady—or really anyone, for that matter. Molly is a very nice little girl. What got into you?" Bruce's pa asked, a little more seriously.

"Molly knocked him over first," Moss said with a smile, and then went back to eating his corn and biscuit while Bruce glared at him.

"Bruce, it doesn't matter if a girl does anything to you, you are not supposed to hit them. The Harringtons are fine people, and I'm embarrassed about the whole thing." Mr. Crawford paused a moment, studied Bruce, then continued, "I would like you to go over there tonight and apologize for your actions."

"Oh no, sir, I don't want to do that."

"Bruce." Lawrence raised his voice a little.

"And I'm going with you," Sarah Crawford said.

"Oh pa, I can't do that."

"Why not?"

"Because Ned said I would have to. This is humiliating," Bruce whined.

"Do you even know what humiliating means?" Mr. Crawford asked.

"Father?"

"Look, you're going, and that's final—and then I want you to tell me about it when you get home."

Bruce mumbled, "Could ma stay here when I go?"

"Speak up, son."

"Could ma stay here? May I go by myself?"

"If that would make it less uncomfortable for you, then yes; your mother could stay here. But Bruce, I expect you to do this with honor and integrity. Don't disappoint us."

With that, Bruce knew the conversation was over. He slipped away from the table with one last look at his little brother who was now feeding Lucy, their baby sister. Bruce gave him a 'thanks a lot' look and then went into his room to find his shoes.

When he walked into his bedroom he glanced on the dresser and something shimmering caught his eye. It was a small bracelet he had made from some old copper fishing hooks. Bruce went fishing once in a while on the Shenandoah River when his pa would take him down to Front Royal. He was proud of the fact that one of his uncles possessed a "Kentucky Reel" and used it for fly-fishing. He had shown Bruce how it worked a few times and that gave him even more desire to spend time on the river.

Bruce made the fishing bracelet last week, twisting the ends together with one of his father's pliers. And though he didn't know if he would ever wear it, Bruce thought he could give it to his ma for a gift sometime. Now, without thinking too much about it, Bruce grabbed the bracelet and put it into his pocket.

When he got to Molly's house there was an unsettling silence around the yard. Usually someone was sitting on the front porch or one of the servants was outside working around the house. Molly's family didn't own any slaves and they wished other people didn't either. Their helpers were freedmen and were paid. Bruce didn't like how quiet it was.

Bruce climbed up the creaky, wooden steps and walked across the wide, front porch to the door. He knocked three times and then turned around and looked down the street. He couldn't quite see his own house because it was around the corner and down the road. Dusk was settling and the sun was just edging down below the downtown buildings. He had lived in Winchester, Virginia his entire life and figured all towns in the United States were about the same.

The door opened and it was Ned, that crazy brother of Molly's. *Oh great,* Bruce thought.

"Ned, could you get your sister for me?" was all Bruce could think to say. He had a mission to do and he wanted to get it over with.

Ned smiled really big when he realized what exactly was going on. "You got in trouble, didn't you? You're here to apologize. I told you, Bruce, you shouldn't have hit my sister. This is terrific!"

"Would you just get Molly for me?"

The back of Ned's head seemed to glow red as he ran gleefully back into the house. Bruce could then faintly hear Ned's ma asking him who was at the door.

"It's Bruce Crawford, mother," Ned shouted.

"Tell him to come in. What does he want?"

Ned ran back to the door. Bruce looked quizzically at Ned and whispered, "You mean she doesn't know?"

Ned opened the door for him and shook his head, "Nope, Molly didn't tell her who did it. She said she fell and she threatened me that if I told the truth she would hammer me."

Bruce grinned at the new information. This wouldn't be as hard as he thought. Molly hadn't told her parents so the whole family didn't know yet. He decided to wait on the porch where it was safer.

Ned yelled, "He's here to see Molly, ma."

Ned's ma walked to the door and smiled at Bruce, "Hello Master Crawford, what brings you here this evening?" Meanwhile, Ned yelled for Molly.

"Nothing ma'am," Bruce choked out. "Just wanted to say hi to Molly and talk to her about something."

Mrs. Harrington's eyebrows rose in arcs as she smiled at him. "How are your parent's doing?"

"They're fine, ma'am."

Finally Molly appeared at the bottom of the steps and looked out the door to find Bruce.

Mrs. Harrington said, "Molly, you have a visitor. Why don't you come out on the porch and talk to Bruce."

Molly gave her mother and Ned a smarmy smile as she walked past them and stepped out on the porch where Bruce was waiting. Then, once the door was pulled near closed she got serious and said in a low voice,

"Bruce Crawford, what are you doing here? Did you come to hit me again—this time in my own home?"

Bruce was a little nervous now because he hadn't thought through the conversation to this point, "No, Molly, I just came because I, well, my pa said I should do the honorable thing and come over and apologize for my actions."

"How'd your pa find out?"

"Moss told my parents everything," Bruce said shaking his head and looking toward the floor.

This made Molly smile a little bit and loosen up. Neither child knew that Mrs. Harrington was standing just inside, hearing every word and was tremendously amused by it.

"Well?" Molly said slowly.

"Well, I'm sorry for what happened today. Will you forgive me?"

"Yes, I forgive you. Will you forgive me for pushing you?"

"Yes, I will." Bruce was relieved that this was just about over.

"Okay then, let's have a truce," Molly said as she stuck out her hand.

Bruce grabbed her hand, shook it pretty hard and then let it go so no one passing by on the street might catch a glimpse of him touching a girl.

Bruce turned to leave, "Okay, see you at church tomorrow." Bruce ran across the porch, touched the first step with his right foot and then stopped. He turned around and ran back up to Molly. He kind of stammered a little as he spoke his next words, "Molly, I, um, I have something for you as a sort of peace offering." Bruce dug in his pocket for the bracelet. "Here. It's just a bracelet I made out of some old fishing hooks."

Bruce placed the bracelet in the palm of Molly's hand.

"Thanks!" Molly said with her eyes shining.

"Thanks for not telling your folks about today," Bruce shouted as he ran and jumped off the porch, almost falling over upon impact with the front walkway. Bruce ran across their yard diagonally and down the street toward his home.

"You're welcome," Molly whispered more to herself than Bruce as she slipped the bracelet over her wrist.

Molly kept the bracelet on for almost an entire week, until the following Saturday when she and Bruce fought again by the stone wall next to Kathryn's stream. Every friendship pact they made that summer was fleeting because of their fights. The summer itself, however, seemed eternal and peaceful.

PART II

THE SOUTHERN DILEMMA

*Do not go where the path may lead, go instead
where there is no path and leave a trail.*

RALPH WALDO EMERSON

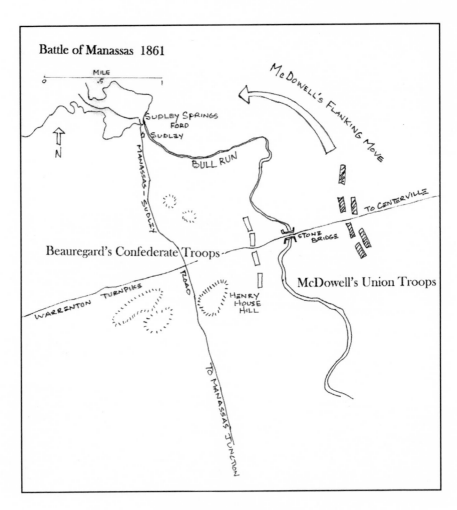

The Battle of Manassas

2.

Twelve Years Later, 1861

Six-foot Riley McNair had a lot on his mind as he walked down Kent Street in Winchester with his wavy brown hair falling partly over his eyes. He disregarded the touch of frost on the hard grass, the leafless trees and the acorns he was crunching under his black boots. He was going to meet his friends in a few moments and he had been dreading this day for a month since he left college. Riley attended Virginia Military Institute—VMI—in Lexington up until December and now, as he walked, he realized he might never see any of his professors again. One professor in particular kept coming to mind, Major Thomas Jonathan Jackson.

There at VMI, due to Major Jackson's rigid mannerisms and harsh discipline, Riley and his friends would sometimes refer to him as 'Old Hickory.' Stiff, boring, old-fashioned and somewhat of an eccentric, he always seemed aloof and too abrupt when talking, even to other professors.

Riley recalled discussions at school centering on Jackson and how he was the most awful instructor his classmates ever had to tolerate. Riley didn't mind him as much as some of the others but he regretted that the Major never felt compelled to make his classes at least somewhat interesting. Jackson's method of delivery was from rote memory. He told his students that each night before class he would stand facing a corner in his house and go over and over his lecture until he had it word for word. It was hard work for him so it was very unfortunate that, despite the effort, the lectures didn't titillate his students at all. It drained them and eliminated any desire to learn the subject at hand.

When not delivering artillery instruction or a scientific philosophy lecture, Jackson was sure fun to tease and the cadets loved to get him riled up. One time a student threw a dirt clod at him, but Jackson caught a glimpse of the prankster and put him under arrest. Riley once removed the linchpins from the practice cannon so at drill the gun rolled down the hill and scattered apart in several directions. Old Hickory was not amused. Major Jackson gave Riley and Bruce, a fellow cadet and Riley's closest friend, hours of delight as they watched the eccentric man try to respond to events as an ordinary professor. It was no use. Jackson was a hopeless cause.

Riley turned the corner and walked down the Millwood Pike. He was now just ten minutes from his destination. Riley recalled that throughout the fall term each carefree day led them closer to the sobering reality that many of the boys there would have to go to war. This point sunk deeply into them immediately after the cadets returned home from college for winter break. South Carolina seceded from the Union over three weeks ago, on December 20, 1860. Riley's father subsequently asked him on Christmas morning if he would consider not returning to VMI until they could tell more about what the future held. Riley and his father and most of their extended family were pro-union and thought what President-elect Abraham Lincoln was trying to do to preserve the country was a necessity. They hoped Virginia would not follow South Carolina and secede from the U.S.

Riley knew the consequences of not returning to Lexington to finish his studies. He could see the scowling faces of James and Isaac, his closest friends there besides Bruce, when they learned he was not going to fight alongside all the VMI cadets if war ever broke out. It was not Riley's desire to leave and disappoint them, but he loved his country and his family more than his school. He often measured out in his mind all the founders had sacrificed for the nation paramount to the ongoing discussion of secession. These founders, men like Washington, Adams, Franklin, Jefferson, Hancock, Jay and Madison worked tirelessly for years to form a group of states into an ideal nation. And though their dream teetered on the brink of disaster at several points during the Revolutionary War they persisted in their rebellious course and found victory. Riley recognized the grit, determination and effort expended and wondered if he himself would have been found faithful to the cause. Riley was proud of the founders but not so confident in himself. *Would he ever be a man like them?* He wondered.

The crux of the problem had to do with where he was born and what he now believed. *Had he turned against Virginia, or had Virginia turned against him?* Riley pondered this a moment. He couldn't retrace with any certainty at what point he had changed his mind about a man's right to own another man. There was not a conversion experience where one day he believed in something and the next day he abandoned the view and clung to something else. Perhaps the foundation of his inner view of the black race as property had been quietly and deeply sapped throughout his life while watching them in bondage. One thing Riley knew, he could no longer tolerate the existence of slavery.

Riley saw his destination in between a slight haze drifting through the trees. Usually pretty self-confident, Riley despised the inner turmoil he was suffering through. The decision to stay home with his family increased his anxiety and hurt his ability to joke easily with others. He hadn't slept well for days. Riley felt overwhelmed and devastated, especially when he thought of the upcoming break with his closest friends. He even fleetingly considered taking his own life. This thought didn't scare him until he developed the plan for how to do it. Jonesy's ma used some type of poison to kill the critters that attacked her garden each summer and Riley knew where Mrs. Jones kept her bottle of death.

Riley, now at his destination, opened the door and stepped his lean body inside. He saw his friends on the other side of the room. He knew he needed these friends more than ever to remind him of happier times. But the very people who could lift him out of his darkness could also corrupt him. As a tiger tamer knows the danger of his cats but spends time in the ring with them anyway, Riley knew the danger of his friends yet needed to spend time with them. He just didn't know how to keep them from attacking him when the truth came out.

Riley walked across the room. They met him here at his own invitation. He wanted to tell all of them at once how he planned to stay with his family and move with them to Pennsylvania if Virginia seceded from the Union. He sat down at their table without saying a word. It was January 12th and the place Riley chose was their favorite pub on the edge of town—the Grey Goose Tavern.

* * *

The Grey Goose would not have been considered a place for aristocracy and was set outside of town for a reason. The Winchester boys liked it because they could be left alone from the gossiping citizens and the place was cheap on the pocketbook. Its hard, coarse features appealed to their sense of manhood.

The Grey Goose was made completely of logs, even the front door. It possessed a large bar across one side with stools to the front and barrels to the back, assorted tables and chairs in the center and at the end of the room an expansive, stone fireplace which always had a crackling fire going during the winter months. The wide-plank flooring was made of pine, but it had so many years of dents and stains from customers that the floor was now as hard as American Chestnut. The walls had mounted animal heads of just about everything that could be hunted in the Allegheny's. There were plenty of large candles and lanterns throughout the room, but it was still dark enough to feel like you could keep your business to yourself.

The overweight, sandy-haired bartender and owner was a jolly good friend to all, yet possessed a keen eye for business and profit. He was a widower who never had any children and his last name was Culpepper. He lived in the two rooms in the back of the establishment and for the most part, kept his personal life to himself.

Thus, it was this non-elegant setting Riley finally delivered to his friends his future plans. None of them said anything at first. *Odd,* thought Riley. Probably suspecting this for awhile, Riley noticed Bruce, his blood-brother since the second grade, didn't look too surprised with the revelation.

Bruce's younger brother Moss, however, glared at Riley with contempt and said, "You're fooling us, McNair. You would not abandon your state in her hour of need would you?"

Riley glanced at Henry and Jonesy who had their heads down looking at the table. "It's hard for me to explain—it all makes sense when I think logically about it but now, knowing I will have to leave you all, it makes me sick."

Bruce, who had much in common with Riley as a fellow upperclassman at VMI in Lexington, looked at Riley and studied him hard before he spoke. "You know Jackson will probably lead a brigade for Virginia if we declare independence."

"I know that. It occurred to me he would be called back into service pretty quickly if war broke out."

"Along with Jeb Stuart, Bobby Lee and all of us sitting here. Family is important Riley, but have you thought this through? Are you resolute?"

"Virginia may not secede," Riley said, surprising everyone. "There is a chance, I'll-be-it a small one, but Virginia may remain neutral through this ordeal."

"Not with Lincoln," Henry finally broke his silence. "He ran on a neutral platform but his party is full of aggressive abolitionists with an agenda. There is no way that longneck will resist them as they attempt to make every state in America a free state." Henry was the one who loved politics in the group and he and Moss were currently students at Emory and Henry College near Abingdon, VA.

"In the last three days Alabama, Florida and Mississippi have joined South Carolina in declaring independence and seceding from the North. You know Georgia and North Carolina will, as well. Do you think Lincoln will stand idly by and allow half the nation to be torn away from his grip? Do you really believe Virginia will remain neutral if Lincoln were to use force and attack those states that depart?" Henry asked.

"Okay, what if Old Dominion doesn't remain neutral and every person in this room raises up their sword and goes to war for their mighty native state? Would that make my decision and point of view any less valid? Does it mean I am a terrible person because I don't believe in slavery?"

"Not all of us are fond of slavery, but we are all Virginians dammit! Born and bred," Jonesy barked out. Big Jonesy, not a college student, was the mildest one of the group and usually never swore. His large size mocked his quiet demeanor and he rarely got this worked up. His outburst sobered everyone.

Henry, a law student, continued the conversation, "Think about it Riley. This is not about slavery but about whether a state may govern her own affairs and choose to continue in a way of life it has had since before there was a United States. You know how many hundreds of years our families have been Virginians? We have been U.S. citizens for only three or four generations. What right does Lincoln and the Northern states have to tell my great grandpappy to quit being a Virginian and start living like a New Yorker? It just ain't right, I tell ya."

"Riley, if the Lord Himself asked me to do what you are doing, I would ask for a second opinion. It is one thing to stay here and not fight and it is entirely another thing to move to Pennsylvania. I mean, if God forbid there should be a war are you going to take up arms and fight for Lincoln? This is madness!" Moss said, disgusted.

Riley was pretty quiet at this point. Then, in walked Daniel Tanner, with the reputation as the meanest person in Frederick County. A mountain man not often seen in Winchester, tall, straggle-haired Tanner walked up to the bar and ordered. As he scanned the room his beady eyes fell on clump of young men in the corner all watching him. He grimaced, flared the nostrils on his pointed nose and turned his back to them.

"I suppose Molly and Ned Harrington and their folks will be going, as well?" Bruce asked.

"Only if Virginia secedes. Our pa's have made tentative arrangements near Pittsburgh. I am hoping to transfer schools and begin again in the fall. And maybe, just maybe, if the current issue gets resolved, I can finish my studies at VMI," Riley said optimistically.

"This is terrible," Jonesy said shaking his head thinking about his old neighborhood. "You are breaking up our group. I may never see Molly again. Have you told Kathryn yet?" Kathryn and Molly were best of friends. Their families were very close. But Kathryn's family, even if they didn't own the current two slaves, would have never considered leaving their home in Virginia.

"Kathryn knows, Jonesy. And so does Julia. They're not happy either. This is a terrible time for everyone."

"It doesn't have to be," demanded Moss.

"Yes it does, Moss," Riley fired back in a way that even surprised himself. Sometimes Moss could really get under Riley's skin. "As long as there is a race of men, women and children who are sold and treated worse than horses and dogs and are separated from their families and whipped and given executions without trial by the whim of their masters,.....then yes, this has to be a terrible time for everyone. You know as well as I do that Virginia is far from being a pillar of moral strength." Riley's unflinching words cut his friends like a knife. He had never stated these thoughts before and usually remained quiet when slavery was discussed.

As the group of boyhood friends absorbed this outburst they did not notice the rapid movement from the bar toward the group. Daniel Tanner had fire in his eyes as his hand flashed toward Riley, grabbed his neck like a vice and thrust Riley's head and shoulders against the back wall of the tavern.

"That kind of talk in here could get you in trouble boy," he said while his other hand made a fist and lunged it at Riley's pinned head. At that instant several things happened at once. The barman yelled, the folks sitting nearby all stood up knocking their chairs over and Bruce, the first one to react, stood, turned and lunged to tackle Tanner at his waist. This forced Tanner's second punch to be off-center but it still made contact with Riley's bleeding face.

No one would have ever entered into a fight with Daniel Tanner if they had a chance to think about it. At six foot three and two hundred twenty pounds he was a formidable foe. He always wore boots which made him appear even taller. Bruce was three inches shorter and about forty pounds lighter but he was quick and agile. They both rolled back onto the floor crushing a chair in the process. Tanner did not let go of Riley easily and Riley almost had his voice box and surrounding tubes ripped out of his neck. He couldn't breathe well for a long while.

Bruce ended up on top and for a moment pinned Tanner to the ground without saying anything. The mountain man's unmotivated malice was shocking.

Others at the tavern were shouting at them saying, "Get out of here!"

Tanner looked up at Bruce and snarled, "You're going to fight for this vermin?" Then, before Bruce could reply, Tanner twisted his body around and got away from his opponent. Not known to quit easily, Tanner then jumped toward Riley again, this time with a sharp knife he had pulled from a sheath tied around his leg.

Riley dodged the blade and his friends tackled Tanner and subdued him, taking his knife. Without them at the Grey Goose that day, Riley would have been dead and everyone knew it. Daniel Tanner eventually left after mumbling something about Riley under his breath.

"Don't come back, Tanner!" Culpepper hollered after him.

"What the devil is the matter with him?" Jonesy asked as he nursed his cut hand. Most people in Winchester had heard of Daniel Tanner but none could say they knew him. He had a mysterious and shadowy quality about him and his soul seemed hidden. It was as if his natural domain was a very dark and furtive world. Tensions were high all over the community and this episode reminded the boys how some people viewed unionists.

Scout, Bruce's retriever and border collie mix, had been waiting patiently outside the tavern. When the group emptied out of the old log building Scout followed behind them wagging his tail furiously.

The young men were temporary filled with adrenaline from the fight, yet depressed. With Riley's confession of loyalty to Lincoln and subsequent move to the North, it forced them all to acknowledge that these were uncertain and changing times. Times in which some people in Winchester would be moving, causing many relationships to change. The social fabric that had raised these citizens since birth would be torn apart.

Scout was oblivious to the turmoil and rubbed against their legs while looking up for approval. After running between them a few times Scout would dash ahead to check his master's chosen path and then repeat the cycle again. They all cherished the hearty dog they had played with since they were grade school boys.

Riley regretted that he didn't take the opportunity to properly thank Bruce that afternoon but he was barely able to speak after the incident. He hoped he would have the opportunity to return the favor to his friend in the future. *What a horrible day,* thought Riley as he put his hands into his coat pockets, turned away from his friends and headed for home.

3.

On April 17, 1861 the Virginia Convention voted 88 to 55 in favor of seceding from the Union. There was loud cheering and excitement in the streets of Winchester that evening. The older citizenry were mixed in their feelings about leaving the Northern states, but the younger generation whooped and cheered wildly. Men shot their muskets and revolvers into the sky and the state flag of Virginia was proudly displayed from the front porches all across town.

This decision was hotly contested for weeks. There was an ardent debate on whether to side with Virginia's Southern sister states, or remain a useless appendage to the Northern Union. When on April 15th President Lincoln issued a call for 75,000 volunteers to go to war against the South, the latter option to remain idle became utterly repugnant to most Virginians. For those siding with Lincoln, the pressure to move laid heavily upon them.

4.

Ned and Molly Harrington's family made a formal decision back in February after Texas seceded from the Union. They decided that if Virginia left the American States, they would move to Pennsylvania with the McNairs. With Virginia's decision finally made, Molly's parents decided to leave one week later with Ned, Molly and Moses. Moses was a black hired hand who many mistook as a slave, but Moses was a servant and worked for the Harringtons voluntarily. A family friend, Moses had played with Ned and Molly as children and was taken into their home when Moses' mother died of tuberculosis.

It was the night before the big move and Molly finished packing and giving her things to her ma and pa to load on the wagon. She was torn about leaving their home. She understood why her folks and her brother felt the necessity to leave, but she processed things differently and did not agree with their conclusion to abandon Virginia. She hated portions of slavery she couldn't change, such as tearing families apart, yet she did not see this war as a predominately slavery issue. Many of her closest friends did not own slaves and the ones who did treated them with quite a bit of respect. It seemed to her that it was in the deep South where most of the abuses lie. She tended to agree more with the theme in town that slavery should be decided by the state, not the national government. She agreed increasingly more with Kathryn and Julia about the issue over her parent's view, yet she had still consented to leave with them at the request of her mother.

Molly was twenty years old and not betrothed to anyone yet. It was socially unacceptable for a proper young woman of Virginia to move out of her parent's house and make a go of it by herself. She was not upset about the situation because she knew she could not force someone to fall in love with her. When the time came the time came. But for her, the time hadn't come. And she was in great company. Her closest friends weren't married either. However, Kathryn was engaged to be married to Henry on June first, Kathryn's 19th birthday, and Molly hoped to come back to be her maid of honor.

Earlier Molly made arrangements to spend her last evening with Julia and Kathryn at Kathryn's home. Molly's parents would sleep on the floor in their empty house on some old blankets, and nobody knew or really cared where Ned would end up on his last night. Because of her overnight, however, Molly would get to sleep on a real bed and she was thankful. She wondered, as she drew nearer to Kathryn's, if they would actually get any sleep or spend most of the evening talking. Molly also wondered if they might be visited by the boys.

Boys! The issue of the opposite sex was a puzzle to Molly. She had always prided herself in speaking her mind and being blunt, but this tended to keep men at a distance from her. On almost every issue Molly had a way to see the heart of the matter and knew what was right and wrong and which side of the discussion the truth was on. It seemed she could do this faster than most so when she would speak out it startled others, not only because of her swiftness, but because of her boldness. Molly felt one of the worst things people could be was disingenuous. She believed if you cloaked your emotions to influence others you were a false friend. If Molly didn't like something she said it. If she was bothered by something another said or did she let them know. *At least people knew where they stood in my company!* Molly thought to herself as she turned onto the lane leading to the Montgomery's home.

She knew her weakness, however, even if others couldn't articulate why they were uncomfortable around her. The hole in her armor was that in her mind she was always right. Molly knew she saw with blinders—usually still with precision and accuracy—but she missed out on some of the details on the edge of arguments or experiences that added to the whole and made the picture art instead of merely colors and canvas. Molly could think deeply but others tended to feel deeply. People appeared to live more joyfully than her because they were not bothered by the details of life. Molly's life was in seeing and searching out the details, and often what she saw bothered her. Molly didn't want to live in conflict and refused to smile politely around people or issues she despised. She was neither a diplomat nor a peacekeeper and her friends told her she had absolutely no mercy.

Molly saw the Montgomery home just ahead and someone sitting on the front porch. Her thoughts drifted back to Kathryn and Julia. What she needed most in life were close friends who could speak the frosty truth back to her and remind her that she was not seeing the picture in total and she might be wrong. Molly felt everyone should see life as she viewed it but this, she knew, was naïve. Her greatest relationship need was to have friends bold enough to stand up to her and not let her get away with her one dimensional view of things.

"Look for the meaning of it," Julia used to tell her. Kathryn would advise Molly to attempt being more loving and forgiving. These two girls were lifetime friends who spoke the truth to her. Just as birds needed air to fly, Molly needed close friends to teach her how to live. She did not want to endure life at a distance from others and in the shallows. She liked to spend time alone and read, but it was her friends who kept her engaged with others. That is why she would miss them so dearly. Molly needed them to learn how to love others deeply. Her heart seemed colder than theirs.

"Hello Molly, the girls are out back behind the barn feeding the horses," greeted Kathryn's father, Conrad Montgomery. He was rocking on the front porch in a chair next to a wooden swing and smoking a pipe. "I am sure sad to see your family leave. They have been stalwart Winchester citizens for many years."

"I'm sad too, sir. You know it wouldn't take too much to talk me into staying behind with Kathryn."

"We were sincere in our offer and that goes for your brother Ned, as well."

"I know, sir, and it was much appreciated. It's just that, without one's family around, then home really wouldn't seem like home, even though you and Mrs. Montgomery have been much like adoptive parents to me."

Conrad smiled yet there was sadness behind his eyes. He had always liked having Molly around—felt like she was a good influence on Kathryn. When Molly was a kid he had called her a pretty little flower. He made his next statement before he thought of how it would sound, "I cannot believe no young man has asked for your hand yet."

Molly immediately blushed and noticed Conrad recoiled a little and looked embarrassed, like he knew he might have overstepped. *Where in the world was Kathryn?* Molly started walking away.

"Young lady," Kathryn's pa stood, took out his pipe and called after her as his wife, Claire, stepped through the front door and joined him on the porch. "Excuse me for what I just said, but I want you to know something before you leave. I fought alongside your natural father. He was my very best friend in this world and no one knows better than I that he was a true patriot and a great man."

"Thank you, sir."

"I have watched you from across town ever since you were in baby britches. I have seen you play with Kathryn and Julia near' every day for almost twenty years. Believe me when I tell you, child, that God has given you a special gift. There is something entirely different about you, Molly, and it is not just your wonderful smile and beautiful head of hair. You are a leader and I have seen you with fire in your brown eyes for injustice and with compassion in your heart for people of less advantage. Remember when you fought with your teacher about letting Moses go to school with you? You are beautiful inside and out, and any single young man would be a fool not to get to know you better and marry you and find the treasure that you are. I've always been amazed with your ease with learning new languages and I will miss having your sharp mind to bounce ideas off of and practice Latin with. You have been a blessing to know, child, almost as if you were an extension of your father who would be immensely proud of you if he could see you now. Thank you for being a good friend to Kathryn. We'll miss you as one of our own kids." With that Conrad put his pipe back into his mouth and he sat back in his rocker.

Molly was speechless and didn't realize until he had finished that her eyes were filling slightly with tears and one had found its way down her cheek. Whenever someone brought up her real father she found it hard to compose herself. But crying in front of others embarrassed her because she did not want to be seen as emotional. *Get over it Molly, remember it's okay to cry,* she thought.

Molly didn't know how to respond to Conrad. Kathryn's ma stood there smiling at her and giving her an approving nod. Finally, Claire held out her arms and Molly rushed up the wide steps and hugged her, burying her face into Claire's bosom as Conrad stayed steadfast and watched a carriage glide down the road.

In a moment, Kathryn and Julia ran around the front of the large house. "Molly, what are you doing hugging my ma for, you're not leaving until tomorrow?"

"I know," Molly replied while she stepped back and wiped her face. "I was just telling your folks how much I appreciate them."

Mr. Montgomery winked at her and whispered, "We know Molly, we know," as he began to rock and squeak the floorboards of the old porch.

Molly, Kathryn and Julia ran off around the house down the back dirt road beside the orchard. They soon found the familiar horse trail that led to a grove of willow trees and wildflowers next to a meandering stream. In the middle of the large trees there was a grassy area perfect for picnics and enjoying the outdoors. The old stone wall the boys built looked ancient now with moss and ivy patches on it, yet it continued as always to circle the willows by the stream and offer a great place to rest against. This was their favorite spot in the world and earlier that day they plotted to spend the last couple of hours of daylight there planning the details of Molly's return for Kathryn's wedding.

"So what were you and my folks talking about?" Kathryn asked Molly after they caught their breath from their sprint on the trail.

"Nothing really, just saying our goodbyes. Your pa is such a gentleman. He has never talked to me like an adult before, but tonight he said some very nice things."

"I think he is going to miss you. He has asked me several times if I thought you would change your mind about leaving for Pennsylvania. My folks were serious about you staying here. I think they realize how lonely the house is going to be once I am married and gone with Henry and only Landon is there."

"They love you, Kate. You have great parents."

"I'll second that," said Julia who had been soaking it all in but not talking.

"Yeah, you would second that because you're always over there eating Claire's cooking," Molly said snidely.

"Hey!" Julia rushed at Molly and grabbed her playfully using too much force and both girls fell over laughing uncontrollably. They were the two wild and active ones in the group compared to the genteel and respectable Kathryn. In fact, ever since Julia was a kid she would take offense at someone who said only boys should do this or that. She was always trying to prove that men were no better than women and would go to great lengths—sometimes disreputable lengths—to prove it. Molly never argued the point and her cool silence on the issue usually left no one wondering.

"Good heavens," Kathryn said. "You two do not look like proper, young, Winchester ladies this moment."

"Oh, you old married bore, who cares about what proper, Winchester ladies should look like?" Molly scolded while still laughing and wrestling with Julia.

"Yeah, you old bore," Julia said as she picked up a handful of grass and threw it onto Kathryn's curly, blonde hair.

"Good grief. Why do I put up with you two?" Kathryn said as she grabbed some grass and tried to throw it at Julia. This started a grass fight that lasted until they were all covered in green. When they began to get it stuck in their mouths and noses, they were laughing so hard that they could barely breathe. Julia had a small snort to her laugh and this made the three giggle all the more.

The girls played and talked until it was close to dark. They started to glance at the trail in the woods that would take them back to Kathryn's and conclude their last night together as girls. None of them wanted this time to end, for they knew it was the end of an era for them and for their country. They had covered the wedding, boys, their futures, all the town news and the last item they discussed was politics.

The recent news was how on April 12th, Southern gunners in Charleston, SC opened fire on Fort Sumter and hit it continuously for thirty-four hours before Robert Anderson surrendered the garrison. Then, President Lincoln issued a call for 75,000 troops in order to attack the South and repress the rebellion. This action is what emboldened Virginia citizens and gave them sufficient reason to vote for secession. Immediately, men were choosing sides and former, heroic officer's in the United States Army were writing their signatures on official letters to the U. S. War Department in Washington, resigning from the military to take up their sword for Virginia. The most famous Virginian officer to do this was Robert E. Lee, the husband of Martha Washington's great-granddaughter. When Colonel Lee resigned from the U.S. Army the news spread like wildfire, and soon he was awarded command of all the Virginian forces and spoke at the Capitol building in Richmond.

As the girls reflected on these events the conversation stalled out as Kathryn and Julia both stared at Molly and shook their head.

"I know. I know. I know!" she somewhat shouted and looked up into the darkening sky. "It is not appropriate for my family to be leaving Virginia right now. I do not agree with my father, but I still must respect his judgment," Molly said.

"How could you, he's abandoning--"

"Don't Julia, not tonight," Kathryn pleaded, cutting her off.

Molly looked squarely at her friend, "Julia, you know my first father fought right beside Jackson and Lee in Mexico. My mother married a man who is also a patriot but he just looks at things in a different way."

"I know," Julia softened. "I just don't want you to go and I'm bitter at the person who is making you do it."

"Now, now, Julia, there will always be disappointments in life," Kathryn stated.

Julia interrupted, "Oh, stop with the philosophical prose and patronizing, would you Kate?" All three girls laughed at this. Kathryn was always trying to say and do the right thing but Molly and Julia saw through her facade of properness. They saw her at her best and at her frailest, and shook their heads when they thought about all that Henry was going to learn about her in the next few months. After glancing at the moon coming up, Molly decided their playtime was over.

"You know, we better go, it's getting dark. I heard Daniel Tanner is back in town and I don't want to run into him in my last twenty-four hours in Winchester."

"Oh, my lan', Molly. Please don't even utter his name, he gives me the chills," Kathryn said.

"He is a grim and miserable man," said Julia. "I wish he was dead."

As they stood up, Molly said matter-of-factly, "Bruce gave me the knife that belonged to Tanner. He took it from him when all the boys got in a scuffle at the Grey Goose Tavern a few months ago."

"Why would Bruce give it to you?" Julia asked.

"I'm not sure. I think he just wanted me to be safe since we are leaving."

Julia gave Molly a puzzled look.

"You're not jealous, are you?" asked Kathryn playfully. She was the one of the three that picked up on people's feelings and unspoken thoughts. Kathryn could tell if somebody in the room was hurting or feeling bad with her keen awareness of emotions.

Julia pushed her lips together silently staring at Kathryn with a serious expression.

"You know Bruce—he is always looking out for us. It's not a big thing. I just hope Mr. Tanner doesn't ever come looking for it," said Molly.

Kathryn wouldn't let it go. "Julia, I thought we agreed Moss was the man for you and Molly would one day have to choose between Riley and Bruce?"

"Please change the subject, Kate," begged Julia.

"Yes Kate, you excel in making us all feel awkward. Besides, I always thought Jonesy was the handsome one of the bunch."

"I'm going to tell him you said that," laughed Kathryn.

"Could we just get going," Julia mumbled as she started walking out ahead of them. They walked about half way down the trail, talking and laughing it up when Julia slowed down and motioned with her hand for them to stop talking. They just about bumped into her but then quickly got the message. They heard it too. Horses were trotting up the trail.

Molly straightened her shoulders, raised her chin up, walked right past Julia and continued down the trail as if she didn't hear a thing. The other two fell in behind her. Around the bend three brown quarter-horses trotted up and came to a halt after their riders gave them a quick pull on the reigns. Molly recognized the first horse before she saw the rider—it was Chris Columbus and belonged to the Crawfords. Moss bounced off the beautiful gelding and Henry and Jonesy followed his lead. The three were looking for the fair ladies in order to give their final goodbye to Molly.

It was a wonderful surprise and could have only been improved if Bruce and Riley were present. *Too bad*, thought Molly.

5.

As Robert Edward Lee lay on his bed at the Spotswood Hotel in Richmond, he couldn't help but reflect on his conversations in Washington just one week before. His first stop was on Pennsylvania Avenue at the residence of Francis Blair who, along with the War Secretary Simon Cameron, had been asked by President Lincoln to make an offer to Lee of high command. They talked about Lee taking the command of a massive army with 75,000-100,000 troops which would be assembled to put down the Southern rebellion. If it had only been to lead the soldiers against a foreign invader then Lee would have accepted it without hesitation.

Later the same day he met with Winfield Scott, General-in-Chief of the U.S. Army, a large man in his build and in his fame. General Winfield was quick and to the point, Lee remembered...

"You are presently on leave of absence?" Winfield asked.

A picture of General Scott from the War of 1812 caught Lee's eye before he answered, "Yes, General. I am staying with my family at Arlington."

"These are times when every officer in the United States service should fully determine what course he will pursue, and frankly declare it. No one should continue employment in federal government without being actively engaged."

Lee's heart at this point was beating wildly. To be in Washington and in the presence of General Scott was one thing. To do his duty to his native state by disconnecting from his mentor, who he admired so much, was another. The heavy general continued the conversation.

"Some of the Southern officers are resigning, possibly with the intention of taking part with their states. They make a fatal mistake. The contest may be long and severe, but eventually the issue will be in favor of the Union."

Lee could barely keep his composure. He did not know what a panic episode was by past experience but he knew it must be similar to what he was feeling now. His heart thundered while his whole career flashed before his eyes; working on the muddy Missouri River as an engineer, serving his nation for a year and a half in the Mexican War, his years at West Point as Commandant.... The sacrifice, the time, the distance from his dear wife Mary and the absence from his children. *Could I possibly utter the words that I myself hate to hear?* He wondered.

Scott continued, "I can tell now by your stoic face you will go with those who are leaving our forces. If you propose to resign, it is proper that you do so at once."

Lee hesitated and thought of George Washington (whose adopted son's home he now lived in), of his father "Light-Horse" Harry Lee, Revolutionary war hero and once governor of Virginia, and he thought of Thomas Jefferson, author of the Declaration of Independence, a former President and also a governor of Virginia. But before he spoke, his last thoughts were of his children.

Lee cleared his throat and stated firmly, "General, I hope with all my prayers to God Virginia stays in the Union. However, if they choose secession, what you and Mr. Blair are asking me to do is to raise my hand against my native state. The property belonging to my children, all they possess, lies in Virginia. They will be ruined if they do not go with their state. I cannot raise my hand against my children. No, I will not, sir. I love my country but my greater loyalty is to Virginia whose land my family has tilled and cherished for over a century. If the Union is dissolved and the government disrupted, I shall return to my native state and share the miseries of my people. I know I disappoint you, sir, but I must, above all else, do my duty."

The silence was maddening and his old mentor wouldn't look at him. Then, abruptly, Winfield Scott replied, "Lee, you have just made the greatest mistake of your life." And with that the interview was over and Lee was escorted by another officer out of Scott's office.

Robert E. Lee rolled over on his bed, looked at the wall and knew that he could have been wearing bright gold stars on a navy blue uniform with a sharp gold belt and tassels. *What if General Scott was right and this was a mistake?* Lee felt as if he had been offered the presidency itself and turned it down. He meditated for a moment on the thought that he could have served as a high ranking Union officer and finished his military career with honor. *His name would have been cherished by Americans forever, but at what cost? Where exactly is honor when you forfeit everything you hold most dear? What is the value of an unstained career gained with an emptiness of personal values?* Lee pondered.

Of course it was too late to moan and look back. For the sake of his sanity, for the sake of his family, and for the sake of Virginia, he must place his misgivings behind him.

And from that moment on, that is precisely what he did. He decided to never dwell on the past but seize the present and every opportunity which developed. On that day in the hotel he resolved to lead Virginia as strong and cunning as his talents would afford. Lee slid off the bed and walked out of the Spotswood into the beautiful sunshine and headed toward the Capitol. He knew that the ominous cloud in the North would soon drift over the Potomac and darken Virginia and he needed to prepare for all out war.

6.

After waving and saying hello, Lawrence Crawford silently walked up the front porch steps of Conrad Montgomery's house. Lawrence sat next to Conrad on a wicker rocking chair and waited for Conrad to begin the conversation. Close friends since childhood, neither had to say anything for them to enjoy each other's company. Both of their grandfathers had served admirably as officers in the Revolutionary War. Both found it hard not to talk about that war or the War of 1812 where Lawrence's father was killed.

Finally, Conrad, without looking at Lawrence and just before putting his pipe back into his mouth said, "Lee's with us."

Those three words spoke volumes, and the two men sat and pondered the importance of having Robert E. Lee fight alongside of them.

"I heard. There was never any doubt," Lawrence said as he studied the floorboards of the porch.

"I was asked by Turner Ashby to be his deputy. I declined for now—still too much to do around here to get the crops in." Conrad was a full-time farmer and a part-time merchant in Winchester.

"I have several loose ends to finish up myself. Right now it doesn't look like I will get away for awhile. The new regiment is starting to form up and perform drills just down the street from us," Lawrence said. He was a practicing lawyer and had partial ownership in several of the businesses in Winchester. In addition, Lawrence was an avid student of history and was regularly asked to give lectures about certain historical battles to students at nearby colleges.

"It seems like a dream, Lawrence," Conrad said. "To think that the U.S. government is actually raising an army to fight us and put our state in its place…."

"I know."

"Where have we come from that this could happen to such a great nation?"

"I've gone over and over the legal aspects of our predicament. Of course there is no precedence for this sort of thing, but this is the kind of testing that Jefferson and Madison actually needed in their generation to prove to the country the importance of nullification and interposition. If this is not a case where a state needs to protect her interest from a dangerous action of federal government, then I don't know what is. We are in compact together with the other states. We entered into this compact freely so we should leave freely. Is this not what the Resolutions of Virginia and Kentucky were all about? The Northern states, in their resolutions, actually did the opposite and delegated the right to the federal government to rise up against them as domestic enemies if needed, but not us."

Conrad chuckled, "How can a state or a cluster of states be considered domestic enemies? And Virginia, for goodness sakes—the home of our beloved Washington." Conrad shifted in his chair. "Anyway, didn't we already discuss this at great length the last time you were here?"

"Of course, but isn't it fun to discuss the minutia of it all?" Lawrence said grinning.

"I don't get the joy out of it that you do," Conrad said.

Both sat still for awhile without talking.

Lawrence continued, "We're trusting our livelihood, our beautiful city, our state and our children to a theory, Conrad, a theory of the inherent rights and privileges of a state within a supreme-state. Thinking about what is at stake sometimes keeps me awake at night."

"Lincoln is wrong to impose the federal will on us," said Conrad forcefully.

"I agree. It contradicts our founding ideals and documents. But, what if slavery is inherently evil? What if Lincoln and his friends from New England are forward thinking and right to compromise our current constitutional structure? What if they are trying to pursue a higher, moral good and founding all of this on the just war principles of Cicero or Augustine?"

"You're thinking too hard, friend. I wouldn't worry about old Cicero. Besides, we both know it is utopian to believe they can cure all the ills of slavery by amassing a large army to enforce how state legislatures govern. It is a belligerent, dark course they have chosen and they have clothed it white with a banner of freedom. This deadly course is a serpent with sheepskin on him," Conrad said and then responded to Lawrence's last comment. "Where do you come up with this higher, moral good, claptrap? Yes, slavery is inherently evil. I don't have to wonder about that."

"I agree. It would also be evil to subvert the laws of the land. Weren't we set up to be collegiate states who govern together in cooperation? One sacred piece of sovereignty a state should possess is the right to secede," said Lawrence.

"Why would any sovereign state form into a union with other states without that right?" Conrad asked.

"Precisely. Our liberty and freedom as citizens in this nation depends on the limitations of the federal government. Without those limitations we endanger our ideals."

Conrad sat up, glanced at Lawrence and then put his eyes back onto the road out front and the old wooden fence beside it. "In my mind they are indeed making this a distinctly slavery issue, which isn't completely unfounded given those sacred words in our Declaration. However, to me, it's a timing issue more than anything. Slavery will eventually be dissolved--but now is not the time. The idea needs to progress and evolve a little more in people's minds, especially in the deeper South where they rely on it for their industry even more than us here in the valley."

"Then you will fight?" asked Lawrence.

"The dye is cast Lawrence—all of us must fight or be disgraced. Yes, I will fight alongside of you and your sons."

Lawrence paused, thought a moment, then said, "The boys are a little too excited. They have never seen what war can do to a man or a nation."

"They will, soon enough."

"This is going to destroy many families," Lawrence said as he stood up to leave. "This will not be like in Mexico where we fought strangers; we'll be fighting some of the family members of our very own community."

"Such as the McNairs."

"Yes."

"Many have already moved. Perhaps by the time we come face to face, they will look differently and we won't recognize them," Conrad said playfully. "Abe Lincoln grew a beard before he took office. Maybe the other Northern-minded men will do the same."

"Perhaps. Secesh, that's what they call us."

"That's also what we call ourselves," chuckled Conrad.

"I have never liked the term," Lawrence called back, walking down the front porch steps.

"So long, Lawrence."

"Good night, Conrad. I suppose I'll be back in a few days to go over all this some more."

"I'm sure you will," Conrad said somewhat to himself.

Lawrence walked down the dirt road, which led away from the Montgomery farm, watching the sun hover for a moment just above the Allegheny's to the west. A few more feet down the path and the red ball melted into the darkness and dropped out of sight behind the mountains shining brilliant beams upward in all directions. Lawrence smelled the fresh grass and blooms in the trees and flowers marveling at the handiwork of the Almighty and that he was blessed to be born and raised in a wholesome town like Winchester.

7.

Henry and Kathryn had set their wedding date during Christmas break after discussing it with their parents and consulting with their minister. They wanted to get married on June first, Kathryn's 19th birthday. They had not factored in that the Northern states would declare war on the South the month before they were to walk down the aisle. Henry came by Kathryn's home to discuss the situation the first weekend of May, his last break before graduation.

"Hello, sir," said fair-haired Henry as he shot a quick wave to Kathryn's father, Conrad.

"Hello, Henry. Kathryn's been waiting for you. How's school finishing up?"

"Very well, thank you. I am done with almost all my papers so I just have final exams," Henry said. He walked into the house before Kathryn's pa had a chance to volley another question at him.

Kathryn was excited to see Henry but had a worried look on her face when they went to the parlor and sat down. "Henry, what are we going to do? Almost all of our bridesmaids and groomsmen have either moved or gone off to war. This is a disaster."

"It's not so bad, sweetheart."

"Yes it is, Henry. It's terrible. You're not involved in the planning. You don't know what it is like to have this project fall apart on you. Last night my mother told me our wedding is like a house of cards the wind was blowing apart. She made me hysterical and now you're acting like nothing is wrong."

Henry could see Kathryn was taking this to a more serious emotional level. He knew he needed to try to calm her some and get her to see the big picture. Henry looked at her with his piercing blue eyes and said, "I didn't say nothing is wrong, Kathryn. I just said it is not a disaster. We can deal with this. Besides, I have an option I want to talk to you about." Kathryn was all ears and looked up at him with near tears in her eyes.

"Kathryn, I know you would like a big fancy wedding, and I did too. The reality however, is that in a few weeks, as soon as I graduate, instead of getting married and having a honeymoon I should immediately join one of the regiments before they go into a battle with the Federals. I really don't want to miss out on any part of this and it is killing me that Jonesy has already been able to enlist. Moss has been threatening to quit school every day. My professors have said they are deciding this weekend whether or not to finish up this week or go the final four weeks as scheduled. If they finish up this week I want to enlist."

Kathryn started to cry.

"That's not all my dearest. Just as much as I want to fight for Virginia's independence, I want to be married to you. I've thought about this quite a bit. Kathryn, will you marry me right now and forego the big wedding?"

Kathryn enjoyed how Henry said her name and didn't shorten it to Kate like her girlfriends. "Well, when are you thinking?"

"Tonight, Kathryn. I've already asked Rev. White if he could meet us at the little memorial chapel in the woods later on."

Kathryn gasped. "You've…talked to Rev. White?" She was happy and sad all at once. She felt the loss of not being able to have her childhood dream of a glamorous wedding. Although, she was excited Henry had been thinking of her and planning this. It surprised her and she loved surprises. Yet something inside her told her this was too impulsive and she should say no.

"We can't, Henry. That simply will not do."

"Why can't we?" They were whispering now because they could not hear any noise coming from Kathryn's ma who was somewhere in the house. Also, the front windows were open where her pa was sitting on the front porch. There was an unusual quietness about the house.

"Because I don't have a dress, that's why."

"Wear what you have on."

"Henry, I don't want to get married in secret. My parents would be disappointed."

"Invite them."

"What? Then your parents would be disappointed."

"I'll invite *them*."

"That's not much of an elopement. Besides, what about school? You have to go back and finish up. I can't go back with you."

"I've made arrangements," Henry said with a twinkle in his eyes.

Kathryn was beginning to be impressed with this conniving young man before her that hadn't yet taken too much initiative in any of the wedding planning.

Then, almost as if in slow motion, Henry got down on his knee and pulled a humble ring out of his pocket. "Kathryn, will you marry me tonight?"

Kathryn began to cry again, but this time it was tears of joy instead of fear and desperation. Alas, she still had one more question for him.

"What about in a week when you go to war? What will our relationship be like then?"

Henry paused and thought for a moment before he answered. "Kathryn, it will be just how we've talked about in our letters for the last few weeks. You will stay here with your parents and I will see you whenever I get a break from the war. Hopefully, we will whip the Yanks fast and furious and this thing will be over by Christmas. Lincoln will then call his troops home. Kathryn, I would like to know you are my wife during this next six months. I would also like to experience tonight and the rest of this week with you as mister and misses. I already think about you every night and day. You're the first thought on my mind when I awake and the final thought on my mind when my head is on my pillow. I would like to make new memories with you that will thrill my soul when I'm lonely or desperate and in the dark of night. Will you take my hand tonight and say "I do?""

Kathryn didn't hesitate, "Okay."

"Okay?"

"Yes, I'll do it."

Henry let out a whoop and Kathryn's ma and pa came running in the room. They had been wondering what all the hushed tones were about.

Later that same evening the bright, young couple had a simple, straightforward ceremony only lasting a quarter of an hour. There were no frilly dresses, no one to stand up for them, no cake and no wedding presents. It was uncomplicated, but brought about the same result as a larger ceremony. Henry and Kathryn couldn't be happier. They had an amazingly romantic week together during Henry's last few days at school.

Though their separation came too soon, Henry and Kathryn cherished the memory of their first seven days of marriage for the rest of their lives.

8.

Jonesy's gear was placed on the porch and he stood in the doorway waiting patiently for his father to finish packing. They both still needed to say goodbye to Mrs. Jones. Jonesy's heart raced as he thought about what they were leaving for. With his senses very much alert, he heard his mutt's tail hitting the knotty wooden floor in the kitchen. He looked inside and saw his pa's favorite blanket draped across the old rocker. He glanced outside and spotted a wooden toy left in the front yard by a toothless neighbor kid. A bell was ringing in the distance.

Jonesy's pa had a birth name of Oliver Jones, but no one had called him Oliver since his mother passed twenty-five years ago. Everyone knew him as Club, Club Jones. The name Club came from when as a kid, he was usually seen with a big stick in his hand and was always hitting things with it. His childhood friends started calling him Club and it stuck, much like Jonesy did for his son, Brian. Most folks in Winchester only knew Oliver and Brian by their nicknames. Even the owner of the sawmill where they worked didn't ever bother using their birth names.

Jonesy watched his pa put his pack and musket outside the door on the porch next to Jonesy's gear. Then they both called for ma. She had been crying all morning. Jonesy was her little boy, though now enormous, and he was perfect in her eyes. Probably no young woman would ever be good enough for Rachel's boy. Although she hadn't had to worry about that yet. With his seventy-eight inches of height and thickness of limbs, he looked like a tree peering down on most everybody else in town. People who knew Jonesy loved him. He was good-natured, well-mannered, affable, never had a bad word to say about anybody else and was simple. He wasn't a simpleton, however, just innocent. He had a broad face that was usually smiling, and a very genteel demeanor to match. His hands were like paddles and his feet were so large that he could never be comfortable in the standard shoe sizes. Jonesy's brown hair, white teeth and blue eyes made him a natural charmer to those girls his size didn't scare off. Jonesy, however, was the most shy of the group around women. He was proud of his friendship with Molly, Kate and Julia and he learned to be relaxed around them. But, besides his ma he had never kissed, let alone touched another girl. All the boy/girl associations, other than friendships, were foreign to him. He did not understand how it all worked yet, how you move past being a friend to being sweethearts. He watched Henry and Kate and it seemed so natural for them, but the depth of love and commitment it would take to be married was as alien to Jonesy as understanding Blaise Pascal's work in mathematics.

He delighted in hearing stories from Riley and Bruce about how Molly had rebuffed them and put them in their place. Each one of those two had denounced women at some point because of Molly's fierceness. She was positively exasperating and provoking in her own way, yet her two courters kept going back for more whenever she would let them. They always had to return to their source of frustration. Jonesy laughed thinking about Bruce saying, "Back to the fountain of fire!" whenever he would try to rekindle his relationship with Molly.

Jonesy was usually content with where he was at in life and in his relationships, except for a few lonely nights when he thought how fulfilling it would be to have someone to enjoy a campfire with. He was always sad to say goodbye to the Winchester girls in the evening. They had a warmth he was drawn to and a natural beauty that attracted him. The older he became, the harder it was to keep the desire to be with them off his mind. A couple of his older, worldly acquaintances from town would take matters in their own hands and look for women who were available on any given evening, but Jonesy would have nothing to do with that. He knew you should never pay for love. He also knew he would never recover from the scorn and shame if respected friends, such as Molly and Kate, found out about the indiscretion. He would never be able to look Claire Montgomery in the eyes again if he was found out.

Rachel finally came to the front of the house and gave Jonesy the longest, tightest squeeze he could remember.

"Ma, we'll be back soon as we give those Yankees a whippin. Some are saying we should be home by the end of summer, once they get a taste of our shot in their backs."

"Oh, son. Be careful." Rachel then glanced at Club, "The war may last a little longer than you think."

She gave him one more tight squeeze as if to suck out his very life into hers.

"Ma, we have to go," Jonesy pleaded.

Rachel released her grip.

"You two are all I have. Come back home to me, you hear."

Club walked up and took Rachel in his arms and gave her a great, mauling hug, "You take care." Club gave her a kiss.

Jonesy watched his folks say goodbye. He knew his ma would be lonely because she had few friends in Winchester. Jonesy knew they were considered a lowbrow family. Some of the Christian ladies tried to reach out to his ma occasionally, but Rachel just didn't fit in too well with them. She was uncomfortable around others. Her course language and mannerisms would draw unwanted attention to her so she told the ladies in town she would rather be left alone.

Rachel smiled, "Club, you keep yourself safe, as well as our boy. I want to see you both back home safe and sound."

"I'm actually hoping Club Jr. will keep me safe," Club said as he glanced up at his tall and sturdy son. Jonesy's only soft area was the blubbery pouch around his middle. "I want you to keep safe yourself. If any Yankees come around here, well, you do the best you can and try to make it through 'til you see us again."

"I'll manage Club, just like before when you were gone. I'll miss the laughter and joyful times at supper. I'll miss Brian speaking in his British accent and asking me for a spot of tea. And I'll miss your big hands on my back, helping my aches and pains." Club gave Rachel one more quick back rub.

"That stubborn Lincoln put in motion something you boys need to stop. So go out there and make short work of a few Yankees so we can end this thing and you'll be back at my table again. I'll be all right, just go and do your business."

"Goodbye, ma," Jonesy said as he slid out the door, bounding down the steps to join the other men moving along the streets to the town's rally point.

"Goodbye, Misty," Club said sneaking in one more kiss before he walked out the door. Misty was his pa's pet name for his ma and he alone called her that. Jonesy glanced back and could see his ma's moist eyes and wet cheeks. She waved her handkerchief at the two warriors. Jonesy and Club turned toward the street and Jonesy took in one last glimpse of the neighborhood for his memory. The trees and shrubs were in full bloom and everything smelled wonderful. Jonesy hoped this war wouldn't last long so he could return to his beloved home. *Perhaps we will be home for Christmas!* Jonesy wished.

9.

The dark rider galloped through the mist down the old, winding road with tall trees on both sides shielding the moonlight. Periodically he would stop to turn his horse and listen for sounds of anyone following him or for anyone on the road ahead. With each stop the rider would travel further than the time before. The air was crisp with a clean smell of budding plants. Most of the birds were quiet now and the rider didn't even hear a dog bark during his three hour journey. Soon he began to see light through the trees and he slowed his horse. He dismounted and walked his horse silently up a narrow trail away from the main road.

About a hundred yards from the road the illumination grew larger and the dark rider could see flames. He knew he must be quiet now. He smiled thinking about his nickname the "Visitor", given to him by an informant and key ally he had in the Union Army. He moved further along the trail until he could hear the sounds of camp and murmured voices through the dense brush and pines. The rider tied his horse to a tree and continued walking by foot, off the trail and toward the voices. A few more steps, now he could make out exactly what they were saying.

"I would like to know where you get your information?" the first voice said.

"It doesn't matter where I get it, it'll change tomorrow anyway. They never make up their mind."

"Are you sure they have a mind?"

"They should put you in charge, Roger."

"I'd march this army right into Washington and give free pints to every foot soldier. And the officers would have to serve them."

The Visitor could hear three different voices. Most of the camp was quiet and through the foliage he could see tents set up all over the pasture. He moved on through the woods until he heard voices talking inside a tent. He stopped to listen for awhile.

"I've never even had a broken bone or a large cut before, Bill. I'm just not sure how my mind is going to work when I see the guy next to me lose a limb by a cannonball."

"Your mind doesn't work now. Anyway, you're going to do fine. Get some sleep and don't worry about it."

The Visitor moved on, very quietly, as he maneuvered even closer to the tents. He approached one where the occupants were obviously using more hushed tones.

"If it's true about moving out tomorrow then I think I'm going to start packing up my stuff," the first voice said.

"Just relax. The boss said he will not have the final word until he talks with *the* boss." This voice was more gruff and aged than the first.

"But you saw the orders. How could that change?"

"Verbal orders are just as valid as written orders. The situation changes, the enemy makes some movement or the President changes his mind about something, and then you need new orders."

"You don't think Lincoln is leading this thing do you?"

"I'm not sure how involved he is. I know he hand-picked McDowell. I know he is frustrated with McDowell's inactivity and has been pressuring him. But I think he defers to McDowell's military judgment."

"Which is…?"

"Not bad so far, but we haven't had a major fight yet."

"Until tomorrow."

"Yeah, until tomorrow. I need to get some sleep. It must be close to midnight."

This conversation verified what the Visitor had assumed. He now needed to know where the assault would take place. He walked very carefully back to check on his horse. He only had a few minutes left to get the critical information he needed or it would not help his friends in the Confederacy. He checked his surroundings and found a little rise in the terrain just down the trail. He was amazed at their lack of security. No cavalry scouts, no patrols, no men on guard duty around the camp. *They must feel secure.* He knew he would have to be more careful in the future once the South began to exploit their lack of diligence.

The Visitor walked through the trees to the rise and clamored up a small hill with large protruding rocks and many dry pine needles making it slippery. At the top he hid most of his body behind a tree so no one could make out his silhouette in the moonlight and positioned his face next to the tree and slid it forward. The Union campsite was spread across a valley that lay horizontal before him. There were two roads crisscrossing the northern portion of the valley. One was the road he rode in on. He shook his head at how close he had come to their position without detection. Even this hill would have been a great place for a scout or guard if the army below had thought about it. *They have a false sense of security*, he thought.

He could see an obvious headquarters area at the southeastern portion of the valley. There was a farmhouse completely lit up with several horses tied up to the posts on the front porch. The commander's briefing. They must be planning something urgent if McDowell was up this late.

The Visitor had memorized the surroundings of the headquarters so he could remember it when he was closer. He moved down the hill and walked over to where his horse had been tied, but it wasn't there. He froze in his tracks with a chilling feeling that someone was to his left. He glanced back. Standing before him were three Union soldiers. The Visitor turned and squarely faced them.

10.

Thomas Jackson had a hard time falling asleep that night. As he reflected on what had been happening recently his mind began to race. He was promoted thrice from Major to Brigadier General. He went from being a college professor to a brigade commander in less than three months. His superior officer, General Joe Johnston, commanded the Army of the Shenandoah, which had 9000 Southern troops. He organized his manpower into four brigades and assigned Jackson as the commander of the First Brigade. Barnard E. Bee led Second Brigade, Arnold Elzey led Third Brigade and Francis S. Bartow led the Fourth Brigade. Each of the last three brigades were composed of regiments from several Southern states, but Jackson's regiments all came from Virginia. In fact, most of his troops came from the Shenandoah Valley where Jackson himself hailed from, being raised by an uncle in Lewis County near the town of Weston.

The five regiments of Jackson's First Brigade (the 2nd Virginia, 4th Virginia, 5th Virginia, 27th Virginia and the 33rd Virginia) were accompanied by the Rockbridge Artillery Brigade led by Rev. William Nelson Pendleton, an 1830 graduate of West Point who became a preacher. In all, Jackson's brigade totaled 2600 men.

In the early morning hours of Thursday, July 18, 1861, Jackson received word from General Johnston that the War Department wanted the Army of the Shenandoah to leave Winchester and move toward Manassas in order to support General P.G.T. Beauregard. Beauregard's 22,000 Confederate soldiers were facing the superior force of Union General Irvin McDowell with a force of 33,000. McDowell was eager to attack Beauregard knowing the Southern Army was divided by over fifty miles of Blue Ridge Mountains and the Shenandoah River.

Jackson assembled his men that morning and made a short speech while walking back and forth on Little Sorrel, a horse obtained by Jackson as a gift for his wife, yet became his favorite steed. Jackson shouted so all could hear, "We are about to go up against the formidable foe of the Union Army. Sure, like us they have some new recruits who have never fought in battle. But at its heart the Union Army has seasoned professionals, hardened men who have served in combat for many months. Some would say if you are scared then you should quit or leave, but I would think that you should be a little scared. Many on your left or right will not make it through the next few days. We have not seen death yet, smelled it or know how we will react when tested by it. I have a message for you who are unsure if you want to be a soldier in this brigade this morning. Consider yourselves already dead. Imagine yourselves on the surgeon's table or in the enemy's prisoner of war camp." Jackson paused to let his words sink in a little. Some of the men dropped their jaws, not expecting such disheartening talk from their leader.

Jackson continued, "It will either be you or the other man--that Union man. And I say.......let it be him! May their surgeons work all night while ours enjoy the Union stores with us. Soldiers, men of my own land, show the enemy the black flag. War means fighting. You were not called out just to set up camp and practice drilling. The more brutal and fierce we are now--our very ferocity--will save lives. We must do the enemy all possible damage in the shortest possible time. Only then can the war be shortened and we return to our families. They are on Virginia soil, First Brigade! We must show them the black flag! Move swiftly, strike vigorously and secure the fruits of victory!" and with that he galloped off to thunderous cheers. The men were beginning to like this former professor.

On July 18th they marched all day. July 19th they rode on railcars of the Manassas Gap Railroad. At four in the afternoon they arrived at Manassas Junction and Jackson reported to General Beauregard at the Wilmer McLean Farmhouse. After receiving his orders, he brought his troops three miles north of the junction and they all bunked down for the night. The next day they rested and prepared for battle. Now, it was after midnight and Jackson knew he could only rest for two or three hours.

11.

"May I ask why you have untied my mount?" The Visitor sounded annoyed.

The Union soldier noticed the dark blue uniform and the gold buttons under the overcoat, "Excuse us, sir, we thought that…."

"You thought what? That it would be appropriate for you to steal my horse? I am a busy man tonight and have no time to be delayed. Charges will be made at a later date." The Visitor's words were uttered through clinched teeth to convey his exceeding outrage.

The frightened non-commissioned officer said feebly, "Sir, we didn't know you were one of us. We found your horse and heard you coming through the trees. We thought you might be a Southern spy."

"If I was a spy, I couldn't accept pay because my job here would be too easy. Now give me my horse, so I can be on my way."

"Why certainly, sir." The leader of the frightened trio took the reins from the one on his right and walked the Visitor's horse over to him. For a moment, the two men locked eyes as the reigns were exchanged.

At once, the Visitor mounted his horse and took off down the trail leaving the three scared men confused and wondering if they would be punished.

"What the blazes was he doing out here?" an enlisted man asked as they walked back toward camp.

"He was about to be shot," replied the other enlisted man.

"I don't know what he was doing here and it would not have been appropriate to ask," answered the leader. "Officers are fools, didn't ya know?"

"I guess so, and mighty mysterious. How is he going to press charges? He didn't even get our names!"

12.

Sunday, July 21, 1861, began at three a.m. for Jackson on his knees in prayer. While praying he remembered it was his wife's thirtieth birthday that day. He reflected how sullen Anna was when he left her in Lexington back in April. Jackson had taken out their Bible and turned to 2nd Corinthians. He had read out loud chapter five to her which spoke of the resurrection. "For we know that if our earthly house of this tabernacle be dissolved, we have a building of God, a house not made with hands, eternal in the heavens......" Then, kneeling down he committed himself and Anna to the protecting care of his Father in heaven. He recalled his voice was so choked with emotion that he could scarcely utter the words. His final plea with her was that God would grant their land peace and they would be free from bloodshed. As they embraced and kissed, he shared with Anna again his belief that the South was committed to a sacred cause. He hoped God would bless their efforts and end this new war soon.

Jackson concluded his prayer to God that early morning on the battlefield for protection of his troops and a quick end to the war.

* * *

Gunfire began at five a.m. and General Beauregard asked Jackson to bring his men to Mitchell's Ford in order to support Bonham's Carolinians. At midmorning there was an urgent request for Jackson to head to the Confederate left because the Union Army was moving their troops in a large arc around them. General McDowell was evidently attempting to flank the Confederate left side. The key intersection was the Warrenton Turnpike and the Manassas-Sudley Road which is where Henry House Hill sat.

The Confederates were soon surrounded by endless blue-uniformed troops pouring in from seemingly all directions. *The South is fighting admirably but is obviously overwhelmed and outnumbered,* thought Jackson.

At eleven-thirty a.m. there was a lull in the battle and Jackson organized his troops in the stone bridge area, just behind where General Bee and the Second Brigade were engaged in battle. Jackson's brigade sat in the woods on the reverse side of the Henry House Hill, just out of sight of the advancing Federals across the turnpike below. First Brigade troops were a tinge affected by seeing fellow Southern soldiers walk through their ranks to the rear with bleeding faces and deep wounds carved into their bodies. One man had an arm partially amputated. Jackson kept his focus and placed several pieces of Rev. Pendleton's Rockbridge Artillery on the crest of the hill pointing them toward the pasture and the road below where the Federals would soon be. Jackson knew if the hill and woods he now occupied were overrun by the Union, the Confederates would be surrounded and the day would be completely lost.

13.

Jonesy gripped his fifty-eight caliber Springfield musket harder than he ever had in his life. He was worked up. He could feel his heart moving his shirt with every beat. He lay behind a tree on Henry House Hill with his unit and practiced in his mind everything he had to do in order to reload his musket. He would reach into his cartridge box and grab a pouch of powder, rip it open with his front two teeth and pour the powder down the muzzle of his 40 inch barrel along with the paper. He would jam it down with his ramrod and then use the ramrod to also push down a minie ball. He would then replace the ramrod, put a percussion cap on the hammer, find a target and squeeze the trigger. When he practiced at home he could fire four shots a minute if he didn't accidentally drop too many percussion caps. *Of course, in combat it might take longer since I'm nervous,* he thought. Jonesy's hands were so large that he had a harder time than most with his caps. He knew he was lucky to have an 1855 rifled model as compared to his father's 1842 sixty-nine caliber smoothbore which Club had rifled recently. Jonesy's musket was more accurate than Club's older musket but both could shoot between 200 to 300 yards pretty effectively.

Jonesy and Henry had been waiting for hours that day for their commander to give them the order. They heard General Jackson was waiting for the right time to surprise the enemy. Jonesy felt the immense heat from the sun, was deafened from the noise of the cannon and almost blinded by the thick gunsmoke in the air. He saw that more and more wounded were hustling away from the battle in the hills and woods below. The afternoon slowly progressed while the cannon on both sides roared and tore to pieces the unlucky victims of their shells. Over thirty men in their brigade died before they saw any action by the incessant hurling of shrapnel from Union artillery. Many rounds were hitting the trees, splintering them and spraying debris on top of the troops below. Jonesy saw Jackson himself, nearly lose his middle finger from a piece of shrapnel as he raised his hand that day. Jonesy watched Jackson ride his horse back and forth while death was hurtling all around him and he seemed not to notice. Jonesy wished Jackson would give the order. *I am ready to go. I am ready to fight for my country*, he thought.

14.

Bruce Crawford loved the smell of the cannon. He ran his hand along one of the twenty pound howitzer pieces of the Rockbridge Artillery, which had just fired. Men were shouting, people were running and it seemed to Bruce as if everything was in slow motion. He walked behind the cannon over to a tree and waited. Jackson did not need him right now, the commanders already knew they were to wait for the order. Bruce sat down in the grass. For now he had time to rest and think.

Bruce was not old enough to help Jackson in the John Brown affair. Over eighty VMI cadets were asked to join in providing security when Brown, an insurrectionist, was hung on December 2, 1859. This time, however, everyone was needed to bear arms against the invaders of their homeland. Even though the invaders were their own countrymen meant little to the cadets. The Northern states were their enemy. Bruce overheard Jackson tell another professor that a fair interpretation of the Constitution and the precedent in the Federal court made fighting in the war justifiable. This was good enough reason for many of the cadets. Bruce saw the situation as a chance for Southern men to serve with pride and prove their mettle. All the drills with the cannon, all the studies in engineering, mathematics and physics were now being put on royal display as grape and canister flew from their artillery.

Bruce remembered how emotionally charged the last several weeks had been. Before he left VMI, a rumor swept through campus that some pro-Union men killed several cadets uptown in Lexington. Without seeking guidance all of the cadets ran to their rooms for their muskets, bayonets and cartridge boxes and poured out into the streets to take matters into their own hands. After being brought to reason, returned to the assembly hall and chastised considerably from Superintendent Colonel Smith, two other professors took their turns and criticized the cadets for their immature and imprudent behavior. Colonel Smith wanted Jackson to say something, as well, before he dismissed the boys back to their rooms.

All the derogatory nicknames they had given him over the years were forgotten with just a few words. They heard a voice from Jackson that night they had never heard in his lectures. Stern and authoritative, Jackson began speaking to the intensely quiet group of young men. "Military men make short speeches," he stated then paused. "As for myself, I am no hand at speaking anyhow. The time for war has not yet come, but it will come and that soon, and when it does come, my advice.... is to draw the sword and throw away the scabbard!" As Jackson sat back down there was a massive eruption of cheers and applause in the assembly hall. For days afterwards cadets could be heard saying, "Hurrah for Old Jack!"

Bruce had written down the sequence of events in his war journal the night before. On Wednesday, April 17th the Virginia convention voted for secession. On Sunday, April 21st at 12:30 p.m. the Corps of Cadets was formed and departed the campus heading for Richmond. All 175 cadets marched away from VMI on the dusty roads led by Jackson mounted on his steed. On April 22nd they boarded a train at Staunton, which was to take them over the Blue Ridge Mountains. The engine derailed, however, inside a long tunnel and it required several hours to get the locomotive in functioning position again. They finally arrived at Richmond and began drilling under General Joseph E. Johnston and John C. Pemberton. For several days Bruce, along with several other VMI cadets, helped Jackson teach basic artillery instruction on the Richmond College campus to scores of new recruits, once civilians, who were flooding into Richmond to join the war effort. Jefferson Davis had assumed the Presidency of the Southern Confederate States and he and Governor John Letcher were there in Richmond (the new Southern Capitol) working furiously to integrate the Virginia militia forces into the new Confederate Army and plan a strategy.

Bruce glanced around as more shells exploded in the trees nearby. He thought of his friends Henry and Jonesy who were waiting patiently to fire their weapons and perhaps kill for the first time. The sun was hot. The hour dragged on. Bruce took off his hat and fanned his face with it. His long, dark hair was wet with sweat and flopped into his brown eyes when he looked at the ground. He thought of Molly. The last time he had seen her was on his Mid-March break when he returned to Winchester.

Jonesy escorted Molly, Kate and Julia over to Bruce's house on Sunday afternoon, an hour before Bruce was to return to VMI. The conversation was somewhat awkward. He mumbled words to Molly about hoping she enjoyed living in Pennsylvania and she said something back about congratulations for almost finishing up college. They gave each other a quick hug and that was that.

Why on earth was he always tongue-tied around Molly? Bruce wondered. He could joke and kid around with Kate and Julia all day long and they would giggle at most of his jokes. He could hug Kate and not feel funny, but if he even stepped near Molly it would be clumsy and difficult and his thoughts would become disoriented. *She was so different than most girls,* he thought. She was ferociously beautiful yet completely unaware of it. Molly had no idea that half the single men in the county wanted to marry her, but were too afraid to ever get to know her. There was something both frightening and exciting about her.

Did he want to marry her? Bruce contemplated. He had never given it any prolonged thought, but he knew his inaction over the idea had finally decided the issue for him. He would have had to follow his friend's lead and propose last fall like Henry did with Kate. Bruce just never knew how to broach the subject with Molly. It was hard to get into a discussion about their friendship. Plus, he was not at all sure she would be favorable to the idea of something more serious.

There was always Julia. She was pretty herself, loved being outdoors and a much easier person to be around. Julia was great riding horses and used to challenge the boys in high school to try to beat her in a race. In the back of his mind, Bruce now realized, Julia had always been his back-up plan. However, she seemed more like a sister than a potential sweetheart. Bruce then thought of his little sister, Lucy, and how much she adored both Julia and Molly. His brother, Moss, had a crush on Julia growing up and used to joke to Bruce about sweeping her off her feet when he became a gallant cavalryman. 'Striking, absolutely striking' was what Moss would say about her. Now Moss was completely focused on the war, as was every other male over the age of fifteen.

Bruce put his head against the tree and looked over in the field and saw Jackson moving back and forth on the horse he had procured at Harpers Ferry at the end of April. Bruce remembered the first time he saw him on the brown Morgan he named Little Sorrel. It was not long after that day when Bruce was marching in a column and a tall, lean, young cavalry officer named Joseph Turnham trotted up next to him on a beautiful brown mare and called his name. Bruce fell out of line while his squad marched on. Joseph jumped off his horse, removed his gloves and pulled some papers out of his satchel. Bruce recalled his words, "Colonel Jackson, who you knew as a Major at VMI, will soon be a Brigadier General." At Turnham's words, Bruce looked quizzically at him. "In anticipation of this, General Johnston wanted me to get some of the administration done so Jackson wouldn't be delayed later on. Jackson recommended to Old Uncle Joe that some of you upper classmen at VMI, who were to graduate, should be given your commissions so you could have the proper authority when you train those less experienced. Congratulations lieutenant."

Turnham, Johnson's aide, pulled out two pieces of paper which looked official. One was a finely-written diploma from Colonel Smith. VMI's graduation for the class of '61 never took place. The other piece of paper was a commission for Bruce signed by Jefferson Davis.

"I know this is somewhat irregular, but here is your commission and rank as a Second Lieutenant in the Confederate States of America. You can take your oath of office later on tonight. Old Jack wants you to serve on his staff as an aide and he would have only picked you if you were thought highly of. When he handed me these papers, he told me you knew what the word duty meant. As you know, those few words are a lot coming from that man, he barely says anything about anybody." Bruce had heard stories about the Alabaman Joseph Turnham and his Mexican War heroics, so he was honored to have been given his rank by him.

Crack! A new series of raking musket fire pummeled the ground and trees where Bruce was sitting, disturbing him from his thoughts. He stood to his feet. Jackson was waving for his aides to come to him. *Here we go,* Bruce thought as he ran toward his commander.

15.

The South Carolinian general of the Second Brigade, Barnard Bee, rode his horse up the hill toward Jackson and gave the report of the collapse of his lines. Bee exclaimed to Jackson, "General, they are driving us!"

Jackson's face was set like flint when he replied, "Well then, sir, we will give them the bayonet."

General Bee rode up to the crest of the ridge along the edge of the woods and shouted to rally the troops of his brigade, "Look, men, there is Jackson standing at the crest like a stone wall! Let us determine to die here, and we will conquer! Follow me!" From that moment, without Jackson's sanction, soldiers began calling him Stonewall because of Bee's rally cry.

As the Union offensive inched forward, hundreds of men were being killed on both sides from the regiments engaged. Several squads in Jackson's lines of men suddenly rushed into battle out of nervousness and a lack of discipline. Most of these soldiers were cut to pieces by the Union cannon and musket balls. Jackson patiently waited. He wanted to surprise his opponent by running out of the woods en masse while the enemy was anticipating a weak defense. Finally, he received word from General Beauregard to counterattack. It was now three-thirty p.m. and Jackson gave the order to advance.

All five Virginia regiments sprang into action against a strong Union offensive led by the 11th New York Infantry. Jackson ordered his regiments to charge within fifty yards, fire and then run upon the enemy and deliver the bayonet while yelling like furies. The wretched screams heard that day would be used often by the Confederates as they advanced upon the enemy.

Jackson's troops cracked into the battle like a thunderbolt, choking the life and motivation out of their opponents in front of them. Forty Federals were wounded or killed instantly and groups of them ran away to form a defense. The surprise attack worked at first, but Jackson's Confederate ranks were repulsed back. A pushing match occurred and both sides seemed to have the advantage at different points for the next hour. Many men found themselves engaged in hand to hand combat. When a bayonet wasn't handy they utilized whatever they could get their hands on to hurt the enemy, even sticks. Some killed another for their first time that day. The yelling, the smoke, the loud cannon and the screaming would never be forgotten. Many, many good men died that hour including General Barnard Bee and Francis S. Bartow, both brigade commanders of the Army of the Shenandoah. Jackson's own coat received several bullet holes.

At first, Jackson's men pushed so hard they left their flank open to another counterattack by McDowell's superior number of infantry. Jackson's unconquered mind led his men to repulse the fragments of the latest Union assault backwards and sideways until Johnston ordered fresh regiments into battle. These new Confederates found open Union flanks with fatigued opponents, who had already been fighting for twelve hours. This damaged the North enough that just before five p.m. General Irvin McDowell, surprised at the strength and resolve of the Confederate Army, ordered a retreat. The Battle of Manassas quickly came to a close.

What happened next was tragic. Jackson watched the Union retreat become so disorganized that all of the roads back to Washington became quickly clogged. Many Union soldiers threw down their weapons and ran at a full sprint, defying the orders of their commanders and first sergeants. Not only were troops returning to Washington frightened to death, but all the tourists from the Capitol who came out to see the show were running back, as well. Politicians, including several senators and their wives, had lined their buggies up and down the roads with other citizens from Washington hoping to see a part of history. Instead of a Union victory, they witnessed the horrors of war, up close and personal, and some of the spectators lost their own lives from the shelling. Many of the Union wounded lay along the side of the path pleading for people to help them while military supply wagons, sutler's teams and private carriages choked the roads. Everyone along the way was fleeing wildly from the ghoulish sounds of war and the violence behind them. For some of the members of the Union Army whose enlistments were up, this first taste of war made them decide to head back home and abandon the uniform.

Jackson later learned that Irvin McDowell, who had hoped for a quick and decisive victory, had 450 men killed, 1,120 men wounded and 1,300 men captured. The South had 390 men killed and 1600 men wounded. Jackson reported 110 of his men killed and 400 men wounded from his newly christened Stonewall Brigade. The 33rd Virginia, where Henry and Jonesy had bravely served, lost a third of the regiment that day. They survived unharmed.

The evening was spent caring for the wounded and burying the fallen. Prayers and memorials were delivered amid the horrific cries from the hospital areas. Loud outbursts from men in acute pain and suffering, sobered those who had made it through the battle unscathed. The steady rain enhanced the eerie aftermath of the battle. Building a campfire was close to impossible, but late in the evening the rain let up to almost a mist. Finally, a group of men near Jackson's tent were able to get a roaring fire going. As the soldiers watched the blaze and pondered the events of the day, the reality of what the Confederate Army had accomplished sank in and the troops began a modest celebration.

From his tent, Thomas Jackson heard a nearby group of men organize a few band pieces together and practice a song some of the men had heard for the first time earlier that summer. Once the band members sounded halfway ready, several other soldiers stood up and began to sing wildly a tune written by Harry Macarthy who was inspired to write the song after Mississippi and other states seceded from the Union. It was called "The Bonnie Blue Flag."

We are a band of brothers,
And native to the soil,
Fighting for our property
We gained by honest toil;
And when our rights were threatened,
The cry rose near and far,
Hurrah for the Bonnie Blue Flag
That bears a single star.

Hurrah! Hurrah! For Southern rights Hurrah!
Hurrah for the Bonnie Blue Flag that bears a single star.

Hurrah! Hurrah! For Southern rights Hurrah!
Hurrah for the Bonnie Blue Flag that bears a single star.

And here's to brave Virginia!
The Old Dominion State,
With the young Confederacy
At length has linked her fate;
Impelled by her example,
Now other states prepare,
To hoist on high the Bonnie Blue Flag
That bears a single star.

Hurrah! Hurrah! For Southern rights Hurrah!
Hurrah for the Bonnie Blue Flag that bears a single star.

Hurrah! Hurrah! For Southern rights Hurrah!
Hurrah for the Bonnie Blue Flag that bears a single star.

Jackson enjoyed the music and wanted the men to celebrate their much earned victory over the Northern Army. He held his aching hand, which Dr. McGuire helped him with after the battle. His sleeve was soaked with blood but he was grateful. Jackson finally drifted off to sleep that evening pondering what he could have done better and thanking God for giving him the cherished victory he had prayed for.

16.

The Northern newspapers prematurely reported victory on their front pages. However, when the truth was discovered of the embarrassing defeat they tried to console the public and refrain from mentioning how vulnerable the Capitol now was. They did not write about their greatest fear—a Confederate advance on Washington.

The Richmond newspapers praised several of the North and South Carolina units and their commanders who bravely fought and withstood the Yankees at Manassas. No mention was made of Thomas Jackson.

When a letter was received by Jackson's pastor, the minister exclaimed to those present at the Lexington Post Office that day, "Now we'll all hear what truly took place at Manassas and have an inside point of view! Here is a letter from Thomas Jackson!" What was read aloud, however, baffled the crowd.

"Reverend, after spending the day in battle with my brave troops, I returned to the bivouac site and there remembered I had forgotten to send my contribution for the colored Sunday school class. Please receive the enclosed offering."

17.

On October 7th, Jackson and a fellow brigade commander, James Longstreet, were promoted to major general due to a restructuring of the forces, making them division commanders. At the end of October, General Johnston, the new commander of the Department of Northern Virginia, ordered Jackson to assume command of the Valley Army of Virginia. Jackson knew this meant separation from his brigade who he had built trust with over the last six months and it tore him apart. He prepared his bags to go and on November 4th he was forced to say his final goodbye and leave.

All of the regimental commanders and line officers stopped by his tent to personally say goodbye. Jackson went outside, mounted Little Sorrel and rode to the front of his entire brigade, which had been formed and brought to attention. Jackson rode back and forth a few times looking at the faces of the men who had served with him on that hot, glorious day in July. He stopped his horse and looked out over the expanse of troops.

In a loud voice he said, "Officers and men of the First Brigade! You do not expect a speech from me. I come to bid you a heartfelt goodbye. This brigade was formed at Harpers Ferry and the command of it assigned to me. You have endured hard marches, the exposure and privations of the bivouac, like men and patriots. You are the brigade that turned the tide of battle on Manassas Plains and there gained for yourself imperishable honor, and your names will be handed down with honor attached in future history."

At this, Little Sorrel moved some so Jackson paused and rode him in a circle until he faced the brigade again. He could hear some of the men weeping when, almost in one accord, the men began taking off their hats and holding them in the air toward Jackson in an honorary salute.

Jackson took off his hat and held it toward his beloved brigade, stood in his stirrups and with a thunderous roar shouted, "You were the First Brigade in the Army of the Shenandoah, the First Brigade in the Second Corps, and are the First Brigade in the hearts of your generals. I hope that you will be the First Brigade in this, our second struggle for independence, and in the future, on the fields the Stonewall Brigade are engaged, I expect to hear of crowning deeds of valor and of victories gloriously achieved! May God bless you all! Farewell!"

Jackson realized the men in front might see the tears forming in his eyes as he turned his horse and galloped away from the formation. The men in formation, many weeping, said, "Hurrah for Old Jack" over and over again until they were hoarse. Jackson, Bruce and two other aides rode away to the sound of cheering. They boarded their train at the Manassas Junction depot and departed for Winchester.

PART III

NORTHERN PRIDE

If war is ever lawful, then peace is sometimes sinful.
C. S. LEWIS

18.

My Dearest Ellen,

I find myself in a new and strange position here. The President, the Cabinet, General Scott and others all deferring to me. By some peculiar operation of magic I seem to have become <u>the</u> power of the land. I almost think that were I to win some small success now, I could become Dictator or anything else that pleases me. Of course, nothing of the kind would please me, therefore I won't be Dictator. Oh, admirable self-denial.

Your Loving Husband,
George

George Brinton McClellan was feeling pretty good. President Abraham Lincoln had recently conveyed on him the highest military honor in the land. He was to command the entire army as General-in-Chief. The President was singing his praises and spoke to others of his hope for McClellan to succeed. Most everyone he encountered those days were enthused about his advancement and applauded his achievements. This was George McClellan's chance to prove to everyone he was a military genius, greater than George Washington. *Perhaps even greater than Napoleon Bonaparte,* McClellan thought to himself.

19.

"How long do you plan to wait here for him?" asked William Seward.

"Until the busy commander returns home," responded Abraham Lincoln.

President Lincoln, his Secretary of State William Seward and the Assistant Presidential Secretary John Hay paid a social call to General George McClellan's home in Washington to discuss strategy with him. McClellan's residence on Lafayette Square was also used as his headquarters building and contained the telegraph office. The President made frequent stops there to see the latest telegrams and to speak with the general in person. General McClellan often kept Lincoln waiting, even after he heard it was the President who called. This greatly annoyed Lincoln's assistants but the President seemed not to notice. This particular evening they were told by the porter the general was not home, but was expected at any minute. They were escorted to the parlor where they now sat looking at each other. They had been there for over an hour.

Lincoln could tell that Seward and Hay were bothered by McClellan's cavalier attitude more than he was. Lincoln took the few moments of rest to think long and hard of the evolution of placing McClellan in charge of the Army. Handsome, confident and especially short when standing next to Lincoln, George McClellan had been compared repeatedly with Napoleon. This bothered Lincoln. Unlike Napoleon, McClellan was not winning wars. Like Napoleon, McClellan possessed an allegiance issue in his personality. You were either for him or against him. There was no middle ground or diplomacy with him. McClellan seemed at times like a narcissist. Yet, he did come across as a competent commander and would hopefully prove the best pick for the job at hand. *Was he a good choice? Time would soon tell*, Lincoln thought.

At last there were some voices in the entry. The general must have returned home, hoped the President.

The porter came to the parlor to report to them the general was home and informed he had visitors.

"Well, is he coming to meet us?" asked Seward.

"He said nothing," replied the porter.

"That rascal!" exclaimed Hay as soon as the porter left the room. "He knows the President of the United States is waiting for him in his parlor and he decides to detain you even longer?"

"Hay, you surprise me by your surprise," said Seward as he pulled out a cigar to smoke. "Have you forgotten we now have a self-important man in a position of leadership? The rest of us are merely impediments to what the little chief wants to accomplish. Don't you know how much he disdains anyone in authority over him?"

Lincoln closed his eyes and tried to reflect again. It was getting late and he was feeling weary. *Now, what was I thinking about before? Oh yes, was McClellan the best choice?* Lincoln continued his thoughts on why he chose McClellan. It was a recommendation from the former General-in-Chief Winfield Scott who presently didn't like McClellan anymore. General Scott had taken offense of how McClellan had avoided him and gave reports directly to the Secretary of War, Simon Cameron. Scott, a national hero, heard how young McClellan had called him "an imbecile, a great obstacle and possibly a traitor." Winfield told people in Washington he didn't deserve to be treated like a scoundrel after fifty years of faithful service in the military. The aging warrior realized his time of effective leading was over and asked the President if he could retire November 1, 1861. Lincoln knew losing Scott would hurt the War Department. Scott was a patriot, born seventy-five years earlier he had participated heroically in the War of 1812 and the Mexican War. What Lincoln couldn't understand was why at first, Scott championed for George McClellan and believed he was an excellent candidate to lead the United States Army. However, as the younger general plowed his trade he unfortunately began to resent Scott and then snub him. The Grand Old Man of the Army grew tired of the games and submitted his resignation. It was time for him to move on and Lincoln allowed him to leave gracefully. Some said Lincoln should have kept him actively engaged in the war. *How could I have prevented him from retiring? General Scott served faithfully since 1808!* thought Lincoln.

"This is ridiculous," Seward said interrupting Lincoln's thoughts. It had been at least thirty minutes since the general returned home. The three asked the porter to remind the general he had visitors. Soon they were happy to hear someone coming down the stairs.

It was the porter.

"I am sorry to announce, but the general has retired to bed."

The three visitors sat dumbfounded. The embarrassed porter stood by the door indicating he expected them to leave.

"This is preposterous!" muttered Hay. "The insolence!"

"I say we go up to his bedroom and wake the inconsiderate charlatan," suggested Seward.

"No, no. Nothing. We will do nothing. This is not the time to educate him in etiquette and personal dignity," stated Lincoln while standing to his feet.

"Astounding," said Seward as the three men were escorted out.

The President made no more visits to George McClellan's residence.

20.

Moses Fry was a humble, well-built man in his early thirties and still not married. He was kind and gracious to all. He didn't know how to write well, but he could read some and continued to work on both of those skills. His parents had been slaves but he was a black freedman. When he lived in Virginia he would sometimes run into the wrong person and be treated poorly, like he was a slave. But his employers always treated him right. Moses called the family 'his folks' and he called Ned and Molly's parents (Lucas and Abigail Harrington) his Master and Mistress, but they all knew he was not a piece of property. He worked voluntarily. His father brokered their family's freedom through his former master on his deathbed. In the plantation owner's last will and testament he gave freedom to Moses' parents and children. Moses' pa died soon after the master died leaving his mother to raise him without any source of income. When his ma passed he was entrusted to the Harringtons to raise.

Moses travelled up to Pennsylvania with Ned and Molly and helped them move all their belongings. As a hired hand, he was essential to just about every project the family had going on. He drove the buggy, he tended the garden, he helped with the indoor and outdoor chores and he kept things organized for the family. Moses definitely earned his keep. One thing he didn't do was cook, but he sure loved to eat. Occasionally, Ned and Molly's parents would invite Moses to eat with them but it was usually only on Sunday. Most other times he ate with their other hired laborers. Both in Virginia and Pennsylvania Moses was given a small, one room building behind the main house for him to sleep in. He called it his lil' shanty and it had one small lantern in it for light.

Moses felt incredibly lucky to be a free man and thankful every day for his father's gift to him. He knew his limitations, however, and that he needed 'the folks' to navigate the obstacles of the racial divide in Virginia, where most black men were slaves. Proud of his heritage he had an old, weathered drawing of his real folks by his bed that he picked up and placed on his heart while he prayed and drifted off to sleep each night.

Moses was actually considered the assistant minister at his old church in Winchester. Moses had been on the deacon board for six years when the head pastor and the rest of the deacon board called him in for a special meeting. Moses could always recall their words verbatim...

"Moses, we have seen you as a man of wisdom and maturity. You know the Gospel of Jesus Christ and you love to teach it to others. You have shown the heart as that of a servant of the Living God. You preach the Word, you are ready in season and out of season to reprove, rebuke and exhort with great patience and instruction. We now do ordain you as a minister for our church and in this state." Moses accepted and all the deacons and the pastor placed their hands on him and the pastor prayed, *"Be sober in all things Moses, endure hardship, do the work of an evangelist and fulfill your ministry to the living God. Amen."*

Moses was the most humble, gracious minister the church could ever remember having serve on its staff. His agreement was for fifty cents a week, if the offerings supported it. Many times they did not but Moses still served faithfully. He also volunteered to lead a Bible Study at old Idalia's home on Wednesday evenings. Idalia was a slave and belonged to the Crawfords. Her little cottage would host Moses and several other slaves from the community. Moses was an excellent teacher and his Winchester friends had written saying they missed his weekly lessons after he moved to Pittsburgh. Moses recollected on some of these relationships when he woke up that Sunday morning.

Today was a good day for him. Mister and Missus Abigail had invited him to dine with them after church. Moses usually went to his new church in the late afternoons on Sundays and tinkered around the yard in the morning until the folks got home. After the move, Moses learned that whites and blacks didn't worship God together even in the Northern states. Most things were pretty much the same for him in Pennsylvania except for the common scenes of slavery in Virginia, which were absent in their new town. Actually, Moses was looked at with more suspicion in Pittsburgh as a possible runaway than he was in Winchester where most white folk knew him and knew his overseers the Harringtons. This wasn't bothering him this morning, however. The folks had invited him to Sunday dinner and he could smell the delicious food as he walked up the back steps, knocked twice and entered the house.

"Hello Moses, are you enjoying your day of rest?" Lucas asked him.

"Yes suh, it's a mighty fine day to be alive. How was worship, suh?"

"Very good, very good. The minister was in the book of Hebrews today. Do you know who wrote the book of Hebrews, Moses?"

Moses thought for a moment. He grew up learning about the letters of the Apostle Paul and Peter and John and he knew the four gospels and Acts. But he couldn't recall. "Dats a good question, but I have no idea."

"You're a smart man, Moses, not to answer too rashly. No one knows who wrote Hebrews and if they say they do then they definitely don't. The book was written anonymously. Most people think it was Paul."

"Hmm, that's interesting. So no one knows?"

"No one knows."

Just then Molly and Ned entered the dining area. "Hi Moses," they both said at the same time.

"How you do, how you do?" Moses jumped like a gentleman and pulled the chair out for Molly to sit in.

When the food finally arrived on the table the family bowed their heads. Lucas cleared his throat, then prayed, "Our great, Almighty God. Thank you for this bountiful meal. Thank you for the treasures we have in Christ and in heaven. And thank you for my family. We ask for you to bless this meal and this home. We ask for you to end the oppression of slavery. And we ask you to end the war and spare the lives of our young men fighting for the dignity of others. In Jesus name we pray, Amen." This was a similar prayer to what he prayed at every meal, but he said it sincerely and Moses always appreciated that.

While the family ate they talked and laughed and enjoyed the time together. They were never in a hurry at Sunday dinner and often they would sit at the table for hours discussing politics, the sermon that morning, the events in the community—anything but work and the tasks they would do on the other six days. They were not strict sabbatarians, like the Amish and Mennonites, but they did as little as possible on Sundays so they would be refreshed for the next day.

Before the folks left the table, Lucas asked a question of Moses. Usually Moses just listened in and laughed with the family and only contributed when asked. That is, unless things got a little out of control and there was hootin' and hollerin', he would slip up and let out some things but that didn't happen very often.

Lucas looked directly at Moses and said, "Moses, what do you think of the war and that the Union Army has lost over 2,000 white men in their battles so far?"

The room became pretty quiet and Molly broke the silence, "Daddy, you shouldn't put Moses on the spot like that. He doesn't read the newspapers and hear all the intelligentsia discuss this war at length like you do."

"It's okay ma'am, I don't mind. I counts it a privilege to share with Master what I thinks," Moses said.

Again, there was a healthy pause while Moses collected his thoughts and took a deep breath. "I don't rightly know whats to think."

Lucas bellowed out laughing at this because it was part of Moses' personality and instinctive humor to act like he would have a profound answer and then say nothing. Lucas had seen this many times.

"Go on Moses, you know I'm not trying to embarrass you, just tell us what's on your mind about the whole affair. We hardly get to hear your side of the story on a lot of the matters that affect you the most."

"Thank you, suh. I do have one small thought on it. I thinks those are pretty brave men out dar going against dose Rebel forces......" At this Moses noticed Molly grimace. *She did not think of this war the same way the family thought,* he remembered.

"I mean, those Southern forces with dem yellin' and hollerin' and sneakin' up on da Union soldiers at night and pokin dem in da chest with dar bayonets when dey is sleepin."

"Is that what you've heard? Where do you get your information?" Molly asked. She no longer felt the need to defend Moses.

Lucas glared at her.

"Molly, let Moses talk, honey. It's his turn now," said Abigail.

"Sorry, Moses."

Moses continued, "Dose are mighty brave men and I is proud of dem. I am proud of Mr. Lincoln and da decisions he is makin. Begin' your pardon but Mister, Ma'am (Moses glanced at Lucas and Abigail), you will never know what it's like to be treated da way we are treated and den not be able to fight for ourselves. My people just take it on the back, workin and whipins on the back, and it changes a man after awhile. Sometimes our people just plain give up. But Lincoln gives us hope. Dat's why dis war is so important for peoples like me—it's giving us hope dat religion means sumpin to you white fokes and dat we are all people on God's earth strivin together to know his will. Dat you white sons will fight for other people, people day don't know and thousands of da black people yet to be born…. dat dey would do sumpin like dat and lay dar life on da line…." At this point Moses got choked up and couldn't finish.

Abigail patted Moses' hand while Lucas spoke, "Moses, you don't have to finish. We all hear what you're trying to say. People from the South will never understand those ideas. In fact our own daughter struggles with it." Lucas glanced over to Molly as he finished his sentence.

"Can I say something?" Molly asked.

"No, Molly, not now. You can have your say later."

"There's another side to it and you know it."

"I know *you* think so but at this moment and at this table I will not permit you to counter what Moses has had the courage to share to us," Lucas said with an edge to his voice.

Molly knew when to stay her tongue. Moses could see she was tired of Master Harrington indoctrinating her.

Ned followed up the conversation by adding, "It didn't occur to me until just now Moses about what you are saying. Our founders felt the same way with the new government they were establishing, that it was not only just for them and their children, but for literally millions of people who would be born into it. To have that kind of vision is sublime. It is like the men of Issachar having an 'understanding of their times.' It is forward thinking and this is why I won't fight for the South. Their cause is of a past generation, not for the future ones. Our times demand we set in place a system that not only works for a few people, in one part of the country, for one small era of history. We need to establish a system that works for all people, in the entire country and in the future of our future." Ned appeared pretty proud of himself for his contribution.

Moses had things under control emotionally now and finished up by saying, "I don't know about no future of a future…." At this Lucas burst into laughter again at the way Moses said it. "But I do knows dat when my people have chilluns, dey posativly cannot be born into slavery. Dar hast to be an end to it. Perhaps da nation could say when all slaves die den it's done, but to allow our chilluns to enter into a life of slavery is beyond my understandin as to how a God-fearin man could allow dat for anyone."

"That's very gracious of you Moses, but I cannot wait until all the current slaves die. I want to see this chapter concluded in my lifetime," Lucas said. "In fact, I demand it."

"It's been goin on fo years, Master. If dey could stop it with the newbones, it would be fine wid me."

"So you don't mind having all your friends in Winchester work the plow for years for nothing and then be sold and separated from their family with sometimes not even a day's notice? You don't mind a Georgian plantation owner coming up and collecting his runaway and mutilating part of his body? I know you do mind, Moses, as much and likely more than me. And that is why we have to put an end to this once and for all. Slavery has got to be abolished and laws have to be put into place so that it can never exist again in any form."

"I admire you Master and I wants to believe dat. I guess I just don't have da faith in yo people and dar plans to believe dat dis is possible and it can all be finished fo good. I also believe dar is much mo dat done needs to be changed dan just slavery."

With that comment Lucas looked up, met Moses in the eyes and slowly nodded his head in agreement.

21.

The Visitor worked hard because it was almost daylight. The sun would soon be coming up over Washington, twenty miles to the east. He had spent the last six hours with a team of men painting logs black and hauling them up the hill in a horse-drawn caisson. Once the logs were all brought to the top, the Visitor mounted some on two-wheeled carriages and others he emplaced on the ground, slanting up so they stuck through the fortifications like large artillery pieces. It was crude, but he knew from a distance it would look like a ridge filled with deadly field guns. These would hopefully delay the Union Army for awhile.

The sun began to rise so the Visitor called his team together and gave them instructions on lighting campfires all along the ridge in the evenings. The campfires, plus daily marching back and forth across the terrain, would allow the ruse to last awhile. *I hope these Quaker guns work*, thought the Visitor. *Perhaps long enough*. His work there was done. He would now ride off and do the same thing in another location.

22.

President Abraham Lincoln dropped his seventy-six inch body into the soft chair and smiled. He was amused that three of the men in the room whom he was so close to presently, had actively contended against Lincoln for the Republican nomination merely a few months earlier. Lincoln was happy it was no longer perceptible that Seward and Chase had suffered immense grief and bitterness because of their loss. Bates, the third candidate running against Lincoln, did not have such high hopes in winning the nomination. The former Missouri Representative had not clung to the mantle of Republicanism much before the 1860 campaign like the other three candidates. Bates was sorely disappointed and soured by the politics of the event held in Chicago that summer, but certainly not debilitated by the results.

Yet with Seward and Chase it was different. Both of these men felt confident they would win the nomination. More so, they both felt they deserved it. William Seward, the former New York Governor and U.S. Senator during the fifties, had spent years building up his support and immortalizing his name in people's minds for the purpose of gaining high office. He was a people person, loved politics and possessed natural abilities which endeared himself to others. This hurled him to the front of the political spectrum.

The Ohio Governor Salmon Chase was in contrast to Seward in personality type. He did not have the natural abilities of Seward and had to maneuver very carefully in politics. He was self-righteous and he appeared never to notice that people felt somewhat belittled in his presence. He desperately wanted to make a positive impression on others, but people often discerned this desire and could not sense true warmness from him. He seemed more self-seeking and self-preserving. While Seward and Lincoln loved to tell stories and laugh with others, Chase had no sense of humor and was never endeared by people outside of his own family. Unfortunately for him, others could easily perceive that Chase's solar system revolved around his singular pursuit of high office. He gave the impression he would never be at peace with himself or the world without this realized goal, yet his very pursuit of it is what got in the way and became his demise.

No one had anticipated Abraham Lincoln could be in the running for the Republican nomination because Seward, Chase and Bates were the obvious leading contenders. It took a mammoth 233 votes to secure the nomination so most supposed a three way tie on the first ballot with Seward, Chase and Bates, and then Seward eventually winning with the second ballot. However, when the first count was tallied in Chicago's Wigwam Convention Center that May of 1860, Seward was a wide margin ahead of the other candidates with 173.5 votes. The shock for the three power politicians (Seward, Chase and Bates) was that, though they had discounted Lincoln, he had garnered the second largest amount of votes with 102. Bates, Chase and Simon Cameron all tied for third place with roughly 50 votes a piece. In the second vote, however, Pennsylvania shifted their votes from Cameron to Lincoln giving him a much needed boost. After the second ballot Seward had 184.5 votes, Lincoln 181 votes and Chase and Bates dropped further behind with 42.5 and 35 respectively. At this point Lincoln's supporters were ecstatic. This was precisely the outcome they had hoped for.

Bates no longer had a chance and his supporters sorrowfully accepted defeat. Chase, waiting at his residence in Ohio for the results by telegraph, was absolutely devastated to learn he did not even garner all of the votes from his home state as Seward, Lincoln and Bates had done. Ohio split its vote between Chase, Lincoln and John McLean, a fellow Ohio man. Later on, Salmon Chase was more upset about this solitary fact than he was at losing the nomination. This was betrayal to him and embarrassing. How could he hope to preside over a collection of states if his home state was not even sure of him? Lincoln recollected that instead of Chase looking at his own failure to mend fences, garner support and secure the votes needed, he looked at others and bitterly enumerated the outcome for months, incredulous as to how it ever happened.

The third and final vote was tallied. Some were perspiring, not from the heat, but because the tension in the Wigwam was so thick you could cut it with a knife. Seward supporters and Seward himself felt sure this final vote would bring him his cherished victory. But, like so many other things in this world that seemingly happen without just cause, Seward ended with 180 votes, Chase 42.5 and Lincoln 231.5, only 1.5 votes away from winning. Immediately upon seeing how close Lincoln was to securing the nomination, a delegate from Ohio switched four more votes from Chase to Lincoln giving the future president 235.5 and a conclusive win.

For a solitary moment there was no noise in the hall as the results sunk deep into the minds and hearts of those participating, then a thunderous cheer and applause for Lincoln was heard throughout the center and out into the street.

The Seward supporters were silent and stunned. That morning their victory had been a foregone conclusion. Now they had to wire their candidate and tell him the bad news.

Abraham Lincoln remembered how he had to be interrupted while buying some things Mary needed from a local shop. When told he had won the nomination by excited passerbys, Lincoln responded calmly and with a wink said, "Friends, this is good news, but if you'll excuse me now, I must return to my home and complete this errand for my wife." Lincoln remembered the look of shock on those rejoicing around him to see how calmly he took the news. Inside he was exuberant but he had learned as a kid to suppress wild joy and raging anger.

Later, after winning the general election in November, Abraham Lincoln astounded the public by choosing his former rivals as Cabinet members. This had never been done and many thought it was a curious, if not an impossible, way to govern the land. *Maybe it is curious but it seems to be working,* thought Lincoln looking at the men in front of him now discussing the war effort.

"Why won't McClellan lead our troops to battle and fight?" asked Seward. "We do nothing while the Southern Army reinforces and expands."

"Give him time William, give him time. The men are doing well and the training is excellent," suggested Edwin Stanton, the new Secretary of War. Stanton was the only one in the room who had not run against Lincoln in 1860.

"More time and more training, you would think we were going up against a mighty empire. Jefferson Davis does not have near the resources we do and the time to attack is now," stated Seward.

"Let me talk to him," said Salmon Chase the Treasury Secretary surprising the others. "My daughter and I have a way of being very persuasive when we have guests into our home. Perhaps we can encourage George to take his men and fight instead of just practicing their marching drills."

There were several chuckles from the group knowing how persuasive the beautiful, young Miss Chase could be. There was also a nervous laugh out of those who knew Chase used his home as the Capitol's gossip headquarters. Lincoln noticed Chase wink at Bates, probably Chase's only friend on the Cabinet.

"That will not be necessary, Salmon, though I do appreciate your eagerness to help," said Lincoln. "I am going to have a war council with all of you and our top generals. We are going to propel our young commander in the right direction and seek to illumine him as to how important it is that he do something. We did not ask him to lead the army from a Washington desk. He must get into his saddle and move these forces away from here and attack."

23.

Riley's depression was not as acute after the incident at the Grey Goose and it disappeared almost completely when the McNair's moved north. Riley felt better internally having his thoughts exposed. The small group of friends worked fragilely around Riley's philosophical dilemma and subsequent choice to move. No talk at that time pinpointed on Riley possibly joining the Northern Army. He was seen more as a pacifist. Though Riley's melancholy improved, Riley's new problem in Pennsylvania was boredom. He was not in school and his family no longer lived on a farm. He also missed his friends immensely, even with the new awkwardness that pierced their relationship.

Surprising himself, Riley McNair was ready to enlist when the summons finally came. He was nearly six feet tall with long dark-brown hair and a powerful upper build. He was good with a horse and asked the draft board if he could join the U.S. Cavalry. After one look at him they complied and gave him twenty-four hours to retrieve whatever gear he needed, secure a healthy horse and make for a camp where new recruits were assembling outside of Pittsburgh.

Riley joined the 4th Pennsylvania Cavalry under Captain Samuel Young and Lieutenant Colonel James Childs. This regiment had been recruiting and forming for several months during the fall of 1861 and using Cooke's tactical manual to perform their drills. Over and over again Riley's unit practiced raids, screening movements, and how to effectively gather intelligence. They learned how to detect small lines of communication, interrogate prisoners and how to demolish railway tracks in a short amount of time.

Mostly the men practiced shooting their musketoons (shortened muskets) while riding. Riley enjoyed the work, but the weather turned cold and they were away from Pittsburgh much of the time. For being noticed as a competent and confident horseman, Riley was given a short pass during the holidays and a promotion to corporal.

The day after New Year's was his last evening at home and he travelled over to Molly and Ned's home to say goodbye to their family. He knew it would be strained with Molly, but he wanted to give their friendship one more chance. It would be the courteous, although potentially painful, thing to do. He always liked Molly and was hoping to have a much closer relationship with her at this stage in life but, just like what happened to his other friends, the war and the differences of belief made them drift apart. She barely spoke to Riley before he moved away.

Riley had a fleeting thought of asking Molly to marry him tonight and wait for him until the war was over. *Would she marry him? Could she marry him?* Riley wondered. Their beliefs were so different now. Because Molly clung more closely to her Winchester friends and to Virginia, Riley knew it would appear it was he who was the rebellious one. This kind of thinking made him anxious. He arrived at the Harringtons just as it was getting dark. As he walked up their front porch steps he remembered something Professor Jackson told his class once, "Meekness is an iron fist in a velvet glove," and he prayed his meeting with Molly would go well.

The conversation was courteous and polite with Lucas Harrington, Abigail and Ned, but with Molly things were strained. Riley asked if he could talk to Molly alone for a moment and her family quickly disappeared.

"I know you don't believe in what I'm doing, Molly. You don't even have to say anything, I can see it written all over your face."

"Don't you feel like a traitor?" she responded.

Riley gave a nervous chuckle, "No, not a traitor. I feel as if I am doing what my conscience and convictions are steering me to do. Look, I don't ask you at this point to believe in what I am doing--."

Molly cut him off in mid-sentence, "Good, because Riley you are going to go to war against our best friends. You will be fighting against Henry and Moss, Jonesy and Bruce. You used to respect Mr. Montgomery and Lawrence Crawford. It would be bad enough to fight against Virginian gentlemen who you don't know, but our neighbors and friends? Our friends, Riley! What will you do if you have them in your sight with a loaded Enfield? Will you fire it?"

Riley knew whatever he said at this point in the conversation would sound trite and possibly demeaning. He was starting to get upset because Molly never looked at an issue from another person's point of view. She was always right and if you didn't agree with her then it was your fault and you were wrong. The problem with communicating with her was that she actually happened to be right most of the time.

With the pause in the conversation, Molly asked, "Do you have nothing to say?"

Riley found himself tongue-tied so with the pause in the conversation Molly turned herself to face the parlor wall.

"Will you not look at me when we talk?" Riley asked.

"No, Riley. I cannot look at you now. You're a stranger to me. "

"Molly, your entire family believes as I do. Do you turn away from them, as well?" As the words came out, Riley knew he was isolating himself from this warm, delightful and spirited creature, but he was unable to control himself.

"Just go," is all she replied.

"Just go and that's it? Molly, you have always had to have things your way! It was always you who wanted to set the agenda no matter what we were all doing. And now you are ordering me out of your house without looking at me? Am I to leave without you giving me the courtesy of nearly twenty years of childhood friendship?" Riley was thankful this seemed to grab her attention. He wondered if she was crying.

Molly turned her face and looked squarely at him. Without any tears evident in her eyes she said sternly, "Riley, leave my presence and this house right now!"

Riley had not accomplished the closeness he had strategized for. He steeled his nerves and gave one more attempt, "Molly, I have more to say to you. I want to talk about us."

Molly glared at him and said nothing.

It finally sunk into Riley that their conversation had concluded and could not be resurrected. He slowly stood up, grabbed his hat and walked out of the room, through the foyer, out the front door and down the porch steps. He turned around and faced the house and stood there mystified at how all of that just happened. Molly was the hardest person to figure out, and though their relationship was problematic most of the time, Riley knew she was the dearest person in his life.

24.

President Abraham Lincoln finished reading a solicited letter from retired general Winfield Scott and began the short journey to his board room where he knew the Cabinet had assembled. As he walked, he recalled how McDowell's failure, a quick show of force which was to put the rebellion down last July, had turned into an ongoing, multi-million dollar enterprise that did not have an end in sight.

All of the president's staff were shocked with what had transpired at Manassas. How on earth Jefferson Davis had the foresight to move reinforcements over the Blue Ridge Mountains so quickly was a mystery. The North was supposed to have excellent intelligence, yet they were outwitted by a movement of troops and supplies which must have been over twenty miles long. *Where was the cavalry report? Where were all the spies we were supposed to have feeding us information on a daily basis from the other side? Where was the secret service report?* Lincoln wondered for a brief moment if the South's spy system was even up and running. *Perhaps it is more advanced than ours,* he thought. Lincoln was getting a headache rehashing it all again. He must put it to rest and refresh his mind for this important war meeting. He stopped by the kitchen to drink some cool water and he continued to think of last fall.

It made the President feel a little better replacing Irvin McDowell with George McClellan, but Lincoln continued to have doubts about the decision. McClellan, roughly nine inches shorter than Lincoln, was fairly young and inexperienced. Though trained in the Mexican War by Winfield Scott himself, McClellan had been in the railroad business the last four years and not in the military. Those things were minor, however, to what really bothered Lincoln about the person of McClellan. It was his arrogance. More than once, McClellan said something so prideful and distasteful everyone in the room would blush. Lincoln knew the others were offended for him but he could take a little verbal abuse from the man if he would fight and win some battles. Victory was Lincoln's greatest goal so he tried to rally people *for* McClellan in order to shorten the war. In fact, he told the Cabinet several times that he would shine McClellan's boots if the general would move out of Washington to attack.

After McClellan was named General-in-Chief of the Army, Lincoln knew there needed to be a change at the War Department and made the tough decision. At the beginning of the New Year, Edwin M. Stanton—McClellan's strong ally—replaced Simon Cameron and became the new Secretary of War. Now, Lincoln hoped that a tight team between Stanton and McClellan would figure out exactly what to do without competition and get this war on the offensive. Though McClellan had been successful while commanding before, this job would require new leadership skills. Lincoln tried to communicate to the young commander the incredibly large responsibility which had been placed upon his shoulders. The response from McClellan was, "I can do it all."

McClellan had fortified positions around Washington and was an excellent army organizer and drill enthusiast, but he had not gone to battle yet. McClellan, or 'Little Mac' as his troops liked to call him referring to his short stature, kept speaking of vastly superior Confederate forces and he simply would not budge toward the enemy. He would not employ for an offense the very army Lincoln had called up months ago and the nation was paying for every day. Lincoln didn't care about the money, but worried there was no progress in the war with all these trained and outfitted troops. Soon, enlistments would be over and they would have to rebuild the army again. *For life and liberty, what was McClellan doing with all his time?* Lincoln wondered.

It was almost mid-January and Lincoln wanted action. In fact, he was demanding it. *Enough with the arrogance and defensive posturing, we have to head to Richmond and strike a death blow to the Confederacy!* He would not take no for an answer any longer. He called a Cabinet meeting for this day and invited General McClellan along with two other generals.

Everyone in the room stood at attention when he arrived, but Lincoln immediately noticed McClellan wasn't there yet. *Another sign of arrogance,* he thought. Lincoln bit his lip a moment and couldn't help but think about the reports over the holidays where McClellan had called him a 'well-meaning baboon' and a person 'unworthy of the office.' *Maybe that's why McClellan wasn't here now,* Lincoln thought. *He's too embarrassed by his insults to the nation's leader.*

"Well, my special guest hasn't arrived yet, but why don't we get started." Lincoln faced Treasury Secretary Salmon Chase, Postmaster-General Montgomery Blair, Secretary of State William Seward, Secretary of War Edwin Stanton, Quartermaster General Montgomery Meigs and former Army of the Potomac Commander Irvin McDowell.

Not long after the meeting began Lincoln's assistant John Hay opened the door and stood back while General George B. McClellan walked in behind Lincoln and crossed the room toward an empty chair. Despite the verbal wounds from McClellan over the holidays, President Lincoln jack-knifed out of his chair and gave McClellan a warm handshake.

"General McClellan, you know everyone here so we will dispense with introductions. The purpose of this meeting, gentlemen, is to decide how to move forward with our attack on the Confederate Army in Virginia. I have heard from the other commanders and I just finished reading a letter from General Scott, which he wrote me in his retirement at my request. Now, General McClellan, I want us all to hear from you."

"I have been busy at reorganizing the entire force—." McClellan started but Lincoln cut him off, which was uncharacteristic of the President, except when he was at his limit.

"I am not concerned to hear about your actions as General-in-Chief of the Army. In fact, it is my thought that having you in this role could be taking too much of your precious attention off of Johnston and Lee. I want to know, and I believe everyone in this room would like to know, what is the commander's intent for the Army of the Potomac? This large mass of men I look out of my windows and see every day—what about them?"

McClellan, clearly perturbed at the President's forceful leading of the conversation, took a second to clear his throat and look once more around the room before beginning to speak. "Mr. Lincoln, I did not know this was going to be an inquisition of confidential plans. I do not feel comfortable in this setting—."

"Then what setting would you like?" Lincoln interrupted. "We can do this anywhere you would like at any time. I believe you will find all of us have been cleared to hear any top secret information you may have." Lincoln was still playing the diplomat. He had one card left to pull by reminding McClellan that it was the President who was Commander-in-Chief, but he hoped never to have to use it.

"Begging your pardon, Mr. President, but I do not want to see my offensive plans printed in the Washington newspapers. Or worse, in a Richmond paper for all to see and give the Rebels a chance to prepare."

"General Johnston and Jefferson Davis have had six months to prepare and we have done nothing," Lincoln said almost to himself.

"Nothing, sir? I beg to differ. I would like to remind you of the shape the army was in when I inherited it from, excuse me sir (he nodded to Irvin McDowell sitting across the table from him), my predecessor. The army was a rag tag, battered mess and completely disorganized and disheartened. I hope everyone in this room has seen it has taken someone with extraordinary skills and determination to put things back on the right path. I had thought the leaders in this room appreciated what has been accomplished so far." McClellan was clearly annoyed as he rehashed some of the same things everyone there had heard from him either one-on-one or in a group.

"No one is doubting your competency, General, and clearly no one would doubt your confidence. It is your plan to push into the heart of Virginia and break the rebellion that we would like clearer information on. We wanted this to be done quickly before Davis ever had a chance to rally reinforcements and equip his fledgling army."

"Mr. Lincoln, it is probably obvious to *some* in this room with military experience that these things take time and great planning. Excuse me for being frank, but we saw the result of your involvement at Manassas. You had thought then that we should push ahead and we were completely overwhelmed," McClellan said with a self-important tone. "Am I not right?"

This stung the President but he kept his composure. He could sense the others squirm at the awkwardness McClellan's words brought to the room. Lincoln had been the only one in the room asking the questions which was protocol until he opened it up for discussion. He didn't say anything but he looked around the room and gave an approving nod hoping someone else would carry the conversation forward.

It was Secretary Salmon P. Chase who asked the next question. "General McClellan, I believe it would be helpful to know whether you do in fact, not only have a comprehensive strategy for beating the South but a detailed plan to attack Johnston's forces, which have been at our doorstep for so long."

"This meeting is beginning to feel like the inquisition. Does anyone else have a question for me?" McClellan retorted.

"General, do you have a plan? This is what we need to know! This is why the President has called this meeting!" Chase was furious. He was not used to being treated this way. Even Lincoln, who Chase disagreed with on most items, was courteous and responded to him when he had a direct question. McClellan was a friend of the Treasury Secretary and an occasional guest in his home. Chase didn't understand why he couldn't be more helpful to them.

"I do have a plan." Everyone in the room breathed a quiet sigh of relief as McClellan continued, "My staff has meticulously put together an offensive operation that will crush General Johnston and his army with one decisive blow."

Now the new Secretary of War, an ally of McClellan, entered into the discussion, "George, could you give us an overview today of how you are going to attack and tell us approximately when?"

"Will you permit me to ask a question first? Sir, you said you have heard from the other commanders and from General Scott. Would you enlighten me as to what they might have proposed would be the best stratagem?"

"You certainly can ask, General, because this is precisely what I wanted to talk about today." Lincoln took a quick moment to organize his thoughts. "The consensus seems to be in attacking Lee's forces back at Manassas, leave a strong contingent to protect our flank and head straight toward Richmond for the ultimate contest. With Manassas Junction in our possession, our supply lines will be unfettered to any avenue of attack we will need to proceed with. Without Manassas in Confederate hands, Davis, Johnston and Lee are declined the opportunity to maneuver their troops so freely. So far, they have successfully kept our army bottled up here defending Washington.

"General McClellan, is that what you would do as well?" Secretary Seward asked. Seward had very little patience with this general who had told others frequently the Secretary of State was 'an incompetent little puppy.'

McClellan actually smiled, "I have two things to say. First of all, Manassas isn't the answer. For reasons I won't go into now, I would not consider Manassas the most promising way toward defeating Johnston and heading to Richmond. Second, I am concerned the war is being run by politicians and not military strategists. This Cabinet and the Congress have given me a task to do and I want you to be sure I will do it, not only exceptionally well, but at the precise moment I have determined it will bring the most success. I have told you I have a plan. I hope this is sufficient for you at this time. When you see my regiments moving forward in the early morning hours one day soon, then you will know the time and the direction of attack."

"If not with Manassas then where, General?" Secretary Seward asked a little more forcefully.

"As I just mentioned I do not want to go into the details, but my plan involves using the navy and approaching Virginia by sea, establishing a beachhead and then driving toward Richmond. Richmond is the next goal, gentlemen. Nothing more, nothing less."

"Are you sure that won't cause unnecessary delays with loading and unloading men on the transports? And won't that bottle up our army at a central point making it more vulnerable to attack?" These questions were asked by General Irvin McDowell.

"Mr. President, I ask to be excused. I have many things that need to be accomplished today and this meeting, if continued, will only work to slow down the very thing you wish for the most."

Lincoln smiled graciously, "By all means, General, don't let us hold you up from planning your attack. I hope you enjoy the rest of your day."

McClellan pushed his chair back, stood up, shook only Stanton's hand and left. Everyone in the room watched him leave in disbelief that the meeting was over so quickly. There was an awkward moment of silence while everyone looked around the room.

Seward spoke first, "My, my. We either have a very confident commander who will definitely win us this war, or a conniver who likes grand plans and strategies more than actual combat. Sir, we have waited for months and I am all but sure it will be several more before we see any kind of assault."

Lincoln studied the others' faces and replied, "We have to hope General McClellan sees what we see, that delaying our assault toward Richmond will only lead to meeting a better prepared adversary. Every day we hear reports of more supplies entering their harbors and more recruits marching up from the cotton states. I am going to give him a couple of more weeks. If he has not made any significant progress toward our opposing forces, I will have to exercise my power as Commander-in-Chief and get more directly involved. Unless anyone has something else to enlighten us today then I suppose we are through." As he spoke the words, Abraham Lincoln knew any intervention on his part into McClellan's control of the army would be seen by the little commander as a mini-act of war.

PART IV

MRS. MONTGOMERY

Women's eyes have pierced more hearts than ever did the bullets of war.
WILLIAM SCOTT DOWNEY

25.

Winchester had seen better days than those that were about to fall upon it during the first half of 1862. The largest city west of the Blue Ridge Mountains, Winchester, boasted a medical college, fifty stores and over 4,000 residents. It was connected to the Baltimore and Ohio railroad and had several major roads crisscrossing through the downtown section. As the county seat, it was the northern gateway to the Shenandoah Valley. As the middle states were becoming the breadbasket of America, the Shenandoah was deemed the breadbasket of the Confederacy. With abundant corn, hay and wheat production, this valley fed many of Virginia's families each year.

The Shenandoah's western border held the Alleghany Mountains and its eastern border the Blue Ridge Mountains. Its southern entrance was Lexington, but the well-travelled Valley Turnpike ran from Winchester only to Staunton, where the Virginia Central Railroad passed through. Whoever possessed Winchester held free access to the 140 mile long valley with its agricultural and transportation assets.

For several months, General Stonewall Jackson occupied Winchester and used it as his headquarters. His office was at the home of Col. Lewis T. Moore's residence who was injured and out of town. Jackson spent most of his nights at Rev. James Robert Graham's house on Braddock Street, a few blocks south from his headquarters.

These were happy days for Winchester and each time Jackson passed by members of his old brigade they would cheer for him exuberantly. Soldiers and citizens alike admired him and enjoyed his presence. Children would shout to him as he passed and hoped for a familiar smile, or wink, or best of all, a personal greeting.

The ladies of Winchester loved walking up and down the tree-lined, paved streets of Loudon, Washington and Piccadilly in their bright-colored dresses and new Jeff Davis bonnets giving salutations to the men and women watching from their porches. Even in the evening hours as gas lamps lit the sidewalks and reflected off of the two story brick homes, men and women would be seen walking and talking. However, when General Jackson and his army moved out of town on March 11, 1862 you could sense the fear and anxiety coming from every home you might pass by.

Now when the women would walk from here to there for necessities they were usually dressed in black as if in mourning. No more were the relaxing evenings and neighborhood strolls by the Taylor Hotel common. Gone were the fine greetings, cheerful smiles and hours of kids playing in the streets. Winchester citizens (who were currently women, children and elderly) wept bitterly in the evenings because their town was occupied by the enemy.

26.

On March 12, 1862, General Nathaniel P. Banks marched his army into the city to the tune of the Star Spangled Banner. The first order of business for the Union Army was to locate appropriate headquarters buildings and to look for supplies and any written reports Jackson's Southern Army might have left behind.

For the entire week before Jackson left, the ladies of Winchester had hauled from the basement much of their food and useful war supplies so their beloved husbands and sons could use them while away at war. All documents and correspondence about the war was carried off by the army or burned so the Union search by Banks proved useless.

Claire Montgomery and her daughter Kathryn sat in their house one morning paralyzed as they heard Union officers banging on the outer door. The knocks became louder and louder. "They're going to knock down the door if we don't open it," Claire said.

"Be careful, mama."

Claire walked to the door amidst the chaos knowing their home could possibly be confiscated. She opened the door and standing on the porch were five Union soldiers, three of whom were officers and one had an eagle displayed on his shoulders.

The colonel spoke first, "Good morning, ma'am. Sorry to disturb you this morning. Are you Mrs. Montgomery?"

"Yes, I am Mrs. Montgomery," Claire replied.

"Ma'am, I have been sent at the request of my Brigadier General Alpheus Williams, First Division Commander of the Second Corps, to secure this home to be used as his headquarters."

At that moment Claire wished the earth would open up and swallow every blue-coated man who had entered their town. Out of the corner of her eye she saw a few other men walk around her house toward the back. She heard her favorite old mare neighing and their chickens being disturbed by the intruders. This was unbearable.

"Sir, could you return and report to your General that this house simply will not be adequate for him. My daughter and I volunteered to teach school here since our city buildings are now being utilized by your army. Even our churches currently have Yankee preachers in them. You have to understand, sir, the children must have a place to be taught." Claire was stretching the truth some and grasping at straws. She had volunteered her home, but no decision had been made yet.

The colonel caught a glimpse of young Landon and beautiful Kathryn behind her, "Ma'am, I will report this to the commander, but I would ask that you prepare to vacate. It would not be appropriate for you and your children to remain here with the general and his staff."

"Where do you propose that we go?"

"Ma'am, it's not my place to provide you new accommodations. I know it is a discomfiture, but we will need you to be gone by this evening."

Claire felt devastated. After the Union officers left, she and Kathryn held each other in the parlor and wept for quite awhile. Claire thought about how much their life had changed since Conrad and Henry departed with the army, but at least they had their home. Now, the rest of their security and safety would be ripped from them. After awhile Claire and Kathryn began to go through the house packing valuables, clothing and food. They loaded a small wagon that Conrad had left for them, ate an early supper and left their beloved home. The wagon was pulled by Claire's horse, Toby, which was too old to be used for the military, but just fine for short trips.

They had been invited to reside at Bruce and Moss's house where their mother, Sarah Crawford, sister Lucy, Gramma Elizabeth and dog Scout still resided. Lawrence Crawford had accepted an offer from Jefferson Davis to be an advisor and judge for the military in Richmond. With the three men gone the Crawford's white house on Loudoun Street seemed cavernous.

As Claire, Kathryn and Landon entered the Crawford home, the old friends gave each other multiple embraces. The Crawford's had also been invaded by the Union Army. A commander of an artillery regiment, a short round man with a red face from Ohio, asked to use the downstairs bedroom for lodging and the Crawford's were compelled to accept. He was a kind man, but he had a voracious appetite and Sarah wondered how she would feed him, her family and the Montgomery's.

Julia Bridgeman came over that evening for a visit and Scout, happy for all the company, went from lady to lady receiving stroke after stroke of affection and praise. Landon and Lucy disappeared to the backyard to play and Scout soon followed. The ladies talked late into the night and Julia ended up staying over so she would not have to go onto the Union patrolled streets after dark.

27.

The next morning Claire, Kathryn and Landon walked over to their home to see how everything was holding up. Their two slaves, Alma and her daughter Genevieve, stayed there to watch things for them and Claire was hoping they had done a good job. Scout followed along behind them, wagging his tail but keeping an eye out for danger.

They stopped first at the Tooley home where there lived six small children. Sarah asked them to drop by with some bread and Claire was happy to do this. Mrs. Tooley, now a single mother, was barely keeping up because half of her children were fighting disease and crying all night. After the Tooley visit, the trio finished walking down the street and turned left to continue to the edge of town.

When they finally rounded the corner of the lane leading to their house, they were shocked at the U.S. flag flying from their porch. As they grew nearer they saw several wagons and horses and carts around their house and several Union infantrymen sitting by the spring across the yard. More troops were near the orchard.

Claire marched up the front steps, opened the door and entered her house.

"Excuse me, ma'am. No one is allowed to enter here without permission," one scrawny, young man told her.

"Do I have to have permission to enter my own home?" Claire asked.

"No, ma'am, I didn't know this was your home."

Just then, the colonel who had asked for the home the day before came out of the kitchen and said, "Why, hello Mrs. Montgomery. It is nice of you to stop by."

Claire just glared at him, still distraught at having her cherished place now soiled with mud and littered with men's weapons and clothing.

A very distinguished looking man with a red, silk scarf around his waist walked out from behind the colonel and said, "Mrs. Montgomery, on behalf of the United States Army I want to thank you for providing your home for our division headquarters. You have a very delightful residence. Being somewhat secluded from town, it is ideal for our work here." The man then glanced at Kathryn who had a scowl on her face.

Claire continued the conversation, "You must be General Williams."

"I am."

"How long will you be in need of my residence for your work General?" Claire asked.

General Williams chuckled, "As long as it will be useful to the Union Army." There was a pause while Williams assessed his landlady and gathered his thoughts. "Mrs. Montgomery I greatly appreciate you giving up your home. I know it is a terrible annoyance for you. I trust you found lodging last night?"

"I have." Even though Claire was upset, she was beginning to warm up to this courteous, older man in her foyer. More soldiers came out of the kitchen to see what the disruption was. "General, must you fly that flag outside of my home?"

"You mean the flag of the United States of America? I must, as this is a major headquarters building of our forces here." With a twinkle in his eye he added, "I suppose you would rather have me fly that Rebel flag we confiscated from your bedroom last night?"

"General, I do not expect you to do that for me, it is just that--." Claire thought a moment, "Never mind, sir. I have too high of expectations for our captors." Claire didn't show it, but she was secretly furious about their discovery and theft of the flag she had sown. She had packed one flag in her luggage last night but she thought Conrad had taken the one from the bedroom.

"You are not being held here captive against your will are you?" asked the general with a twinkle in his eye.

Claire despised his patronizing tone, "No, but my house is."

There was an awkward moment before General Williams, a former judge from Michigan, smiled and continued the conversation. "May I ask you a question, Mrs. Montgomery?"

The general did not hesitate for a response, "I have been curious, why are the women and children in this town so sour and unpleasant to us? I have been getting reports from all of my subordinate commanders as to the extreme displeasure the citizens of Winchester have displayed to the troops, especially from the ladies. They are downright bitter toward us, washing their porches where we have sat and looking the other way when we wish them good day. Some of the younger women have even spit in soldier's faces. Apart from needing a few homes and garnering some sustenance, we have tried to be hospitable and accommodating when able. Yet one woman tried to poison us with some food she anonymously donated to the men. Many women here are walking around town in black as if going to a funeral. I had heard of Southern hospitality, but I am very disappointed with the hospitality of Winchester."

"The hospitality of Winchester has never been finer, sir. A few days ago we gave up our livestock and wagons, wine and drygoods, all for our men who left with General Jackson. What do you expect, General? You have made us a dominated people. We are in enemy hands. We despise your cheerful trumpetry and gallant uniforms and wagons of weapons and ammunition. We know the contents of those wagons will kill our husbands and our sons. General, some of our young soldiers are still just boys. We despise your fancy boots, knowing many of our young men from poor farms have shoes barely stitched together." Claire just paused to catch her breath and continue but General Williams interjected.

"Mrs. Montgomery, you are not in enemy hands. I work for the United States of America. Virginia is one of those states and Winchester is a fine city in our country. I deeply regret you would treat us as foreign invaders. Abraham Lincoln is simply--."

This time Claire interjected, "This is Seward's and Chase's war, General. That New York Yankee and the Ohio abolitionist have despised the South and our traditions for years. Even now Seward is negotiating with foreign nations against us."

"Mrs. Montgomery, this is not a war between two nation states as we have had in the past. The Southern states will never have sovereignty and be joined by a European power. As President Lincoln explained in his House Divided speech, this nation will either be slave or free. Lincoln is for union, not disunion. Because Lincoln holds the value of unity, when South Carolina seceded he was forced to take action. He had to govern according to his interpretation of the Constitution and that is what he is doing now, by sending troops into your town to pursue the Rebel Army."

Claire pressed her lips together silently so Williams continued, "I realize that if he had not called for volunteer troops in April, Virginia may not have seceded so soon and diplomatic relations might have prevailed. However, Abraham Lincoln sees in our nation what many Southern men do not. A powerful, united, sovereign entity that could never cease to be one, even if several states assemble an army and revolt. Whatever the cost, our unity must be maintained. We can no more be two nations as we can be three or ten or twenty. The preamble of the Constitution, Mrs. Montgomery, reads 'We the people of the United States, in order to form a more perfect union.' These words alone have inspired many from the North to send troops and supplies forward. It's their love for their country that compels them to do this, no less than your love for Virginia and the South."

The General had spoken a lot and knew his words were not well-received by the look on Claire and Kathryn's face. Landon was tired of the conversation and had walked into the parlor and sat down. Scout was still on the porch waiting.

"I also know history and politics, General, and I suppose now you will quote for me Andrew Jackson's toast at the Thomas Jefferson dinner?"

Williams smiled graciously and shook his head no.

"Has not the Constitution been interpreted by our courts that states are to decide for themselves as to what laws are just or unjust? Have not all the recent laws decreed that slavery is legal and just and Southern states are free to exercise this right?" Claire took a second to compose herself because she was getting overly excited.

With eyes blazing she continued, "What you Northern men will never understand and our Southern men see clearly is that Virginia was and is for the union and unity. Men in blue uniforms do not have the corner on what it means to be united. I have heard many a man in Winchester say that even if Lucifer himself had been elected president they would vote for union over disunion. Many veteran soldiers in Winchester, like my husband Conrad, are against war with a passion and have declared war the sum of all evils. Yet now, these same men are fighting in this civil war. Have you considered what could make such staunch unionists fight a war? Have you considered for a moment what it would be like to have your own city attacked? If your home was under siege, would you lay down your arms and accept the terms of whoever came to take you over? Or, would you also be horribly offended that this friendly overseer, the federal government, whose only powers are given by independent states, decided to attack one of its own limbs--?"

Appearing slightly annoyed with the conversation the General decided to interrupt as Claire slowed to inhale, "And I suppose now, ma'am, that you, like Lee, will tell us that Virginia has been in existence since the early

1600's and part of the Union only since 1776, so your loyalty lies with your state?"

"No sir, I will not. That would be wasting my breath. I will conclude this conversation with a question. How could Northern men who say they want union send an army into other states and not expect a war?" By now there were officers all along the staircase who had come out of their new offices (former bedrooms) to hear the debate. "And now I must go. Do not fear, General, I am positive the residents here will one day be joyful and courteous to you--."

"On the day of my departure?"

Claire smiled, "You are starting to understand me General. Thank you for your kind demeanor and listening ear. May I ask you a parting favor?"

"Of course."

"If I have grievances about destruction of my property or theft of any of my possessions may I bring these to you?"

"You certainly may, Mrs. Montgomery. You have my word they will be reviewed and taken seriously."

"Thank you, General."

"Mrs. Montgomery, I know you would like to leave, but if I could ask one more question? Have you read Uncle Tom's Cabin?"

"Yes, General Williams, I have read Stowe's book and I have had my children read it."

"What did you think of it—I really am curious?"

"General, it was written from a Northern perspective by a self-righteous abolitionist. What more would you like me to say?"

"You didn't think it was good literature?"

"Yes, she writes well, no doubt. However, I do not agree with her accusations and conclusions."

"You wouldn't agree, then, that one of the most harrowing parts of slavery is the separation of families at the will of their masters?"

"Not all Southerners treat their slaves in such a manner. Each person has to choose whether to do evil or good on a daily basis."

"Then you do not believe slavery is inherently evil?"

"No, sir, I do not. It is a mechanism by which labor is wheeled for a positive outcome to our economy. One could have an honorable slave/master relationship and one could have a dishonorable one."

"What do you think of the words in the Virginia Declaration of Rights, written by George Mason, a Virginian himself, that all men are by nature equally free--."

"Equally free and independent, and have certain inherent rights," Claire interjected the last words of the general in unison with him. "I know it, General Williams, and I also know Franklin and Jefferson put Mason's thoughts into the Declaration of Independence. However, it says 'men,' and it is implied 'white men,' not women or the African race. Women were just recently given the right to own property and we still cannot vote! I am sure with time women and the black race will evolve to where they have the same rights as white men. You know that Taney and the Supreme Court ruled against Scott. The African man simply doesn't have any rights--yet."

General Alpheus Williams hesitated a moment to consider whether or not to pursue this delicate subject. He could tell by her mannerisms that his hostess was ready to depart.

Claire made the decision for him. "Thank you for this conversation, General. Good day." And with a parting glance, Claire, Kathryn and Landon walked out of their house and hurried down the street led by Scout.

Several of the officers in the Montgomery home laughed heartily at the properness and dignity of Mrs. Montgomery. General Williams merely shrugged his shoulders, looked up at the men while walking back into the kitchen and declared, "Now you know what a 'died in the wool' Southern woman thinks and the mentality we're up against here in the fine city of Winchester."

28.

By the middle of March in 1862 things were desperate for the Confederate Army. The Union Army under General Ulysses Grant had secured the surrender of Fort Henry and Fort Donelson and captured over 14,000 Southern prisoners. The Federals took over Kentucky and most of the state of Tennessee to include Nashville. Many of the major Southern seaports were also at risk and Roanoke Island, North Carolina was taken. The Confederate supply of powder was almost depleted and their arsenals were empty. The Confederate Army had merely a fourth of the strength of McClellan in Virginia and even most Virginians thought it was a matter of time before Richmond would be in Federal hands.

With more inactivity on the part of McClellan, Lincoln issued an executive order called General Order No. 1, which told all of the army commanders they would "move out" on February 22nd toward their new objectives. To make sure General McClellan (who was already feeling soured by this interference) understood Lincoln meant business, the President issued another order directly to McClellan. This order declared the Army of the Potomac would move on February 22nd to seize and occupy a railroad point southwest of Manassas Junction and move toward Richmond from there.

Young Napoleon McClellan underwent an emotional convulsion and then registered complaints with the Secretary of War. He suggested using his own plan which called for a massive naval assault with his army of almost 120,000 troops. His proposed assault would require thousands of sea vessels to move not only the soldiers, but 4,000 horses, 1,100 wagons and over 200 cannon. The logistics were expensive, time consuming and not very strategic in case of a retreat. President Abraham Lincoln and the

Congress were already concerned because the war was costing the Union over two million dollars a day. Lincoln wanted a quick and decisive end and he looked again at his very own picked high commander of the armed forces and pleaded with him to go overland from Manassas to Richmond.

General McClellan was used to getting what he wanted and with great persuasion spoke some of the words Lincoln wanted to hear. Little Mac told the president his own plan would bring the nation a quick, brilliant success and he would stake his life and reputation on it. In fact, he told Lincoln he would stake the very cause of the Union on this one great plan of his.

With his customary patience and humility, Abraham Lincoln allowed McClellan to move forward with his own plan. However, February 22nd came and went without any troop movement. In fact, General McClellan did not perform any serious movement until mid-April and his first assaults would be weeks beyond. Lincoln was beside himself with anticipation and disgust but could only watch and wait. He was not completely discouraged, however, for he was told by his spies the Confederates were on the brink of defeat. *May it please be true,* thought Lincoln.

29.

As Jackson walked through the leafless trees in the rain to locate his aide, he reflected on the events of the last few days and the urgent messages from Robert E. Lee in Richmond. Because of McClellan's Peninsula Campaign up the Chesapeake Bay in pursuit of Richmond, Confederate General Joseph E. Johnston ordered most Confederate forces to concentrate east of Richmond. Jackson was told by Lee, Johnston's intermediary, that his small contingent of 3,000 was being used as a diversionary force to keep Nathaniel P. Banks (Commander of the Union V Corps) occupied at Winchester. This would alleviate the pressure the Southern Army felt from McClellan's leviathan force coming from Washington. Both Union armies, if combined, would surely be lethal for the Southern Capitol.

Because Jackson moved toward the Shenandoah River near Rude's Hill after his escape from Winchester, the Union Army stopped pressing their advance with James Shield's Division. In fact, the Union generals were convinced Jackson had vacated the valley entirely giving them freedom to reposition and send troops toward Richmond to assist McClellan.

Jackson had just left the tent of Jedediah Hotchkiss who was a geologist and cartographer. He commissioned Hotchkiss to make some maps of the valley and the mountains to the east. Jackson specifically wanted to know about passes and trails which might be overlooked by the larger Union Army and utilized by Jackson's more maneuverable force. He also asked Hotchkiss if he could make some crude maps of any major encounter their army might have with the Federals. Jackson finally spotted what looked like Bruce's abode and kicked some mud off his boots on a rock outcropping just near the tent.

"Who are you writing to, Lieutenant Crawford?" Jackson asked his aide when he walked into the small tent and saw Bruce at his field desk. Jackson, at five foot eleven inches had to duck under the straps to come in. He pushed his brown hair back and rubbed his beard straight again.

"A friend," Bruce replied as he stood up at attention.

Motioning him to relax with his hand Jackson asked with a grin, "Is this friend a male or a lady friend?"

"A lady, sir."

Jackson smiled, "It is amazing how God has designed there to be two sexes. And that one can scarcely live without the other one. I know I miss my bride and she has only departed a few days ago. Is this a friend from Winchester?"

"Yes, sir. But presently she is residing near Pittsburgh with her mother and adoptive father. You might remember her birth father, Cotton Matthews. He fought in the Mexican War and fell in the battle of Chapultepec."

"I do remember Cotton. He was a fine officer. I heard his widow and her new husband had travelled north, didn't want to fight for—." Jackson abruptly ended his sentence. "No, it was their right, just as it is our right to stay and try to work vigorously to end this."

"I miss their daughter, Molly, but I am not sure how she feels about me. We played together as children, but as we grew up it became more and more awkward to communicate with each other," Bruce shared. "She can look at me and make me feel as if I am still six years old and she twenty."

Jackson stared at him a moment with a thoughtful look and a twinkle in his eye, then abruptly changed the subject. "What have you heard from Colonel Ashby?"

Colonel Turner Ashby was the head of Jackson's cavalry and commanded the 7th Virginia Cavalry. Ashby's beloved brother, Richard, had been his companion at the beginning of the war until last June. Overrun by Federals and fighting alone, Richard was wounded and part of his skull was cleaved off by a Union saber. While he lay on the ground writhing in pain, he was asked if he was a secessionist to which he replied "yes." His horse and spurs were taken from him and Richard was thrust in the belly with a sword and left for dead. Turner Ashby heard about the ruckus and pursued the party who had destroyed his brother. During his fierce attack on them he was wounded and three of his men died while the Union contingent was routed. He returned to search for Richard and finding him close to death, Turner diligently took care of him for a week before his brother finally expired.

"I have not received a report, sir." Bruce knew the Ashby brothers and their sister well because they grew up not far from Winchester and visited often. Now, Colonel Ashby had over 500 men under his command and he led them with ferocity and vengeance. Jackson and Bruce sometimes worried over his recklessness. The loss of Turner's brother and subsequent grief gave him a savage hatred for the Federals. "Wherever he is," Bruce added, "I am sure that he and his horse Tom Telegraph are enjoying their ride together immensely."

"I am sure they are, Lieutenant."

30.

When Jackson left, Bruce resumed writing his letter.

General Stonewall Jackson just left my tent, Molly, and it is a powerful, yet strange experience working for him. He is not at all as I remember him when he taught in the halls of the Institute. Gone is the awkwardness and deftness that seemed to surround him. With the secession of Virginia, a warlord was born who is focused on nothing except the full annihilation of the Union Army. His bravery and forcefulness in battle have won him the respect of all the men. Their only complaint is that he is too strict. He refused to give passes to the men when we camped outside of Winchester. This was an impossible order to obey for men like Henry who had a new bride. Others, like my brother Moss, were able to ride into town on their horses to gather supplies once in awhile. I heard even Jonesy snuck into town once or twice to check on his beloved ma. Because I am Old Hickory's aide and at his side night and day, I was at his headquarters on Braddock Street a great deal. This allowed me to have constant communication with those in town and I was able to give messages back and forth. Kate was especially grateful for this privilege and she wrote Henry often.

We are currently awaiting word from Colonel Turner Ashby as to the disposition of the Union forces in and around Winchester. My gut tells me Jackson will attack there as soon as possible but he will never reveal his plan— even to his ablest commanders. You would be amazed at the daring adventures Turner has taken my brother Moss on. They defy the Union altogether and gather information about them as if they were allowed to be in their very camp and attend their meetings. I am sometimes scared for Moss's life. When we fled Winchester, just after midnight, Colonel Ashby and Moss remained behind until the next morning. As the Union Army slithered into town, Ashby and Moss took off on their horses just ahead of them. Moss has grown a slight beard and his hair is long. I am proud of him, but he is too cavalier with his life.

Molly you might be wondering why I am writing to you now after so many months apart. The answer is simple. I miss seeing you. My hope is that soon this war will be over and our families will all be reunited and I can see you again under the willows by the old stone wall. I am glad you are safe and with your family, though I know you would rather be in Winchester. The ladies there have helped us out immensely with clothing and boots and food and comfort items for our tents. You would be proud of them. I hear their homes are now invaded by the Union commanders, but they are holding their own and tolerating the unpleasantness well.

I miss you Molly, and I hope we can see each other again soon. Your good friend, Bruce Crawford

His mind began to play tricks on him. He remembered how Jackson used to say to the cadets, "Never take counsel of your fears." Bruce decided it was appropriate for him to call Molly a friend. Thinking of her possibly being married, he also felt it was too forward to write the line about seeing her under the willows. But, he didn't want to cross it out or start over. Besides, what did he have to lose? If she was with someone else she would simply rip it up and continue with her life. He decided to leave it alone and give it to the quartermaster to send on the next mail run. *Sometimes I think about things too much,* Bruce thought.

31.

That afternoon a note came from one of Colonel Ashby's riders to the headquarters where Jackson, Bruce and Sandie Pendleton (Jackson's other aide) were making plans. The message was from Ashby to Jackson stating Shields was retiring northward and a long procession of loaded Federal wagons were moving from Winchester to the northeast and back over the mountains toward the Potomac.

"Banks must be taking his corps south to join McClellan!" Jackson announced. "This would be devastating to our cause. We must not allow this to happen. Sandie and Bruce, notify the commanders at once to assemble here for their marching orders. Though they outnumber us heavily, it is essential we prevent Banks from connecting with McClellan—that is our sole duty here. If we fail at this task, it will jeopardize the entire Confederacy."

32.

George McClellan took another smoke from his pipe as he looked at his subordinate commanders; Generals Irvin McDowell, Edwin Sumner, Samuel Heintzelman and Erasmus Keyes. These four men, along with the absent Nathaniel Banks, were all made corps commanders under McClellan by Lincoln's second general order.

"Well, this should wrap things up quite nicely. I just received word Jackson is out of the Shenandoah hiding scared somewhere and most of General Banks' corps shall arrive here in a few days. That will give us enough firepower and reinforcements to penetrate Johnston's Army and capture their nerve center Richmond. With Grant's gains in the west this war should be about over. Perhaps we'll celebrate the Fourth of July in Atlanta gentlemen," McClellan laughed, very amused with himself.

McDowell and the others were more hesitant, having experienced the battlefield at Manassas.

"Strike up the band!" General McClellan ordered.

Immediately the little band huddled at the far end of their large meeting room began to play the "Gary Owen" and all sang heartily together:

Let Bacchus' sons be not dismayed,
But join with me, each jovial blade,
Come, drink and sing and lend your aid,
To help me with the chorus.

Instead of spa we'll drink brown ale,
And pay the reckoning on the nail;
No man for debt shall go to jail,
From Garryowen in glory.

We are the boys who take delight,
In smashing Limerick lamps at night,
And through the street like sportsters fight,
Tearing all before us.

Instead of spa we'll drink brown ale,
And pay the reckoning on the nail,
No man for debt shall go to jail,
From Garryowen in glory.

We'll break the windows, we'll break the doors,
The watch knock down by threes and fours,
And let the doctors work their cures,
And tinker up our bruised.

Instead of spa we'll drink brown ale,
And pay the reckoning on the nail,
No man for debt shall go to jail,
From Garryowen in glory.

We'll beat the bailiffs out of fun,
We'll make the mayor and sheriffs run
We are the boys no man dares dun
If he regards a whole skin.

Instead of spa we'll drink brown ale,
And pay the reckoning on the nail,
No man for debt shall go to jail,
From Garryowen in glory.

PART V

DEATH AROUND A STONE WALL

One man with courage makes a majority.
PRESIDENT ANDREW JACKSON

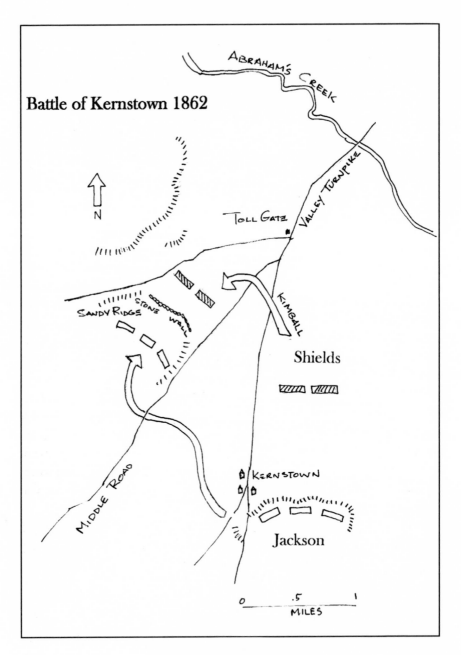

The Battle of Kernstown

33.

General Jackson looked intently at his three brigade commanders and his cavalry deputy. In the room were Brigadier General Richard B. Garnett, Colonel Jesse S. Burks, Colonel Samuel V. Fulkerson, and Colonel Conrad Montgomery (Kathryn's father) who was representing Colonel Turner Ashby and the 7th Virginia Cavalry. "Gentlemen, General Lee has asked us to stop Bank's corps from leaving the Shenandoah Valley and heading southeast to join General McClellan for a rendezvous at Richmond. They are trying to put together a deadly force to win this war with one bold push. We need to perform our own bold push. Our actions here will save many lives and protect the residents of our Southern Capitol from defeat if we are sharp and attack impetuously and continuously. We must keep our enemy bewildered and not give them time to think. A furious, wild attack back into Winchester will make Banks rethink the safety of any contingent he might have left there. We all know these forces were left there to protect Washington. Now my good Colonel Montgomery, what is the latest you have heard from your commander?"

"Sir, Colonel Ashby is pursuing several of Shield's men toward Winchester as we speak. He sent word asking for a strong infantry reinforcement. He believes there is no more than three or four regiments in front of him at Winchester and a few pieces of artillery," Conrad answered.

Jackson's eyes pierced through Conrad as he spoke, "Good, Colonel. If he is correct and it is no more than a brigade and we catch them off guard, we might have a chance. We must follow Colonel Ashby on foot starting immediately. Commanders, have your units secure two days of rations and begin the march before first light. We do not know how long it will be until our men will be fed again and they may have to march right into battle. I will give final battlefield instructions after I am there and have seen the terrain. Let us depart from here now and may an ever kind Providence direct our path."

34.

Riley volunteered for a special duty which called for one cavalry squadron. He and four others were winding their way through the mountains south of Pittsburgh and heading southeast toward Maryland. They were an advance party and the remainder of their unit would soon follow their lead, and all of them would eventually join forces with McClellan's Army of the Potomac. Riley was not told their exact destination, but as he grew close to the northern border of Maryland, he couldn't help but believe he was heading home. It had been eleven months since he had seen the place of his childhood and his friends.

He enjoyed the memories he shared with his band of Winchester friends. Yet, when he thought of seeing them now, possibly in battle, it brought a grimness over him like a dark cloud, pregnant with a wicked storm. As he pondered the situation, Riley tried to be careful not to allow his thoughts sink toward the abyss. He had talked positively to himself over and over again about this war and the necessity to prevent the Southern states from secession. He knew what was at stake for men like Moses, and for the millions of slaves who were still unfortunate enough to be living south of Mason and Dixon's line. *This is a fight for justice and freedom for people who cannot fight for themselves,* he thought to himself. These noble ideas gave him little comfort, however, when he imagined the faces of Bruce, Henry, Moss and Jonesy. Just as Riley knew he could take his own life if he willed it, he knew he could also kill his friends. The thought made him sick.

His small unit was preparing to halt for the night. They had covered nearly forty miles that day and everyone was exhausted. At this pace they could be across the Potomac and in the northern part of the Shenandoah

Valley in one and a half to two days. Riley fed his horse and then himself. He scavenged for and found some straw in a nearby yard to make himself a fairly comfortable bed. He closed his eyes and tried not to think about the possibility of fighting the people he held so dear.

35.

Moss finally found them. The three soldiers huddled near the small fire were laughing. Moss dismounted from his fine horse, Chris Columbus, and tied the reigns to a tree branch. He appeared the epitome of a brazen cavalryman with his western hat, sword and overcoat. He approached the group slowly and said, "I wondered if I would find you all tonight."

"Hey, our gallant knight is here," Henry said.

"If Ashby is the black knight then what are you, the gray knight?" asked Jonesy.

"No, Moss is the white knight," corrected Henry.

"Three cheers for the white knight," said Bruce.

"Funny. Very funny. It's not so gallant being with Ashby after a day like today with all the riding."

"How are you able to be here now?" asked Bruce.

"I just delivered a message to Jackson from my commander. Ashby wants me back by his side yet tonight so I cannot stay long—just a moment to rest old Chris and stretch out my backside. I asked Sandie where you were and he told me you had come down here by Cedar Creek to visit these noble footmen of the famous First Brigade."

"Yes, your ass might get tired but my not-so-tender feet are aching after the cruelty of that grueling march today," shared Jonesy.

"What feet? I can't feel my feet," Henry replied.

"I admire you all, walking everywhere you go," Moss replied. "I have never appreciated a horse so much as the last few days moving from Mount Jackson to north of Strasburg, then northward toward Winchester." Moss looked behind him at all of the small fires and makeshift tents and shelters almost as far as his eyes could see. "It is surprising how much our strength has grown over the last few weeks since we left town," he said.

"Yes it is. Besides receiving the hundreds of men from the Augusta County militia, we've taken in scores of men from all over the valley wanting to serve with Old Jack and give a jolting blow to the Yankee invaders," Bruce said.

"I hear many of the new men have religious convictions and will not touch a weapon, so Jackson is allowing them to be teamsters and have other duties of service in administration of some kind," Henry said.

"My religious conviction is to pick up my weapon and shoot it at the enemy so that we might end this war and I can go back home," said Jonesy.

"Where's Club?" asked Moss.

"Oh, he's sound asleep over there. Can't you hear him snoring?" Jonesy laughed as the others listened and chuckled.

"Did you all hear about what happened to General Shields earlier today?" Moss asked.

"I heard somebody mention his name at headquarters, but I have not heard the details," Bruce replied.

Jonesy and Henry now looked intently at Moss.

"General Shields was shot by Bruce's classmate, Preston Chew."

"You're kidding."

"I'm dead serious, and I hope Shields will be dead soon, as well. Word is, they amputated his arm and already have it in the mail headed back to Ireland for his mother," said Moss.

"That can't be true. Shield's ma can't still be alive. I've heard he's one of the oldest men on both battlefields," snorted Bruce. "Besides, you can't mail an arm."

"The Levite did with his concubine's arm," offered quick-witted Henry.

"I don't know gentlemen, but I do know there is turmoil in the Union camp tonight thanks to Preston Chew, Ashby and yours truly."

"How many of our men were wounded?" asked Henry.

"Several, but most of them are now doing pretty well. We know tomorrow is probably going to bring a good fight for us, if Jackson steps it up and gets you all to Winchester."

"Hopefully tomorrow night I'll be sleeping in my own bed."

"I wouldn't go that far Jonesy. Even if we get all you boys up there, we still have a couple of Union regiments to deal with," Moss replied.

Bruce chuckled a little, "Jonesy, you know General Jackson won't let you go home to be with Club and your mama. Even if we win back our beloved town, I am sure passes will be given out only at a bare minimum."

"Well maybe with a victory he will relent for a pass for us for one night," hoped Henry, thinking of Kathryn.

"Bruce, at least let them have that hope before they go to battle tomorrow," Moss pleaded.

Bruce closed his eyelids and thought for a moment of the unlikelihood of Jackson waving off protocol yet said, "All right, maybe Old Jack will be so beside himself that he will not ask for accountability right away. Regardless, we have little left of the night for sleeping and I better go see if he needs me for anything else tonight."

"I've got to go, as well. This has been a pleasure. If I see you three on the battlefield I will do my darndest to help you out," Moss said before he departed.

"I feel the same way," Henry said. If I see any of you in danger, I will quickly attend to your aid."

"Wild horses couldn't keep me from helping one of you," Jonesy said.

"Then it's decided; all of us will be the rear guard of the other," Bruce said. "What was it Alexandre Dumas wrote, *un pour tous, tous pour un*? May that be true for us tomorrow."

"I don't know what you just said but count me in," said Jonesy earnestly.

"I pledge my life," Moss said.

"Here here," hailed Henry.

"Here here," echoed Bruce.

"Here here!" concluded Jonesy.

"Duty! Strength! Courage!" The four young men said together as they broke out in grins and clasped each other's hands. No one mentioned Riley that evening, but they all took mental note of his absence.

Moss was off in a moment, trotting his horse between all of the sleeping soldiers. Big Jonesy and Henry rearranged their gear once more and bunked down for the night. Bruce walked back up the hill toward their headquarters tent noticing the bright stars in the sky. As he looked out across the valley he wondered if there could be a more beautiful place on earth.

36.

At the Union Army headquarters in Winchester, General James Shields did not waste time handing off battle command to Colonel Nathan Kimball that evening. Previously, Kimball was the First Brigade commander in Shield's Second Division of Bank's Fifth Corps. General Shields had been shot, and learned a lifelong lesson to think more seriously about staying in the rear of the action. The rumors swirling around on both sides of the picket line were exaggerated. Shields had been knocked unconscious with a wound to his shoulder. He did not need to have his arm amputated and soon he was alert enough to discuss with Kimball what he should do the next day.

In the early morning hours, Colonel Kimball planned out how he would approach the next day's battle. Kimball, a physician from Southern Indiana, had taken swift action earlier in the day which prevented Ashby from getting all the way to Winchester. As soon as Shields fell, Kimball sent his brigade forward in a collaborated effort in order to push Ashby south of Kernstown. Kimball's brigade was now encamped for the night in Kernstown, without a stitch of bedding. Colonel Jeremiah Sullivan's brigade was bivouacking just north of Kernstown at Hillman's Tollgate. And as the rear guard, Colonel Erastus B. Tyler's brigade was still in Winchester. These three brigades made up Shields division, which was now led by Nathan Kimball.

In Winchester late that night, Kimball tried to convince the other commanders, including Shields and Nathaniel Banks, that it appeared to him Jackson was determined to return and make an advance on Winchester. The other commanders wouldn't believe him. They reminded Kimball that Jackson's column was fragmented and at least two to three days away from where Ashby's men were skirmishing. Besides, President Lincoln, Stanton and McClellan would have a heart attack if they had to turn the rest of Bank's corps, that of Alpheus William's division, around and not continue toward Richmond. General McClellan was counting on those reinforcements.

But Kimball had been fighting against Ashby and personally saw his opponent's determination and boldness.

"Please, gentleman, you have to believe me. That was no casual skirmish. These men were pushing to see how far they could go. Their bravery mocked what you are proposing," Kimball pleaded. "I believe there will be an all out attack in the morning, possibly with all of Jackson's men."

Banks held firm, "I need to remind all of us that even if by some miracle, Jackson was able to garner his entire force up here, counterminding our spies and reports of those residents faithful to our cause, he would not be strong enough to attack. We have interviewed deserters from the Confederate camp saying the men do not have proper clothing and rations. How could they wage war against us? We are too strong."

Kimball gave up. After a long day filled with motion and emotion he was fatigued. He did not have the stamina to press his commanders. He suddenly realized that if he went to sleep immediately he would at best have two hours of rest before he needed to rally his troops at four a.m. *They are wrong,* he thought. *They didn't fight Ashby today.*

37.

President Abraham Lincoln wasn't getting much sleep that night either. He asked his assistant John Hay to accompany him on a walk so he could visit Secretary of State William Seward. It was an hour before dawn when Lincoln arrived, but Seward was still sitting in his parlor in his robe. Lincoln walked in and sat down. No one said anything right away. The President stared at the floor.

Finally Lincoln made eye contact, "Were you sleeping in that chair, Secretary?"

"Not very well," replied Seward.

"Sorry to bother you tonight, or actually this morning. You deserve time away from your official duties," Lincoln said.

"I'm guessing this is not urgent, but that you just needed some fresh air and wanted company. Am I right?"

"You're spot on as usual. I wish I could tell you that McClellan's Army has landed and they are pounding toward Richmond, but there has been no news from him. All that Stanton told me last evening is that General Shields received a slight wound, and also about some skirmish activity south of Winchester by the Confederate cavalryman Turner Ashby."

"Ashby? The sympathizer folks around here are making him out to be a god or a spirit or something, saying to people that he is invincible."

"I sure hope not," responded a dreary Lincoln.

"How's Mrs. Lincoln?"

"She's not bad. Head hurting. Still aches for the boy."

"I miss Willie," said Seward.

"Tomorrow will be one month since his funeral."

Lincoln closed his eyes for a moment and seemed in deep thought.

"He was a dear, dear boy. I have vivid dreams about him and sometimes we two are conversing at great length," said the sober Lincoln.

Seward sat there a moment and looked at the pitiful, weary figure sitting across from him. *That man, just a few feet away, was the nation's leader, yet while embroiled in a stagnant civil war, God still saw fit to take his eleven year old son,* Seward thought. The loss of his Willie was torturous for all around the Lincoln's to bear, but it was nine year old Tad, Lincoln's youngest son, who took it the hardest.

"It's comforting to know that so many cared for him. Judge Taft and his boys, all three told me how much they miss Willie. They used to climb to the roof and watch for spy boats on the Potomac together. All we have left when we die remains in other's memories." Lincoln paused, a little choked up. "We can still hear Tad crying at night for his brother and that so bothers Mother," Lincoln said.

Both men sat there without saying anything for awhile. The birds outside started singing. Seward dozed a little bit and then sat upright and asked, "Do you ever blame God?"

"Blame him? No. I pray to him. I am thankful for my two other boys and for Mary and for this great task he has chosen to give me."

"To inflict upon you," offered Seward.

"Sometimes it does feel like an affliction. But most days I am energized by the responsibility." Lincoln thought for a moment, looked sharply at Seward with a set jaw, then said solemnly, "I want to free the slaves William. I want to do it once and for all with a proclamation that declares all slaves free, everywhere in our nation."

"Then why don't you?" Seward was always bold with Lincoln when they were one on one.

"Because I am still too worried about our border states—it might push a state like Missouri over the edge to side with the Confederate cause."

"Wrong, sir. The reason you cannot do it now is because it doesn't look like we are winning the war. Sure, we have had success in the west and with our navy, but McClellan, with his imbecile pontoon plan, hasn't caused anyone to believe in him or frankly in your administration—which also incriminates me. What we need is a victory! We need a battle that is clearly won and shows the American people, all of them, we are going to eventually win this war. The largest image in people's mind around here is of Manassas and the Rebel Army making short work of McDowell and his wonderful escapade of marching drills he practiced around here for weeks. And I ask, where was the marching after the battle? Our troops ran as fast as they could back to Washington, as if the hounds of hell were after them. That image does not instill confidence! We need a win, sir. A win that will unite the country and give hope to the pro-union people everywhere, including the slaves. If you free them now, it will not do you or the slaves any good."

Lincoln took a deep breath and blew it out slowly. "You thrive on always telling me the cold hard truth. You're useful to your country for that. There are too many men who are quick to slavishly agree, or who try to flatter you with their words, but then retaliate when you are not looking. Thank you." Lincoln paused a moment and then returned to an earlier idea, "I sure hope this Ashby fellow doesn't live up to these rumors and do something definitive in the valley. What do you know about him and about his leader, Thomas Jackson?" Lincoln asked.

"Pretty much just what you do; Jackson, they say, is sort of an eccentric fellow that a few are truly inspired by, but others, including Davis I hear, are not so sure about his competency. He is a hard man to work with, I think, because he doesn't communicate well. Usually he is fairly stoic. As you know, General Scott worked with him in Mexico and thought quite a lot of his efforts there. A religious man, I think he is Presbyterian, and halts most activity on the Sabbath. They say his strong Christian faith is what inspires the citizenry the most.

"Turner Ashby is another case. He comes from the lower valley and lost his brother before the battle at Manassas. He and his brother were close and I hear it is a type of blind rage that drives him now—looking to avenge his brother's death. They say he has no concern for his own safety."

"Yes, that's what Mr. Stanton says, as well," responded Lincoln. "It's what makes Ashby so dangerous. Tell me, do you remember who Shield's three commanders are, I can only recall the names of two of them at this late hour."

"Let's see; Jeremiah Sullivan for the Second Brigade, Erastus Tyler for the Third, and Nathan Kimball is the commander of the First Brigade."

"Well, Kimball is now in charge of Shield's division," Lincoln told Seward. "May God grant him success against Ashby and Jackson."

38.

Henry and Jonesy woke up as the first beams of sun were shooting over the top of the Blue Ridge Mountains to the east. It was Sunday, March 23rd. They marched for what seemed like an eternity to them. Their tired feet now had sores on top of sores. The two men actually felt sorry for some of the other men they marched alongside whose shoes had either worn out and they were marching with just one; or, they never had any to begin with. A few of the young men right off of their farm were ill-prepared for all the walking they were going to do, but most of them adapted quickly. They would usually collect a pair of boots from a generous citizen, procure a pair from a local shop or borrow a spare pair from a fellow soldier tired of carrying the extra weight. To compound matters, the roads had large ruts and were muddy from days of rain and wagon tracks that formed deep gullies. The good news was that the terrain was fairly flat and alongside of the road there were occasionally some oaks and scattered pine trees that gave the men something to look at and lean against when on break.

They marched for several hours before hearing the first artillery shot. Henry and Jonesy thought of Moss who was most likely near the front and already engaged with the enemy. Club was at the head of their company because he was one of the non-commissioned officers in charge. Though they heard the cannon for several hours, it wasn't until the afternoon that they were close enough to be able to hear the cracking sounds of the muskets when they fired. After marching nearly twelve miles, they were relieved when Stonewall Jackson, Bruce and a few other aides rode at a quick pace past them with cheers from the men all along the line. Soon, the order was given to leave the highway and enter into a grove of trees and rest. The men were thrilled. Though they were not supposed to, Henry and Jonesy laid completely down on their backs and shut their eyes. They knew they were not quite to Kernstown yet and would have several more miles until they reached Winchester.

What mystified them, however, was how much cannon and musket shots were being fired just up the road from them as if the war had suddenly changed to south of Kernstown instead of north of it. According to what Moss told them last night, they thought they would be running a few Union regiments out of Winchester that afternoon, at most, one brigade.

Finally the order came for the 33rd Virginia Regiment. Their brigade, the First Brigade (Stonewall Brigade) led by Brigadier General Richard B. Garnett, would follow Colonel Samuel V. Fulkerson's brigade out of the woods, through a wide meadow and up the side of a hill called Pritchard's Ridge, which was heavily occupied by Union cannon. Their mission was to flank the ridge and silence the cannon beating heavily down on the meadow and the north side of the woods where Fulkerson's lead elements were. Henry and Jonesy were happy the other brigade was going first but they were, all of a sudden, a little nervous. Thrusting immediately into the chaos of a battle after their long march was not something they liked very much.

A few of the men were pulling out their New Testaments and reading passages as they waited. Some were scribbling little notes to loved ones which they would tuck inside their coat pocket. A few of the younger soldiers were trembling or holding their ears. The cannons were deafening as the men huddled together and watched the last of Fulkerson's brigade make it out of the woods and crash into the meadow. Club came by to see how the boys were doing and he, Henry and Jonesy decided to borrow from others, as many cartridges as they could, so they would be prepared in case of a drawn out firefight. Some of the men were in a panic and didn't have a gun or a cartridge box thinking they would have a chance to get them from the wagons before the battle. One of the lieutenants told them to calm down, they would have to use their buddy's muskets once they didn't have need of it anymore. This wasn't something that inspired those with a musket.

Suddenly, Bruce raced up to Henry and Jonesy on his horse and asked them, "Why haven't you all moved out? You're supposed to be following Fulkerson."

Henry exclaimed through the loud bursts crashing into the trees, "We haven't been given the order from Cummings to move on yet."

"Where is your commander?" asked Bruce.

Henry and Jonesy both pointed toward the west where a huddle of men were standing. Bruce bolted off.

Soon the order was passed down the line to form into columns. The 33rd Virginia was the lead regiment of the five infantry regiments and was commanded by Colonel Arthur C. Cummings. Henry and Jonesy were in company D and close to the front of their pack. Before they were ordered to leave they glanced back through the woods in the opposite direction of where they were about to run and they saw the lone figure of Stonewall Jackson sitting on his horse like a statue. The funny thing was that he had his left arm in an upward position as if to give a signal or something. Whatever he was doing, it was inspiring to see their commander near them.

"Let's go!" the men shouted right in front of Jonesy and Henry. Soon they were all fast-stepping it to the edge of the woods where a barrage of shells were hitting the trees. They hesitated a moment, took a deep breath and lunged out into the meadow, running as fast as they could with musket balls whizzing by their heads and loud explosions all around them.

In that small instant of time as they ran through the meadow, all Jonesy could think about was his warm bed back in Winchester, sitting down to a hot meal at his ma's table and hunting with Club on Christmas Day. Jonesy was right behind Henry and as they ran he watched Henry's back the whole way. Their unit ran across the meadow and then across two muddy roads before dashing into another clump of oaks and yellow pine trees. No one was killed during their maneuvering over the rolling countryside because many of the shells were exploding ten feet or more above their heads. As they huddled around in the trees trying to get behind the largest oak trees they could find, they realized one man from their regiment was wounded and a couple of men seemed petrified, not responding to their leaders when spoken to.

Henry and Jonesy looked at each other and nodded a little bit. They had successfully passed the first test of death unscathed. They awaited their orders, wondering if they were going to have to dash back across the meadow again or forge forward through the trees ahead of them. They could see some of the soldiers from Fulkerson's brigade and knew they hadn't moved on yet. More men piled up behind them, all very thankful to have made it through the meadow alive. So far, the two Winchester boys had never heard such a thunderous barrage of cannonade, even when they were waiting behind Henry House Hill at Manassas when they rushed into battle and captured several Union Artillery pieces the prior July.

They waited there for almost an hour as both side's artillery pounded each other, breaking through timber and wreaking havoc. Sometimes debris from the impact would hit a Confederate soldier just a few feet away from where Henry Gallagher and Brian Jones were positioned. Several times during the pause their brigade commander Garnett rode by them and encouraged the 33rd Virginia to remember their success at Manassas, to be brave and to move forward when the order came with all haste. Henry couldn't rest at all, he paced back and forth around their little section of the woods. Jonesy sat on an old tree stump and rubbed one of his feet. Club was running around making sure everyone had water and ammunition and taking anyone wounded to the rear where they could escape to get some help. Jonesy had never seen his pa so worked up. Jonesy was excited. He knew being there and participating in the battle was helping him come of age. He felt a little part of his boyhood slip from him.

Soon the order came to move out and Henry and Jonesy hustled back to their spot near the front of the pack. The 33rd Virginia, led by Cummings, was to the right of the 21st which was led by Lieutenant Colonel John M. Patton Jr. As thy hustled up the gentle slope of Sandy Ridge and left the trees, Jonesy was saying over and over to himself, "Duty, Strength, Courage. Duty, Strength, Courage." When, almost in slow motion, Jonesy saw the soldier immediately to his left struck by a cannonball, which took off part of his right arm nearly severing the entire limb in the process. Jonesy screamed to his front "Henry, Henry....they hit Tommy Hays! He's down!"

"Keep moving Jonesy and get your musket up! Don't worry about Tommy now." The front line of the regiment all took aim and fired at the Yanks who were just past a stone wall on the ridge. Jonesy didn't say another word and he raised his musket and found a Yank and let him have it. They shuffled forward while they reloaded. Soon, they managed to arrive at the stone wall before the Yankee soldiers did, but the Federals were very close and their officers were yelling at them to charge. The Confederate line all took another deliberate fire and sprayed shot out all across the front of the Yankee line. At least twenty of the blue coated Yankees fell. Jonesy and Henry sat down behind the wall for a moment and reloaded as a shower of balls whizzed over their heads. The Confederate soldiers who were climbing up behind them were riddled with musket balls and many crumpled up and fell over. Jonesy and

Henry both let out a moan when they saw some of their friends suffer a direct hit by a minie ball. They agonized at the pummeling some of the comrades in their squad received.

Jonesy started shaking his head and then shouted over the din of the battle, "We have to help them get to the rear before they die, Henry."

"Not now, do what you're told and hit those in front of us."

Henry and Jonesy both stood up, took aim at the fast approaching Yankee soldiers and let loose a barrage of shot with their comrades to the left and right. Again, another scattering of blue coats fell to the ground. With that attack many of the Yankees in the front of the line dropped down to the ground in fear, trying to find something to hide behind. Their immediate line was broken but more blue coated soldiers were coming in lines behind them. Jonesy thought he saw several regimental Union flags in that part of the battle and was wondering where they all came from based on what Moss had told them the night before. *Besides, where was Moss?* The boys hadn't see him the entire day. Now they could hear the cries coming from the soldiers who were wounded on both sides. Some of the crying was pure anguish wrenching at Jonesy's heart. Other men without weapons were moving forward now to 'borrow' the musket's and ammunition of their fallen comrades.

"Don't worry about the ones who don't make it, there'll be time for that later," Henry said to Jonesy as he placed another percussion cap onto his weapon.

"I hadn't seen an arm shot apart like that before, that's all" Jonesy said. "I'll be all right."

"Don't think about it now, just focus on those Yankees in front of us." Henry himself was worked up with adrenaline and talking fast.

"How could I not focus on them Yankees?"

"Hey, Jonesy," Henry grinned. "Were still alive—be thankful."

"I can't wait to get this over with," Jonesy said.

"It can't last too much longer because it's almost dark."

The boys stood back up took careful aim and squeezed the trigger. Jonesy, an expert at rabbit hunting, had little difficulty connecting with his target.

The Union soldiers were a little farther away now but there were more of them. Reinforcements had arrived and new regiments were pouring in from the northeast. The Winchester boys could see the Union commanders on horseback rallying their troops and encouraging them on.

"This can't be going as planned," Henry said as they sat back down behind the wall again. "Stonewall must have somehow miscalculated. We have fought at least one brigade today, maybe two, since there is another group fighting toward the east."

"Looks like Old Jack might have met his match this time," Jonesy mumbled while he pushed his ramrod down the muzzle of his musket.

39.

"President Lincoln, I received a wire from General Shields, and it's not good." Secretary of War Edwin Stanton was escorted into the President's study by John Nicolay.

"What do you have?" Lincoln asked the fretting Stanton without peeling his eyes away from the paper he was studying.

"Shields was short and to the point. He said Jackson's Army attacked his division at Kernstown. Many casualties on both sides. Banks had already departed for the east and was no help to them."

Lincoln jerked his chin upward, locked eyes with Stanton and with almost a grin said, "Was I to doubt General Banks when he told me he was sure Jackson's forces had left the Shenandoah Valley?"

"Sir, I don't understand," Stanton said a little impatient, not wanting to play a mental game with the President.

"It's not a puzzle, Secretary, but merely a question. So far, each of our generals have been convinced of things that simply aren't true and I am merely asking you if we can believe anything they tell us? You see, General McDowell was convinced that Jefferson Davis' Army was isolated and unable to be reinforced so he attacked it; only to wonder later how Jackson showed up on the battlefield to reinforce Johnston. General McClellan was convinced he needed a grand movement of forces to counter the strong opposition west of Washington, only to find the fortifications there empty. Not to mention the fact the cannons there, which we had spies watching for weeks, were actually logs painted black!" Lincoln was starting to raise his voice, "Now, two weeks later, after I was told by General Banks he is convinced their opposition is at least ninety miles away and incapable of making an attack, we find they are on the doorstep of Winchester again and very capable of an attack.

"So, my question to you Mr. Stanton, and I hope you are not annoyed with it, is this; should I now doubt my head generals when they tell me they are convinced of something?" Lincoln paused, stood up and walked over to the window to look out on the lawn. "We have the Pinkerton Agency, we have our intelligence and our spies, we have railroads and telegraph and over a hundred fifty thousand soldiers in Virginia alone and we cannot seem to find out where our enemy is or where he isn't until he strikes us in the face. Now I know it is not your fault. It's always no one's fault, but the American people are being delayed again and are going to have to stomach more bad news. And I am going to have to explain it all to them. So please, Edwin, go back to your office and wait diligently for more news and keep me updated. No, actually, I am coming with you. I will not be able to rest until I hear how this all turns out. Tell me one more time, how many troops does Shields have there in the vicinity and how many troops did we think Jackson had?" Lincoln asked as they both started moving toward the door.

Stanton coughed a little bit to clear his throat and give himself a moment to think. "Sir, I believe we estimated Jackson's force at around 3,000."

"And the Federal forces there?"

"Even without William's division, General Banks would still easily have over twice that many troops on the ground there plus cavalry," Stanton estimated.

Lincoln stopped and turned to face Stanton, "So the Rebels attacked us and we had twice their forces? A bold man that Jackson. Either his intelligence is faulty or he thinks very little of his opponent."

40.

In the town of Winchester you could hear the distant sound of artillery shells exploding. The citizens were wondering what was happening and many hoped that soon their beloved Confederate Army would be marching back into town to the tune of "Dixie."

Kathryn's little brother, Landon, was sitting on the front steps of the Crawford home all by himself looking toward the south and listening to the distant explosions. The residents of Winchester were not allowed to leave town or go anywhere near the battle by order of the general.

While deep in thought about what could possibly be happening south of the city, Landon saw two boys walking slowly down the street toward him. It was Harry and Allan McDonald.

"What are you two doing?" Landon asked.

"None of your business," Harry responded.

"Well, I'm going to follow you," Landon said and stood up.

"Suit yourself," the older boys said and kept walking.

Landon followed the two McDonald boys down to the southern end of town on Loudon Street and then the three veered to the southeast on the Valley Turnpike. The boys left the road after a while because Federal troops and wagons were assembled in front of them. They cut through an orchard and walked behind some trees and up a slope until there was a nice opening and they could see some action. There was smoke coming up from the cannon and they could identify clearly the movement of troops and their unit's flags.

"I'm going closer," said Harry, the oldest of the three boys. He started moving down the hill and through another patch of trees. The younger two followed him and he led them up to another high area just behind the battle where a lot of the action could be seen. There was an old fence there and all three of them climbed up onto it and sat mesmerized by watching thousands of blue-coated men with muskets and supplies keep filing past them toward the front.

Most of the action was taking place on the next high spot over from them called Sandy Ridge. There was a stone wall on top of the hill and it appeared the Confederates were using it as a defensive position, holding it against onslaught after onslaught of Union reinforcements. The boys watched intently as scores of wounded Union soldiers were helped from the ridge back to the wagons, which were lined up just below where the boys sat. They would grimace as they heard the crying and screaming coming from the men who were loaded on the wagons to be driven away back up into town. Some of the birds singing beside them acted like this happened every day and they went ahead with their music and dancing here and there. The boys wondered about their pas who were on the other side and they hoped Angus McDonald and Conrad Montgomery were alive and well.

41.

After being successful against Ashby's cavalry earlier in the day, Colonel Nathan Kimball made a serious error a few hours later by not putting troops on Sandy Ridge to protect his right flank. His focus had been on Pritchard's Hill, but Sandy Ridge looked down on Pritchard's Hill. After the Confederate's took the Ridge and lined the stone wall on top of it with infantry, they were then able to bring up Jackson's Rockbridge Artillery to fire from the position. This gave the Confederate forces a distinct advantage, one Jackson apparently hoped he could use to win the battle, but he was obviously unaware of the thousands of troops Kimball still had at his disposal. At the same time, Kimball didn't know how many troops Jackson had because they were covered in the trees west of Kernstown. He assumed the Southern general must have another army marching toward him to help the Confederates. *No one would attack this aggressively if they were not well strengthened,* thought Kimball.

Nathan Kimball looked to Colonel Erastus Tyler's Third Brigade for the answer to his problem. He sent him forward to the right side with the directive to take Sandy Ridge and use the stone wall for a Union advantage. Tyler wasted no time deploying his five regiments and led off with the 7th Ohio. The men affixed their bayonets and left their baggage in neat rows where they hoped to come back and pick up their gear before dark. None of them knew exactly what was going to happen in the last two hours of daylight, but they were anticipating a quick victory.

After marching through some trees a few hundred yards north of Sandy's Ridge, they encountered a Southern skirmish line that let out a deadly volley at their front column. Fifteen to twenty Union soldiers fell down. When the men not wounded reorganized, the Union regiment decided to head right for the stone wall where the Confederate's were assembled. This was a drastic mistake. After receiving several murderous volley's from the Southerners behind the wall, the Northerners recoiled because the Confederates left the wall and charged at them. Kimball's blue hordes scampered back the way they came into the woods about seventy yards away from the wall. While running away the Union infantry heard the continuous zinging of musket balls flying by their heads and ripping through loose clothing, sometimes finding flesh.

The young men from 7th Ohio and 7th Indiana found that seeing the fallen warriors lying dead around them, men that they knew, was a terrifying experience. For most it caused them to aggressively pursue their attackers. For some it immobilized them from making any worthy contribution to the fight. Just as men were being physically paralyzed from wounds, some were becoming mentally paralyzed by the trauma around them. Heads were blown apart so that large pieces of the skull and brain were missing, legs were torn off or dangling at their owner's side and stomach's and mid-sections were riddled with holes from minie balls. Splinters of shredded timber were everywhere. The grass and shrubs around them were stained with red and a few of the trees had pieces of flesh stuck to them. Muskets, cartridge boxes, canteens and clothing littered the battlefield and the cries from the wounded, not yet dead, were horrific. Some of the youth from the fair farms west of the mountains took off with fleet feet away from the fight

Colonel Nathan Kimball, seeing how Third Brigade did not succeed at taking the stone wall, sent up First Brigade (which was his former brigade). The first few regiments were just as unsuccessful at trying to take the ridge. Nearly two full brigades of almost five regiments each had failed to take Sandy Ridge. Fortunately for the Federals, because of the waves of Union soldiers trying for that high ground, the Southern Army was foiled at moving forward and gaining any significant amount of new ground. Whenever they tried they would soon be repulsed back to the protection of the stone wall.

The sights and sounds of the battlefield sobered every man who made his way toward the stone wall with his regiment. As they scurried through the heaps of fallen men, the wounded horses and the smoke-filled air, they began to hear the whizzing noise of lead balls all around them, from head to heels. This caused them to slow down and look for places to hide to defend against the spiraling death balls. A few key leaders in the 14th

Indiana inspired their regiment and held them steady against the so far victorious Confederates.

Then, all of a sudden, with the sun already below the trees and the last few moments of daylight soaking the terrain before twilight, the Southern Army unexpectedly gave a call to retreat from the wall. The 14th Indiana took full advantage of this opportunity and scampered up to the wall and placed their flag into it. They used the wall to stand behind and shoot at the fleeing soldiers. The momentum had turned and the advantage immediately changed to the Union Army. More Federals rallied behind the Indiana men. Their bravery had paid off. They had been successful. They had done their duty.

42.

Moss had been in constant motion for almost fifteen hours. Earlier in the day he, Turner Ashby and his cavalry were reinforced with infantry from the 2nd Virginia regiment. They had attempted to make a push directly for Winchester on the eastern side of Pritchard's Hill. Ashby had miscalculated the Union strength, however, and their Confederate forward guard was no match for the artillery and infantry strength of the enemy. Kimball had directed several of Sullivan's regiments directly at Ashby and at first, the boldness of the Southerners began to penetrate the Union line. But their success was fleeting. Ashby's men and the infantry who accompanied them fell back into the woods southeast of Pritchard's Hill. To their astonishment they were not pursued by the superior forces opposing them. They waited and helped screen Jackson's movements into the woods to the west and then they retained a firm position on Jackson's right flank.

During the late afternoon Moss asked Ashby if he could ride around to check on his friends and see if any of the brigade commanders needed cavalry support. They had heard nothing from Jackson for awhile and knew most of the fighting was now to the northwest of them. Ashby consented and Moss rode off into the woods to look for the 33rd Virginia or for Bruce so he could gather some more information on the battle.

As Moss rode through the trees he saw many soldiers falling back to the rear, some carrying wounded men. He finally found Bruce who was dismounted from his beloved horse, Copper Jake, and said, "What's going on Bruce, why are the men retreating?"

"It's not what Jackson wanted," Bruce replied hastily studying his little brother to make sure he was not harmed. "Most of the men were running out of ammunition so General Garnett ordered them to retreat a few minutes ago."

"Because of ammunition?" Moss asked in disbelief.

"Stonewall is irate! He had two new regiments coming up to support the effort at the stone wall on Sandy Ridge, but the order had already been called and the men retreated. You've got to get word to Ashby that we need our retreat screened. Tell him to leave his current position and come to the front of battle."

"Is that from Jackson?" Moss asked.

"Directly! He just sent a runner to find Ashby, but you know exactly where he is. Please hurry, Moss, we need this to prevent a complete rout."

"I'm off," Moss yelled behind him. "Let's go Chris!" he said as he shot back through the forest the same way he had come.

When Moss reached Ashby it took them no time to halt operations where they were and provide a large contingent of cavalry to help screen the movement of Jackson's massive retreat. When Moss finally rode as near to Sandy Ridge as he could without being too close to the Union snipers, he could see how many men had fallen. There appeared to be hundreds of Confederate soldiers lying dead all along the southern portion of the stone wall. It was getting pretty dark and he was unable to see as clearly as he would like, but it seemed like a great slaughter had taken place. There were shouts of pain and agony and shrieks from the men who had to be temporarily left alone while the Union Army stormed over the wall and took advantage of the high ground.

Moss slowed Chris Columbus down to a trot as he studied the masses of men. There was much shouting and soldiers running past him from everywhere. A few of the soldiers seemed delirious and confused. Moss tried to point them in the right direction. *Look at this battlefield,* he said to himself. The terrain now lay beneath a haze of smoke in the twilight, and Moss suddenly realized there were no other riders around him. There was still a straggler or two making their way between the clumps of the dead and wounded, but Moss suddenly became acutely aware he was detached from his cavalry squadron and security. He picked up his pace and headed directly south behind some limping men and then heard the shouts and musket fire of a group of Union soldiers behind him. *They must have come over the wall at a sprint. I can actually make out what they are saying. I must be too close!*

Moss kicked Chris hard in the ribs urging him to move hastily. Chris jumped, but right to their front another group of Union soldiers appeared from behind some scrub pine trees. Moss turned his horse around and began charging in the direction without Union soldiers when he heard a forceful volley of shots. Moss felt a stinging in his ribs as Chris collapsed underneath him and threw Moss forward where he somersaulted onto the field of death he was riding through. Moss jumped up, found his sword and glanced around him. He was completely surrounded by Federal infantrymen.

43.

Landon Montgomery and the McDonald boys watched the epic conclusion to the battle unfold before their eyes in disbelief. They were extremely proud of their Confederate soldiers holding the line and repulsing the attack of regiment after regiment of blue-uniformed men. They would cheer out loud until some of the Federal soldiers looked toward them and ordered the boys to quit their hollering. They were so close to the battle that a Confederate artillery round made direct contact with the neck of a soldier and his head rolled nearby to where they were sitting. The three boys would never forget the experience.

With the encroaching darkness on the terrain and the darkness in their heart over the retreating Southern Army, they decided it was time to head home. They asked a Union officer if they could help with the Confederate wounded and bring some of them water. They were denied and told to go home. They did bring some water to a few Union soldiers who were wounded and the men were grateful to the boys for their sympathy.

When they had finally slipped back through the fields and woods and up the main street of Winchester they said goodbye to each other and departed for their homes.

44.

Landon ran inside with tears in his eyes. As soon as he found his mother he buried his head in her breast and sobbed and sobbed. He tried to tell her of the gallant defense of the soldiers, but that they suddenly turned and fled and the Yankees took over the stone wall and pursued the army into the night.

Landon was surrounded by both women of the Montgomery home and their hosts the Crawford's along with Julia Bridgeman. He told of the head that rolled by him, of the cries of the wounded from both sides, of the hundreds of Yankees that kept pouring into the Confederate line only to be repulsed. This brought tears of joy and pride to Claire and Kathryn and Sarah Crawford. Scout licked Landon and sat proudly on the boy's feet as he told the story of the battle to the women. There was crying and frustration as the Montgomery women told Landon they had tried to come find him and were not allowed to leave town. Lucy and Landon eventually went upstairs to get ready for bed.

"Mother, our men need our help!" Kathryn gasped. "Henry could be lying out there in that cold field tonight injured."

"I know dear. All of our men could be out there, but we must pray to the Lord that he has spared them," Claire said looking up at the eyes of all of the other anxious women in the room.

"He hasn't spared all of them," said Julia stoically.

The ladies decided to pray together again for the safety of their family members and for the protection of General Jackson and his troops. They had hoped that Jackson's Army might march into Winchester that evening, but it now appeared it was not meant to be.

After hearing Landon's report, Julia left for home hoping she might run into someone who could offer more news from the front. Scout saw her safely down the street and then ran back home as fast he could, not wanting to miss a minute of the action inside. Sarah Crawford did not permit Scout to go outside most of the day for fear he would run toward the battle and be lost forever. She so loved Bruce's dog and knew it would be too much for her to be separated from him, as well. Besides, he was a good watchdog and she always felt a little more secure with all the strangers in town knowing that Scout was at the bottom of the stairs keeping guard.

None of the women slept that evening but kept a vigilant eye on the front door, waiting for word from the battle or for a loved one to stop in out of necessity because of being wounded or on the run. They could see from their windows the scores of men being brought into the makeshift assembly areas in town for the wounded, including the Taylor Hotel, the churches, the banks and the county courthouse. It began to rain and the women suffered mentally thinking of their darlings perishing on the cold earth. They couldn't sleep and they couldn't eat. Deep into the night they finally laid on their beds in the dark, listening and waiting for the unknown.

* * *

Early in the morning, before daybreak, the women arose and went to help with the casualties who were brought into town. A handful of the wounded brought into Winchester were from the Southern Army so the ladies were able to hear more about the battle including the courage and the loss behind the stone wall. They found out Conrad, Bruce, Henry, Club and Jonesy all were spared with minor wounds, but that Moss was missing. They heard of Garnett's command to retreat and of Jackson's regret of the order. They heard of the terribly long marches the troops endured the hours before the battle and the lack of food and rest. They heard how most of the wounded and dead were still lying out in the field by Sandy Ridge, and how the Union Army continued its prohibition against the citizens of Winchester leaving town and entering the battlefield area. The Federals were still working out there, burying their dead and gathering weapons and other equipment, along with any intelligence they could find from dead Southern officers.

The women of Winchester, especially Claire, thought this business of not letting them go to their friends and neighbors lying wounded in their hour of need was pure madness by the part of the Union. They knew lives could be saved if the soldiers could be brought to the hospitals before they expired. It infuriated the women and made it hard to be kind and caring to the soldiers they were nurturing who wore blue uniforms. Nonetheless, they tried to smile at and comfort those near death with soft words of compassion. When Union officers would stop in to check on the wounded the women would bite their tongues and try not to speak their minds about their prohibition from the battlefield.

Kathryn worked hard, going from wounded man to wounded man until she stepped into the operating room and saw a large mound of sawed off legs and arms. She broke down. She ran out of the tent and fell onto the ground on her hands and knees, staring at the soil underneath her trying desperately to regain her composure. The image which kept flooding her mind were those ghastly body parts. She was sick to her stomach and took a long while before re-entering the hospital.

Claire and Sarah worked feverishly attending to each man's needs. Finally, late in the day, the carts brought into town both the dead and wounded Confederates. Some of the injured soldiers were delirious or unconscious. A few had wounds that were festering and already with maggots. The stench was horrific. The pain and suffering unbearable. The women exhibited stomachs of steel and willed their way to help each soldier brought in.

However, not all the women that day obeyed the Union orders and stayed in town. Rachel Jones slipped away and entered a remote part of the battlefield taking away as many pistols as she could from dead Union officers and hiding them in an old stump to retrieve later. Julia, even after being told not to leave town, tried to sneak down a back trail and was subsequently refused by force from leaving Winchester. She was threatened that if she tried again she would be locked up.

Julia found Kathryn and together they decided to head over to the prisoner cantonment and bring food and water to the Southern soldiers there. They discovered the Union had captured over two hundred Confederate soldiers the evening before and they were being held under a heavy guard at several different places. One location was across the street from the largest makeshift hospital near the Taylor Hotel. Julia and Kathryn walked there first.

When they arrived with their food they were first inspected to make sure they were not concealing any weapons. Then they were allowed to proceed to the humbled crew of dirty, tired men. Their food was received with much gratitude, but it was not enough. Other women had arrived with the same idea but all of them soon realized it would take many kitchens to satisfy the scores of prisoners. The women were heart-wrenched because many of the men were fellow citizens and sometimes family members. They hoped the Union Army would have compassion and feed their trophies with the train loads of food amassed in Winchester.

Eventually, between the women and compassionate Union officers, all of the prisoners had their first after-battle meal. For this they were grateful.

45.

Riley's squadron of Pennsylvania Cavalry arrived in Winchester on March 24th, the morning after the battle. Realizing they had missed a major engagement the day before, they asked permission to enter the battlefield and help with the wounded. This was granted. Riley decided to walk alongside the ridge where there were still masses of men laid in heaps on both sides of the wall. Several squads of Union infantry had their coats off and were digging long trenches to put the dead. All of the Union wounded were cleared from the battlefield, but there were still moans and cries coming from the Confederate fallen. As Riley walked along the ridge he saw a litter team of two Union soldiers make their way over the wall, place a Rebel soldier on the makeshift bed and walk him back over the stone wall toward Winchester.

Riley looked around at the devastation. The wall he was standing on was soaked red with blood. Most of the trees in the area were cut off a few feet above ground by cannon canister. Down the hill a few birds were flitting here and there curiously poking at some of the fallen. There was a pile of dead bodies near where Riley stood and he could see the frozen faces of the men who yesterday fought for the South. Two of the young soldiers lay dead, skewered with the same sword. Another dead man had his arms out as if pleading with someone to come and help him. As Riley gazed at it all he stopped walking and sat on the wall facing south, listening to the moans of the dying. He yelled out a loud groan of compassion springing from deep within and began to weep. This momentary flash of anger and sadness lasted just a split second before he stood up, ran to the nearest wounded man and gave him a sip from his canteen. The man had a horrific leg wound. Riley helped the man sit up and lean against a tree because the wounded man was stiff and sore from lying on his back so long. Riley called for the nearest Union ambulatory team to come and help him. He then ran to another man with a wound in his abdomen. This man also was thirsty so Riley again opened up his canteen for a sip.

Riley approached a dead Confederate lieutenant who looked familiar to him except for the beard. When he stepped closer he recognized him as his friend Isaac from the Institute. Riley knelt down and put his hand on his friend's lifeless shoulder. "Isaac, Isaac. You were always so much alive," he said. Riley noticed Isaac still had his sword in his hand as if he had dismounted and was ready to enter a swordfight. However, he must have been shot before he encountered his opponent. Isaac had a hole the size of a quarter-dollar in his chest.

Riley wondered if he would soon find Jonesy, Henry or Bruce among the dead. He thought of Molly, how she would love to have been there to tend the wounded, and he worked harder. Riley personally carried over ten wounded soldiers back up to Winchester over his shoulders like he was carrying a large sack of potatoes. He led Union litter teams, now all solely focusing on the Confederates, to the soldiers with the worst wounds. He dug a grave for Isaac and made sure the Union soldiers in command had a plan for the dead Confederates still lying in heaps. As the sun set behind the mountains to the west, Riley found he was exhausted and laid down to rest a moment. He fell into a deep sleep and did not arise until the next day.

46.

Stonewall Jackson wasted no time making sure his unit departed Kernstown as quick as possible. He knew the Union cavalry would be right on their heels, nabbing up last minute prisoners and seeking to capture a wagon of goods that just couldn't keep up. He didn't let his disappointment with General Garnett poison his mind. His men needed sound leadership with the advent of this blow and there would be time to deal with Garnett later. He moved his troops to the nearby town of Bartonsville where pure exhaustion forced many of them to stop.

Jackson couldn't figure out how the battle had changed momentum so quickly. He had planned to bring up the 5th and 42nd Virginia regiments to support Garnett at the wall and did not anticipate Garnett moving his men backward. Instead of forming a new offensive, Jackson utilized the two fresh regiments to provide heavy defensive fire toward oncoming Union soldiers as the rest of his army retreated into the woods and disappeared into the night.

The next day, the Army of the Shenandoah consolidated and restored discipline. Marching onward to Strasburg, they briefly stopped there and then continued speedily to Woodstock. The Union Cavalry appeared to have been called back and no more skirmishes took place after Monday, the 24th of March.

Jackson's total losses were 80 killed, 375 wounded and 260 captured. He later learned that Shields and Kimball counted 118 Union killed, 450 wounded and 20 soldiers missing or captured. This did not console him.

47.

Moss was in a foul mood. His trusted horse Chris Columbus had perished, his grandfather's Revolutionary War sword was taken from him, and he was now a prisoner of war, captured by Lincoln's Union Army. Moss was ashamed. His heart burned for victory that long day and he worked tirelessly helping Turner Ashby fend off the Union attacks. Pure exhaustion and confusion left him vulnerable in that twilight hour when he was surrounded. He had planned for that day his whole life as a boy—usually surrounded by wild Indians—he always pictured himself attempting one last heroic deed, saving himself and the army for which he was fighting. But it did not happen that way at all and the Union was now proud to have him, one of Ashby's chief helpers.

The first night was cold and restless. The Union guard had Moss and about sixty other men outside of Winchester on the side of a hill awaiting word from higher on how to proceed with them. Moss and the other captured men were given time to reflect on the battle and many began feeling the sting of shame and remorse. Winchester, for some reason, had evaded Jackson's attempt at re-capturing and they couldn't help but feel personally responsible.

Moss's wound in his ribs turned out to be superficial. A Union medical aide gave him a bandage to wrap around his chest to stop the bleeding and to help it heal up. Some of the prisoners were interrogated by the provost marshal but, possibly because of his wound, the Union guard left Moss alone.

In the middle of the afternoon, on the day after the battle, the Federals readied all the prisoners for a march to the train station. They were to be rout stepped right through the middle of town in humiliation.

As Moss loped up the hill and walked alongside other down-faced Confederate soldiers he thought of his brother. He wondered where Bruce might be heading with Jackson and if he knew yet the trouble Moss had gotten into. Bruce was usually around to get him out of whatever mess Moss found himself in at the schoolyard or downtown on Saturday. Moss would sometimes attempt fighting older boys or groups of boys instead of just one. His big brother was always just around the corner, ready to rescue him from complete defeat. But not this time. This was something different and gave Moss a feeling of desperation he had never felt before.

Losing his horse, Chris Columbus, completed the picture of total defeat for him. It made him think of his pa who was an excellent cavalry officer. Lawrence Crawford had raised and trained Chris Columbus since he was a suckling foal. *What would his pa say?* Moss wondered.

A strong Union guard contingent marched the humbled Confederate prisoners up Market Street toward the Winchester and Potomac Railroad depot. It turned into a type of parade. Some of the prisoners were marching past their homes and on the streets they used to play on as boys. The women of Winchester lined the streets waving handkerchiefs and cheering their husbands and sons. There were more than two hundred prisoners walking up the middle of the street and Moss tried to cower in between others so his face would not be seen. Out of the corner of his eye, Moss saw Claire and Kathryn Montgomery waving to the troops. They yelled to him, but he offered them no more than a simple nod. He was ashamed. There they marched in humiliation and defeat, but the residents cheered them on. Moss then saw his younger sister, Lucy, standing up ahead. When fourteen-year-old Lucy caught sight of Moss she began to yell for him as loud as she could. Moss tried not to look her way.

All of a sudden, Lucy ran out into the street and called to him. "Put your head up Moss, you'll get 'em back. Put your head up and think of how you'll lick them. Put your head up, Moss, and think about riding with Ashby again." Tears streamed her face.

Lucy ran alongside the column of men, encouraging her brother who was acting as if he did not hear her. She was warned by the provost marshal's men more than once not to get too near, but she did not listen. In desperation for Moss to notice her, she ran into the group of prisoners and put her arms around Moss's waist and wailed, "Oh, Moss!" while burying her head into his sore ribs.

Finally, unable to keep up the pretending, Moss stopped and put his arms around her. He leaned over a little until his eyes were level with hers and he held her face in his hands. "I'm sorry, Lucy," Moss said painfully.

A guard was yelling at them and walking over to where they were holding up the line of prisoners. Before he arrived, Lucy took both her hands and put them on Moss's cheeks. Staring at him with fire in her eyes she said, "Don't give up, Moss Crawford. Remember what Jackson says-- Give them the bayonet!"

This made Moss smile, but immediately Lucy was yanked backwards by a private in the Union Army who found it his duty that day to help keep the prisoners on the right side of the road moving forward. He pulled Lucy out of the gray-coated men and pushed her back to the side of the road telling her to stay away. Moss had a notion to level the scrawny soldier, but thought he would wait until a more opportune time.

"I'll tell mom you're okay, Moss. I'll let her know you are just temporarily held up. Be careful."

Moss turned toward her and smiled and waved mouthing the words "thank you" to her.

He was better now. Despite the shame of yesterday, he knew what he must do and would begin to look for his opportunity.

48.

The Visitor watched as the group of Southern soldiers were marched up Market street. He kept his hat down low almost covering his eyes and he drew his overcoat around his shoulders. He knew what he had to do this evening before it would be too late. He just didn't think there would be that many of them—*almost too large a group to do what I have in mind,* he thought.

49.

Jackson's attack caused a considerable stir in Washington. A stir that would have the exacerbating effect of irritating General McClellan beyond repair. President Lincoln and Edwin Stanton ordered General Banks to return to Winchester. All of the Federal brigades, once in route to help McClellan with his grand attack on Richmond, were turned around and ordered to march back over the Blue Ridge Mountains again. General Jackson's attack on the Union forces at Kernstown ended with the Confederates retreating as the Union advanced. However, the sheer audacity of Jackson attacking over 9,000 men with only 3,000 caused the leaders running the Union Army to be much more cautious in the Shenandoah Valley at the expense of their assault on Richmond. George McClellan sat in his tent in silence, astounded the President would interfere so much in military matters.

50.

Stonewall Jackson did not know what to think. His thoughts on the battle seemed muddled. He rode Little Sorrel up the Shenandoah Valley that Monday evening pondering why the good Lord willed him to assault on the Sabbath. *Especially with the horrific results.* The thought never entered his mind that the eight hour battle at Kernstown had just saved Richmond, the Southern Capitol.

51.

The Visitor left supper early that evening and walked out of the house, found his horse, and took off in the direction of Harpers Ferry to ride the 29 miles to where the Winchester and Potomac Railroad connected to the Baltimore and Ohio.

"Run straight and true, Torch," the Visitor whispered to his beloved stud.

The Visitor covered the distance in under two hours because Torch was restless and ready to run. He arrived to the station and saw the freight cars filled with Confederate prisoners resting on the track prepared to move eastward.

The Visitor thought quickly of his options. He knew that as soon as he freed the first prisoners they could help him with the rest. However, the tracks were guarded with heavy infantry forces and some cavalry. It was a prized possession and, no doubt, General Shield's personal trophy he was sending back to the War Department so he could receive his next promotion. The Visitor was just one man and he had an enormous task to accomplish.

All of a sudden, two things happened simultaneously. The whistle on the train blew twice indicating it was ready to depart, and a Union officer caught sight of the Visitor and shouted at him. The Visitor turned his horse around and shot through the trees and out of sight, hoping he wouldn't be pursued. He had gotten too close, too careless. Even though he was in a Union uniform, he would have a lot of explaining to do to justify being this far from his command.

The Visitor was not pursued, but as he turned Torch back around and walked up the path to look at the train, he saw it had already taken off.

He was too late. He had a back-up plan, but he would have to go over the bridge to pursue the train. He did not anticipate such a large security force attending to the train or the bridge. All his plans that evening were thwarted, so he turned his horse around and slowly made his way back to Winchester.

52.

Moss rode in the train for what seemed like hours. He knew the direction they were going and he knew they would be in Washington soon. What he did not know is if it would be his final destination or not. When the train stopped, it took over an hour for the guards to open the doors. Some other prisoners were yelling for help, complaining of being sick or having to use the latrine. There was no sympathy from their captors. Finally, the railcar doors slid apart and all the prisoners were allowed to hop off the train and follow a guard out of the station into a secured outdoor area on a street with Union soldiers forming a large U-shape around them. The area was illuminated by street lamps.

Moss looked around to see where they were. They were told they only had a few minutes to use the latrine and stretch their legs. Some asked about rations and they were laughed at. Moss got up next to one of the guards and asked him where they were.

"You're at President Street Station in Baltimore. Have you ever been to Baltimore, boy?" the guard asked.

"No."

"Where are you from?"

"Virginia."

"I figured that, ya pie eater. What part of Virginia?" the guard asked Moss.

"The country part." Moss didn't want to be too specific knowing he had to make a break for it and he didn't want anyone knowing which way to look for him.

The guard was now tired with the conversation and turned his back to Moss. People were shouting at the prisoners to get ready to get back on the train. Moss took a look around and wondered, *is this a good place to escape?*

Some of the captives began to shuffle closer to the train station ready to move out when they got the order. Moss was slow at moving and kept studying the far end of the lot they stood on. He figured the odds were not in his favor at all. But he also knew if he was shipped north he would have a much farther distance to get to Virginia. He needed a diversion, something to draw the guard's attention away from him. He thought about the train station. It was pretty empty, but there were a few more obstacles in there than outside. He realized it was pure insanity to think of making a run for it, but it was dark and there were back roads he could run into if he wasn't shot. Moss knew that Maryland was mostly Southern-minded and believed it would have easily been Secesh, if Washington wasn't in such a strategic place between Maryland and Virginia.

"If any of you try to escape, we'll put a bullet in your back faster than you could say "Dixie,"" one of the guards suddenly said.

Moss thought it was almost as if they were reading his mind. They must have seen the anxious look on the prisoners faces as they glanced up and down the street. All of the guards stood with loaded guns and looked ready to use them.

Moss whispered to the man next to him, "Do you think we should make a break for it?"

"Are you crazy? You heard what he just said," the fellow prisoner said. "I'm not going to die here tonight. I'm going to get to where they're taking me and then try to escape when they're not expecting it. They are all on high alert just waiting for us to make the move. No, I'm not going to make any break for it tonight."

"So, you're going to wait until were hundreds of miles from home?" Moss replied.

"I already am—I'm from Florida."

It started to rain and the guards hollered at the prisoners to get back in the train station to board the train. Moss walked back over to the guard who he had spoken with earlier and asked, "Where are we headed?"

The guard smiled, "You're going to Washington and from there I'm not sure where you'll end up."

As Moss and the other Confederate prisoners headed into the large, brick building, Moss keenly observed the inside area to see where he could make a break for it. He thought if he slipped out of line and ran between cars he could possibly exit on the other side. However, he had not seen the other side and didn't know if there was an exit on that end of the building. He peered through two of the cars and saw several Union soldiers on the other side of the tracks. Chagrined, Moss followed the men in front of him and clamored back up into the train.

Soon the train departed from President Street Station and eventually stopped in the Capitol. The prisoners were escorted out of the train. They marched over to the Old Capitol building, a temporary structure built by the House of Congress after the British burned the Capitol building in 1812. Most of the prisoners went into the main building, but a smaller number of prisoners went into a home adjacent to it. Moss was with the latter group.

The men were hungry, tired and dispirited. Far from them now were thoughts of home and victory and reclaiming Winchester. They were each given a cold biscuit, a sip of water and an old blanket before being told to lie down on the floor in the upstairs rooms. Their guards would remain downstairs listening for any noise coming from above. The upstairs windows were all boarded over and there didn't seem to be any exit except for the front stairway. Moss laid himself down on the floor with the other men and listened to his stomach growl. It felt good to stretch out, even though the floor was hard.

Late that evening Moss tried to escape out the front door, but he was caught and beaten. He decided to be patient and wait for a subtle opportunity which might actually give him a chance.

53.

Lucas Harrington slapped Molly hard across the face. Tears welled up in her eyes, not because of the pain or the mortification of being humiliated in front of others. Tears came because she knew she and her father had crossed a divide. Their relationship would never be the same. The veiled closeness which permeated their relationship had completely dissolved over the last few months. Once, her father was somewhat of a hero who had helped to rescue Molly out of the darkness of death that had fallen on her home since the Mexican War and the absence of her father. Harrington was not perfect but he challenged her to excel and read books and sermons. They loved to discuss Jonathan Edwards and George Whitefield. Molly used to rely on him when her mother was acting senseless. Harrington would usually come through for her and be a voice of reason. Today, however, his character evaporated before her eyes. The once giant man in her life became a dwarf. Molly closed her lips and did not dry the tears that streamed her face. She kept her hands at her side, turned around and walked up the narrow staircase to her bedroom wondering how things had escalated so quickly.

* * *

It was Sunday and Moses had been invited to join the family for dinner. Their pastor was also invited. Lucas led a discussion about slavery and the latest news about Jackson's push north toward Winchester. Moses discussed with the pastor the feelings of many of the blacks there, who had run forward and escaped into the lines of the Union.

During the last few months, the Harrington's table company had discussed many aspects of the war and of slavery and freedom and of religion and politics and how they were all connected. Molly usually bit her lip in these discussions as the lone voice of Southern sympathy. Her brother, Ned, was especially colorful in how he coined phrases and used his wit to turn the table on an argument before it was fully discussed. Often, he interrupted Molly before she could get her main points across. But on this day it was her father who cut her off as she discussed the legality of the slaves running away from their masters in the middle of the night and entering into General Banks' command and the security it afforded them. The Southern landowners temporarily had no recourse unless they were to destroy Banks and reclaim all of the black contraband.

When Molly said, "Justice cannot be served until the Northern invaders have been displaced from Virginia," the conversion turned serious.

"Justice?" Lucas asked. "It was justice that allowed those Africans to finally escape their affliction. As a Christian person it should not be so hard for you to grasp the inherent evil of slavery and the stain it has placed on our government and ideals," Lucas said.

Reverend John continued, "Molly, you can never separate your theology from your sociology. They are one in the same. Science and Politics and Scripture have authority in their respective lanes but the theology of Scripture wraps up everything and trumps all of these areas. You can never misuse Biblical language when discussing secular topics."

"Reverend, I respectfully disagree," Molly bravely said, feeling the scorn of her father as she spoke the words. "Didn't we see the Plymouth dream fail to make that a reality? The city on a hill that was to be a Bible commonwealth was lost as soon as the second generation failed to embrace the values of their parents."

"What is your point?" red Ned asked.

"The Pilgrim fathers assumed that when redeemed parents had children and placed them into the covenantal community through baptism that the children would one day own the promise. The leaders believed the redeemed parents would have prodigy who, when hearing the gospel, would own the covenant for themselves and make a profession of faith after a conversion experience. But we all know that within a generation, children who were baptized, grew up in the church but did not make a profession of Christianity. They married and beget children and then the Pilgrim Fathers had a dilemma. What do you do? Do you not baptize the children and cast the entire family out of the church?

"One solution was what Solomon Stoddard called the half-way covenant. This was not Biblical. This paved the way for people to take short cuts. People who had no conversion experience were allowed to participate in politics as half-way citizens. Society creates rules and distinctions which our theology does not always shine light on. What if theology and the rules of a society could remain distinct without having to bend the Bible? Would that necessarily be evil? What if some of our problems occur because we are trying to put things on parallel levels, things that cannot be parallel? Theology deals with our heavenly relationships and sociology deals with our earthly. Theology will never be subordinate to sociology because God is the center of our lives--."

"Molly, get to the point!" interrupted Lucas.

"The politician does not have to integrate his faith into every speech and decision he makes. He might think slavery a terrible woe, but if he believes the immediate undoing of slavery could bring greater harm into society then he could forego pushing abolition until a riper time. Still a person of prayer, still a true believer and reader of Scripture, still hearing from God, but patiently waiting for God to act instead of using force, and breaking laws, and halting justice, and killing one's own neighbors--."

Slap!

Lucas had heard enough, even though Molly had only just begun. She had started to bare her soul and reveal some of the frustrations bottled up inside her that evening to the group at the dinner table. She knew it was not what they expected to hear. She also knew some of her thoughts were controversial. What she did not expect, however, was that her speaking her mind so infuriated her father that he would feel forced to spill out his anger in a physical way.

Molly refused to depart from her room the rest of the day. She was packing a few clothes for her trip. Her father's actions actually helped her to make her decision easier. She had been planning to leave and return to Winchester but she could not decide when to do it. She would leave that evening and say goodbye to her family, not in person, but in a note so they could not try to persuade her to stay. She slipped into her parent's bedroom to borrow some of her own funds her parents were storing for her in a drawer and she found quite a surprise on her father's cherry dresser. It was an unopened letter from Bruce Crawford addressed to her.

54.

In April of 1862 General Stonewall Jackson's command of 6,000 troops congregated to the east of the Valley Turnpike at Rude's Hill near New Market. The extra 3,000 men came from the conscription law that the Confederate Congress passed. All white men between the ages of eighteen and thirty-five were subject to three years of military service. Most of the new men were young and strong and Jackson was elated at the boost in strength. Jackson closed a letter to his dear Esposita (Anna), "I am thankful to God for sending so many of His children into this army and my prayer is that He will continue to send them, and that He will bless them and those with whom they cast their lot." However, his veteran fighters were not elated with him at the moment.

On the first day of April in 1862 Jackson not only fired the Stonewall Brigade Commander, Brigadier General Richard Garnett, but had him arrested pending a formal investigation and court martial. Dick Garnett was charged with incompetence. He had broken his brigade away from the battle without orders from his superior. In Jackson's eyes, Garnett had not done his duty and the Shenandoah Valley Commander wasted no time in replacing him with someone else. However, the soldiers of Jackson's old brigade did not agree with this decision. They liked Dick Garnett and felt he had performed admirably. For weeks after the decision troops halted their joyful shouting after Jackson when he rode by them. It further frustrated them that he seemed not to notice or care.

General Jackson asked Bruce to see to it that the commanders had their men working hard at battle drills along with mending foot wounds and other potential medical delays. He knew many miles of marching were upon them and he wanted all of his aides working hard to ensure the forces were ready. Jedediah Hotchkiss drew up more topographical maps for Jackson, Sandie Pendleton helped with the paperwork and endless transitions of officers and enlisted, and Reverend Dabney (Jackson's new assistant) ministered to the troops as a chaplain.

Confederate high commander, Joseph Johnston, asked again for all available troops in Virginia to meet him in Richmond. General Lee gave Jackson private permission to temporarily continue movement in the Shenandoah Valley. While the rest of the Confederate Army was planning a defense, Jackson was formulating a new surprise attack. He wrote to General Lee and requested permission to consolidate his forces with those of General Ewell before Ewell embarked for Richmond. Lee apprehensively approved of this hoping perhaps Jackson might still be able to do something significant.

General Richard Ewell commanded a full division of four infantry brigades and five artillery batteries of four guns each. They were currently bivouacked at Orange. His forces of over 8,500 men would put Jackson's strength at nearly 15,000.

Jackson was excited to unite forces with a man so much like himself. Thomas Jonathan Jackson was born in Virginia on January 21, 1824. He was thirty-eight and had graduated from West Point in 1846, seventeenth in his class of fifty-nine cadets. He had served admirably with Winfield Scott in the Mexican War and was now a general. Richard Stoddert Ewell was born on February 8, 1817 and was forty-five. He was raised in Virginia and had graduated from West Point in 1840, thirteenth in his class of forty-five. Lastly, Ewell had also served admirably for Winfield Scott in the Mexican War and was now a general. However, Thomas Jackson did not know their personalities couldn't be more dissimilar.

Jackson seemed at peace with his destiny, spoke with a low, soft voice, loved to playfully tease people and attended diligently to his relationship with Jesus Christ. Major General Dick Ewell had a swearing tongue and a high-pitched voice. He was a bitter and agitated man who didn't care to talk much about God. Both men loved their troops and both were excellent commanders, but Jackson was the senior commander.

Jackson had time to formulate his plans while waiting and watching from his new headquarters at Swift Run Gap near Harrisonburg. Nathaniel Banks had pushed Jackson south for miles, but had resisted pursuing him past Harrisonburg. After listening to General Lee and hearing from his spies, Jackson supposed the strength of Banks' forces in the valley at 18,000-20,000 soldiers. Besides Ewell, Lee had also authorized Jackson to utilize General Edward Johnson's troops of approximately 3,000 who were located west of Staunton to guard the rail lines there. In Jackson's mind this made it an even match and he wondered momentarily about how exactly to proceed until some unimaginable news came from General Lee. President Lincoln was again considering the option of having Banks send a division east for assistance with the Richmond campaign. Jackson hoped this astonishing news was true and waited for an opportune moment.

55.

As men become closer in war, women become closer in the hollows of warfare. Sarah Crawford and Claire Montgomery were always close, but the days following the battle at Kernstown cemented a familial closeness which would bond them for a lifetime. They became family that week. Landon and Lucy grew closer, as well, by spending hours entertaining each other while the women worked. They would often fight, but navigated most of the boy/girl problems because they knew their moms needed them to be good.

The women of Winchester worked tirelessly for days following the battle. After they attended the Union and Confederate critically wounded men, they went to work to bury the dead they found on the battlefield or who had died in the hospitals. Rows of men lined the porch of the courthouse. Some of the men had papers pinned to their coats telling who they were. As the women ministered to the wounded in the hospitals, they saw things which routinely turned their stomachs. Many legs and arms were damaged and amputated, but the more hideous wounds were to the face. One man was still alive yet had his eyes and nose taken off by a small caisson ball. Another man had his lower jaw missing, but was somehow still conscious. The women scribbled notes to families from severely wounded men grasping for the next breath and fighting for their lives. As the women took shifts to rest, they would return to men they tended the day before who had passed by the time they returned to their side the next day. They would arrive at an empty cot, unable to help the wounded warrior any longer. The surgeons were limited in what they could do in their rough environs with the few supplies they possessed. The bleeding could be stopped, but the bleeding of the soul could not.

Claire, Sarah and Kathryn worked hard on both Union wounded and Confederate alike and were exhausted by the end of the week. But their efforts made no difference to the press. The Baltimore American Newspaper commented several times how the ladies of Winchester showed a great lack of concern for the men in both armies.

The Baltimore American Newspaper also told of Jackson's Army fleeing farther and farther south. Toward the end of April the report was that his army had disbanded and was in search of clothing and shelter. They rarely heard good news those weeks and mourned the thoughts of longer time away from their loved ones. However, the Winchester ladies were delighted that Generals Nathaniel Banks, James Shields and Alpheus Williams had departed with their staffs to attend to the retreating Confederates. They heard the new Union headquarters was in Strasburg. The Montgomerys were still not allowed to re-enter their home, however, because the Union Army commanded it now to be used as a hospital.

56.

One day in May a very icy encounter took place between the Winchester women and the Union rear guard. Several officers came to the Crawford home with none other than the notorious mountain man, Daniel Tanner.

"Are these the women?" the Union officer in charge asked.

Rough, stringy haired Tanner grunted and pointed to Sarah and said, "Her husband works for Davis down in Richmond." Then he pointed to Claire and said, "Her husband never leaves Turner Ashby's side."

The women were appalled and outraged at the betrayal by a Southerner. They knew Tanner was probably only in it for the money and they were haunted by his demeanor and savory appearance. Sarah was thankful Daniel Tanner obviously did not know about Bruce being Jackson's aide de camp.

The Union officers took Claire and Sarah down the street to another home where a balding, fat officer sat behind a desk smoking a cigar. He had red blotches on his neck, face and head. His eyes were narrow slits and his ears stuck straight out of his head rather than laying flat. They could see beads of sweat on the skin covering his large skull. The women knew he was short and had somewhat of a limp because they had seen the man walking in town several times. He was never polite to them when he passed by. Daniel Tanner thankfully backed away from the group before they entered their interrogation room.

"Ladies, I hope you are not frightened by coming in here to talk to me. I only want to ask you a few questions," the officer said. The ladies did not move a muscle.

"I hear that you both have relations which are influential to the Confederate Army. This makes me question whether or not you might be feeding them information you learn from around town about our forces or strength. Somehow, the Confederate War Department is learning intricacies about the location and size of our troop strength and we are trying to crack down on all spying within this town, which has served as a central headquarters for the last few months. No doubt you have had plenty of opportunity to solicit information and pass this along to your loved ones, which is treason based on the ordinances we set when we came here."

The officer did not stop to let them respond, "Both of you have a relationship with a man who has a key role in governing the affairs of Jackson's movements. Not only do I want to hear from you now what types of information you have passed to them, but I am going to ask you to pass our official and approved information to them as well." The Major paused to allow the last phrase to sink in a little.

The clever ladies knew exactly what the man was proposing. It was Claire, who noticed the golden oak leaf clusters on the man's uniform, who spoke up first, "I am not sure exactly, Major......?"

"Major Welch."

"I am not sure, Major Welch, who you are and how you fit into the chain of command. Up to this point we have had fairly stable relations with General Banks and General Williams especially, who has used my home for a headquarters and whom I have spoken to on numerous occasions. However, assuming you are legitimately working for them, of which I am highly suspicious, I would like you to go to them and tell them at no time will I ever pass along any approved information I might gain by you for the purpose of deceiving or confusing the Confederate Army as to what the truth is about your status. I am appalled you would even consider asking us about this betrayal to our fledgling Southern government and I am further disturbed you would take counsel with a dark villain the likes of Daniel Tanner whose very name is anathema in these parts."

There were several other men in the room lining the wall who raised their eyebrows at Claire's forceful comments. Major Welch put his cigar down on the wooden table and looked back at Claire, and then to Sarah. Sarah remained silent.

"First of all," Major Welch began, "You are in no position to tell me what you will or will not do here. As far as I am concerned, you are an agent of the enemy who is occupying some of our important headquarters space, which could otherwise be used for our troops who have to sleep outside. Second, I do not appreciate your tone or your unwillingness to answer my questions in a direct manner. Look outside and see our Federal dead and wounded. I have been tasked with preventing another surprise attack by that foolish man who used to be a schoolteacher. Nobody ever seems to consider the weight I am under with this job and how terrible it is for me to be in this position. Now, I want you to rethink your position here and answer my questions." The major began to raise his squeaky voice, "Tell me if you have ever passed along any information about the Union forces here to your loved ones in the Rebel Army."

This time it was Sarah who took the lead. She quickly grabbed Claire's hand because she knew her friend was about to explode at the pompous little man and she took a slight step forward. "Sir, if I could ask you a question first?"

"What?" Welch said clearly annoyed.

"May I ask, Major Welch, who it is you are working for and by whose authority do you occupy these premises and remain here while most of your army is miles away conducting real soldier work?"

"I resent your belittling and how dare you ask me for any clarification. Is it so you can pass along more information to your Rebel allies? I work hard, every day and never receive an ounce of thanks. I don't have to accept more abuse from women who are obviously up to some type of treachery. Listen, I am only going to ask you this one more time and then--."

"And then what?" Claire now raised her voice. "Are you going to put us into the city jail like a common thief? Is this what you are insinuating?" Claire glanced around the room and did not like how the men there were studying her.

The Major actually smiled at Claire. "No, I wouldn't keep you in Winchester. I could cart you off to Washington, ma'am, where they will not be as gracious with you as I am. I work for powerful men and don't think we don't know there are many women serving as Rebel spies in this town. One of you maggots actually took a shot at one of our soldiers the other day."

Inwardly Claire and Sarah smiled because they knew of whom the Major spoke. It was Rachel Jones who did not take mischief from anybody. They did not want their knowledge to be transparent on their faces and so Sarah started speaking again.

"Sir, I have written my son precious few letters, which your own couriers offered to take for me with a flag of truce to the Southern camps.

As to the information it was personal in nature as a mother would write to her son."

The Major smiled knowingly, "So, you're telling me you gave him no information as to our forces here?"

"If I had, your own courier might have opened the letter and read the contents before it was delivered to him. If it was treasonous I would have been apprehended."

"Who is this courier?"

Sarah hesitated because she did not want to get the kind young man in trouble.

"Listen, I have worked hard today as I do every day for a thankless government. I demand some respect, and I demand you answer my question. Who was the courier?" the plump major growled standing up.

"Look Major Welch," Claire interjected. "We are neither trying to hurt you or help you. We are neutral and non-participants in this war. We tended your wounded and dying for days after the Kernstown battle and have given our homes and cattle and gardens and blankets to comfort your troops. I have made meals for hundreds of Union soldiers, officers and enlisted alike. I petition that you speak to General Williams himself as to our status as traitors."

"How dare you, madam! I am not going to talk to anyone else about this, but I am going to have you answer my questions immediately," the short officer stated gruffly, pointing at them with his cigar hand and slamming a fist on the table with the other.

Claire sensed the self-important man might be bluffing and this time she grabbed Sarah's hand and stepped right up to his desk and said, "Listen, Major Welch, you have unlawfully detained us and I am going to report this at the very first instance I see a senior ranking officer. Furthermore, we will never be Union spies for you. This interrogation is concluded and my friend and I will be on our way. Attempting to prevent our departure would be extremely unwise and unpleasant for you."

At those words Claire Montgomery spun on her heels, weaved her arm through Sarah's and they marched out of the room the way they came in. Amazingly no one stopped them and Major Welch did not say anything as they left. In the front room of the house Daniel Tanner was sitting on a wooden bench waiting. Claire gave him the meanest scowl she had ever given anyone in her life and Tanner returned the favor. Claire and Sarah walked out of the house and up the street to the Crawford house without turning around or saying anything to each other. They were so determined to arrive at their home safely they had no time to admire spring's beautiful tulips, violets and orange blossoms throughout Winchester. Once inside the Crawford home they immediately put several pieces of furniture in front of the doors before they relayed their experience to the rest of the family.

57.

Molly traveled from Pittsburgh to Somerset without much of a problem. She was a good rider and had enjoyed spending many hours on her horse, Daisy, when back in Winchester. She met several nice people who helped her on her journey home. She would usually stop at a church in town in order to meet someone with which to stay. She was taking her time and enjoying the spring weather.

Because of the rains, the roads after leaving Somerset were treacherous. It was north of Cumberland, still in Pennsylvania, when Molly's horse, Daisy, was getting spooked by the loud cracks of thunder.

"Whoa, Daisy. It's okay girl. Settle down. We can take this easy," Molly tried to speak calmly to the mare in order to help her settle down a little. She could tell by Daisy's eyes that the horse was petrified.

Molly was just about to stop and dismount when, all of a sudden, a loud snap of thunder clapped close by them and Daisy jerked to the right and flung her rider to the ground. Molly landed crooked, twisting her ankle. Daisy ran off as it began to rain. Molly sat there stunned and frightened. *Oh Daisy, what am I supposed to do now?*

58.

Just after midnight that evening the Crawford home had an intruder. Scout was resting at the bottom of the stairs, protecting the front door and listening to the whole house. Kathryn and Claire were in their makeshift room, formerly the bedroom of Bruce Crawford. Sarah and Lucy Crawford slept in the largest room (Lawrence and Sarah's bedroom), Grandma Crawford was in her usual room on the main floor and Landon was in Moss's old room. The Union commander had recently moved out freeing up Lucy's small bedroom, but the young girl had decided to keep sleeping with her mama.

Something startled Kathryn awake. She arose and walked over to the window in the dark to close the drapes. When she looked out into the night she thought she saw the squatting figure of a man with stringy hair and a long blade in his mouth. His hands were fiddling onto the window as if trying to open it. Kathryn shrieked. Scout barked and raced up the stairs and into the room. Kathryn took several steps backward and sat on the bed while Scout attacked the thin window pane barking fiercely. Next, a light appeared in the bedroom doorway. It was Claire with a host of people behind her including Landon with a musket in his hands. When they looked out the window no one was there.

The room froze for an instant as Scout recalibrated in order to lunge through the window seemingly begging for someone to open it for him. Sarah ran over to the window and opened it. Scout sprang through the opening, skidded down the porch roof and leaped into the air, tumbling onto the back yard. He ran away barking violently, chasing the intruder who seemed to vanish into the darkness.

The family huddled together and comforted Kathryn as she whimpered. Landon finally put down the musket after Claire pried his fingers away from the stock and bore. Kathryn was not sure if she truly saw anyone or just imagined it because it all happened so fast. Just in case, it was decided that for the next few nights someone would stay awake, sitting in a chair with a loaded musket on their lap. Scout returned later that night with a cut on his snout and a patch of red-stained clothing between his teeth.

Part VI

Oh Shenandoah, I Long to See You

I have, I know, but few and small claims upon Divine Providence, but something whispers to me - that I shall return to my loved ones unharmed.

Sullivan Ballou, written in a letter to
his wife during the Civil War

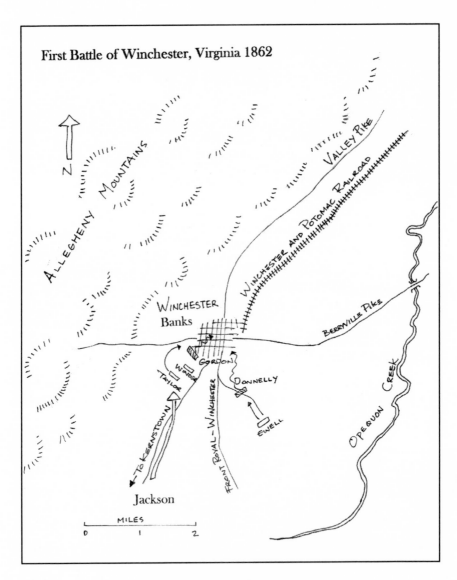

The First Battle of Winchester

59.

"President Lincoln, the press is reporting General McClellan has called you two-faced," War Secretary Stanton told Lincoln. "He claims you are withholding troops from him needed for his assault on Richmond."

Lincoln looked thoughtfully at Stanton a moment and then with a grin replied, "If I *were* two-faced, do you really think I would be wearing *this* one?"

Both men laughed heartily.

"I've been thinking about McClellan and pondering how I can show him I support him. He obviously feels discouraged with some of my decisions."

"Sir?"

"I believe we must send Shields and his division to General McDowell. This would give a greater force to McClellan when McDowell marches to Richmond," Lincoln told Stanton.

Much had changed in the last few days and Lincoln was feeling more confident in his commanders. The Union saw victories in Pea Ridge, Arkansas, Shiloh Church on the Tennessee River and also New Orleans, which was captured by Captain David Glasgow Farragut. The most notable victory was the one on the Tennessee River by Corinth, Mississippi. Over 100,000 soldiers were part of the battle and 3,000 men were killed. Another 15,000 were wounded and finding a hard time of getting proper medical attention. General Grant buried the Confederate dead quickly in several trenches. One of the trenches was filled with over seven hundred bodies, in many places stacked seven bodies high.

With these encouraging offensives from other commanders, President Lincoln had had enough of trying to appease General McClellan and hearken to his whims. Lincoln believed that things would be easier if he, himself, assumed a stronger role as Commander-in-Chief since communications flowed in and out of Washington. He was tired of being a go-between for General McClellan, the man with whom he daily lost his patience. The President issued an executive order dividing off the parts of McClellan's command except for those forces that were with him. General McDowell was now the commander of the Department of the Rappahannock, General Banks became the commander of the Department of the Shenandoah and General John Charles Fremont was the commander of the Mountain Department. General McClellan was limited to just the Army of the Potomac and President Abraham Lincoln now operated as General-in-Chief.

"But sir, Shield's Division is the nucleus of General Bank's force. You want them to march over the muddy mountains to join General McDowell? Didn't we settle this issue after the Battle of Kernstown and made McClellan painfully content with McDowell's smaller force?" War Secretary Edwin M. Stanton asked.

"Yes, we did. And oh, how McClellan grieved the decision even though he already has over 100,000 men. Remember me questioning how many soldiers he needed? Johnston and Lee cannot have more than 60,000 troops in that area. I suppose he wanted to triple their number before he would fight them. However, General Banks assures us Jackson is on his last leg and out of the valley. They have chased them all the way down to Harrisonburg. Banks said the Rebels are on half rations and sickly. Plus, if I was the Confederate general in charge I would tell Jackson to move with haste to help them defend against the largest army ever amassed to the east of Richmond. Wouldn't you?"

"I suppose," responded Stanton.

"Do you think they are aware of the grave danger they are in?"

Just then, Secretary William Seward was introduced by John Hay and walked in, putting his papers on the mahogany table. The Sewards and Mrs. Stanton had visited the Kernstown battlefield together at the end of March and had reported to the President all they could glean from the residents and commanders there.

"Good evening Mr. Seward, we were just about to make a decision. Perhaps you could sound in with your opinion?"

"Let me guess, Young Napoleon has returned to Washington because of a lack of troop strength and you want to know why everybody is planning a parade for the charlatan?"

"No, sir. We are not talking about parades. I have decided to send General Shields and his division over to McDowell in Fredericksburg before he moves in force down to Richmond. General Banks reports that Jackson is pushed out of the Shenandoah Valley and is probably already limping back to Richmond by now. I thought it might encourage McClellan to fight, but Secretary Stanton doesn't see any wisdom in it. What do you think, Secretary?" Lincoln asked Seward.

"I visited Winchester and I will tell you that those people are holding out for Jackson to come back there and reclaim the city for the South. The women walk around as if wounded, praying daily for the destruction of the North and the return of Jackson. If Jackson knows about this, and I am sure he has some knowledge of it, then it must play on his mind. He was headquartered there over the winter and probably derived a fondness for the people. I would bet on Jackson returning to Winchester which re-threatens Washington, putting her in danger."

"You know, that may not be all bad," the President slowly said.

"What do you mean?" Stanton asked.

"I am thinking about the forces we have out west. General Fremont is located in the Alleghenies. I believe you said, Edwin, that he has roughly 20,000 troops. What if we send Shields east now as suggested and this entices Jackson to move northward down the valley toward Winchester. Those forces, if Fremont were to head due east toward Staunton, would be cut off from their supply route and main body in Richmond. Then, if we were to send a couple of divisions back west from Fredericksburg to oppose Jackson head on, we could crush him regardless of what gains he makes in the valley."

"That sounds pretty risky, Mr. President," Stanton said carefully.

"It is a risk. All of war is a risk. The side that wins is usually not necessarily the larger force, but the more cunning force, the more daring and audacious force," Lincoln responded.

"Twenty thousand soldiers to the north and south of him would pretty much do the job," Seward added.

"Look, let's send Shields over to McDowell at once. Banks is probably right and Jackson's paltry force is no doubt limping into Richmond as we speak. There is no reason to leave them in the valley when their mission is done there," President Lincoln concluded with his gracious style and warm smile.

Ed Stanton couldn't help but notice a gleam in Lincoln's eyes as he closed the meeting.

60.

Henry, Bruce, Club and Jonesy all huddled by the warm campfire discussing what they remembered about that fateful day in Kernstown when Moss was taken prisoner. None of them had seen him in his final minutes. Bruce was running messages for General Jackson and Henry and Jonesy had already fallen back, following General Garnett and the rest of their brigade. They did not realize until the following day that Moss had not reconnoitered with his cavalry unit. Bruce asked Jackson if he could go on a mission to look for him and he was denied. Jackson was in no mood to grant a favor or a leave of absence. The Valley Commander had similarly refused his quartermaster, Major John Harman, who asked to go home to attend the funeral of his child—the third one to die from scarlet fever in a matter of days. Jackson wrote the major explaining his position, "We must look to the living, and those who come after us, and see that with God's blessing, the freedom which we have enjoyed is transmitted to them. What is life without honor? Degradation is worse than death."

Henry walked off by himself into the darkness and sat on an old stump just past the glow of the fire. He missed Kathryn terribly. He had not seen her since a few days before the Confederate Army had left Winchester two months ago. He closed his eyes and thought of being with her. He had to be thankful with only his memories of her for now. He decided to take out a pencil and scribble her a note even though he could barely see the paper.

My Dearest Kathryn,

The taste of victory is sweet and enjoyed immensely by all of us foot soldiers. Near the town of McDowell on Sitlington's Ridge we encountered Yankees and had some fierce fighting. We got to serve with General Johnson's men. They all call him Old Allegheny because he looks and smells like the hills. The important thing is that he and his men fight hard and we destroyed the dirt out of those who opposed us. We lost over one hundred brave men and we took the time to properly put them to rest before moving on. We never did catch up to the remainder of the enemy, for they got away very hastily after their loss.

The indications are strong that we shall move in a few days. I do not know whether we will move northward toward Winchester and into your arms or southward to defend Richmond from McClellan's hordes. Whatever may befall us in the weeks to come, I want to reaffirm your position in my heart. My love for you is boundless. When I think of the fire in your eyes and words and spirit and the humble manner that you approach everything in life, it reminds me why you are the star of my heart. Please have patience and ask the Keeper of our souls to protect the sovereignty of statehood and the freedom of Virginia. Please also give my love to my family and yours. Your crushed husband, Henry

Henry folded his letter and placed it in a small, square envelope. He returned to his friends and asked if Bruce would give the letter to the quartermaster when he saw him next. Bruce obliged. The conversation at the fire was pretty subdued. Club Jones had joined the boys. Club kept a blanket on his back while his front was warmed by the fire. Though the days were getting much warmer, the nights were still cool.

"So, no word from Winchester or from your brother Moss? I say he could be hiding out up there." Club said with a twinkle in his eye pointing toward the mountains.

"He's not like that, Club," Bruce responded firmly.

"I don't mean in a bad way, but gatherin' information about the Union for us. Perhaps he's spying on them," Club coughed as he finished his sentence.

"If that were true we would have heard something about it by now."

A horse was approaching them and the Southern men all turned toward the rider. It was Sandie Pendleton who shouted to Bruce to collect the 1st and 2nd Brigade Commanders to headquarters at once.

"What's it about?" Bruce asked.

"You know General Jackson, he never tells anybody anything for security sake. Too many spies around," said Sandie.

Club chuckled, "I'm not a spy, Brian, are you?"

Sandie added as he rode off, "I think this meeting is important because Jackson has sent for General Ewell." This caught everyone's attention.

61.

The staff and the commanders all assembled in Jackson's headquarters building, but he was not going to start without General Ewell. It was an awkward hour as they waited for the General to ride up from his own headquarters in the mountains. Finally, in walked Richard Ewell, or "Old Baldy," as some of the men called him.

Stonewall Jackson began, "Gentleman, thank you for coming. We have received word that a large contingent of Union forces are leaving the valley. This gives us the opportunity to strike a terrific blow to our opponent if we act quickly, before he can be reinforced." Nobody said anything.

"My proposal is we leave at first light tomorrow and put a sharp knife into the throat of our enemy. That is all, you are dismissed," Jackson concluded. There was a long, awkward pause.

"That's it, sir?" spoke Dick Ewell.

"What do you mean, General Ewell?" asked Jackson.

"I mean, I thought I was summoned all the way here to discuss the details of a plan. Where are we going to first, where are we going to meet, what is the order of march? What do you want my cavalry to be doing?"

Jackson grinned at the edgy Ewell, "General, these plans will be revealed to you at the appropriate time and not a moment before."

"So, we are supposed to prepare our troops and get ready to move and not know what direction to assemble?"

"Yes, General."

Ewell still looked confused.

"Point your forces northward," added Jackson.

"Northward?"

"Yes. You will know more at precisely 5:00 a.m. tomorrow morning. Gentlemen, this completes the meeting."

Jackson's three brigade commanders, Brigadier General Charles S. Winder, Colonel John A. Campbell and Brigadier General William B. Taliaferro, all sat speechless, unmoving. They were getting used to Jackson, but Dick Ewell's face turned bright red and he stormed out of the house. Everyone could hear him swearing as he walked over to his horse and rode off with his aide.

62.

Before he went to bed that night, Bruce stopped once more at Jackson's quarters to see if he needed anything.

"Hello, Lieutenant Crawford, not asleep yet?"

"No sir, I was just checking if you needed anything," Bruce responded to the general. There was a shadow over one side of Jackson's face where the lantern didn't illuminate.

"What did you think of the meeting?" When Jackson asked the question he shot Bruce his characteristic half-grin with a twinkle in his eye. When Bruce saw the expression it communicated to him Jackson knew exactly how exasperated he could make people. Everything he did and said seemed calculated—including the present conversation.

"Well, sir," Bruce gauged his words before he continued. "I would say that your commanders did not gain from the meeting what they had hoped."

Bruce hesitated, but Jackson looked at him with raised eyebrows suggesting he continue.

"I guess I don't understand why everything has to be so secretive," Bruce finally offered. "Your commanders are not spies." Jackson didn't respond and continued to look over some reports on his field desk.

Bruce continued, "However, sir, I couldn't hope to be half the leader you are. My aspiration is to command troops with the authority and earnestness you exude."

Jackson looked up, "I suppose your dear, captive brother and friends from Winchester look at us commanders with what Thomas Hughes would call rose-colored spectacles, but I wouldn't get caught up in trying to emulate anyone. I also wouldn't try to seek too much advice on leadership or service. You've got to learn those things in life, in battles. I've done twenty things wrong and ten things right. Thankfully the wrong things haven't destroyed this army. There is no magic formula for success." Jackson then looked at Bruce with his jaw set and Bruce knew something of import was about to proceed.

"Success comes when we act out of principle and character over time, and it is often not seen as success." Jackson paused, then looked toward the side of the tent and said, "It is your systematic approach to life that makes you successful, not your spontaneity."

Bruce looked at Jackson somewhat quizzically before Jackson continued, "Success comes with faithfulness. You should never set all your hopes to command troops or ask for it prematurely. Focus on the details of life and obey what orders you are given each day. Many of the commanders in this army proved themselves as good followers in Mexico. Some of them were common foot soldiers, infantry men. You and your friends might be tested in this war for future opportunities to lead. So never get consumed about the rank that is placed on one's collar. Greater rank means a greater servant's heart for the soldiers you lead, more obedience to the leaders above you, and usually more time away from home."

"It sounds like it will take a long time before I do much of anything important," Bruce said.

Jackson shot Bruce a fierce glance and exclaimed, "What you are doing every day for this army is of the utmost importance! There is tremendous honor in doing your duty, no matter how small the task! I like to remember Brother Lawrence peeling potatoes in perfect tranquility knowing he was doing precisely what God had assigned him. Right now you are young and untested. There is too much of your character left hanging in the balance—too much impulse and too little time of service. Impatience! You have yet to be tried in the crucible of life. I am not looking down on your enthusiasm, but you never promote someone based on their eagerness or intentions. You promote someone based on their past performance and potential to serve. Remember lieutenant, strength does not ever spring from our spoken words, it comes from within, from our character." Jackson paused while this last phrase soaked into his apprentice.

"Character, in my opinion, is just as important as competency. Character cannot be learned. It cannot be counterfeited. It happens when a man allows his integrity and purity to forge his inner person into someone who has depth and is unshakeable in regards to the most important things in life.

"Lieutenant Crawford, I have a question for you."

"Yes, sir?" Bruce dryly croaked out.

"Actually, I suppose it is now time to get some rest. We can finish this conversation later."

With that said, Jackson escorted Bruce to the door.

Bruce left in a daze. He had never heard Jackson speak about service and leadership so openly before. Being told he was young and untested disturbed him a little bit, but he was more happy than upset. Bruce thought of some of the words Jackson had used, *crucible of life* and *strength from within*. He had developed a fondness for Jackson and wondered where all these experiences were leading him. Bruce's thoughts then shifted to Molly and wondered if she was receiving counsel from a wise, older woman about how to be strong and successful. *Why was Molly seemingly born with strength of character and he had to work at it?* Bruce wondered.

63.

Molly was in a warm bed wondering what she would have ever done after her accident if she had not been saved by David Peachey that day.

A few hours after her accident, Molly was surprised to see her horse slowly walking up the hill toward her being led by an older man with a black hat. The man was Amish and his name was David Peachey. David helped Molly to remount Daisy and he carefully led them in the rain down the hill and toward his small farm. The older gentleman took her into his home and introduced Molly to his wife Grace. They offered Molly a place to stay so she could heal. Molly's ankle had swelled terribly and she was in tremendous pain so she accepted.

Thankfully, the old Amish couple knew a few home remedies. They also did not mind company because they were missing having their own kids around. Their children had married off and moved to Smicksburg to raise their families. In the days that followed, Molly would feel that this man and his wife were as dear to her as her own family members. She was amazed at how close they could get in just a short time.

David and Grace Peachey were very pleasant and straightforward people. They spoke in a variation of German, but Molly could understand them because she had studied and learned German as a child. The Peacheys worked very hard all their lives and now, with their children gone, they just managed to eke out an existence from the small crops, large vegetable garden and few livestock that remained on the place. Molly viewed their hospitality as a gift and she was grateful for the dry roof and warm bed.

The Peacheys nursed Molly back to health and while Molly was there she learned a lot from them. One thing she learned was their view about the war and slavery. Molly kept most of her opinions on the war to herself and decided to do more listening and learning than talking. That was easy to do since she struggled with coming up with the right German words for her thoughts. The Peacheys had a very plain view of how to live and how to follow the Scriptures. Molly found it refreshing, but knew she would not be able to limit herself to the same kind of lifestyle they chose.

Molly could get around on the crutches David had made for her, but because they never pressured her about leaving she decided not to rush things. It seemed they truly enjoyed having her around and having someone young in their home again. They were fascinated with her determined personality and her grasp of the Scriptures. Plus, Molly helped with the cooking and a few of the chores that she could do while on crutches. After several weeks, Molly was able to move around without a crutch or a cane, but she tried not to spend much time using her ankle because it remained tender. She knew her time was limited and she had a couple of questions for her hosts.

Usually for supper the Peacheys did not have a large meal. They would eat some fruit and perhaps some cooked zucchini. It was at one of these simple mealtimes Molly made her expected announcement.

"I need to be leaving in the next day or two," she said in German.

The Peacheys did not say anything. Both of them had their heads down studying the meager meal on their plates.

"I have so enjoyed your hospitality to me during my time here," Molly continued.

Mrs. Peachey looked up at her with glistened eyes and raised her old arm up and placed her hand on top of Molly's right hand.

"You have been a gift from God to us," Mrs. Peachey said choking up.

Mr. Peachey still did not say anything and continued to look straight down at the wooden table he had made with his own hands in his father's barn almost fifty years before.

"I have a couple of questions I wanted to ask you before I leave," Molly said.

"Yes, dear?" Mrs. Peachey responded.

"Well, you and Mr. Peachey have been so kind to me, I have truly felt loved by God while in your home through your caring hands. I have also greatly enjoyed using my German and learning your dialect."

Mrs. Peachey smiled while David still looked down.

"I have something to say that I did not tell you before. When I left my home in Pittsburgh, my father struck me in the face because of my

Southern views and acceptance of slavery. You have gotten to know me over this past- nearly a month- and I wonder, what do you think of my views? Am I wrong in your eyes? I know you don't believe in ever fighting in a war." Molly had asked a lot and waited patiently for their response.

It was David Peachey who cleared his throat to begin talking. "Molly, we have enjoyed your stay here." He was broken up and had to stop a moment. "When you first came I told Grace it would be wise if we brought you to an English person's home to care for you, but I told her it was her decision. She decided to keep you here and I accepted. Now that you are leaving I cannot imagine what our quiet home will feel like without you. Our children are supposed to come for us or move back here, but they have ignored their responsibility. We are too old to live by ourselves and manage a farm all alone. I know the day will come when they will return, but perhaps God had them delay just so we might meet you and get to know you."

Molly smiled when she heard these words. She knew David was especially fond of her, but she was glad to hear just how special their time together really was for him.

"As far as your questions," David hesitated, "You know our people are afraid of slavery and being enslaved ourselves. That is why we go to the effort to put into place minimal government rules and duties. We do not like being a part of the government, but we do just enough out of fear. We know if we do not participate at all our own people may be in jeopardy of being enslaved.

"We do not think or talk much about other races. We do not judge them, but they are not part of our everyday lives. We do not think slavery is good even though the Bible speaks much about it. We have been persecuted since our existence. We know what it means to suffer and be despised. Because of this, we can identify perhaps more with the black man than with you. I have heard of one Amish family helping escaped negroes on their journey north to Canada. Grace and I are glad that we have not been asked to participate in this. We are a quiet people and want to live at peace with God and our neighbors."

"As far as what we think of you and your views," David paused again as a lump formed in the back of his throat.

"We love you, Molly," Mrs. Peachey finished for him. "We do not care that you believe different from us. You have been a bright light in our home. When our son left us we were sad, but when our daughter left I thought I would die. It was nothing but darkness in this home for many months. When you came I remembered what it was like to have laughter again and activity. I was excited to get out of bed and get to work because I knew you were here and that we would spend the day working together. Helping you with your ankle and your journey through these parts is nothing compared to the gift that you have given Mr. Peachey and I with your company."

At these words, David looked up from the table with a big grin on his face. Evidently, Grace had spoken the words that were in his heart, but he was unable to get out. Mrs. Peachey took both her hands and clasped Molly's hands tightly. "Miss Harrington, you are our second daughter. We love you and if there is anything we could ever do for you then please let us know."

David began to reach out and join in the loving embrace, but then thought better of it and placed his arm by his side. His smile gave away everything that was in his heart.

"When you pass back through, if it would not be too much trouble then we would like you to stop and say hello," David said.

"No, it would not be much trouble at all. I just do not know when that might be. I do not know if my parents will stay in Pennsylvania when the war is over. I would very much like to introduce them to the couple who has helped me so much. My ankle is strong now and I do not limp at all. I am able to ride my horse well and be on my way. I have stayed the last few days because I knew it would be hard to say goodbye," said Molly.

"Whatever your views of the war and slavery," David began, "We are proud of you."

"Oh, Mr. Peachey, that means so much to me." Molly then stood up and hugged him around his neck quickly with a glance at Grace who was grinning from ear to ear.

Molly went to her bed that evening with a heart full of love and trust again in her fellow man. This simple couple had made such an enormous impact on her and she knew it would take awhile to sift through all of the ramifications of her experience with them. She knew she felt differently than before about the war, but she was unable to isolate what exactly was different. She was also trying to view slavery through the Peachey's eyes—ones who were afraid of being slaves. Molly had never had that fear. In many ways, she knew she was sheltered and pampered from some of the ugliness in the world. Her view of slavery was tempered by the fact that she lived in northern Virginia and not in the cotton states. She knew that, but she had never spent long in calculating what it might mean if she went south and hated what she saw. She could live with Virginia slavery, but that was not the predominate way slaves were utilized in America.

David and Grace Peachey had imprinted something on her conscience. They were not abolitionists, but simply abhorred the very concept of slavery. What they had communicated with her over the weeks she spent with them had changed her worldview. They wanted to serve God in thought, word and deed. They desired to live peaceably with their fellow man—things her own father and mother wanted. However, the Peacheys were willing to take their beliefs to the extreme, even if it meant seclusion and being despised by the public. This was something her parents, who loved recognition and their social standing, would simply never do.

Molly fell asleep that night without pain in her ankle for the first time since her fall. She had completely healed, and now it was time to depart for Winchester.

64.

General Ewell noticed the cloudy skies in the morning as he rode northward with his troops out in front of the Army of the Shenandoah. Each day started cloudy, but soon the hot sun would scorch the marching troops. They were headed to Front Royal before going to Winchester, in order to deny the Union an eastern escape and supply route to Washington. This strategy might also isolate and trap the blue forces in Strasburg where they could be destroyed. It was a bold move against an enemy whose strength in the region was not exactly known.

Ewell's mood was better than the night of the staff meeting. He knew there would be a fight soon and he was excited. The march started May 19th and continued for three days with only a brief stop for overnight sleeping. Each day they covered at least fifteen miles. The soldiers under Ewell's command were weary, foot sore and barely given enough to eat. But they were motivated. Whenever they would see General Jackson they would cheer or sing a song for him. Ewell had yet to understand their admiration for the man. He hoped to God Jackson wouldn't disappoint them.

65.

Federal General Nathaniel Banks never felt adequate with the amount of troops he was given to defend the Valley. They were scattered between the three towns of Front Royal, Strasburg and Winchester. These towns formed a triangle with Winchester at the northern apex, Strasburg on the bottom left western point (with the Valley Turnpike running through it), and Front Royal on the bottom eastern point (near Manassas Gap). Banks had roughly 1,000 soldiers at Front Royal, 4,400 men in Strasburg and 1,500 troops acting as a rear guard at Winchester where stores of supplies were being held.

General Banks heard word that day that President Lincoln was near Fredericksburg consulting with General McDowell about beginning his movement of troops toward Richmond. Banks would now be the important rear guard and his army would provide the covering force for the Capitol. Banks knew that if he failed to hold Winchester, Washington would be exposed to unmitigated danger.

66.

Bruce walked alongside of Henry and Jonesy for a couple of miles while holding onto the reigns of his horse. It was Friday, May 23, 1862 and they were almost to Front Royal. They had marched on the eastern side of Massanutten Mountain in the Luray Valley the day before. Now they were hiking up a narrow mountain road with tall pine trees on both sides. If they would have taken a moment to look up, they would have noticed the beautiful sight of the blue sky above the green woods. But they were too weary to think of anything but the pain and drudgery of the continuous marching. Every bodily joint was stiff and sore and many could no longer feel their feet. The only thing keeping most of them marching up the steep hill was knowing that just over the peak and down the other side were Yankees. Yankees that were living luxuriously in a quaint little town and enjoying all the fruits of bivouac and their rich government supplies.

Bruce couldn't get his mind off of Moss, but didn't mention it to the others. He wondered where his little brother was and if he would ever see him again. Moss was more daring and impetuous than Bruce and that scared him. He hoped Moss hadn't done anything stupid and been killed for it. There was no word yet from the Southern government about the prisoners taken at Kernstown. Bruce was also saddened thinking about their fine horse, Chris Columbus, being shot. The whole episode at Kernstown was a catastrophe and he hoped today's venture would go much better.

The boys spoke of their pains and of home. They laughed at thoughts of Landon, Lucy and Scout and they amused themselves with childhood memories of growing up and playing from Fairfax and Piccadilly Street and across town to Southwark. They all hoped for a quick, easy rout of the enemy and for an end to the war. They despised Lincoln, Seward and

McClellan. They loved Stonewall and thought Ewell was a rascal. They all felt sorry for Dick Garnett and believed he was treated poorly. None of them spoke of Riley, Moss or Kathryn out loud. There were certain subjects too sacred to speak about while marching. Bruce thought of Moss and Molly. Jonesy thought of Molly, Julia and his ma. Henry's quiet thoughts were consumed with his fair-haired Kathryn and memories of her from their brief honeymoon.

A few men behind them broke into a simple song one of them made up while marching that day and put it to the tune of the first part of "My Bonnie Lies Over the Ocean."

We love you Virginia we love you,
We love you so much and so more,
We have trust in our Virginia,
So much we will win the war!

While the three friends were deep in thought and mechanically marching together, General Jackson quietly rode up alongside the column and requested for Bruce to ride with him toward the front. Soon, the other two boys peaked the ridge and as they descended the clatter and noise of the battle greatly increased. They could see General Ewell's regiments pouring into Front Royal and the Union Army hightailing it out of there. The residents were cheering even as the federal Parrott guns desperately pounded the community being flooded with Confederate forces. The Union command at Front Royal disintegrated and fled northward over Richardson's Hill and the South Fork of the Shenandoah River.

The Winchester boys were delayed by their commander who wanted to await word from Jackson before proceeding. By the time Henry and Jonesy and the 33rd Virginia Regiment arrived into town the action was over. The afternoon sun was evaporating behind the hills and the region now belonged to the Confederate Army. The two infantry soldiers found plenty of goods in town to make life more comfortable. Henry nurtured his aching feet, Jonesy his aching belly. They camped north of Front Royal, a little south of Cedarville. The order was out from General Jackson, they would leave early the next morning and head towards Winchester. Stonewall's infantry were now known as "foot cavalry" for they had marched 80 miles in the last four days on the rocky, muddy, almost impassable terrain.

67.

Turner Ashby missed his young aide Moss Crawford. The cavalry chief had been sent west to Buckton Station to intercept any enemy forces which might try to escape. Ashby was also rapidly destroying their telegraph communication lines. Though he tried to overtake the Federal position at Buckton Station with successive cavalry charges, Ashby could not penetrate the strong Union defense. The Union shot deadly enfilade fire into their advance. Several of Ashby's key officers fell dead right next to him and the glow of hatred in his eyes grew stronger. Ashby's deputy, Conrad Montgomery, was able to finally convince him to withdraw from Buckton Station when it was obvious there was no hope. The three hundred horsemen eventually turned and thundered toward Cedarville. Though they did not take Buckton Station, they had at least captured two locomotives and ruined the enemy's communication lines for awhile.

68.

General Nathaniel Banks was in a stupor. The reports he received that evening all seemed to contradict each other. One report had General Jackson and his army at Front Royal, and another near Strasburg. It was obvious a strong Confederate push moved the Union forces out of Front Royal. But Banks wasn't sure yet if this was a decoy or the main effort. A large cavalry contingent had also been seen on the turnpike.

More messages came in from runners helping him solve the puzzle late that night. The forces at Front Royal opposing the Union guard appeared to be over 5,000 strong. Banks now had no doubt about his situation, but unfortunately he had wasted the entire evening pondering. Banks did not want to retreat from his main effort at Strasburg, he knew it would be a sign of weakness. However, he could not take the chance of Jackson attacking from the north, from Winchester. It took him so long to formulate a plan that General Banks' aides wondered if he was mentally okay up to the point of his delicate decision.

After midnight, Banks finally gave the order to retreat the infantry and all necessary supplies up the Valley Turnpike eighteen miles north toward Winchester. Winchester was the pearl of the Shenandoah Valley, possessed a critical crossroad and a strategic railroad junction. It was also the easiest avenue to the Union position at Harpers Ferry across the Potomac. Whoever held Winchester could take the Ferry and then march easily to Washington. Winchester had to be retained. Strasburg could be taken again later, but if the Union Army lost Winchester they would not only lose their major regional stockpile of supplies, but they would be forced to depart from Virginia. Banks now realized he was in a desperate race for the high ground south of town where they had held Jackson's Army back last March. He did not go to bed that evening and his troops were on the road well before dawn.

69.

Jackson relished having his own independent command and performed magnificently as a tactical commander. The evening before, he personally superintended the attack on the retreating Union forces formerly in Front Royal. The Federal contingent raced across the fields away from Front Royal in order to cross the South Fork River and then the Pike Bridge over the North Fork. As soon as they crossed over they tried to set fire to the bridges. This slowed down the Confederate pursuit, but the cavalry men in gray were hungry for battle against their fleeing enemy. They quickly rebuilt portions of the bridge and drove on toward their opponents. Jackson commissioned Major Thomas Flournoy with the task to give hot pursuit to the Yankee column moving northward. Flournoy was one of Ashby's subordinate commanders and he was a good soldier who followed orders. Thomas Jackson told him to press the enemy and to attack as soon as he caught up with him. This happened at Cedarville when, with the second cavalry charge, the Union line broke and the Northerners were either captured or escaped by running away like wild men. A stunning victory, and Jackson directed it from the very front.

It appeared that every citizen of Front Royal came out to welcome the troops and throw a party for them. Songs were sung, hogs were butchered, chickens were cooked and lots of merriment occurred in town that night. Jackson could hear the celebratory excitement, but chose to stay near the front. The house he decided as a meeting place for his commanders had a large family living in it who were all very proud of him. Over seven hundred Union soldiers were taken prisoner and almost half-a-million dollars worth of supplies were garnered. The father of the family told Jackson his nine-year-old daughter wanted to sing a song for him. Jackson, deep in thought and planning for the next day, paused what he was doing and smiled at his host in agreement. The commander took a seat in the living room while the father dusted off his violin. A young girl with braided hair and light brown freckles on her nose smiled at Jackson and began to sing with everything inside she could muster.

I wish I was in de land of cotton
Old times dar am not forgotton
Look away! Look away! Look away! Dixie Land
In Dixie Land whar I was born in
Early on one frosty morning
Look away! Look away! Look away! Dixie Land

I wish I was in Dixie, Hooray! Hooray!
In Dixie Land I'll take my stand
to live and die in Dixie.
Away, away, away down south in Dixie.
Away, away, away down south in Dixie

Old Missus marry "Will-de-weaber"
William was a gay deceiver
Look away! Look away! Look away! Dixie Land
But when he put his arm around'er
He smiled as fierce as a forty-pound'er
Look away! Look away! Look away! Dixie Land

I wish I was in Dixie, Hooray! Hooray!
In Dixie Land I'll take my stand
to live and die in Dixie.
Away, away, away down south in Dixie.
Away, away, away down south in Dixie

Dar's buck wheat cakes an 'Ingen' batter
Makes you fat or a little fatter
Look away! Look away! Look away! Dixie Land
Den hoe it down and scratch your grabble
To Dixie Land I'm bound to trabble
Look away! Look away! Look away! Dixie Land

I wish I was in Dixie, Hooray! Hooray!
In Dixie Land I'll take my stand
to live and die in Dixie.
Away, away, away down south in Dixie.
Away, away, away down south in Dixie

At this point all the children were dancing in a circle and Jackson, Bruce, General Ewell and several other officers and staff members were clapping to the violin and singing heartily. It was a worthwhile break to take their minds off the battle for a few moments. General Jackson took the youngster who sang the tune into his arms and told her how much he appreciated it. He patted her head, asked her a couple of questions then graciously excused himself and departed back into his bedroom. He still needed to prepare the final details for his attack on Winchester. Jackson got very little sleep that evening.

70.

Following the Battle of Kernstown, Riley was temporarily attached to the 29th Pennsylvania Infantry as an escort. Several of their original riders were killed or taken prisoner and they desperately needed a few good men to fill their ranks. Riley's own cavalry unit, the 4th Pennsylvania, was slowly making its way down toward Richmond, stopping in Washington and then on to Fredericksburg. He was to join them as soon as he received word from his commander.

The morning of May 24th started early for the young Winchester lad. He and his unit were to advance along the chapel road between Middletown and Cedarville. Once they encountered Rebel skirmishers they were to report it immediately so General Banks could know exactly where the enemy threat was positioned. They only advanced a mile or two when they started to receive some fire from the east. Riley thought they should continue to charge and penetrate the Confederate line but his commander despicably ordered them to retreat. Riley was infuriated. They had not even ascertained how many of Jackson's troops were on the road and in the vicinity. Their report would do nothing to help General Banks.

When they arrived back at the turnpike, they saw wagons slowly moving in both directions. Strasburg was evacuating, not just the military, but it appeared the entire town. Most of the civilian wagon drivers were black men and some of them were pulling large white families. Entire kitchens, stoves, parlor furniture, bedroom sets and smaller barnyard animals were all being transported by a massive array of wagons. Some of the carts were pulled by a single mule. Some of the extra-large wagons were pulled by six-horse teams. There was every combination in-between.

Military units were trying to get themselves organized and make progress around the civilians. Riley was mesmerized by the chaos. Scores of women and children were following the wagons on foot. Around the many wagons raced dogs and tiny children. One young boy was pulling a goat, but at times the goat was pulling the boy back to Strasburg. Some people were screaming, many were discussing and most looked wide-eyed and scared. Behind them there were large billows of black smoke where Union soldiers had set fire to warehouses of supplies that could not be moved in time. The intensity on the turnpike was as if Stonewall Jackson was entering Strasburg and taking prisoners. But as Riley assessed the situation, it was becoming clear Jackson was probably headed to the same place these wagons were. *They might be running into him!* Riley thought. *And they had no idea.*

"Hey corporal, let's keep moving." Riley's thoughts were interrupted by an officer reminding him they were to move back toward Strasburg to receive further orders from the command. *How do some of these guys convince people to make them officers,* he wondered.

71.

Jackson wasted no time that morning surmising exactly what Banks had as his options. Jackson predicted that Banks would flee from Strasburg northward to Winchester. This was not confirmed, however, for several hours. When he finally had conclusive evidence of where General Bank's main force was headed, he made all the final decisions he needed to in order to maneuver his army. General Ewell was to head directly to Winchester with his division and Jackson would head west to Middletown in order to pursue the enemy from the rear.

When Jackson finally fell upon the turnpike with his artillery pieces, it was a very sad day for the Northerners unfortunate enough to be in his line of sight. For hours, Jackson and Ashby pounded the turnpike from the high ground between Strasburg and Winchester. The caravan of wagons and supplies and soldiers became a massacre. The entire line was disrupted for at least a mile in both directions. But what Jackson soon realized is what he had feared the most had already occurred. The bulk of General Bank's forces had passed that point on their journey toward Winchester. *They might possibly reach the high ground south of Winchester before Ewell!*

72.

Bruce had never heard so much moaning and complaining from the troops as he did that Saturday afternoon. Even though they were headed back to Winchester to retake the city, their moods were not joyful. Shouts and complaints were even blatantly being made about Jackson, which Bruce was loathe to hear. Everyone's feet were in terrible pain. Their limbs were stiff and their neck and shoulders tired of the strain of the straps of their bags. People were not throwing their muskets down yet, but Bruce knew it was almost to that point. The officers refused to reprimand their troops because they were sympathetic with the men. It was fun to joke about being foot cavalry when not marching, but when back on the road it was unbearable.

Bruce caught up to where Henry, Jonesy and Club were marching. He dismounted his horse and walked alongside of them for awhile.

"Stonewall has to know what were going through—but it seems he doesn't care," Jonesy said.

"He knows," Bruce responded. "And he's proud of you. It's just that he knows we have to get to Winchester before General Banks or there will be hell to pay."

"We're paying for it right now," said Henry.

Club laughed. He was in as much pain as the younger ones, but his pride as an old soldier wouldn't allow him to reveal it.

The foursome walked past a squad of men sitting on the ground by the side of the road. Several in the group were completely prone with no evident desire to continue on. Again, Bruce noticed, there was no officer yelling at the men to get back into the column.

It appeared to Bruce that Jonesy and Henry were biting their lip quite a bit so as not to wince or cry out in pain from the cuts and bruises on their feet. They happened upon a soldier who sat down in the middle of the road and wept while rubbing his feet. No one said anything. Everyone fanned out on each side of him and silently advanced leaving him alone on the road. Bruce knew the marching was a necessity, but he also wondered how much you could push human endurance before it cracked. *And when would you know? Would hundreds of soldiers simply fall over at once?* Bruce wondered.

"Bruce, you've got to tell him what's going on here," Jonesy said. "You've got to explain to him how foolish it is to keep driving us on like this. We're not a herd of cattle. The march to Front Royal did us all in and we're through. We did not even get one day to rest."

"He knows Jonesy. He probably also knows not all the men will make it. But the ones who do will—."

"Will what?" Club interrupted. "What kind of fighting will men do after marching over 90 miles in a few days? I'm not going to complain because it does no good and I will be there to fire my musket tonight or tomorrow morning when ordered, but there is a limit and Stonewall went past it long ago. Please don't try to explain his reasons to us."

Club said no more. He didn't need to. Bruce didn't respond. He knew they were right. His back and thighs ached from riding his horse so much without a break, but his feet felt fine. He looked at the limping soldiers all around him slowly following the man in front. Bruce was amazed at what he saw and he almost allowed tears to come to his eyes. The sheer bravery and commitment of what he was witnessing suddenly came alive to him. These men were marching possibly to their death, but they kept putting one foot after another. *Why would a man carry a weapon into battle knowing others were firing at him and it could be his last moment on earth?*

Bruce was proud of these men. Proud of what they were accomplishing. Proud of what they were sacrificing. He mounted his horse and left his friends with new resolve to perform his best in order to end this war as fast as possible.

73.

Colonel Turner Ashby had been with General Jackson during the Valley Pike attack. Some of the cannon being used were his from Preston Chew's mounted artillery unit. The large guns were brought up the hill overlooking the crowded road and began a devastating raking fire. After about an hour of watching men lose their arms and legs, horses falling down and wagons exploding, Ashby was satisfied. Blood was flowing down the turnpike from the many soldiers unable to get past the tremendous burst of firepower. Ashby moved on to search for his next target. The road he left behind was completely clogged with burning wagons, dead men and wounded horses. His work there was finished.

His next task was to pursue the Union wagon trains that were scurrying toward Winchester. Jackson's troops would be behind them, but he was to push the Union retreat with cavalry skirmishers and take as many prisoners as possible. The wagons left by the Federals, however, were too tempting for many of Ashby's men. As the sun was setting that Saturday, a large contingent of his troopers were taken over by their impulses. The wagons were filled not only with military rations, clothing and ammunition, but with candy, vegetables, fruit, chocolates, jellies and whiskey. Some of Ashby's men disappeared looking to steal horses or favors from the cheering women.

Turner Ashby never had good control over his cavalry companies and today was no exception. Yet Ashby remained in good spirits for several reasons. They had overtaken a far superior enemy in Front Royal and Strasburg, the prospects were high that Winchester would be re-taken as well, and he had just received word that the Confederate War Department was promoting him to Brigadier General. Ashby hoped to have the rank pinned on the next day in downtown Winchester once the Northerners were routed. That he would wear the new rank for less than two weeks could have never entered his mind.

74.

Corporal Riley McNair had ridden hard all day. He and his team helped provide protection to their infantry regiment who were scurrying north toward Winchester. One stray enemy musket ball luckily missed Riley's head, but did tear through his hat. Once his unit was safely in Winchester, Riley volunteered to return to the crowded Pike to personally assist the struggling civilians. The black laborers, the farmers and the shopkeepers were all at wits end trying to navigate the Valley Turnpike along with over 500 military wagons and sutler's teams. They needed some military supervision. Riley watched the sun go down while helping a gentleman replace a wagon wheel which had slipped off the axle of his wagon.

In the twilight hour, just south of Winchester, Riley saw Ned Harrington marching along the Valley Pike with a squad of men from Pennsylvania. Despite the fact that Ned had his kepi hat pulled too low on his forehead they made eye contact. Riley ran up to him and grabbed his shoulder.

"Ned Harrington, you've enlisted!" Riley exclaimed.

"Yeah, rub it in," Ned said mournfully.

"What do you mean? Aren't you proud to serve?"

"Absolutely not. I'm a pacifist," Ned said proudly.

"A pacifist? I knew you didn't want to go to war, but a pacifist? I see you are carrying a musket—what gives?"

"I may be carrying this death device, but I will never fire it toward anyone. Or, any creature."

"Then why'd you enlist?" Riley asked incredulously.

"My father made me," Ned replied not very happily. "After Molly left, he told me he was tired of watching me waste my days away while most other young men my age were off to war."

"What do you mean Molly left?" Riley asked with concern.

"She ran away from home a few weeks ago and we haven't seen her since."

"Ran away? Whatever for?"

"Father struck her in front of the reverend and I think it bruised her pride, so to speak."

"Why did he hit her?"

"You know Molly. She always thinks she's right about everything, including about why this war is being fought. Hey, I've got to get going."

Ned's squad was waiting for him and beginning to be agitated. It had been a long day and they were almost to Winchester. They knew Jackson's Army would be on the road they stood on very soon. Current reports were that his cavalry was already spotted north of Newtown.

"Hey Ned, one more question. Where do you think she is currently if you had to guess?"

"I thought she would be in Winchester when I passed through a few days ago, but the women folk there said they hadn't see her. They marched us down to Strasburg yesterday just to turn around and send us back up to Winchester today. That's almost thirty-six miles! I despise marching. These leaders are nuts."

"Hang in there, Ned." Riley smiled. Red Ned never lasted long when work was being done. He was always the first one to take a break or more often, just plain disappear. Riley imagined the conversation when old man Harrington ordered him to enlist—how delightful that must have been.

Fun thoughts aside, Riley was extremely concerned over the news about Molly. There were some pretty rugged areas in Pennsylvania and during this war there is no telling who might be on the roads or take an interest in *helping* a beautiful young woman along.

It was almost 200 miles from Pittsburgh to Winchester. The terrain was mountainous and the roads were thick with mud this time of year. There were some areas of the route where there were no communities for large distances. Without good planning it could be difficult to have enough food and water for the trip. Riley imagined Molly taking off on her horse without planning out all of the details. *What would she do if she was caught out in the open in a terrible thunderstorm?* He wondered.

Riley spent two to three hours in the darkness helping civilians pour into Winchester and assisting them when their wagons would get stuck in the mud between the tremendous furrows now on the road. Soon he could hear the sound of the battle closer to his position. *The Confederate Army must be pouring up the road and almost to Kernstown now,* he thought. Union defensive positions were being hastily put together around the south of town. As Riley listened to the crack of musket fire from the south, he walked over to the command headquarters to receive his next assignment.

He was assigned as an aide in Bank's First Division. When he left the building it started raining for the fourth time that day.

75.

The Winchester ladies received some unexpected visitors that evening. Just after Scout barked, they heard a knock at the front door which had been guarded cautiously after the Welch and Tanner affair. They thought it might be Ned Harrington again, but when they opened the door it was three wide-eyed Union infantry soldiers from a Maryland regiment. Sarah noticed they looked pretty haggard and frightened. The soldiers asked for some food and possibly a place to stay for the evening because they had just marched from Front Royal.

"Come in, boys," Sarah Crawford graciously offered.

When the young men had huddled around a little table and eaten some biscuits, bacon and coleslaw left over from supper, they began to loosen up a little and look less anxious.

The women had heard reports that afternoon of how General Jackson's Army was on the move and the Union Army was retreating, but they had not met any soldiers who had direct knowledge of what was happening.

Assuming the women were Union patriots, two of the soldiers talked openly about all the happenings. The third soldier said nothing the entire evening, but looked at the women suspiciously.

"Our regiment has been decimated," one of the men said. "And the worst part is that we were beaten by fellow Maryland men. Those Confederate traitors put their Maryland regiment out in front of their battle lines because they knew they were going up against us."

At the sound of the word traitor, seven year old Landon glared at the soldiers for a moment and then ran upstairs to retrieve his wooden sword. Lucy smiled because she saw the unspeakable joy and pride in her mother's eyes with the revelation of a Confederate victory.

"So, the whole Union contingent was routed?" Sarah followed up trying not to reveal the triumph in her heart.

"Completely. We were overrun. And word is, Jackson will be here before midnight," the other talkative soldier revealed.

"Tonight?" Claire asked.

"Yes, ma'am, he's hot on our heels."

"Why aren't you three with your unit?" Claire asked.

"Well, begging your pardon ma'am, but our unit doesn't exist anymore. We're it as far as we can tell. When the Southern cavalry made their last charge we saw most of our leaders fall to the ground. A few of us made off into the woods. Jacob, Lo and I found our way onto the road headin' up here, so we took it. But there was no one behind us from our unit."

"What about General Banks? Is he still in Strasburg?" Claire boldly asked. Sarah was surprised at Claire's directness, but did want to know the answer.

The men sized up the women one more time before answering holding their gaze the longest on Kathryn. "He's here," they said.

"He's here in Winchester?" Claire asked.

"Just got in about a half hour ago. We wouldn't have known, but he strode into the command quarters after we went there looking for some folks from our unit and for food. He had his aides and, by the looks of the roads out there, all of the wagons and goods from here to Strasburg are flowing into town."

Claire and Sarah were stunned. They had not realized that the threat Jackson was causing in Front Royal yesterday was forcing the entire Union command in the valley to consolidate in Winchester that evening.

"So there might be a battle tomorrow?" Kathryn asked.

"Young lady, there is *going* to be a battle tomorrow! Jackson is supposedly right outside of town. Our folks are digging in and preparing for a defense."

Kathryn couldn't hold it in any longer. She was so excited her beloved Henry would be home soon, tears of joy flooded her eyes. She held her hands to her heart and then to her face and then back to her heart. Suddenly she dashed out of the room and fled upstairs because she did not want the men to be disheartened by her pleasure.

Sarah walked over to the front door and opened it to look out into the street. Soldiers were moving about hurriedly while citizens lined the sidewalks watching them. There was obviously something very important happening in Winchester that evening. Sarah stared for a moment at nothing in particular, but deep inside she imagined seeing Lawrence, Bruce and Moss all walking up the front porch, taking off their hats and smiling at her. Scout's sudden bark brought her back to reality, and when Sarah turned around to look at him it seemed that the dog was smiling, as if he could read her mind. Sarah closed the door again and returned to her company, not mentioning her vision to anyone.

Claire looked at Sarah and said, "In a day or two when this battle is over, I will need to go back over to the place to see if it is still occupied. Perhaps Alma, Genevieve and I can start putting a few things back in order." Alma and Genevieve were two of Conrad and Claire's slaves who were left at the home to sleep there and tend to whatever the soldiers needed, and most importantly to protect their personal property that couldn't be carried over to the Crawfords. More than once Alma or Genevieve had run over stating how a Union officer was 'messin wid da furniture' or paintings or clothing or beds, etc. Claire always had her guard up. She had learned to trust General Williams a bit, but he wasn't always there and the other soldiers who were passing through would sometimes think things were *available* and up for grabs when there was little activity in the house. Some nights, Claire stayed at her house but she couldn't bear the sight of the thick mud on the floors and the constant disarray in the kitchen. Claire had not seen Alma or Genevieve for at least two weeks.

The soldiers laid down on a soft carpet in the parlor and fell right to sleep, snoring loudly. Scout kept watch over them and did not leave the parlor entry all night.

76.

The iron hand of Stonewall Jackson was in action now and there was no trace of the velvet glove. He force-marched his troops throughout the entire day, fighting the Union as they went. They didn't stop for a meal or to take a rest break. Soldiers were ragged and weary, bumping into each other while they marched. Half-asleep and staggering, the men did not arrive to the sloped land south of Winchester until three in the morning. Though Stonewall wanted them to march a few hundred more yards to the crest of the rise, his army could go no further. They had reached the breaking point of human endurance, just shy of their commander's goal. At the order, almost every marching soul immediately collapsed where they were standing and dropped into a dead sleep. They did not notice the chilled, moist grass or the beautiful stars occasionally poking out between the clouds.

77.

Before General Banks went to sleep, he positioned close to 1,000 troops to the southeast of Winchester and over 4,000 troops to the southwest facing Kernstown. He knew the largest contingent of Jackson's Army would be coming from the Valley Turnpike, but he did not know what else Jackson might throw at him. He kept over 400 soldiers in reserve, ready to switch from one side or the other, along with his cavalry.

Like Jackson's men, Banks' soldiers were exhausted. Several regiments, such as the 2nd Massachusetts, were charged with forming picket lines and turning around to deliver volleys of musket fire at Ashby's oncoming cavalry. The fire was deadly to the Confederates, but it was time-consuming and petrifying to the Union foot soldiers who were ordered to turn south and fight. The extra marching and intensity of combat took its toll. To frustrate them further, nearly none of the Union line which emptied into Winchester that evening had eaten anything in twenty-four hours. Plus, there was still nothing to eat before they went to sleep. There were no blankets to cover with so there was nothing between them and the dewy clover. But being tired, hungry, cold and wet was not their main discomfiture—it was the thought of Stonewall Jackson.

78.

Henry and Jonesy woke at four a.m. to a murky fog. It was Sunday, May 25th. They were closer to home than they had been for several months. They had no joy, however, because they had no breakfast. They marched for over an hour through drenched fields of wheat, clover and wildflowers. Finally, through the shifting fog they could see they were just south of their beloved Winchester and they could also see men in blue uniforms waiting for them with Parrott guns.

The cannon fired up and roared for almost two hours with skirmish lines taking deadly shots at the artillery teams. Both armies tried to push forward on the flank to secure the high ground first. When Jackson rode by the 33rd Virginia they were ordered not to cheer because of how close they were to the enemy line. The men simply raised their hats in adulation until he disappeared into the fog.

Henry hadn't said anything all morning. Jonesy had grumbled a little about the lack of food and the wet grass. They were both prepared to fight, they had kept their cartridge boxes dry.

John F. Neff was their commander. He was strict, a former VMI cadet, the son of a Dunkard minister, and, at 27 years of age, the youngest regimental commander in the Valley Army. Neff took his orders directly from Jackson that morning to hold a key hill on the western side of the battle line so Union artillery could not be placed there. Neff saluted sharply and agreed to the mission before ordering his men to attach their bayonets.

Henry and Jonesy were waiting patiently for the next set of orders and were crouched low behind some shrubs and old stumps with their company spread out to their left and right. Bruce was nowhere to be seen, but they were told he was sent back south to retrieve more batteries. Club was at the far right consulting with the company commander. Most of the men were shivering uncontrollably.

"I'm cold," whispered Henry.

"What do you think is going to happen this morning?" Jonesy mumbled.

"What do you mean?" Henry asked.

"I mean, do you think we will win or lose?"

"Don't think about possibly losing. We have to win this, Jonesy. If we fail to enter Winchester this time our army will be easily overtaken. Look at us. Everybody is on their last leg. There is no conceivable way we could outrun them to the south like we did after Kernstown. Every bone in my body aches as I know yours does. We simply have to win and I think everyone here knows that. Plus, we all want to see our families in the worse way. They are just beyond those hills, just one mile away."

"I'll bet you can't wait to see Kathryn?" Jonesy grinned. They usually didn't talk about her.

Henry was going to scold his best friend for bringing her up, but instead let out his next breath through his nose and said, "Yeah. She's all I think about."

"Well, you better think about war now, here comes Colonel Neff."

Neff came by encouraging the men and told them to keep waiting for a little bit longer. Their regiment was chosen to be kept for the second wave of attack that morning. Henry and Jonesy were relieved at the news and went back to talking.

"You know, Jonesy. It looks like we are going to make it through this one. Yet, every time we go into battle there is a chance, however small, that one of us will be killed. If this is my last day, I want you to take the letter out of my breast pocket and make sure Kathryn gets it, you hear?"

Jonesy was shaking his head warning his friend not to speak of such things.

"No Jonesy, listen to me. I will do the same for you and make sure Club and Rachel get your belongings. Don't let those Yankees find anything on me. I couldn't stand to think of them reading what I wrote to Kathryn."

"Would you just knock it off, Henry! I hear what you're saying, now enough. Quit talking like that. You can give it to Kathryn yourself."

"I know—I will. I just want to make sure we are clear on that point."

"We're clear. Just, no more okay?"

Silence.

"Duty?" Henry offered.

"Strength," Jonesy answered.

"Courage!" they said together.

A few minutes later the word came. They were marched up Brower's Hill with their entire brigade. Dick Taylor's 8th Louisiana Brigade (attached from Ewell's Division) had cleared the Union from the adjacent stone wall and sent them scattering backward into town. Now, three brigades were heading north toward Winchester. Stonewall Jackson held up his hand and gave the word to let fly the 'Rebel yell' and nearly every member of the Confederate Army in the vicinity let loose in unison a fierce, terrible scream.

Chaos ensued on the Union side. Northern muskets were unloaded a final time toward the mass of gray-coated men and then their owners turned and fled. For a moment there was jubilation from the 33rd Regiment and others on the hill, but men kept dropping from stray minie balls. The cannon proved somewhat ineffective that morning but things were happening so fast, occasionally a cannon ball would rip through a Confederate line taking a limb or two with it.

Colonel John A. Campbell of Jackson's Second Brigade fell wounded so Colonel John M. Patton Jr. (formerly of the 21st Virginia) took command. General Charles S. Winder (1st Brigade Commander) was nearly killed several times by a hail of canister and musket balls. Many Louisianans were wounded during an earlier charge and several of them were making their way back past Henry and Jonesy. One soldier from New Orleans had a bayonet wound to the left side of his face which removed much of his skin and ear. He was still very much conscious and walking past them to seek aid. That sight, along with the scattered dead men and pools of blood they had to step over, rattled the Winchester boys a little.

As they maneuvered around the hilly slopes, the Union regiments left fighting were getting to be fewer and fewer. Soon, as the Rebel infantry and artillery continued to flank the Union right side, the 27th Indiana and the 29th Pennsylvania left for a retreat, some throwing their weapons to the ground so they could make haste back toward Winchester. It was now only the 2nd Massachusetts and the 3rd Wisconsin left between Henry and Jonesy and Winchester. Two more Union enfilade of raking fire punched the Johnny Rebs. More cannon shot and then the Union sprinted back toward the trees. General Williams gave the last orders to his Union troops on the southwest side of Winchester that morning before he disappeared into the city roads and safety. As the Confederates approached their darling town, occasionally one butternut coated lad would fall to the ground from a stray musket ball.

Jonesy and Henry were within one hundred yards of the outskirts of town when Henry called out to Jonesy, "I think I might be hit, Jonesy, but it's not bad. I just need to sit down and rest a moment." He was already down on one knee.

Jonesy leapt back to where Henry was. "You're coming with me, and don't try to argue about it." Jonesy reached down and with brute strength picked up his friend, laying him over his shoulder and backwards.

"That hurts my wound, Brian, careful," Henry pleaded.

Jonesy was struck with the fact that Henry had used his birth name— it meant he was indeed in a lot of pain. He hesitated, then thought, *if I can just get him into town and into the hospital.*

Jonesy pressed on.

Henry slipped out of consciousness.

79.

Riley McNair's opportunity to be a general's aide was short-lived. During the night his horse had somehow cut his leg and was now limping so Riley couldn't ride him. With no horse he was no good as a messenger. This made him an infantry soldier for Colonel Dudley Donnelly. Donnelly was the First Brigade commander for General Alpheus William's first division and he commanded the 5th Connecticut, the 46th Pennsylvania, the 28th New York and the 1st Maryland. Riley asked if he could support the Pennsylvania unit since part of the unit was made up of enlistees from Pittsburgh, where his folks now resided. Plus, Ned was in that unit so they would need someone to shoot their weapon accurately to make up for his antics. Riley's day started at 4 a.m. and before an hour had passed the sky lightened some and a dense fog was discovered all around them.

Colonel Donnelly had his men on the far left of Bank's Winchester defenses. Though the ground to the southwest (where Colonel George Gordon's Third Brigade was defending) held nice hills with wooden groves, the terrain to the southeast where Riley awoke was smooth with a long rolling field. They were guarding the Front Royal Road which forked about a mile east of town to also form the Millwood Pike. Rebel skirmishers had been making a nuisance of themselves all morning through the fog. The Union cannon tried to find them, but it was a challenge with only twenty to thirty feet of visibility.

Riley's Pennsylvania regiment was ordered to retreat back into a wheat field since the Confederate cannon was beginning to indiscriminately find some targets. They were to lie down in the stalks of wheat and wait for further orders. The 28th New York had maneuvered farther back and formed behind an old mossy stone wall right along the main road. The most forward regiment was the 5th Connecticut. They hunkered down beside the road one hundred and fifty yards ahead of the other two regiments. The Maryland regiment was in the reserve.

Soon they saw the grayish-looking coats carefully marching up the road. They were whispered at to hold their fire for another minute until more naïve Confederate soldiers passed by. Soon the order was given.

"Fire, fire, fire!" screamed the officers. The 5th Connecticut squeezed their trigger first delivering a mortal blow to the surprised Rebels. Many of them crumpled where they were. Immediately the 28th New York stood up from behind the wall and delivered a flanking volley all across the length of the enemy. Then Riley and the 46th Pennsylvania fired. All of these death blows, plus the four that followed, would have been enough to send most regiments slithering back the way they came. However, the Confederate commander despicably called for his remaining men to charge with the bayonet. Before they could get close to the New Yorker's wall they were struck again. Many shot right in the vital organs. With this shot and the continued firing of the Connecticut and Pennsylvania men across their flank the Confederates had no choice but to run away. Some of their officers were casualties. The troops who were not wounded soon disappeared into the fog down the Front Royal road.

This was the first time Riley believed he had actually killed another man. He shot his newly issued musket four times, and with two of the shots he saw men fall down directly at where he was aiming. He laid himself back down onto the ground and thought about this for a moment. It was a peculiar feeling knowing he had just removed the life from another. He knew he couldn't dwell on it too long or he might get to thinking like Ned who he had not seen the entire morning.

Soon the Union soldiers heard cries from those they had wounded. Some of the Confederates were just in front of the wall they sat behind. A few of the Northern men ran out to talk to them and see where they were from and who was leading them. It was quickly passed back to Riley that these were men from North Carolina and they were being led by General Ewell.

Riley secretly let out a sigh of relief. He still did not have to face his friends in battle. They were surely with Stonewall Jackson and must be on the other side of town. The thunder of cannon from the west lasted for what seemed to Riley like hours. He knew Bruce, Henry and Jonesy were all there, a few hundred yards from where he was, but they would have no idea Riley was in Winchester. There was not any activity from the Rebs for awhile so he sat back against a tree and tried to doze.

It was mid-morning before the thick fog lifted its veil. Riley and the soldiers lying around him were speculating on how many Southerners were to their front and if they would be able to repel the next charge. They also wondered where they would be setting up camp that night, in Winchester as victors, or across the Potomac humiliated. Riley hoped it would be Winchester. He wanted to find out from Mrs. Montgomery and Kathryn more information about Molly.

As if in answer to their question of where they would camp, Riley heard the troops up front shouting that the Rebels were coming. And as this information was trickling back from the front, new orders were being passed from the back to the front. They were to retreat into town as orderly as possible, not leaving any personal gear behind. The commanders did not have to ask twice. Immediately, rows with hundreds of blue-clad soldiers were seen on both sides of the road. They all turned and marched at a quick step down the avenue and into the bustling city of Riley's birth. The Rebel Army pursuing them would find the ancient stone wall with the Confederate dead in front of it. But all the defenders would be gone.

80.

Winchester came alive as morning broke and the sun appeared. With Stonewall Jackson's push from the southwest and Richard Ewell's push from the southeast the Union Army was forced to retreat and evacuate northward, through town and try to escape from their attackers. Citizens of the fine town were rejoicing. They emptied out of their houses and lined the streets to say goodbye to their captors and welcome their sons and husbands. The women of Winchester were not very sympathetic to the Federal forces and a few of them were downright hostile. Rachel Jones took out a musket and shot from her window at squads of men running through her yard. She hit at least three Yankees but only one was not able to limp away. She dragged the poor fellow who couldn't get up to the back of her house and left him to die. She wanted to kill an officer. Another squad of Yankees passing by decided to fire back at Rachel and riddled the front of her home with lead.

Some of the women used boiling water to punish the enemy from their upstairs windows. Some used knives and whips. Others used pistols and broken glass. A few used rocks. The women had been plagued for months with a band of armed men who were able to enter their houses whenever they wanted, take things out of their residences whenever they desired and procure items from their vegetable cellars, gardens, orchards and livestock from their barnyards. These women had no recourse. Yet, many of the women who acted hostile toward the fleeing Union (and it was only a handful that day who fought back) felt guilty afterward and discussed this with their minister the following week. But not Rachel Jones.

The abundance of the citizens threw a makeshift Sunday parade for the Army of the Shenandoah that 25th of May. This caused the Federal

Army to slow down even more as they scurried away on every road and alley available to save their lives. All the women were waving Southern flags or handkerchiefs and bringing their beloved army water or snacks. Some were singing "Dixie." Many were saying "Hurrah." Reunions were made as some of the men found their way to their own front porch for a brief hug and kiss. The commanders were driving them on to pursue the Northerners so they had to say hello and goodbye quickly.

Then, as General Stonewall Jackson entered the city for the first time since early March there was a jubilant mob of admirers encircling him and cheering his great triumph. People were frantic with joy and excitement. Children were running around Little Sorrel in circles. The aged citizens showed wide, toothless grins. All of them laughed and waved at the passing troops. Jackson himself was exhilarated by the enthusiasm and fervor of the crowds. The energy and joy being displayed was breathtaking. This was a homecoming like no other. Their conquering hero had returned and given them a stunning victory over a larger army. He had also given them a chance to see their loved ones again.

As the troops continued to march into Winchester, the entire town lit up with escalating waves of elation. Women were running into the arms of their husbands. Children were jumping up and down and running behind the soldiers passing in the streets. The people were so overwhelmed with emotion at that moment they were shaking each other's hands and hugging each other as if everyone possessed the same heart and mind. People held on to each other and were weeping, even with those they had scarcely said "hello" to before. The citizens of Winchester became one and knew they would never forget this incredible day.

81.

As Sarah, Lucy, Grandma Crawford and Scout along with Claire, Kathryn, Landon and Julia all looked on from the front of their house, there was desperation from Kathryn to find Henry. More and more troops passed but there was no Henry. Finally the 33rd Virginia began marching by and Kathryn saw Club Jones toward the front of one of the companies so she ran up to him and said, "Sergeant Jones, have you seen Henry? Do you have any idea where he could be?"

Club hesitated briefly, looked away from her and said, "Young lady, your husband has been wounded. My son took him to our medical folks, so they will be a little delayed."

Tears instantly welled up into Kathryn's eyes and she searched Club's face for a clue as to how serious Henry's wounds might be. She started but stopped, "How—?"

Club said, "I don't know how bad he is. I believe it was a shot in the leg because he couldn't walk. Brian had to carry him on his back." With that, Club turned away from her and continued to march along the road with his troops.

Kathryn collapsed onto the ground. She did not pass out, but at that moment she forgot to tell her legs to keep standing. Her inner thoughts lost all meaning and she buckled at once. The women gathered around her, raising her head and putting it on Claire's lap. Kathryn began to gently weep tears of anguish. Sarah Crawford wept as well, but Claire was keeping her composure. As more soldiers from the unit marched by they found out additional information. Henry and Jonesy were at the southern edge of town and Henry was being looked at by the brigade surgeon. Kathryn asked if he would have to lose a leg, but no one could tell her that information. Landon took off down the street to find Henry, and Scout followed close behind.

82.

After his short moment of intense celebration with the citizenry of Winchester, Stonewall Jackson advanced himself and his army north of the city to pursue General Banks. He was frustrated. Inconceivably, Ashby's cavalry were nowhere to be found to capitalize on their success. His troops were dog-tired and unable to pursue the enemy at the speed their opponents were running away. Furthermore, there was no organization in the ranks following him. Jackson was pushing his men with tone deaf ferocity, but they had nothing left to give. Soon, he halted the advance and had his men set up camp north of Winchester at Stephenson's Depot. Jackson himself rode back to the Taylor Hotel and fell fast asleep.

* * *

Stonewall Jackson's reputation as an ingenious, daring and competent commander now took root even in the most doubting hearts. The Union Army was scattered and fleeing over the Potomac River. The Federals had forfeited not only more than 300 casualties and 3,000 prisoners of war to Jackson, but vast stores of supplies also had to be left in Winchester. Almost 100,000 small arms stored there were now in Confederate hands, along with half a million rounds of ammunition and hundreds of thousands of dollars worth of medical supplies and instruments. The food acquired by Jackson's Army was so voluminous it took a long time to inventory. There were several tons of hardtack, over a hundred head of cattle and thousands of pounds of salt pork, sugar, salt and other commissary stores.

Jackson had sixty-eight of his own soldiers killed during the campaign. He grieved every one of them. To one family he wrote, "The loss of your noble son is deeply felt by me. Tears come to my eyes when I think of his death." He also declared May 26th as a day of rendering thanks to God for the success he bestowed on the Army of the Shenandoah. Yet his soft side was limited, for he was tough as nails when it came to discipline in the forces. Whatever the army was doing, fighting or practicing drills in cantonment, he required his men to follow his rules. Despite the celebration following their victory at Winchester, Jackson organized a firing squad to kill three former deserters who had been captured. He also placed several of his men into a prisoner of war camp who were caught wearing Union clothing. Finally, he denounced to Richmond some of his fellow officers who disgraced themselves in Winchester following the battle. None of it was personal, but rules were rules.

83.

When Henry awoke he could see everything going on around him, but he couldn't hear anything for a moment. It was as if everything happened in successive frames—things appeared to move slower than they would in normal life. Then, abruptly the sound accompanied the motion of the room and he was for the first time fully conscious. He did not feel his body, neither of his legs, feet or hands. But he could bend his neck some.

There was someone's head buried in the bed covers next to his chest and it was attached to a slumped-over woman's body. Henry raised a numb arm up and tapped on the shoulder of the woman laying there a few times until her form began to move. The head turned toward him while one cheek still gently rested on a sheet. The face he recognized as Kathryn's. Another freeze frame. No noise, just a smiling, blond-haired, rosy-cheeked, beautiful, delicate-featured face looking back at him.

"Oh, Henry!" Kathryn gasped as she raised her head up and lunged at him to hug him. Henry was happy he could feel her arms around his sides and back. He reached his arms up and hugged her back the best he could. Everything began to come to mind now, the shouting, the sounds of war, being hit in the leg, being carried by Jonesy. Kathryn was weeping. Their lips met once or twice and hers felt like feathers across his lips and cheeks.

"How am I?" Henry asked. "My leg?"

"The doctor said you should be okay. He said you lost a lot of blood and that is why you passed out. If Jonesy hadn't gotten you to the aid station within a few minutes of your wound you would have died."

"They did not have to amputate?" As Henry spoke the words he tried in vain to wiggle his toes and feel something.

"No, my brave soldier, they didn't have to amputate. The doctor said unless your wound gets infected you should be back on your feet within days. Look." Kathryn stood up and pulled the covers off of Henry's feet. "Both legs and feet are attached." She smiled at him.

Henry was noticeably very thankful. "I cannot feel them," he said.

"The doctor gave you some medicine for the pain. He said it might cause you to have some numbness. You're fine, dear." Kathryn looked thrilled.

Over the next two hours the young bride relayed to Henry all that had happened since he was in the hospital. Of Jackson's stunning victory the morning Henry was wounded. Of the glorious time the Winchester citizens had in welcoming home their warriors. And of her own grief and agony over his being wounded. She told him of Landon finding him at the aid station and of Turner Ashby's promotion ceremony to brigadier general. Of General Bank's retreating across the Potomac and rumors Jackson would soon be going to Washington. She then told him where Jonesy currently was waiting for him.

"You know he absolutely wouldn't leave your side. I had to invoke my authority as your wife for him to budge on the matter. Only after he made me swear several promises to him would he step a foot away from you."

Henry laughed for the first time, "What did he make you promise?"

"First of all, that immediately upon you awaking I was to notify him through a messenger. Also, that I would take good care of you until he returned. And finally, I was to tell you that you were stupid to discuss dying that morning because he felt it put a curse on both of you."

"On both of us? What happened to him?"

"While running with you on his back, Jonesy's foot got caught in a groundhog hole or something and he twisted his ankle. He limped the rest of the way to get you to the surgeon."

Henry smiled and shook his head. *Oh, Jonesy.*

"Henry, you better talk to him. I had to convince him of the fact that as your spouse I was just as capable of staying by your side and taking care of you as he was."

"He is somewhat like a large child, Kathryn. He never went to college so Winchester and his friends and family are everything to him. He means well—don't be dismayed at him."

"All right, dear. I just don't like having to compete for my own husband."

Kathryn sat with Henry at the field hospital until it was time for both to get some sleep. She promised to be back early the next day with food and new bandages for his leg. She kissed him tenderly and playfully reminded him of his promise to grow old with her.

"I remember, Kathryn. You are my first and last thought every day. You are the dearest, most precious gift I have ever been given. And, I cannot wait to hold you again like a husband should hold his one true love."

With that Kathryn smiled sweetly, gave him a parting kiss, and rushed out of the hospital before she cried again.

84.

Bruce was in his tent when a quartermaster soldier came by to give him a package.

"Came in this morning for you, sir."

Bruce told the soldier thank you and took the package. He opened up the brown paper wrapping that came from Pittsburgh, Pennsylvania and in his lap were seven letters. They were the letters he had written to Molly and all of them were unopened. There was a note that came inside the package. Bruce unfolded the note and began to read:

Dear Master Crawford,

I am returning these letters to you which you have sent to my daughter. She has no desire or need to receive them from you and I have spared her from the embarrassment of having to issue you a reply. Here is the cold truth of her current situation; she has another suitor. She is pledged to him and will be wedded to him as soon as this war between states has concluded. Hopefully you can see that my returning these letters to you is for your benefit as well as hers. It will save you the awkward embarrassment of having to face her and her new husband after you have tried to pursue her, but missed your mark. You are a noble lad and I am sure you will find the right wife once the war is over, but it will not be my daughter. I would write for God to bless you, but as I am adamantly opposed to the cause for which you are fighting, I will simply write 'good day.'

Sincerely,

Lucas Harrington

The words dripped into Bruce like poison. He read the letter three more times and then examined every one of the seven letters ensuring they were never opened. He was stunned.

Riley. Mr. Harrington had to be speaking of Riley, Bruce thought. Bruce had not seen Riley or heard of his whereabouts except for a brief conversation Bruce had with his own mother and she told him that Ned Harrington and Riley McNair had been in Winchester the day Jackson's Army re-entered the city. She had said nothing about Molly.

Bruce was sick to his stomach. It felt as if a cannonball had exploded in his heart. His mind was racing. He had not kept track, but he was pretty sure he had written eight letters. He opened the last letter and read part of it. It was one he had written a couple of months ago. He knew he had written one after it. Whether she ever got it he would probably never know. Bruce remembered what Jackson had told his class once, "when life punches you in the gut then jump into your work. It will not only take your mind off your pain, but you will accomplish something as well." Bruce decided not to dwell on it and to get back to work—yet it wasn't easy. He was trampled in the heart.

As he would attempt to sleep for the next few nights he would feel enveloped with feelings of despair and disillusionment. What frustrated him was that he couldn't shake the morose feelings. He wondered what Molly might be thinking of the entire affair if she knew about it. *Oh Molly, where are you and what are you thinking?*

85.

Claire and Landon stepped foot into their deserted home and Claire had to sit down for a moment to wipe her eyes. There was mud caked throughout the entire residence. The beautiful rugs her mother had given to her were all ruined. The parlor, which had been used as a surgeon's operating room, had a significant amount of bloodstains on the floorboards. There were bandages, both used and new laying throughout the house. There was trash and some of her china, silverware and teacups, all filthy and sprinkled throughout the downstairs.

Claire managed to collect herself and walked to the back of the house and into the kitchen. What she saw was unimaginable for an orderly, proper woman like Claire Montgomery. It appeared that a hurricane had ripped through this one room leaving everything topsy turvy. The brick floor and countertop were cluttered with rags and trash. There was a hair comb, a shoe tied to an odd-looking boot, small, empty munitions boxes and discarded items of half-eaten, rotten food. The dishes were piled high and completely caked with stains of several meals. The whole kitchen was filthy and the ants had found the bowls where sugar had once been kept. Every item of dishware was out of the cupboards and in disarray throughout the room. The cupboards and drawers were all half-open and either empty or crammed with old metal parts of some makeshift weapon that never worked. Claire noticed several dirty rags, possibly used for cleaning, but obviously not for cleaning the kitchen.

Claire scanned her eyes around the room once again. She saw a nutmeg grater, two soiled handkerchiefs, twine, old newspapers, numerous crumbs from bread and crackers and a piece of a biscuit. There were pieces of torn-up paper, a rolling pin, part of a shirt, a tiny mound of sugar (not in a bowl), some discarded tobacco and grains of coffee throughout. There was a key, a couple of dirty table-napkins, a sock with holes in it, several spoons and a darkened rind from some type of melon. Claire tried to take a deep breath and think for a moment about where to start. All of a sudden she was struck with a painful punch into her left kidney.

She turned to her left and saw Landon there who tried to hit her again, but she grabbed his wrist and held on tight.

"Landon, what are you doing? Why did you hit me?" Claire asked in painful curiosity.

Landon didn't answer, but tried with his other arm to swing around her and hit her again. Claire was too fast for him and now had both his wrists locked tightly in her hands.

"Young man, it is time to calm down and take a moment to explain to me what has gotten into you. Landon, do you hear what I am saying to you?" Claire could see that Landon had a blind fury in his eyes and this little boy she was holding was temporarily not the well-tempered son she and Conrad had raised with delight.

Finally, tears began to form at the corners of his eyes and drip alongside his cheeks and his little nose.

"Why Mama, why?"

"Why what?" Claire asked.

"Why do you help those Northerners with food and everything?"

"What do you mean, son?" Claire could feel the intensity leave his body so she released his wrists.

"I don't understand why you spend hours at the hospital helping the Union soldiers and fixing their wounds and why you give them food and cold water that we could eat and drink ourselves. Why Mama? They shoot at papa and try to kill him and look what they did to our house. How can you be so nice to them? It doesn't make sense!"

"Oh Landon, you are having to endure so much as a seven year old. I have failed to appreciate how all of this must be affecting you. You always seem so happy and content. It must be confusing to you how this war is being conducted."

Landon said, "The other night you and Mrs. Crawford allowed those three Union soldiers to spend the night and you fed them a nice meal. Those same soldiers could go outside the next day and kill papa. I mean, why wouldn't you try to hurt them—aren't they the enemy?"

"Yes, they are the enemy, Landon, but they are also human beings."

"I would have poisoned them if I had prepared their food."

"Landon, those men were desperate and in need!" Claire took a breath and thought about how she should explain this to him. "Landon, as a Christian, it is our duty to help the down-trodden and poor in the world just as Jesus did when he was here. Just because there is a war on does not mean we change our views as His followers."

"But mama, isn't it a crime to give aid and comfort to the enemy?"

"It is at certain times, honey, but this war between the states has kind of turned everything upside down. Do you remember when Ned Harrington stopped by the other night to say hello?"

"Yes."

"He was the enemy. Should we have shot him?"

Landon smiled at the thought.

Before he could answer his mother said, "No, Landon, we shouldn't have shot him. He is a friend of ours and the brother to Kathryn's best friend in the world."

"I'll bet pa could shoot him."

"Yes, your father could shoot him, but not in our home. There is a difference between pointing your musket at someone and shooting them on a battlefield when they are shooting at you, and when you see them casually in your home or on the street."

"I don't understand, they are still the enemy."

"They are still the enemy, but it would be uncivil to harm them unless they were shooting at you."

"Then why did some of those ladies in town shoot at the soldiers as they ran away from our army?"

"Well, Landon, they were angry and bitter. And sometimes you know what's right to do, but because you have been so hurt and wounded by others it blinds you to what is actually right and wrong for a moment. Some of the Northern soldiers did not act like gentlemen when they were here and hurt some of the women. The women who shot at them were still outraged and angry."

"I would have shot at them if you had let me."

"Landon, you cannot let your anger make you act unlawfully."

"But you don't have to help them! Why did you and Mrs. Crawford spend so many hours at the Union hospital cleaning bandages and nursing those soldiers back to life? Those soldiers could kill papa. I know we are not to harm them, but why help them? It doesn't make sense," Landon said.

"No, I suppose it doesn't. And Landon, sometimes I don't even understand it all. But when you see those young boy's faces and know they have a mama somewhere praying for them and hoping they are being treated well, it is hard to do anything different. I know when Sarah wipes the sweat from their brow and gives them medicine she is taking care of Moss who is in some dark place right now. When we care for these boys we are merely being decent human beings. Sure, in many ways these troops in town are imposters and the enemy, and we would be justified to try to kill them or give all of their secrets away that we could gather. But you know, when you see they are hurting from this war, just as much as you and your loved ones, then it makes one stop and think. These soldiers need a smile and sometimes a piece of bread just as papa does when he is away and in a strange town."

"So, do you do it because you are a Christian or because you are a decent human?" Landon asked very innocently.

"Well both, I believe. Jesus taught us to do to others as we would have done to ourselves, and that no greater love has a man than that he should lay down his life for his friends. Jesus even laid down his life for people who were his enemies. He gave us the supreme example of how to be a decent human being. Remember how he prayed for those people who had just put him on a cross to die? He asked God to forgive them. How could he do that, Landon? No normal person would ever have the courage to do that just before they were killed. He taught people to love others in a meaningful, entirely unselfish way. He taught us what being a real human being is all about."

"Why don't the Crawfords pray before they eat?" Landon asked.

"My, oh my. There's a question out of the blue. They don't believe quite as strongly as we do about matters of the faith."

"You mean they are not Christians."

"Well, no. I wouldn't say that. They just don't take it as seriously as we do."

"They usually don't go to church, either."

"I know Landon, but I don't want to try and judge if they are true believers or not. They have shown Christ's love to us these last few months and allowed us to stay in their home. They have given us a tremendous gift. They do not have the same fervent faith your father has, it is true. But they love others deeply and they love Virginia and the Southern cause very much. They are good friends."

Landon took a moment to think about what his mother had just explained to him.

Claire gave him a big hug. "You have so many questions about life, please never be afraid to ask me anything and please, don't ever hit me again or you will not be able to sit down for a week with the whipping you'll get. As for today, let's just keep it between us."

"Okay," said Landon with a slight grin.

"What do you say we start cleaning up this place. Now that General Jackson is in town we will be able to move back here and live on our farm again. Won't that be nice?"

Claire and Landon started with the kitchen and worked for several hours. Soon their home was looking much better. Kathryn joined them after she completed some good Samaritan work at the Tooley home. Alma and Genevieve did not help because they were nowhere to be found.

86.

Heavy Jonesy sat beside Henry's bed. The lighting was poor and there was moaning across the room. Jonesy was filling Henry in on all the excitement he had missed the last few days.

"I'm sorry about your hurt leg, Jonesy."

"No bother—just an inconvenience." Jonesy was talking in his English accent again. "Did you hear about my pa, yet?" he asked.

"No, what happened to Club?"

"He was making his way up the orchard slope just before town and he was hit hard right into his chest. He fell down and landed square on his back. Several around him thought he was dead. A piece of canister or a large musket ball hit him in the front part of the haversack slung over his shoulder. He had a clump of old hard tack in there and it stopped the death ball cold, yet it knocked him over like he was hit with a cannon. In a real way, some sorry, old sheet iron crackers saved his life."

"Bully for him. That is a great story," Henry said as he thought about it. "I've heard of a man being shot into his Bible that was in his breast pocket or in his canteen, but not in his rations. The funny thing is they expect us to eat that armor."

Both sat for a moment without saying anything. Jonesy grabbed his friend's hand and stood up. Squeezing it and then letting go he said, "I'll look for you in one month—no longer."

Henry smiled. "The doctor said if it doesn't get infected I should be good in about six weeks."

"Okay, five weeks. By Independence Day I will be looking for you every day."

"All right, Jonesy, Independence Day."

"Don't forget. And don't get too spoiled by the Missus and leave me to fight the Yanks all by myself."

"I won't. I'll be there my friend. Save some of them for me, and don't you dare allow McClellan to enter into Richmond."

Jonesy walked out of the room without turning around.

87.

Molly Harrington found herself in the wrong place at the wrong time and she was now being held against her will by a feisty Union officer. Molly left the day after her farewell conversation with the Peacheys. Her hosts loaded Molly up with food supplies and filled her canteens with water. David had also taken good care of Daisy. The mare with her new shoes had been in no finer shape.

Molly rode through the beautiful mountain passes slowly, taking in all the sites and thinking deeply while she travelled. She rode east, crossed the Potomac River and made for Martinsburg and the Valley Turnpike. She soon discovered that her timing was terrible. Near Martinsburg, she came across the routed Union Army making their way northward away from Stonewall Jackson and his army. Molly drew the suspicion of several soldiers as she sat on her proud horse perched on a ridgeline overlooking the turnpike. She was curiously watching the soldiers flee for their lives when she was noticed by the wrong person. Soon, a dispatch of three horsemen were sent in her direction. Fear paralyzed her and she did not know what to do. If she ran away it would look blameworthy, so she hesitated. She knew her best defense was the truth. She was passing through, returning to her home. Surely they would leave her alone and let her pass. She thought for a moment of speaking only in German, but then she decided that would make her look even more vulnerable.

The soldier's did not afford her the opportunity to bargain with them. Their orders were to bring her back to their supervisor to be questioned. She could either obey them or be shot. By the looks in their eyes she knew they were in no mood to play games. She asked who their supervisor was, but they did not reply. They tied her horse to one of theirs and led her back down to the main body. She was given to a Major Welch for a brief questioning. Once he learned she was from Winchester he took her horse and tied it to his wagon. He commanded her to sit in the back of his wagon cluttered with some supplies and he rode on and on without explaining to her where they were going. He did not let her explain she had not been in town since the war started, and he refused to accept her demands to see his superior. He merely said if she tried to get away he would not hesitate to shoot her at once. Despite his orneriness, it was clear to Molly he liked what he saw of his new prize, and he was delighted to have captured such a beautiful spoil of war on such a depressing day.

Molly was scared when they rode back across the Potomac and halted to make camp away from the main body, but dread poured into her heart when she saw the individual that came up to Welch, as if reporting to duty. It was the disreputable mountain man, Daniel Tanner. The two men were plainly talking about her and laughing coarsely. The other three men who had taken her near the turnpike joined them. One of them, with three gold stripes on his sleeve, approached her and told her to take care of her horse because they would be spending the night there. She asked again why she was being held captive and the man gave her a wild grin and told her that they always had to interrogate prisoners of war to see if they are spies for the enemy.

"I am not a spy," Molly said icily.

"We'll see about that," said the man who smiled like an elf and had one of his front teeth missing.

After taking care of her horse, Molly found an old stump and sat on it waiting for one of Welch's men to talk to her. She did not know exactly what to do. She felt powerless. She believed once she explained everything they would be forced to let her go, that is, until she saw Daniel Tanner. Once she saw him she knew she was not being held by normal military procedures. She prayed for God to release her and allow her to continue on to Winchester the next day. She was so close. The journey which started weeks ago had some delays, but she had never gone backwards. Re-crossing the Potomac was disheartening to say the least. She decided to think of nicknames for the unseemly gentlemen who had her captive. For Tanner, she thought of the word Mohican because he had long, stringy hair, darkened skin and always carried a knife. For the one who had told her to take care of her horse, she thought of the name Toad, because of his course skin and arched back. For Welch, the only name that kept popping into her mind was Bullethead. Welch had a high forehead, a pointy red crown and reddish hair on the sides and back. In fact, she thought, his whole body looked like a bullet because, though short, he was broad from toe to head. The other two men looked somewhat normal, but appeared pretty ignorant. One of them did not have a hand on his right arm, just a bandaged stump. Welch commanded them like you would two little children. And that was the name she chose for those two, the Children.

Molly was beckoned to join Welch inside a tent the Children had put up for him. The sun was setting as she walked by the fire toward the tent. She walked into the small area lit up by the lantern then saw Bullethead, the Mohican and Toad all glaring at her and studying her in a way that made her feel extremely uncomfortable.

They had a wooden stool for her to sit on and she sat there while the men kept staring.

"Okay missy, what is your name?" Major Welch asked in a business-like manner.

"Molly Harrington," Molly replied.

"Where do you live?"

"My family lives in Pittsburgh."

"But you said you were in route to Winchester?"

"Yes, that is where we used to live. My family moved because they are not sympathetic to the Southern way of life and felt Virginia made a grave mistake in separating from the Union."

"I'll agree with that analysis," Major Welch said. "Tanner, you're from there. What do you think of her story?"

"It's true. I know about them," he replied.

"So, I guess the question we need to ask is why were you traveling back to Winchester?" Welch continued.

"I was returning to my home to see my friends."

"You don't sound convincing."

"Pardon me, but why do I need to sound convincing? It's the truth and I would like to know on what grounds you are detaining me?"

"Look, little plumb, don't start asking us questions, we've got the goods on you. You were standing on that hill watching us depart town in order to communicate with Jackson exactly where we were and what we were doing. If we had let you pass on then he would have very little doubt as to what our situation is, now wouldn't he?"

"Major, I'm not a spy. I was returning home to see my friends."

"Yeah, yeah, I've heard your alibi."

While Molly was inside being interrogated, the Children had been searching her belongings as prearranged by Welch. They suddenly entered the tent with a letter and a long knife.

"Look what we found," the Children triumphantly showed their oily boss.

"Hey, that's my old knife!" Tanner shouted out. He stood up, grabbed it from them and studied the blade for a moment. He turned to Molly and asked with venom, "Where did you get this?"

"What importance is that to you?" she said, weighing each word.

Slap!

Tanner hit her hard across the face. "Answer me!" He yelled.

"What if I cannot recall?"

"You will recall!"

Slap!

"You're a lying she-devil!" Tanner said with clenched teeth.

Molly's lower lip was cut open. She did not try to say anything else about the knife Bruce had given to her over a year ago.

Welch and Toad had been studying the letter the Children had brought to them. Welch removed his spectacles, looked at the seething Tanner and said, "Have you ever heard of a Bruce Crawford?"

Suddenly Tanner's eye's opened up wide and he smiled knowingly and said, "Yes, I have. It was his little group of friends that attacked me in a tavern awhile back and one of them took my knife. I'll wager you it was her little boyfriend Bruce that jumped me and took it from me."

Welch looked at Tanner quizzically, "How big is this person that bested my six foot four inch warrior?"

"He's not bigger than me, but he had four or five friends with him."

"Interesting. You know, those women we detained awhile back that were so feisty—wasn't one of them named Crawford?" Major Welch asked.

"That's right," said Tanner. "It's the same people. She has two sons and her husband serving in the war." Tanner kept looking at his knife in disbelief.

"And here we have the lover of one of the sons—just one big happy Rebel family."

Molly glanced up at this comment, "I'm not his lover, we are just childhood acquaintances."

"No matter, missy. It is still pretty fortuitous that we should find you before you hooked up with your Rebel partners." Welch was studying her with a cagey eye.

Molly glared back at them while they all laughed at her and her predicament. Welch started reading lines of Bruce's letter out loud to raucous laughter. Molly hated this part of her evening and hoped Bruce would never find out about it. After reading it in its entirety, Welch tipped it in the candle flame and let it burn into furled ashes.

"May I please speak with your commanding officer?" Molly asked as nicely as she could.

"May I please speak with your commanding officer?" Welch echoed in whiny derision. "No!" Welch stood up and began walking around Molly while he talked, "That's all you people want, isn't it. A chance to be free of me and not have to answer my questions. This is my work little girl and whether you like it or not, you are stuck with me. Oh yes, you are stuck with me. You're going to join my world for awhile and understand my pain. You're going to see how hard I work at my job and you're going to see how little thanks I get from it. I have to put up with these morons and buffoons they give me as assistants and still make something creative with it."

"Hey, boss! That's not very nice," Toad yowled.

"Shut up, fool. Do you think my commanders appreciate my efforts? Do you think I'm ever rewarded? No, I've never been told 'good work Major Welch', or 'splendid piece of intelligence, Major.' They expect top notch work, in fact, demand it and they never offer any help or one word of thanks. So, I don't want to hear your little whines about seeing my commanding officer. As far as you're concerned they don't exist. I am the commander here. Imagine I have an eagle on my uniform and call me colonel. I'm the eagle here. Do you understand? I'm the eagle. I want to hear you say it! Eagle!"

Molly hesitated, but one look at his face told her that complying would be the best method with the maniac. With a bruised eye and a battered lip she mumbled, "You're the eagle."

88.

President Abraham Lincoln received the news that Winchester was lost with forceful determination. It was a setback, but Lincoln felt with a little repositioning of the Union forces in Northern Virginia, their plan to go after both Richmond and Jackson could still succeed. War Secretary Stanton, however, became paralyzed with fear. He felt the Capitol was in danger and was beside himself until he took action. Issuing a call to all Northern governors, he told them Rebel forces were now moving upon Washington in great force and that they should dispatch all militia and volunteer forces in their state. He further told them Banks was completely routed and Harpers Ferry was about to be overrun.

Lincoln looked at the events as another opportunity for success, but first he had to make sure there were enough forces to do the job. The original plan in sending McDowell south from Fredericksburg was to have over 150,000 attacking Richmond with a defensive force of 60,000 remaining near the Capitol. Could McClellan attack Richmond with less? Lincoln was sure of it. He told McDowell to stand down his machinations for Richmond and to send 20,000 soldiers to the Shenandoah Valley. McDowell immediately directed the fiery Irishman Shields to move his 11,000 strong division westward from Fredericksburg. Shields had just recently returned with his men from Winchester. He knew his men were shoeless and not prepared for the march so he gave a few choice words about the Lincoln Administration to those who would listen. General Edward Otho Cresap Ord followed Shields with an additional 10,000 men.

General John C. Fremont was directed to move at once his nearly 14,000 soldiers from Franklin to Harrisonburg. This would put his force between Jackson and Richmond. Fremont, however, chose another route—much to the ire of the President. He took his troops northward to Moorefield because of the bad roads toward Harrisonburg. Lincoln and Stanton wanted him in Strasburg as soon as possible so they could close a trap with McDowell's 20,000 men coming at Jackson from the east, Banks with 7,000 men to the north ready to re-cross the Potomac, along with Brigadier General Rufus Saxton's 7,000 men at Harpers Ferry. The 'hammer hitting the anvil' Lincoln called it. If Fremont could get there in time, Jackson would not have an escape route.

No, we are not in danger Mr. Secretary, this could be our chance at victory, thought Lincoln. He knew the Union forces had no better opportunity to crush a major element of the Southern Army than at that hour. *I think we will soon see the light of day.*

89.

The Visitor rode hard and finally came within view of the Union forces he was looking for--Shield's division. They were just outside of Front Royal and tasked with reaching Strasburg by the following day, Saturday, May 31st. The Visitor knew this would prove fatal for Jackson's Army because it would trap them. He had to be convincing. His trusty horse, Torch, got a little fidgety when they were halted by armed guards on the outskirts of the encampment area. The sun was just going down. It was Friday, the 30th.

"Please take me to your commander, I have a very important message for him," the Visitor pleaded.

"And who should we tell him wants to talk to him?" the forward guard asked.

"For right now, all you need to know is that I am a lieutenant colonel in the Union Army. But you could also tell him I work for Pinkerton."

"Pinkerton, huh," the guard looked suspiciously at the Visitor and then spit out some of the chew from his mouth.

"Sergeant, there is not a lot of time, you are wasting precious minutes for your commander."

"Okay, okay." The guard had the Visitor follow him as he wound his way through the camp. There were rows of wagons and makeshift camp preparations going on. Hundreds of stacked muskets and munitions were laying in organized piles throughout the camp. As men looked up to see who was passing through their bivouac area the Visitor could see uncertainty in their eyes. If they only knew how close they were to their target, thought the Visitor.

The Visitor was introduced to an officer on Nathan Kimball's staff.

"Good evening, I have some urgent news for your commander. I work for the intelligence community and was tasked with screening the southern roads for any movement coming up from Richmond."

"Go on."

"It appears that there is a large force heading north. It is General James Longstreet's division. Their purpose is to help Jackson proceed to Washington."

"You've got to be kidding me!" the officer said incredulously.

"I wish I was," the Visitor said. "Look, I cannot stay. I have to return to Washington tonight."

"Tonight, that's impossible."

"I have to try, that is the urgency of my mission."

"What am I supposed to do with your information?—you offer me no proof." The Union officer truly wanted some advice.

"No, I cannot show you a written order or a sketch of Longstreet's troops all camped out at Luray….."

"Luray! You mean they are that close?" the officer was flabbergasted.

"Your leaders do not expect a threat from that region?"

"Our threat is supposed to be to the west of us."

"Not any longer. I must be going. Please tell your commander that if he pursues his course tomorrow and heads for Strasburg, he will leave his rear element completely exposed to an advancing corps of Confederate regulars. He could put the entire Capitol in jeopardy," the Visitor said.

"A corps?"

"Yes, at least a corps."

"Hey, how did you know we are going to Strasburg?" the officer asked.

"We all know it. I was on the council that decided your commander's orders. Now I really must be off."

The Visitor turned to leave, hoping his words would be enough. He grabbed Torch's reigns and began walking the way he was escorted into camp.

"Wait, one more question." The Visitor stopped and did not turn around. The guard, noticing the meeting was over, walked back up to escort his guest out.

"Who do I tell Kimball and Shields that you are?" the officer asked.

"I appreciate your wanting to protect yourself, but you cannot be responsible with that kind of sensitive information. Just tell them a kind visitor stopped by. They will know who I work for."

No more was said. The Visitor was escorted to the edge of camp and released. He rode away in the general vicinity of Washington until he was out of sight. He hoped that his plan would at least delay Shields, if not stall him out completely.

He usually relied on two tactics for his deception. The first was the impeccable uniform he wore and the genuine manner in which he carried himself. This had to be unquestionable. Everything down to his buttons and type of sword were all cunningly chosen so he would be absolutely believable. The second tactic was the way in which he delivered his information. He always sought a lower level officer and he tried to be quick with the facts and appear to be in a hurry. He tried by his haste to convince his listener he was not actually trying to convince him of anything, that his mission was simply to deliver the information. He did not over-embellish and he did not give ideas as to how the unit should now proceed. In fact, he under-emphasized everything and implied that he didn't care if his intelligence was accepted or not. This wasn't true, of course, making it a very delicate task. He always attempted to put the risk on the shoulders of his listener. It was their job to persuade the command, not his. He was simply sowing seeds of doubt in the minds of their superior officers. Sometimes it worked and sometimes it didn't. He would circle around the camp later in the evening and see if he could pick up any morsels of information from the bivouac area. *We'll see if I've prevented a catastrophe,* he thought.

90.

Nathan Kimball and James Shields did not receive the news well from the Visitor. They scolded their aide that he should have brought the man with the report right to their headquarters. A search went out to try to find the Visitor to no avail, so a scouting party was hastily put together for the next day to check this new intelligence of the Confederate offensive. They were to ride all throughout the Page Valley, to the White House Bridge and along the Massanutten Mountain. Shields did not take his division to Strasburg the next day, as ordered by Lincoln. He just had to be certain.

91.

General Thomas Jackson made the tough decision to depart Winchester and head south on the Valley Turnpike before it was cut off. Early on May 31ˢᵗ, Jackson said goodbye to his friends, the Grahams, and led his army southward. He had asked for reinforcements from Richmond, but there were no other Confederate forces for many miles which could assist. Jackson felt he was getting boxed in. He did not know exactly how many Union troops were around him, but he guessed they might possibly double his numbers. He was thankful when he approached the outskirts of Strasburg there were no Union guns waiting for him and blocking his line of march.

His sudden departure crushed the residents of Winchester. Their conquering hero and protector would be gone. They were now left totally exposed to the Union Army. And this time, the Federals who fled from Jackson amidst cheers from the residents would not be as gracious when they returned.

* * *

Unknown to him at the time, all the Union forces within a day's march more than tripled Jackson's 17,000 strong army. Two of the armies were within an hour's ride. As Jackson passed through the town of Strasburg, General Fremont sat in place with 15,000 Federals just four miles to the west of the Turnpike. General Shields had another 10,000 Federals waiting twelve miles to the east of the Turnpike. Unimaginably, neither

Union Army moved forward that day to attack their target. Their enemy Jackson was as exposed and vulnerable as a piece of ripened fruit, ready to be picked off the vine for consumption. However, the Union general's inaction allowed Jackson to slide through Strasburg and slip through their fingers.

92.

In Richmond, top Confederate General Joseph Johnston fell seriously wounded in his right shoulder and his chest. His forces were up against those of General McClellan on the Chickahominy River. It was getting dark and a desperate hour ensued. President Jefferson Davis and General Robert E. Lee had ridden down toward the battle to learn some news when Johnston's litter-bearers came by them. The information of the fallen commander caused Jefferson Davis to turn to his friend and say, "General Lee, I shall assign you to the command of this army. Make your preparations as soon as you reach your quarters. I shall send you the order when I get to Richmond."

Robert E. Lee was now the commander of the Army of Northern Virginia. This assignment was a tremendous honor and carried massive responsibility. The fate of thousands of young lives would rest on his decisions. For Lee, the time had finally come to expose to the world who he was and what kind of leader he would be.

PART VII

THE SUMMER OF YOUNG NAPOLEON

Quinctilius Varus, give me back my legions!
CAESAR AUGUSTUS

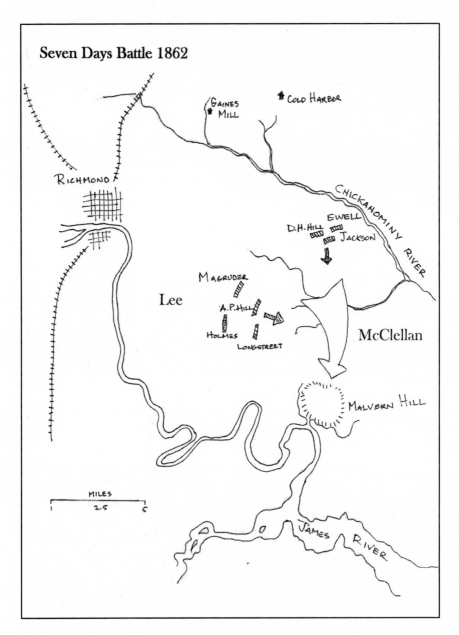

The Seven Days Battle

93.

My Dearest Ellen,

I know how proud you must be of your conquering warrior hero. With the great battles of Williamsburg and Hanover Courthouse behind me, it is not any wonder how you must think of your man. I know the press taunts us and suggests I am never with the troops when they go to battle, but it is not true. I know who I am and what I am about. I simply must not take unnecessary risks with my life, for the fate of my army depends upon me and they all know it. You should see how my very presence inspires the men. The whoops and cries for joy when their commander passes through camp are heard even in the streets of Richmond. They continually tell me my presence on the battlefield is what saves the day. You know I have written you before about Norfolk. Some critics now say I never gave proper credit to his Excellency for his visit to Norfolk with Chase and Stanton. But why should I? It was the result of my movements that Norfolk was abandoned by the Rebs, the Merrimac was destroyed and the Monitor now protects the waters unhindered. His Excellency does not deserve credit for my strategic planning, does he?

I am proud of my men, Ellen. Once boys, I have worked them hard and watched them grow up into the fighting tools they now are. None of us are innocent in regards to cold-blooded fighting any longer. Fair Oaks and Seven Pines brought an awful sight for any eyes. The bloating corpses, the awful stench of rotting flesh, the disfigurement…. I cannot tell you how I am beginning to loathe this war. I also loathe stupidity in people who should know better. I will not now remind you of the struggles I have had with my corps commanders. The utter nothingness and immense worthlessness of some of the leaders I have to endure every day is even harder than fighting the opposition.

To think of the enemy actually gives me hope for tomorrow. Secesh is building up as strong as he can in front of me, just before Richmond, and this is a good thing. I will deal with these Rebels with one strong, crushing blow and end this war. The reports say even now hundreds of wagons and citizens are fleeing their Capitol in anticipation of my advance. You must have heard from the papers that Jefferson Davis has replaced Old Joe Johnston with Robert Lee. This will only seek to serve our cause. I know Lee, he is cautious and will not make any bold moves. His attempts to command in western Virginia were futile. He is an administrator who would best serve his government as a secretary. Yet, I am glad they do not feel the same as I do about him—it will only serve to my advantage. And, I need an advantage over the Secesh leadership because I do not have a single friend in the high councils of my own government. I'm afraid that even honest A. is not for me. The abolitionists who think I'm a traitor have poisoned his mind like so many in our Congress. I am only comforted by knowing I am far away from Washington and the heat which continues to radiate from the Republicans.

You must know this venture is one of the greatest historical battles of the world and that is why there are so many difficulties. I see now I am God's chosen instrument to perform his desire and to heal our land of this fracture of North and South. This is a sacred cause and the right side will win. I am thankful for this task. I am thankful for your respect and faithfulness.

Your loving husband,

George

Major General George Brinton McClellan finished his letter to his wife and reclined in his chair that evening. He was smoking a cigar and celebrating a recent report from the battle-line when several of his commanders joined his company.

"It was only a matter of time, boys. Those Southern gentlemen had to realize they could not last that long. I mean, we have some twenty-three million people compared to their nine million. We have ninety percent of the factory production, over seventy percent of the railroads and three quarters of the farmland. Any idiot could ascertain with these lop-sided figures, along with our genius in military strategy, it would only be a few months before their gay dreams of independence would come crashing down around them. Look, we have gone from Washington to the doorstep of their Capitol. How long do you think it will be after the Capitol is taken that they will fight this war?"

"They could move it back to Montgomery where it was before," said Fitz John Porter, a newly appointed corps commander and friend.

"Nah," said McClellan. "It'll never happen."

"You forgot to note they have over ninety percent of the cotton production going for them," said Edwin Sumner. His nickname was Bull Head because it was rumored that a musket ball had bounced off his head.

"Yes, and now no ports in which to ship it out of." McClellan laughed heartily. He knew the European powers were steadily giving supplies to the Northern factories and increasingly isolating themselves from the South and their desperate cause.

McClellan then turned his thoughts to his own political future. "I'll tell you what," said McClellan airily, "No one is going to regret it when the Lincoln family leaves the White House."

Several of the generals chuckled knowing the controversial relationship their commander had with their Commander-in-Chief.

"The only defenders in Congress he now has are radicals and I hear even his own Cabinet barely tolerates him," snorted General McClellan.

"Why are you always so sour on the man?" William B. Franklin asked him.

"Because he meddles in matters that are not his to meddle in. He promised me McDowell's corps and then maneuvered them west, away from Richmond without consulting me. That is the act of either a coward or a traitor—you choose. Have you seen his last telegram? It says 'Hold all your ground. Yield it only inch by inch and by good order.' Isn't that ridiculous? Why would anyone think they needed to tell a master military strategist to yield their ground only slightly? He meddles in things too serious for him. He is like a little child trying to understand engineering techniques. He would do better to host tea parties with his crazy wife. He has no respect from me."

"That is obvious," said Porter.

"At least we have had solid victories up to this point. What is the latest casualty count?"

"Sir, we are at 780 dead and over 3,500 wounded in action. Also, we cannot account for another 650 of our soldiers."

"Staggering, yet Secesh had more, correct?"

"Well, sir, we estimate they had around 1,000 killed and twice as many as ours wounded."

"Seven Pines was a bloody affair. Has everyone in critical condition seen a physician yet?"

"Almost. I thought they had all made it to the little town of White House but today I found out they are still trickling in."

"We've got to do better next time at caring for our wounded and allowing them to see a doctor sooner. I have heard many men died on the short train ride from the battle," McClellan said sullenly. "I have never heard groans from men as I did that day after the battle." McClellan paused. "There were some fine men out there."

No one knew what to say as McClellan seemed to be taking a rare moment to grieve the loss of his men.

Abruptly he said, "The only good news is now with old Joe Johnston out of the fight and Robert Lee as the commander, the battle should go much faster for us."

"What do you mean?"

"I know Robert E. Lee. I fought with him in Mexico. Lee's an engineer, not an infantry officer. Sure, he can make maps and survey land like no other. He can also decide the best place to build a dam. But lead troops into battle? He does not hold the moral firmness or the steadfast will of a true commander. I predict he will be very cautious and weak in his leading and then after the press hounds him awhile he will simply fade away into retirement. He is definitely not a fighter. Once we roll through Richmond, whatever support he must have garnered from Davis will be dissolved."

"What if old Lee surprises us like Jackson did to Banks?"

Little George McClellan took the cigar out of his mouth and stared straight through the officer who asked the question with his steely eyes. "It'll never happen. We're too powerful."

94.

General Robert E. Lee did not waste a single moment. He wrote his daughter that he wished the commander's mantle had fallen to an abler man and his only ambition now was to drive the enemy back to their homes. He concluded by saying he would do this speedily and thoroughly. Lee immediately set out to prevent the capture of Richmond. He had earthworks constructed on the eastern side of Richmond, he fortified all the main roads, he mounted a heavy gun on a railroad truck and he reorganized the Confederate artillery making them more mobile. He wrote to Jackson congratulating him on his recent accomplishments in Winchester, but told him he could not provide him the requested 40,000 additional troops in order to conduct an offensive on Washington. He told Jackson he needed him to unite with the main army in Richmond first and drive McClellan off the peninsula before he could give Jackson the forces he needed. Without Jackson, Lee knew his chances against McClellan's behemoth force were slight. Yet, despite the odds, Lee decided to begin his tenure in leadership by hitting General McClellan in the nose and conduct a surprise attack.

95.

Salmon Chase received the short telegram. It was marked 'confidential.' Only the clerk who carried it to him would know of the contents. Chase paid the clerk a sizeable gratuity and reminded him of the importance of secrecy during wartime. He returned to his study and sat in his oversized chair behind the beautiful wooden desk. He thought of the master plan he had developed to turn the Cabinet one by one against Lincoln and then seize power with the support of the Union Army. This telegram would surely tighten his ever-growing control of Washington. What he read was not what he expected, however.

Dear Mr. Secretary,

I have decided I will not be content with being your Vice President. I have determined through watching the administration you are a part of and hearing from friends of mine in Congress that I, myself, would be the best choice for President. I will gladly offer you a position on the Cabinet when the time comes and I am elected, or perhaps an ambassadorship. This departure from our original plan in no way changes my feelings of friendship for you. And I know you feel the same way about me.

G. McClellan

96.

The first week of June found Thomas Samuel Jackson in a hurry to arrive at Port Republic before Shield's division. Jackson had learned from a spy that due to Shield's embarrassment of letting Jackson slip by him at Strasburg, he was going to try to beat Jackson to Port Republic. By maneuvering through the Luray Valley to Conrad's Store, Shields hoped he could cut Jackson off and force him to fight. Jackson, however, was marching his men relentlessly. He ensured security on their flanks and rear and listened to a report from Colonel John M. Patton of the 21st Virginia regarding a skirmish toward their rear with Federal Cavalry. Patton was remorseful he had to kill three Union horsemen.

"Why are you remorseful?" asked Jackson of Patton.

"Because they were brave and gallant and with no regard to their own safety they charged into the middle of my strong regiment."

"Colonel Patton, why would you not shoot them?" asked Jackson.

"I should have spared them, General," Patton answered, "because they were men who had gotten into a desperate situation."

"No, Colonel!" Jackson replied forcefully. "Shoot them all. I don't want them to be brave."

Patton left the meeting with the same remorse, but with a better understanding of his commander.

For days Jackson pushed his troops. The men were exhausted, hungry and footsore. No one was happy. Troops were scattered down the turnpike for eleven miles. Jackson kept pushing. He knew he had several Union Armies surrounding him, with the greatest threat just to the east of the Massanutten.

One commander told him he was afraid that his men would not keep up and his unit would fail him. Jackson said unflinchingly, "Lead them without fear. God will give them strength and courage to do their duty."

Jackson decided to make his stand against Shields at Port Republic. He simply had to get there first in order to be in a menacing position when Shields attacked. He sent twelve of Ashby's riders to destroy the South Fork Bridge at Conrad's Store. He now had to push his men for one more march. They had already marched over one hundred miles from Winchester and were almost delirious. More than one of Jackson's subordinates began to question his sanity. Jackson's decision was resolute however, and he kept the men marching. He received word from Richmond that no reinforcements would be coming so he wrote Lee again of his situation hoping for him to change his mind.

On Friday, June 6th, Jackson's Army limped into Port Republic. The commander set up his headquarters at the home of Dr. George Kemper. Major John Harman, his quartermaster, maneuvered all of their wagons safely into town. General Ewell's division was to the north at Cross Keys and Ashby was at Harrisonburg. They had arrived there first and it was a tremendous relief. Things were looking positive until later in the evening when Jackson received word that Turner Ashby had been killed.

The 1st New Jersey Cavalry, led by Sir Percy Wyndham, traversed through Harrisonburg, and on the southeast of town he fell into an ambush of Ashby's cavalrymen. Wyndham, a British colonel, was captured because his men did not follow him into battle. His troops all scattered. When the Union brigade commander George Bayard heard the news, he returned to the area with some fresh cavalry troops to go and find Wyndham and the rest of the wounded who were left on the field. They ran into Confederate infantry which Ashby had garnered from General Ewell. Both groups fired deadly volleys at each other. Turner Ashby led the 58th Virginia Regiment and as he advanced his horse was shot from under him. Ashby jumped to his feet and drew his sword high above his head, shouting out to his men to charge with him. He fearlessly ran into the Union line and Ashby, the solitary attacker, was shot and mortally wounded.

The news sobered Jackson. He was not always happy with how Ashby led his troops but he respected him. Lately, Ashby had done much better at being attentive to order and discipline. A brigadier general for less than two weeks, Ashby's death was not only sudden but shocking to the entire command.

The next day, Ashby's body lay in a pine box in the front parlor of a home in Port Republic. Confederate soldiers came to pay their last respects to the brave cavalry commander.

"He was the most gallant man I ever saw," said Colonel Samuel Fulkerson, Jackson's third brigade commander.

General Ewell said, "I have always had the highest admiration for Turner Ashby."

Jackson stated of Ashby, "I never knew his superior. His daring was proverbial. His powers of endurance incredible. And his tone of character heroic."

Bruce's words to memorialize Ashby were to call him a fearless lion without any concern for his own safety. "Some commanders surround themselves with body guards. Turner Ashby was the bodyguard for this army and sought not to uplift himself, but to uplift his entire unit. He was as brave as any man I have ever met," Bruce concluded.

Conrad Montgomery reminded all that Ashby was the son of Colonel Turner Ashby who fought in the War of 1812 and the grandson of Captain Jack Ashby of the Revolutionary War. He remembered a time when Turner was riding his beloved mount, Tom Telegraph, destroying bridges before the oncoming Union Army at Narrow Passage Creek and at Edinburg while Union infantry were peppering the ground around him with minie balls. Ashby, Conrad recalled, seemed not to notice nor care about the danger around him and continued to lead and direct his troops as if in garrison.

Jackson left the memorial service knowing he would grieve over Ashby the rest of his life. They had a unique relationship of respect and trust. Ashby's emotions were hurt early in the war when Jackson instinctively turned to Jeb Stuart instead of him. Then, Jackson was hurt by Ashby with his lack of organization and discipline. There were several times when Ashby had lowered Jackson's trust in him. Once or twice their friendship was disrupted, such as at the conclusion of the Winchester battle when Ashby couldn't be found. But those memories did not seem as sharp as before and they did not lighten the dark mood that was now cast over Jackson's thoughts. Jackson decided to trust in the Almighty and rely on the fact that God's plans were always larger than the individual players. Ashby was replaced by Thomas T. Munford.

June 8th, 1862, was a Sunday and Jackson's men were resting. The order of the day was to write a letter home, take a long nap or attend a religious service. Major Robert Dabney, in fact, was writing a sermon to deliver that day. However, a Union raid from Colonel Samuel S. Carroll (Gen. Shield's Fourth Brigade commander) made the men grab their muskets and return to duty quickly. The raid ultimately failed and Carroll's men retreated. General Erastus Tyler led an all out Union attack against Jackson and he failed, as well. At Cross Keys on the same morning General Richard Ewell's men received an attack from General Fremont. General Isaac Trimble (Ewell's Seventh Brigade commander), bravely led his men to repel Federal forces twice his size. Ultimately, almost three hundred of Ewell's men were killed during the fight, but nearly seven hundred men of Fremont's command were killed. This cost sobered up both sides and sent the Federal Army far away from Jackson to lick their wounds.

97.

"Absolutely incredible, sir!" balding Chase exclaimed.

"Not so much. I'm getting used to this type of news from my commanders," said Lincoln thinking how pleasurable it was to see the stoic Chase annoyed.

There they sat. President Abraham Lincoln was reclining in his favorite chair in the green room after several hours of receiving visitors at the White House. He was accompanied by War Secretary Edwin McMasters Stanton, Treasury Secretary Salmon Portland Chase, Attorney General Edward Bates and Secretary of State William Henry Seward. This impromptu Cabinet meeting began when Stanton and Chase entered the room and gave Lincoln the most recent report from the front. Seward and Bates were already with the president, debriefing him about their day.

Edwin Stanton continued the conversation in the East Room underneath a large chandelier, "What do you mean, sir?"

"I mean stalemates and setbacks."

No reply, so Lincoln looked around the room at the forlorn faces. All of a sudden a tired feeling swept over him and he wished he was alone. Soon the feeling passed and he found he wanted to talk about some of the 'whys' of operations in the valley.

"Let's discuss the situation a little bit and reason together. General Jackson's Army was trapped at Port Republic, weary and probably hungry from their long, fast march up the valley away from our strength. We have him in our sights with Shield's and Tyler's men on the East and Fremont's forces to the west. Instead of them coordinating an attack at the same time, Fremont remains idle! Why, I ask? Also, why is it that Jackson's junior commanders of Winder, Patton and Taliaferro with their brigades can put fear in all of my major generals who lead divisions? I knew precisely what Jackson was doing with his force, causing us to keep our forces bound up around Washington and away from Richmond, and though I endeavored to countermine him and have my generals outsmart him, they have let me down with their slowness and hesitations and lack of courage on the battlefield."

"Sir, it is a complicated matter of affairs," Stanton mumbled. This comment hinted at patronization and drew some sneers from the others.

"Complicated? I see nothing complicated about it. It seems pretty straightforward. Jackson and his commanders do not run away from battles, but choose their ground. Jackson and his commanders keep fighting even when overwhelmed as they did in the battles at McDowell and Kernstown. Our men seem to turn and run when things do not immediately go their way."

Stanton choked a little, wiped his nose and said, "Sir, with all due respect, Tyler reports they were vastly outnumbered, yet continued to push against the Confederate line until it broke several times. However, Jackson was able to keep reinforcing his weak points as soon as there was a hole made in the line. He used Ewell's troops he had in reserve. Our men had no reinforcements. It sounds like they performed admirably despite drastic odds."

"Fine to know, Secretary, but our forces are halfway back to Washington now and Jackson has control of at least half the valley with his whereabouts presently unknown! Plus, I keep hearing about how bad the odds are for our side, yet we have over 150,000 men in Virginia alone, 100,000 with McClellan and over 50,000 with McDowell, Fremont, Banks, Saxton and Shields. The Confederate Army could not possibly be as strong as us, yet we continue to lose battles."

Seward and Bates exchanged quick, knowing glances toward each other before looking at the floor. Chase was sitting upright and held his usual disapproving face. *For some reason he seems a little different this afternoon,* mused Lincoln. No one said anything for a moment.

"Isn't anyone here as irritated as I am about this? Our Capitol remains persistently in danger as long as Jackson remains unchecked!" Lincoln said as he rested his head against the back of his mahogany and velvet chair.

"Yes," Seward solely said, but then remained quiet. He could feel Lincoln boring his eyes into him. The Secretary's thoughts drifted to his beautiful gardens in Auburn, New York and his early morning walks. Slowly, Seward continued, "They say Jackson thanks God for his victories and wishes Virginians would attend more to thanking God for his successes than to look at him. This is much different than McClellan."

"What are you suggesting—that God is fighting for the Rebel Army and not for us?" asked Lincoln.

"No, not at all. It is merely an observation that came to mind and I was attempting to make a subtle comparison with a few of our own commanders. I don't know if we could give you any of the answers you are specifically looking for..."

Chase blurted, "Absolutely not."

Seward continued, "We have been foiled in our efforts to mass sufficient strength to destroy Jackson. All of us sitting here know our focus the last six months has been overly drawn toward our impetuous commander with his grand peninsula strategy." This drew sudden ire from Stanton, McClellan's one remaining friend on the Cabinet.

"If we had been able to move our main force toward Richmond from Manassas, as all of us in this room unanimously proposed to Young Napoleon, then we could have dealt with Jackson while moving toward Richmond. I hate stating the obvious, but we have achieved close to nothing in Virginia in the last six months and Salmon, you know how many millions of dollars it takes to support our army for that long. What real gains have been made?" asked Seward.

Salmon shook his head and looked at the floor.

Bates, with a warm grin said, "Though he moves like a glacier, we now own a peninsula we did not have before." Bates and his family had enjoyed a tour of the peninsula with Seward at the invite of the Navy Secretary Gideon Welles after Norfolk was taken by the Union.

Chase entered into the discussion by adding, "If we delay any longer, Secretary Seward, might Britain come alongside the South and try to save her?" He asked the question rhetorically and did not expect an answer, but then looked toward Lincoln and continued, "From what you were saying before, sir, I have received word from friends of mine that the Confederate strength is not the 200,000 that McClellan believes it is, but more around 90,000. He is afraid of shadows. For months he thought that painted logs were actually cannon. He is timid. He could crush the Rebels if he went against them immediately, yet he persistently grieves not having McDowell's forces." At this comment Chase looked intently at Stanton for approval but Stanton kept a bland expression. Lincoln thought how odd it was that Chase didn't defend McClellan like he had on previous occasions.

Just then John Hay came into the East Room with an eager look for the President. John Hay and John Nicolay were Lincoln's principal assistants. Nicolay was Lincoln's private secretary and Hay was the assistant secretary. They worked well together, loved Lincoln and affectionately called him the Ancient because of his chiseled features and mythical countenance. When Lincoln let them look deep into his eyes it was like peering into history. They called Mary, Lincoln's wife, the Hellcat—but not to her face.

Twenty-three year old Hay waited until he had the proper acknowledgement. Lincoln was the first to speak, "What is it, Mr. Hay?"

"Sir, the War Department just received a telegram from General McClellan's headquarters. He said we will be seeing in the newspapers tomorrow the description of the Confederate Cavalry Chief, James Ewell Brown Stuart, riding with his brigade completely around the Army of the Potomac. McClellan said the report is true but not to fear, apart from destroying about 70 supply wagons, they were unable to cause any significant damage and it is again business as usual."

The news from Hay validated the emotions and tone of the meeting so far. No one knew what to say. Several of them looked out of the large window in front of them. *Business as usual?*

Lincoln refocused, studied Seward a moment as if to deduce what the Secretary of State might be thinking, and then said, "Men, it is mid-June. General McClellan started his campaign months ago. Richmond was the goal and they are on the doorstep. Let each of us pray to Almighty God that he will help McClellan take action and his mission will be successful. I cannot imagine the despondency of our people if he were to fail at this quest. It all hangs on McClellan."

98.

Moss Crawford had been incarcerated in a prisoner-of-war facility for almost three months when his lucky day arrived. He had gotten to know the other prisoners and guards fairly well and though he had planned his escape over and over again, he never implemented his plans and remained passive. He endured harsh interrogations from some guards and kindness from others. He was with approximately ninety Confederate soldiers who had been captured from various battles over the last year. Rarely were they ever allowed to leave their annex compound and see the prisoners from the larger building next door, but they knew they were there.

Moss looked like a different man from when he was first captured. He had lost weight and appeared fragile. His hair was long and matted together and he had a tremendous beard and mustache.

Moss was routinely called out of their secure room and into the upstairs hallway. Sometimes he was escorted down the stairs and into a living area sparsely furnished with just two chairs and a small table. Moss saw the room every day when he passed through the house with the other guards and a contingent of prisoners during their daily routines of relieving themselves, work projects and special humiliation parades where they would line up outside and march while visitors would come by and gape at them. On most occasions interrogations took place upstairs in a little room the prisoners did not like to go to because sometimes they were mistreated there. They referred to it simply as 'the room' and Moss had been beaten there his first night of captivity when he tried to walk quietly out of the front door. He had also been beaten by some of the other Confederate prisoners once because they suspected him of thieving someone's rations.

He had heard little news from the war and what he did hear was usually exaggerated in favor of the Union.

Moss had been living in an over-filled, dusty room with wooden floors and cracks in the walls which let the cold seep in. He had an irregular size mattress without much padding left so he could feel the hard floor whenever he turned. He made three important friendships, which he believed, had been the only way he endured his confinement period. The first friendship was with one of the other prisoners named Lewis Powell. Lewis was from Florida and spoke with a strong Southern swamp accent. Over the weeks in confinement, Moss and Lewis had grown to trust each other and then count on each other, always watching each other's back and protecting what few little trinkets they could accumulate. The guards would pass them things when they were in a good mood like a wooden top or a Jew's harp. Lewis was one who Moss entrusted all of his escape plans to and Lewis usually talked Moss out of them.

The second friend Moss found was a stray cat that had been allowed to be inside the barracks and live with the men and come and go as it pleased. At first Moss did not ever pay any attention to the feline creature, but after petting it one day for two hours the cat came back to him the next day for the loving strokes. Moss always looked for the cat after that day so he could spend time with her. He named her Elizabeth after his grandmother. In a mysterious way the kitty cat gave Moss hope for the next day and reminded him of some of the simple pleasures of home like the privacy of his own bedroom, the freedom to enjoy Scout and Chris Columbus whenever he wanted to pet them, and the freedom to spend time with people he loved whenever he wanted to. Elizabeth would purr and curl up on Moss's lap not caring whatsoever if he was a poor prisoner or a rich king, Elizabeth enjoyed his attention and returned unconditional love. Unfortunately, she stopped coming by about a month ago. It tore at Moss's heart. He searched for the feline in vain when he was allowed to go outside for something and he called repeatedly for her, but he never saw Elizabeth again after her disappearance.

The third friend he made was a few days after Elizabeth had disappeared. When he was outside calling for his cat he met a young boy who was eight years old named Wilfred. Wilfred was a little chubby, fairly polite, had a dimple on his chin and a couple of freckles on his nose, like Ned Harrington, but he did not have any red hair. Wilfred was a curious child and asked Moss what he was doing calling for the cat. He also wanted to know why Moss had joined the Confederate Army, if Moss liked the color red, what was his favorite food and if he had a best friend. The first day or two Moss was not very appreciative of the little menace and all his questions. But soon he grew to enjoy the boy's desire to hang on to the back fence and call for Moss when he would see him. Moss and the other prisoners fought boredom each day so they cherished any conversation with someone on the outside, including an eight year old named Wilfred. The conversations were always short and they were usually in the late afternoons when Wilfred was returning home from school. He told Moss his mother did not like him hanging out by the high fence and talking to the prisoners. She told Wilfred it was unsafe and uncouth and that he was to leave those godless Rebels alone. Wilfred said he didn't know what godless meant.

One warm day Moss was waiting out behind the annex of the old Capitol building near the fence where Wilfred would come and chat with him. Sure enough, about the usual time, Wilfred loped slowly down the street, walked past his house and entered the narrow alleyway that led back behind his house to where the fenced annex was located. He smiled when he saw Moss.

"Why don't you ever shave off your beard? It looks gross," Wilfred said straightaway.

Moss chuckled and responded, "Why don't you ever tie your shoes?"

Wilfred looked down at his untied laces surprised that Moss had noticed through the fence.

Moss was anxious inside because he had a question he wanted to ask Wilfred, but he was not sure if Wilfred could keep it a secret from his parents being only eight years old. Moss knew how parents could pressure information out of a child, especially if the child looked guilty and was trying to hide something. Moss decided that he had to take the risk. The days were getting warmer and he had heard discussions of the guards speaking of transporting the prisoners up north, possibly to New England in order to discourage any of them from escaping. That move would be devastating to all of them—moving them farther from the border.

Moss had contemplated escaping ever since his first night when he made a futile attempt and suffered horribly for it. Another time, a month later, he had his heart set on it, but a fellow prisoner set forth to accomplish the deed a night before Moss's chosen day. The individual was caught and beaten almost to death. The guards were talking about tar and feather for him, but it never got that far. Thankfully, at this prison located in the heart of Washington, they did not practice corporeal punishment so none of the other prisoners were punished when one did something criminal. Another time he had wanted to escape one of his so-called friends gave the information to the provost marshal and Moss was taken to 'the room' and summarily tried, convicted and beaten, all in the manner of thirty minutes.

He had put off another date of escape because they were supposed to have a special visitor that day from the White House. In the morning they were told to clean up their living quarters extra well for the visitor, but they were not told who it was going to be ahead of time. When the gentlemen showed up it was the Attorney General Edward Bates. He walked upstairs, checked the teeth and backs of some of the prisoners and merrily went on his way to some other important meeting he had that day. He never spoke to the prisoners and was not too interested in the mechanics of the operation, at least in the annex building where Moss was.

Moss finally gathered the courage to ask Wilfred his question. "Can you keep a secret, Wilfred?"

"Yes. I keep secrets better-an any other boy in my class."

"How can you be so sure?" asked Moss.

"Because I never tell anybody anything—even if it kills me."

"Not even to your parents?"

"Nope. I don't tell anybody nothing."

Moss could tell he was lying, but he did see some resolve in Wilfred he hadn't seen before.

"Wilfred, I've got something I need to tell you, but you have to keep it a secret."

"What's that?"

"I'm going to escape tonight."

"Are you serious?" Wilfred asked.

"I'm dead serious," Moss replied

Wilfred didn't say anything for a moment and appeared deep in thought until he asked, "How you going to do it?"

"Trust me, I've got a plan," Moss answered.

"I don't think I'm supposed to trust criminals."

"True, Wilfred, but I'm not a criminal, I'm a prisoner."

"What's the difference?"

"The difference is that I have not done anything illegal in the eyes of either nation. I have been apprehended for fighting for a cause I hold deeply in my heart, but I am not a criminal."

Just then the guard watching Moss who was friendly toward him and allowed Moss to have these extra moments in the yard after their afternoon outdoor session, motioned with his arm that Moss's time was up.

Moss finished the conversation quickly, "Wilfred, I'm trusting you. Don't tell your parents or I'll get quite a whipping by these old guards, you hear?" Moss started walking toward the guard.

"I hear. I told you I could keep a secret. Best in my class!"

"Best in your class. That's good Wilfred. Keep up that record," Moss shouted behind him.

Wilfred shouted after him, "Where you going to go to?" Then, as soon as he said it, he covered his mouth with both hands realizing he had spoken loudly enough for the guard to hear him. Wilfred turned about and ran away toward home.

Moss froze inside but kept walking without changing the expression on his face. Perhaps the guard would think nothing of Wilfred's comment. Moss winked at the guard waiting by the door as he passed by him and nothing was said about the comment.

Moss spent the whole evening as nervous as a cat in a tree. He had shared the escape plan with Wilfred to see if he could trust him. If nothing happened before the next day then Moss would know Wilfred hadn't told his parents, and his parents never reported it to the guards. If Moss was suddenly taken in 'the room' he would know the little boy slipped up and couldn't be a trusted confidant. Moss had to take the chance because he needed Wilfred for the escape plan he had concocted. There was only one way Moss could conceptualize ever leaving that makeshift building and making a go of it. He had to have a horse and a map and some tools in order to try to break out of the building and cut through the fence. Wilfred could get those for him if he set his mind to it, and hopefully he could be secretive about it.

Moss did not tell his friend Lewis Powell exactly what he was working on with Wilfred. Lewis thought it was just a normal day with no new stories to tell. Moss laid awake half of the night wondering if there would be a knock at the front door or if the guards would storm in unexpectedly and seize him. When Moss did doze off he dreamed the worst dreams of being whipped and beaten across the face with a wooden pole.

When Moss opened his eyes at the first call, daylight was poking its way through the cracks in the old wood placed over the windows. He knew then Wilfred hadn't told his parents about his escape and that he could trust him. There was one other possibility—Wilfred had told his parents and the guards were playing a terrible trick on Moss, testing him to see if it was true. Moss decided to watch the guards carefully that day and to be a little brazen just to see if they might overreact but they never did. Lunchtime took forever to arrive and Moss counted nearly every minute of the afternoon until he asked to go outside for his afternoon break. The guards were being more generous with the warm weather arriving and they preferred to be outside as much as the inmates, so they were lenient.

Moss didn't mind his chores that day, the scrubbing of the front and back staircase and helping out in the kitchen. He whizzed through the work as if he had gotten a good night's sleep. He couldn't wait to see Wilfred and congratulate him on his great achievement of secrecy. That afternoon Moss brought outside with him a harmonica he had received in a recent trade with another inmate. Wilfred had earned it and Moss wanted to give it to him as a gift.

Moss waited not at the fence, but near the little privy in the back of the yard. He did not want to draw the attention of a guard who might wonder why he was so close to the exterior fence in the back lot. Some of the guards knew his routine of talking with Wilfred, but not all of them because sometimes the guards would switch assignments and perform duty in another building.

Moss looked intently down the alleyway for what seemed like almost an hour. He wished that Wilfred would still come by in order to see if Moss had actually left or not. Hopefully Wilfred was as curious about Moss escaping as he was with everything else in Moss's life.

Soon he saw him coming and Moss's heart jumped skyward. However, the next instance he saw a man walking behind Wilfred and it appeared they were both coming from their house and toward the back fence. Moss didn't know exactly what to do. Should he walk briskly back to his quarters or wait and see what this was all about? He had a terrible feeling in the pit of his stomach as Wilfred walked up to the fence and motioned for Moss to come closer. By the time Moss stepped over to the fence, both Wilfred and someone who looked an awful lot like the little boy were standing there looking at him. Wilfred was beaming at Moss with a grin from ear to ear.

"That's my pa," Wilfred said proudly.

"I see that, Wilfred. What's he doing here, I thought you weren't going to tell anybody—remember best in your class?"

Wilfred dropped his grin a little bit, "Oh yeah, I didn't really tell the truth about that."

"Thanks......." Moss didn't know what to say.

The whole time they were sorting through the dilemma Wilfred's pa stood there and was looking Moss up and down.

"After I told my pa your plan, he said he wanted to meet you."

Moss was glaring down at Wilfred, exasperated, when Wilfred's pa began to speak.

"Well, hello. You obviously know now we don't keep secrets in our family. I could see something was going on with Wilfred the instant he got in from school yesterday."

"Nice family," Moss replied.

"Say, do you really want to escape or are you just kidding around about all of this? I mean, you're still here today," Wilfred's pa said truly curious.

"Why, is this some kind of trick? Do you work for the Federals somehow?" Moss asked. He noticed Wilfred's pa was around forty-five years old, a little heavy in the middle and not very tall. His hairline was receding and he had hair coming out of his ears, but he had a pleasant smile and a friendly demeanor.

"No, I'm not on one side or the other. I'm definitely not a spy for the army. I do perform some contracts for them, however. I'm a business man."

"Okay."

"When Wilfred told me you were going to escape yesterday I had something come to my mind I thought I could ask you about—if you were ever going to truly escape. I assure you, I will not turn you into the guards. My wife would. She is a Unionist and a Lincoln lover."

"You're not?" asked Moss.

"Oh, no. Like I said, I'm a business man. I don't get too concerned about politics."

Moss glanced around to see if the trio was drawing any attention from the guards, but so far the men in blue had not taken any notice of them. Wilfred walked a couple of feet away to chase a cricket.

"Well, what if I did run away?" Moss said.

"I could help you—that is if you tell me how to do it. I'm not good at this kind of thing. But the point is, if I help you I would ask you a small favor."

"Go on," Moss said.

"I would ask you to carry a letter for me to one of the generals in the Rebel Army."

"What would the letter say?"

"Well, that is really not your concern but since you would have to trust me I will need to trust you so I will tell you. I own two small factories nearby that distribute durable goods for the army; canteens, cups, silverware, plates and other items. Lately, Edwin Stanton has been giving some of my monthly contracts away to his personal friends. This really bothers me. And, I don't know what to do about it. I have warehouses of good material that needs to be sold. If you were to alert one of the generals in your army about it and they could pass the message up to General Lee or Jefferson Davis himself, I might be able to broker a deal with them and ship these goods around to one of their harbors. It's a business contract I am proposing. And I would make the Confederate Army a good deal."

"What's in it for me," Moss asked dryly.

"Well, I'll help you escape from here. I can supply you with a wagon and a team, or just a horse and anything else you can think of. I mean, I cannot help you break out of this facility—that would be breaking the law. You would have to do that yourself, and I also can't supply you with any transportation."

"I thought you just said you could?" Moss asked.

"I mean directly. You would have to steal them from me but I could have a horse all saddled up and tell you where he was tied."

Moss thought a moment. "You'd let me take your horse, mister?"

"I look at it as an investment. Hopefully it will pay off with big dividends. I hear your army needs supplies."

"What's your name?" Moss asked.

"Lefty, Lefty Sanders, owner of Sanders and Foote Supplies."

"Who is Foote? Does he know about your desire to do business with the Confederate Army?" Moss asked.

Lefty smiled at him, "Foote doesn't mind at all. He's been dead for almost three years. The name is what's important in business. People have trusted Sanders and Foote for near a score. They wouldn't know what business just a Sanders was," Lefty said proud of himself.

"Well," Moss glanced back and saw a guard walking toward them.

"Listen. Have Wilfred here tomorrow and I will make arrangements through him. Don't come back here, it will raise too much concern among the guards for them to see me talking to you. We might have already blown our chance with today's meeting."

"Okay, so you want just Wilfred tomorrow, but you will think about it and let us know?"

The guard was almost up to fence where they were talking when Moss said, "I hope to see Wilfred tomorrow."

Moss turned around just as the guard approached and Lefty and Wilfred darted off down the alley back to their home.

"What was that all about?" the guard asked.

"The man wanted to come out here and see who had been talking to his son in the afternoons," Moss said not lying.

"Well, was he upset that you were a prisoner?"

"Didn't seem to be. Said his wife would be, however."

"So are you supposed to stop talking to the boy?" the guard asked.

"No, the man said he didn't mind as long as I don't swear or say anything mean to him."

"Oh," was all the guard said as they walked back to the annex.

This was sure a lucky day, Moss thought. Then, he shook his head and chuckled thinking about Wilfred and his astral ability to keep a secret. *Best in his class? Must be a small school,* thought Moss.

99.

General McClellan was almost prepared to attack Richmond. His army was within ten miles of the Confederate Capital and he was pleased with the reports he was getting from his intelligence officers, some of whom had slipped into the city to see what was going on. The streets of Richmond were clogged with people loading wagons and fleeing the city in anticipation for his attack. For once things seemed to be going McClellan's way. The Army of the Potomac was gargantuan with ten full-sized divisions. He was just given over ten thousand replacements from Washington, which put his total strength at a little over 105,000 men. These men were anxious to fight the Rebels and make proper amends for the Battle of Manassas the summer before. The itch for atonement was at high tide. It had not been fully scratched with the battle at Fair Oaks. Though McClellan called it a solid victory, he knew some of the men were focusing on the failures that day. Regardless, with the morale, the strength of this force, the abundance of supplies and the terrain before Richmond in Federal control, it was thought by all a major attack was imminent. McClellan told his corps commanders he needed just a few more days because he believed the Confederates had around 200,000 troops and he still hoped that perhaps McDowell's Army would make it down to support him on his right flank.

* * *

George McClellan finalized his plans and briefed his corps commanders while showing them a sand table of the region his aide had prepared. McClellan was deepening his friendship with Fitz John Porter and William

Franklin, his two new corps commanders and he was glad they were in the room. "Thankfully, it has just been reported that General Jackson and his troops are at least 120 miles away, still in the Valley. This will help us not be so outnumbered as we enter into the final phase of this campaign. Banks, Fremont and Shields, though bumbling idiotically the last few months, have somehow managed to adequately engage Jackson so he will not be a bother for us.

"We will begin this final battle with artillery until we have battered the hell out of Secesh. Then we will move in force. With Heintzelman and Sumner in the middle we will attack and take Old Tavern, the surrounding field and the woodland to the south. This will put us in the vicinity of Nine Mile Road and a bold thrust will enable us to put our heavy guns on that high terrain. From Nine Mile Road we will sweep with a hook formation from the east of Richmond and around to the northeast with Fitz crossing the Meadow Bridge. Once the Rebs are dispersed back into Richmond we will move up our large cannons and assault the city ruthlessly until they move out to the west where they will be trapped with other Federal forces coming behind them. If they are stubborn we will siege Richmond and surround them, cutting off all their avenues of escape. It is simple, really. From north to south the lineup will remain Porter, Franklin, Sumner, Heintzelman and Keyes. Fitz, you have an extremely important position because if the enemy decides to flank us by crossing the Chickahominy in your northern sector, you will have to repel their attack—even if the hounds of hell are let loose and you think you are being obliterated, you must retain your defenses. If they turn our right flank then any necessary movement backward by one of our middle corps' would be put into jeopardy along with all of our supply lines. These Rebel rascals are strong and outnumber us considerably. If by some slight chance they take an advantage on us it will only be because we were withheld the necessary troop strength by my antagonists in the White House and Congress. It will not be your fault. It will definitely not be my fault. I have pleaded for more troops, for the necessary strength to pull this off. No one knows like I do what it takes to go up against a desperate foe, a mama bear that's cornered with her cubs. The White House sends telegrams asking us when we will fight. *When we are ready!* And not a day before! What more do they need to know?"

McClellan looked around the room at all of his commanders and said, "It is now time for Secesh to pay for past wounds. I intend to implement this plan as soon as the weather cooperates. Does anyone have any questions?"

"What if Lee makes the first strike before we make ours?" This time it was General Franklin who asked. William B. Franklin graduated first in his class at West Point in 1843 and had been a close friend of McClellan for over 20 years.

"Remember William, I told you all the other day, I know Bobby Lee. He is cautious. We can count on him to delay until we have attacked."

Franklin looked appeased at this comment but not all the men did. McClellan looked around the room and locked eyes with each commander for a moment.

"We are the United States of America! We defeated the Mexicans! We will defeat these Rebels despite the odds!"

100.

After the Battle of Winchester, Riley McNair secured a couple of new horses and convinced Ned Harrington to join the cavalry with him. Ned was agreeable because it would mean he no longer had to carry a musket and could focus more on reconnaissance. Plus, he would not have to march anymore. The two joined up with Riley's original unit on their way toward Richmond. Colonel James Childs, the commander of the 4th Pennsylvania, was glad to see Corporal McNair again and thankful he brought along a friend. For the Peninsula Campaign, Child's cavalry unit was attached to the Third Division of Fifth Corps under Brigadier General Fitz John Porter.

Riley was happy to have two solid friendships as they bivouacked near the Chickahominy River. The first was Ned Harrington. Ned, an unlikely friend considering their casual distaste for each other in Winchester, had grown on Riley. Ned was no soldier, but he made Riley laugh and he kept him updated with the Harrington family. Riley's other friend was an excellent sharpshooter from the New York and Pennsylvania border by the name of Thomas Hans Draeger who liked to be called by his middle name because it was his grandfather's. Hans had two girlfriends back home, Chelsea and Mary, and he would write a different one each night. Riley and Ned loved to tease him about accidentally putting a letter to Chelsea in an envelope addressed to Mary.

Hans told them, "Thank you, I will no longer use their first name at the beginning of the letter, but will merely write Dear Sweetheart."

It was Thursday, June 26th. General McClellan issued orders for Porter's cavalry to be ready to perform a scouting mission that afternoon. The men had a later than usual lunch in anticipation of a late supper.

They were chewing on their meals with their haversacks next to them and lounging on the banks of the river.

"I don't suppose either of you have anything to put on my biscuit?" asked Ned.

"No, Ned," answered Hans.

"I cannot stand to eat biscuits plain. They don't taste right. Are you sure you don't have any long sweetening you could loan me?" Ned asked twisting his long neck around as was a habit of his when he was flustered. Ned would move his neck in jerks and look from side to side. The young man's dexterity with his neck would often perplex others. Riley and Hans thought he looked somewhat like a goose.

"Look, be thankful you have food. I've gone days without food in the past month," Hans said.

"Any jam?"

"Ned, too much sweet food when you're hot and miserable will give you the Virginia quick step, now quit your jawing."

Just then a member of Brigadier General George McCall's staff rode behind them and shouted, "You men there eating, it is time to get ready. I just informed your commander he is supposed to start his mission now. Be quick, General Stonewall Jackson and his army was sighted just across this river and moving this way and looking for a fight."

The three young men just about choked on their last bite of lunch. *Stonewall Jackson?* It seemed impossible. He was supposed to still be in the Shenandoah Valley. The three gathered up their belongings, ran over to their horses to mount them and join the rest of their preparing unit. *Did General McClellan know Stonewall would be here?*

"I don't like the sound of this," Riley said, turning his new horse Danny around.

Hans laughed at him. "Really, you don't like to hear that the one who decimated your army in your hometown has now followed you here and wants to make war. Who would have thought?" He said sarcastically. "These Rebels will not give up until they are beaten into oblivion. Jackson is a decisive leader and allows no room for our mistakes. My aim is to find and kill him and be the hero of this entire war. He is their most glamorous fellow."

"Have you ever met him?" Riley asked.

"Nope. Just heard stories about him."

"I would not call him glamorous. I have sat for hundreds of hours in class with him and he is anything but glamorous," Riley said matter-of-factly.

"Well, he's a little bit different now, isn't he?" Hans fired back sharply, kicking his horse lightly with his spurs.

Riley was silenced.

Ned didn't say a word throughout the exchange. He stoically put back on his kepi hat, watched the other two move quickly on ahead and hoped he would not have to fight anyone that day.

The threesome joined the rest of their unit and Colonel Childs gave them their orders and everyone moved out. Many of the soldiers were petrified. They had heard of Jackson's exploits in the Shenandoah and wondered how he had gotten down to the Chickahominy so fast. They did not want to go on a mission to see if they could find him. Riley could tell by Ned's expression he was thinking why couldn't we just let a sleeping dog lie?

Riley didn't say too much while riding through the fields north of Mechanicsville. Hans wouldn't shut up.

"Why isn't our infantry moving with us? I don't understand what we are supposed to be doing out here. If we know Jackson's Army is out here then why not just move our infantry into place and start marching toward him? With our luck our little regiment is going to run into Jeb Stuart's brigade," Hans said.

"Would you quit talking?" asked Ned.

"Why?"

"Because I don't like to hear about Jackson."

"It just doesn't make sense to me, that's all I'm trying to say."

"Me neither but I'm trying not to think about it. It makes it tough when you keep chattering away."

"All right, all right, Ned, hold your horses. No need to get redder than you already are," Hans said with a smirk.

With that comment Ned moved his horse forward to ride in front of Riley and away from Hans. Hans then started bending Riley's ear on a number of things.

Their patrol produced very little useful information for their corps commander Fitz John Porter. They had poked all the way to Pole Green Church and had not seen any of the enemy's pickets. They began to hear heavy artillery and musket shots to the south. A major encounter was happening near or in Mechanicsville. The cavalry unit returned to headquarters to see if there were new orders. Later, after dark, a squad of cavalry, not including the Pennsylvania trio, found out that Jackson's Army was near Beaver Dam Creek. Porter reported this to McClellan and the commander of the Army of the Potomac ordered Porter to withdraw back to Gaines Mills. This withdrawal was to consolidate into a new defensive position they could utilize to stop the advancing Confederates and hopefully regain the initiative.

101.

Moss had planned for this evening very carefully. He had his friend Lewis Powell spread the word that Moss was deathly sick and in no mood to talk to anyone. Moss had coordinated with Wilfred to have a horse saddled and ready in his stable. There was a part of the fence that the prisoners were not supposed to go near because it was rotten and falling apart. The guards made sure the prisoners stayed away from that area during the daytime. The far corner of the forbidden part was butted up against Lefty's stable. Lefty had told Moss, through Wilfred, that he would have an opening there with a few loose planks and if Moss would just kick in the rotten fence where Wilfred told him to, a gaping hole would appear which Moss could fit through. The horse would be waiting for him with letters for General Lee regarding a business proposition in a saddlebag. Lefty was in as much danger as Moss if he were to be caught and the papers were discovered. Moss just hoped Lefty's wife wouldn't find out about the plan.

Moss was so scared he was sweating while lying in his bed waiting for darkness. He knew he could easily be shot while charging the horse down the lane between Wilfred's house and the fence where he usually spoke to him. If he wasn't shot and killed he would probably be hanged the next morning. *My ma would definitely not approve of this,* he thought. Even with the risk of being killed that evening Moss concluded it was worth the chance at freedom.

Lewis was going with him. Lefty refused to provide two horses and went back on his suggestion about using a wagon, so Moss had to think of an alternate plan. He could not outrun the guard's pistol fire with two men on the horse. Plus, the extra rider would make it unstable and Moss would have to run the horse through some sharp turns. Lewis might easily fall off. Plus, both of them would not be allowed out of the building at night. It was only by special exception that a guard would allow a prisoner to go out past dark to use the latrine. But protocol required only one prisoner at a time was to leave the prison room. Moss finally thought of another way to bring Lewis along without drawing attention to their plan. Lewis would attempt what Moss tried the first night. Perhaps with the raucous in the back, Lewis would make it out and Moss could circle around and allow him to mount the horse. It was very risky for Lewis, but he was willing to give it a go.

Lewis came over to where Moss was lying. "It's time Moss. I am going to go get the guard for you."

"Okay Lewis. If this fails I want you to know that I have appreciated your friendship."

"Me too."

Moss began to cough loudly. Lewis stood up and walked briskly over to the door of their large room and knocked on it to get the guard's attention. Soon the door was unbolted and Lewis spoke to the guard on duty about Moss. He explained how Moss hadn't been outside to relieve himself all day because of his sickness and he smelled really bad. Moss slowly got to his feet and shuffled over to the door while they were talking. He tried to appear miserable and he was doing a good job at it. The guard agreed to take him out to the latrine, even though he was not happy at this interruption. Lewis asked if he could help Moss down the stairs and back up when he returned and the guard also agreed to that, not wanting to touch the foul-smelling, sick prisoner. The guard re-bolted the prison door and escorted the two men down the steps. When they reached the bottom of the stairs Lewis agreed to wait until Moss returned. The guard looked thankful that he did not have to argue with him about why he couldn't let them both go outside to use the latrine and nodded at Lewis to wait there.

Moss sat in the latrine awhile trying to get his nerves up. He had envisioned this moment all day as the crucial part of his plan. He would wait until the guard knocked and then Moss would open the door and attack him with everything he had. He hoped he could get back on his feet to run away after he pushed the guard into the ground. There would be a second guard waiting at the back door who would either try to shoot his pistol at him or chase him. Then more guards would pour out of the house.

Knock. Knock. Knock.

Moss took a deep breath. He stood up, pushed the door open and lunged at the unsuspecting guard. The man went down in an instant and Moss was on his feet running to the far back corner of the yard. While sprinting he heard some shouting behind him and knew he only had one chance to find the right spot and be gone. He shuffled to a stop, counted off ten paces and then kicked as hard as he could. There was more than enough room to slip through the fence and into the stable. Lefty had done a bang-up job for him. Moss heard the shouting behind him getting closer as he adjusted his eyes to the dark and walked over to the horse. He quickly untied him and led him to the half-open door of the stable. Moss mounted him inside and then catapulted the fine horse out of the stable and into the lane, just as a prison guard had found the hole Moss had crawled through.

Moss kicked the horse as hard as he could. This was the true test, he whispered. His thoughts were muddled. Before he reached the end of the lane he heard gunfire. He turned the corner and raced down the street toward the front of the old Capitol building. He turned again riding quickly and felt the breeze in his face. *Euphoria*—Moss was free and it felt wonderful. His eyes were watering. He could see the form of a man in the street in front of him and Moss hoped it was Lewis. His horse fled forward. *It is Lewis!*

Moss slowed down to a trot then stopped and helped Lewis mount the horse. Neither one said anything as Moss gave a loud giddy up. His friend had snuck out the front door without being noticed and now they were off without any idea as to which direction Virginia was. In all his planning he forgot to ask Wilfred to ask his pa which way to go. *If that don't beat the Dutch*, thought Moss as he ran his horse down the lane he hoped would take them to the Potomac.

102.

Bruce Crawford woke up in the early morning hours and could not go back to sleep. He was weary both physically and emotionally and knew his body needed rest. After he received his letter from Lucas Harrington, he couldn't stop thinking about Molly. He tried different techniques but nothing worked. Her very existence, knowing she was alive and out there somewhere, was consuming something vital inside of him. His thoughts for her were unshakeable. Molly was going to reign in his heart as either a soul mate or a forbidden and lost opportunity for the rest of his life. Not knowing where she was or how she was doing was disturbing to him. But if he found out she was truly betrothed and madly in love with another man, it would ruin him.

Besides telling him repeatedly not to take counsel of his fears, General Jackson encouraged Bruce to go to Sunday chapel services and to start reading the Bible. The commander explained to Bruce it was his faith in God that was the most important thing in his life and what sustained him through tough times. He further explained how his love even for Anna was subordinate to his love for the Master. Bruce, however, had never taken an interest in spiritual things. He had gone to Sunday School as a child, but needed a little more proof as an adult that it was necessary to be as close to God as Jackson was. It seemed a little superfluous for the life of a warrior, almost contradictory. But Jackson, of course, did not see it that way. He thought he was on a holy mission with God directing his every step. He sure prayed enough. Late at night, when all the other commanders had gone to bed and Bruce would poke his head into Jackson's tent to make sure he didn't need anything, he would find him praying. More often than not he would find General Thomas Jackson, the mighty war hero of the South, earnestly pleading with God for forgiveness of his sins, for a humble heart and for protection of all of the soldiers assigned to him. On the evening before a battle Jackson would sometimes commit the entire night to prayer.

There was an element of Jackson's faith that was appealing to Bruce. After doing all he could do and then praying about it, Jackson was at utter peace and could sleep like a baby even in the most dire circumstances. He had a clean conscience. Bruce couldn't sleep at night and often worried. Jackson would quote Scripture to no one in particular, it was like a continuing conversation he was having with God. Bruce used to laugh because early on in the war Jackson would take walks in the woods where he would spend long moments confessing and praying to God. He would have his eyes shut and occasionally bump right into a tree or be poked by a branch, sometimes cutting his face. Jackson told Bruce one day he had decided that it was okay with God for him to walk and pray with his eyes open.

Besides being emotionally tired Bruce felt ultra-fatigued physically. He had marched and ridden his steed for hundreds of miles over the last couple of weeks with very few break periods. He was usually the last one of the aides asleep and the first one awake. Bruce had always been a light sleeper and had the annoying habit that once he would awake he could not go back to sleep. This did not help him at all, especially during wartime. Some nights, like this last one, the artillery would fire off and on all night. Bruce felt almost delirious that morning yet climbed out of bed to re-stoke the fire and make some coffee. His mind kept racing and it would do no good to continue to toss and turn.

Soon, the rest of the Valley Army and Ewell's brigades were up and preparing themselves for the day of war ahead. Jonesy stopped by to speak to Bruce and see if he had heard anything regarding Henry. Henry had stayed behind in Winchester because of the wound to his leg. Bruce hadn't heard anything but reassured Jonesy none of them at headquarters expected him back before the end of July. Jonesy walked off, seeming a little disoriented by not having his best friend along for the fight. Bruce made a mental note to check on him during the day to make sure he was okay.

It was Friday, June 27th and the stakes of today's battle were incredibly high. If Commanding General Robert Edward Lee could secure a victory here and drive General George Brinton McClellan off the peninsula then perhaps the war would be over or perhaps foreign powers would help the South with trade and with fighting men. However, if McClellan was successful today and pushed Lee into Richmond, he would siege the city with the Army of Northern Virginia inside of it and eventually bring about their surrender. This would be absolutely devastating to the entire cause of the South and the war would most likely be over.

Bruce marveled at how Jackson had entered into the story of the Peninsula Campaign and McClellan's assault on Richmond. A few nights ago without telling his subordinate commanders where he was going Jackson, Major Harman, Bruce and two other aides rode over fifty miles to meet General Lee at the Widow Dabbs house where Lee had his headquarters just northeast of Richmond. Jackson met with Lee, D. Harvey Hill, Ambrose Powell Hill, and James Longstreet. These five generals planned their strategy to attack McClellan's much larger army. The complexity and sticking point to the plan was in that their enemy was more resourced, more mobile and less tired. General Lee estimated they would ultimately have close to 90,000 soldiers for the battle and they would be going up against nearly 110,000, odds that Lee didn't like—no commander would. *Except for Jackson,* thought Bruce.

However, the numbers didn't matter, suggested Lee to his commanders. The Confederate Army was battle-tested and had become a family. They did not have as many new recruits as the Union Army and the leadership in place was sound. With initiative, boldness and exploitation it might provide them an unlikely opportunity to sweep McClellan's awesome force away from Richmond. McClellan would not be expecting Lee to attack him. The generals agreed with Lee and were in one accord. After the meeting, the five tired valley officers re-travelled the 50 miles back to their encampment at Frederick's Hall. Though most of the group dozed during the journey while in their saddles, only Bruce fell off his horse, Copper Jake, a couple of times because of sleep. Not only was it embarrassing, but it was very painful.

As Bruce saddled up his horse he thought about yesterday's battle. The Union had delivered a blistering repulse to the Confederates who were led by A.P. Hill. Hill moved his men forward hoping and anticipating that Jackson would already be sweeping the Union Army off their high ground according to what Lee had laid out, but that was not the case. Jackson did not make it to his intended destination in time and did not attack on Thursday the 26th. Ambrose Powell Hill grew impatient and stormed across the Chickahominy with his division and marched them east through the village of Mechanicsville. Once through they found the Union Army in a fortified position and on high ground. Jackson had not come, the Union had not been routed, yet Hill proceeded to throw his entire division into the enemy's lanes of fire to be butchered. A. P. Hill lost over 1,500 soldiers that day and the estimate for enemy losses only 300.

Bruce finished his thoughts of yesterday's battle and kicked out the morning campfire. As the other men finished getting ready and struck camp, Bruce mounted Copper Jake. He needed to find Jackson. *Yesterday was long, but today is going to be even longer,* he thought.

103.

General George McClellan telegraphed Secretary Stanton at the War Department,

"Victory on Thursday against Secesh was complete even though against great odds. I am beginning to think that my army is invincible."

104.

General Robert E. Lee was so exasperated Friday he could barely talk. Lee, a magnificent looking officer, was known to be decisive and ingenious along with possessing a calming presence. With his silver hair giving him a distinguished look, most who met Lee walked away thinking he was the most splendid officer they had ever seen. The Confederate general had a natural ability to inspire others and have people warm up to him quickly. Children especially clung to Lee as a person of trust and friendliness. Robert E. Lee smiled warmly and gave the impression that he was a perfect gentleman. Despite his gifts of character he was also a bold and fearless warrior who, with over thirty-two years of military experience, had a good grasp on what was possible with the resources available to him. For example, Lee knew George McClellan was somewhat shy and timid in battle and if given the opportunity of being attacked or imagine he was out-numbered, McClellan might pack up, move away and plan another battle which could take six months preparation. This is what Lee was counting on. This is what Richmond needed. Lee had to take the initiative and make the Union commander believe he was being hurt badly, but this is not what had happened with the first major attack.

With his audacious offensive, Lee had actually exposed himself to a demoralizing counterattack with the prize being Richmond. Lee had two thirds of his soldiers swung to the north in order to flank the Young Napoleon's lines. This moved them away from the central part of eastern Richmond. If McClellan attacked in the center with strength, Lee would only have around 30,000 troops to try to repel him. Lee knew the risk he was taking and that is why he was furious when his commanders did not follow his carefully made plans.

Lee was agitated because he had wanted Jackson to attack on the afternoon of the 26th in order to drive the Federals east of Mechanicsville and from their entrenched high ground. This would allow A. P. Hill to attack there without being pummeled by artillery fire pointing down on them from the north. This had to be a coordinated attack of the first order or there would be great loss of life. However, Jackson did not attack that day and A. P. Hill, without orders from Lee, went ahead and attacked, thus enduring considerable casualties. Both of his subordinates had some explaining to do because their failures might have allowed McClellan to fortify his position with another corps which would easily hold against anything Lee might throw at him the next day.

But soon Lee thankfully found out George McClellan did not re-fortify to the north. At some point in the middle of the night McClellan had inexplicably changed his mind about what do with the news of Lee pushing into Porter's Fifth Corps, and the surprise of Stonewall Jackson being present in the battle on his far right flank. Lee heard from his scouts very early in the morning that Porter's Corps had struck their camp and abandoned their post. The scouts had seen great blazes of fire where large amounts of supplies were being destroyed. Lee knew this was standard operating procedure when a displaced army had supplies they could not transport quickly and did not want the enemy to obtain them. Lee was curious, however, as to what this retreat might mean. Either McClellan was giving up the fight in the north in order to sweep around to the southeast, or he was pulling back to regroup and plan for a massive Northern offensive.

General Lee rode to the front on his beautiful horse, Traveller, and met with Thomas Jackson. Lee began to feel somewhat better about the situation. He was still bitter and thwarted at what had transpired the day before, but he suddenly saw he had a new opportunity to bring harm to McClellan's imposing army. General Lee asked D. H. Hill and Jackson to continue to push to the east and south until they found the enemy position and when they did, to take it over. From earlier reports Lee knew that General A. P. Hill and General Longstreet were making progress and already engaging the enemy at Powhite Creek near Dr. Gaines's residence. *Perhaps there was still time,* thought Lee. *Perhaps yesterday's fiasco had not cost him all of the initiative and they still might have a chance.*

105.

The commander of the Army of the Potomac, General George B. McClellan, never mounted a horse in order to ride out to the front to consult with his commanders like Lee. He spent the entire day in his headquarters building miles away from the action responding to telegraphs and thinking about his future.

106.

"Move, move, move!" shouted Club while he chewed on an old cigar and hit each soldier from Delta Company on the back as they passed. There was an hour left of sunlight on Friday, June 27th and the men were about to wade through the swamp at Gaines's Mill. It was the last push forward. Stonewall Jackson had finally arrived on the battlefield and arrayed his brigades and their regiments all along the trees west of the swampland.

As Jonesy waited for his company to move ahead he could see through the tree branches the thick layer of smoke hanging all around the base of the hill to the east. He would have to march almost a mile to get to the creek bed and base of the plateau where the Union Army was entrenched. He could not make out their forms through the trees but the whole hillside seemed to be moving. *There must be tens of thousands of them shooting our direction,* Jonesy thought. *They can't miss!*

Jackson rode by Brian's column shouting at Sergeant Club Jones and whoever else would listen, "Move forward quickly! Do not stop to fire your musket! Sweep through the field and give them the bayonet!"

Jonesy caught a glimpse of Jackson as he rode by on his horse, Little Sorrel. His face was grim, his eyes were steel and he was holding up his sword while he talked. As fast as he came up and issued his directive, he disappeared again. The men all cheered as he rode off.

Jonesy scampered past Club and his father hit him on the back a little harder than the other men. Jonesy was proud of his father. Though he was ornery and would swear at the soldiers he supervised, they loved him like no other. Club was a man's man. He continued to live off the land even when times were good and most items could be purchased at the local market. Club loved fresh deer meat, turkey and duck, and even enjoyed rabbit more than most. He drank freshly squeezed milk from their dairy cow each day and he delighted in Rachel's fresh bread and the vegetables she harvested from the garden. Club told others summer was his favorite time of year because he ate like a king.

Jonesy moved past Club out from under the cover of trees and instantly he was stepping in several inches of bog water. This slowed him down and made their ordinarily straight regimental line look distorted. Now Jonesy could see to his north and south and there must have been ten or twenty thousand other soldiers doing exactly what he was doing. It looked like a massive consolidated charge that couldn't have been better even if planned, but Jonesy knew the perfect line was an accident. Each brigade had simply started out as soon as they arrived and could get organized in the woods.

He could now see what he was up against. In one or two hundred more yards he would be dodging artillery, and a quarter to a half-mile past the artillery he would be dodging a maze of bullets. Jonesy was sweating and it was dripping down the sides of his nose into his eyes. He kept moving as fast as he could. His bayonet was attached and he remembered what Stonewall shouted to the commanders. Jonesy missed Henry but he was proud to be moving across that field. He was proud of himself for taking a stand against the aggressive North trying to invade Richmond and he was proud of the fact the Stonewall Brigade had won so many battles in the valley. He was proud he had been with Jackson since the beginning.

Canister shot was whizzing through the air swiping at the men as they moved forward. Some men to his right were wounded. He could hear the cries of the wounded he was walking up on. He followed the man in front. He thought of home, of his ma, of his elementary school teacher, of Julia, of the Grey Goose Tavern, of Daniel Tanner and he kept marching. He had heard that Tanner tried to break into the Crawford home and he was working for the Union and Jonesy grew more angry. The minie balls started to fly by him making a deathly whizzing sound. More men wounded. The man to his front fell down. Jonesy bent over and kept moving, now at a jog. The noise was horrific. The sound of a ball going into the flesh of a man was a terrible thing, like a rock the size of your fist being thrown hard into soft mud.

Jonesy looked up and could see the plateau just before him. He would have to dip down a small incline, pass over a creek and then start to climb the plateau where the Yanks were entrenched. It was a terrible position to have to breach. He was wishing he was on the defense, not the offense. The plateau was thick with trees, looked about eighty feet high and had breastworks at the base of it. The cannon and musket firing coming from the small bluff was ghastly. Jonesy did not think about death and he kept running. He must have passed a third of his company on the way to this point.

Jonesy thought about Riley and Ned and wondered if they were on the plateau. He grabbed his weapon harder. He couldn't think now because the enemy was so close. The Rebel yell went up in his company. Everyone still standing let out a long, loud shriek. Jonesy raised his bayonet over his head and charged with all his might. He climbed up part of the plateau with others from his unit and made his way through two sets of breastworks. He had to step over fallen Confederate soldiers, some were friends. He kept going. The smoke was thick and lead was flying by him. He glanced up and unbelievably saw the blue coated defenders leaving their positions and running. *They were running!* He kept charging and running after them. He was at the top of the bluff now and there were no more trees. Someone yelled out that they should fire at the defenders. They stopped, took aim and fired their muskets. They could not miss. Jonesy reloaded and shot again. Others from his regiment made it up the plateau. Many were cheering. Club was there congratulating him and then he disappeared. Jonesy ran ahead with some of the others. They captured several prisoners. Some volunteered to guard them until later. Jonesy wanted to continue on and did. On the ground were some discarded regimental colors. They soon found a pocket of resisters. Jonesy was shot through his hat and coat. The Union cavalry then came charging at them, but Jonesy and the others in his unit shot their horses out from under them and took more prisoners. He thought he saw Riley on a horse. Colonel John Neff, his regimental commander, rode by him trying to organize the wild pursuit. It was loud and men were crying and dying. The momentum kept Jonesy and the others going. It was almost too dark to see who was in which army. He kept going and fired into the mass of blue coats. *At least ten thousand,* he thought. *I can't miss!*

Jonesy heard the order to stop. Time to reconsolidate. Take a breather and a drink. Help the wounded. Pick up what the Union dropped. There were new Enfield muskets, canteens, haversacks and crates of food. The men were exhilarated. Ten pound Parrot rifles were captured. Jonesy smiled, relieved. He was alive and uninjured. He did not know the importance of this plateau and why they took it. It did not matter. They had done their duty. They had overcome.

107.

Riley, Ned and Hans had a time of it. Not because of the fighting, but because they all wanted to fight—except for Ned—and were not allowed. For awhile they were running errands and scouting out enemy positions. They saw Jackson's and Ewell's men marching down the Old Cold Harbor Road and reported it to their higher command. They were to protect the far right flank of their infantry and give an account of any movements north of them. They could hear the battle and hear men dying. They desperately wanted to enter into the fight in a significant way, but they could not disobey their orders. The day ended badly for them and their entire corps. Their position on the plateau behind Powhite Creek was routed and their unit fled away. They helped out stragglers and tried to screen their army from the Confederate infantry running toward them but it was taxing.

Twice Hans was knocked off his horse and twice he remounted and kept moving. Ned stayed clear ahead of the other two, afraid of being taken prisoner like so many other Union soldiers. Riley often dismounted from Danny to help men get up and he escorted several wounded to a wagon. He took the time to help one soldier climb aboard his horse even though the Confederates were within fifty yards of his position. Thankfully the two weren't captured. Riley also cared for a few seriously wounded men and spoke the much needed words of encouragement to those who had no hope. There were no medals given out that day and no commendations for honor. For hours the infantry withstood wave after wave of the Rebel assault and for most of the day held them back and decimated them with their artillery. It was in the last few minutes before darkness, when Jackson's men were thrown into the battle, it seemed many of the tired men gave up and lost heart. Their theory was 'live to fight another day.' Riley hoped this would be just an aberration in their plans to capture Richmond. He hoped they would be able to reconnoiter to take up another position in which to continue their advance on the Southern Capitol. He did not realize a final decision had already been made at the headquarters building of the Army of the Potomac.

108.

All day long General McClellan stewed about what to do and when to do it. He never went onto the battlefield but monitored all telegrams from his headquarters at the Trent house. He continued to receive reports from General Fitz John Porter stating he needed extra men because of the increasing intensity of the Rebel attacks. McClellan responded by sending Slocum's division to him. He had four other corps at his disposal with over 80,000 soldiers between them, but McClellan felt he could only spare an 8,000 man division.

Confederate General John Magruder led a large contingent west of Old Tavern on Nine Mile Road, outside of Richmond, and was skirmishing off and on throughout the day. McClellan thought a major thrust might suddenly come from Magruder in the middle so he shouldn't shift too many troops away from his north to south line of Sumner, Heintzelman and Keyes. He sent some reinforcements from the nearest position to the north, that of William Franklin's corps, and waited on telegraphs from Porter.

Little Mac appreciated the initially positive reports from Porter in the early afternoon and hoped his friend would remain content with the extra division. Porter, however, asked for even more troops so he could mount a counterattack, but McClellan had to turn him down. His strategy, which everyone had agreed to, didn't call for shifting too many units away from the middle. *We dare not open the chance of being overrun,* McClellan mumbled to himself.

McClellan overheard an aide say something about him being mentally paralyzed, but he didn't have the energy to correct him just then. He overheard another whisper something about him being "a brilliant self-promoter yet unable to make decision." *I will deal with them later. I have a war to run.*

When the battle escalated and Porter became utterly desperate and concerned for his own survival, McClellan asked his other corps commanders how they were faring. He presumed the answer he received, none of them could spare any men. McClellan saw the entire battlefield in his mind. *We are far too outnumbered.*

George McClellan issued a final telegraph to his friend Porter, "*Hold your own. You must beat them with what you have.*"

The young commander knew he had to finally make up his mind when General Sumner reported back to headquarters that it looked like Lee's troops were ready to attack him from Richmond. McClellan debated with himself another instant as to whether to travel out to Sumner's position to see for himself, but then decided he should stay in the rear where he could oversee the sinking of the ship. *We are doomed,* he thought. *But it is not my fault.*

109.

There was an eerie stillness at the Trent House that evening. The tents were taken down, the equipment was moved out, and the supplies they couldn't move were added to a large bonfire in the middle of the yard. This was the largest army that had ever walked on North America and its commander, George McClellan, sat for hours on a stump staring at the large fire and watched the flames lick up the new wood thrust onto it. The Young Napoleon appeared to others to be in a stupor. He issued an order for Erasmus Keyes to retreat his two divisions and move backward towards the James River. Porter wanted Keyes' men for reinforcements, but McClellan thought it was no use. The final decision had been made and time had now come to telegraph Washington. The Peninsula Campaign was concluding.

The fury in the mind of the former railroad president grew while watching the flames rise higher and higher in the sky. As McClellan began to dictate his telegram to the clerk he seemed in torment like a child in a maze who could not find the exit. Finally the words came together,

"I now know the full history of the day. I have lost this battle because my force was too small. I again repeat, I am not responsible for this. The government has not sustained this army. The president is wrong in regarding me as ungenerous when I said my force is too weak. I merely intimated a truth which today has been too painfully proved. Finally, if I save this army now, I tell you plainly I owe no thanks to you or to any other persons in Washington. You have done your best to sacrifice this army."

As he concluded his telegraph, he knew he was accusing his own government of treason, but he didn't care. McClellan sat back on his stump and continued to be mesmerized by the fire.

110.

As the evening sky was darkening, Bruce reported to Jackson that Colonel Neff of the 33rd Virginia had a substantial number of his regiment killed as they made their way toward the Union breastworks. Jackson told Bruce he wanted to find and congratulate him and his unit for their bravery. On their way to find Neff, they ran into the leader of the Texas troops, General John B. Hood, who was attached to Jackson under Whiting's division. Hood's men had been the first to cross the field while over fifty cannon fired at them. They were the tip of the spear and the first to break over the entrenchments of Porter's Fifth Corps. Jackson told Hood, "The men who carried this position are soldiers indeed!"

Bruce received a message from their cavalry chief, Tom Munford, that Conrad Montgomery was taken captive during one of their skirmishes with the Union cavalry. He had been slapped broadside by a sword and knocked off his horse. Before the Confederates could return to reclaim him, he was placed on a Union horse and led away to a place of entrenched Federal infantry. As Munford described it to Bruce, this was a psychological blow to the entire unit losing the Mexican War hero. Bruce felt it was a blow to him, as well. He had known Conrad ever since his first memories.

Later, while Jackson was riding forward on Little Sorrel with Bruce next to him on Copper Jake, they found themselves suddenly surrounded by approximately twenty Federal soldiers. Though the Federals had them outnumbered and outgunned, Jackson yelled at them all in a fierce, authoritative voice, "I demand your immediate surrender!" and the young Union soldiers laid down their arms and were marched by Bruce back to the rear.

Before bedding down for the evening, Bruce had to try and tally up the casualty count for Jackson. He reported that in their three divisions they had approximately 300 killed and 1500 wounded. This grieved his commander. Bruce noticed Jackson closed his eyes in prayer even before he dismounted his horse for the evening. He raised his head toward heaven and communed with his God, no doubt thanking him for another victory and praying for the families of those taken.

When Bruce finally closed his eyes to sleep that evening he realized he hadn't thought of Molly once since daybreak.

111.

In the days leading up to the Battle for Richmond, President Abraham Lincoln, the Ancient, worried ceaselessly. He could not sleep. He could not eat. He was losing weight. He physically felt the intensity and stress many of the soldiers on the field of battle were experiencing. His wife, Mary, was deeply concerned for him and tried to encourage him to eat at mealtimes but he could not.

When the telegraph came to him, early in the morning on June 28th, President Lincoln felt sucker-punched in the gut. The Union losses were stunning. Almost 900 soldiers killed during the one day battle at Gaines's Mill and another 6,000 wounded or missing. He was mortified for the American people. He was thoroughly disappointed. Lincoln, retired General Winfield Scott and Secretary Stanton knew approximately how many soldiers the Young Napoleon had at his disposal and how he greatly overpowered even the highest estimates of what General Lee might possess. *There is no reason why McClellan should give up so soon,* Lincoln thought. He seemed a competent, albeit slow, general who could make things happen. But with this telegram the Ancient was ashamed for him. Lincoln resolved to take full responsibility for what happened and place it all on his shoulders. He would painfully tell Congress and the public what had happened. He would cautiously remind McClellan of his strength and encourage him to attack before he left the peninsula. *In the meantime, I will look for another general who can fight in this war and be victorious. The American people deserve a victory. The slavery issue can wait no longer.*

112.

General Lee was disgusted with the slowness of the attack at Gaines's Mill. He knew if there were better coordination and movement, the plateau behind the Mill could have been overrun. A more devastating defeat to the enemy might have been accomplished. *We need to deliver a death blow to McClellan, not just bruise him,* he thought. However, Lee was happy for the victory, no matter how limited. He worked hard the next few hours trying to discover what General McClellan might be planning. He could not tell if he was repositioning himself to continue his conquest of Richmond or if he was fleeing the area completely and heading for the James River. Saturday the 28th had very little activity and the Confederate Army had to play a waiting game until the Federals revealed what they were going to do. Meanwhile, there were massive burying operations for the dead and transporting the wounded west into Richmond for those needing a hospital. The total casualty count for the Confederates was almost 1,500 killed and over 6,000 wounded. Surgeons worked on patients and performed amputations throughout the hot summer day. The cries of agony and pain broke Lee's heart, but it could not be helped. *There would be more crying before it was all over,* he thought.

Robert Lee found out a crucial piece of information later in the day from Jeb Stuart. The York River Railroad was undefended and the major bridges leading toward the James River were destroyed. Lee believed this had to mean McClellan was giving up any notion of positioning his troops again where they used to be. The tall cloud-like images of black smoke toward the east and south confirmed to Lee supplies were being burned before the anticipated Confederate pursuit. *McClellan must be leaving,* decided Lee.

Sunday, June 29th, 1862 was filled with more disappointment for Robert Lee. General John Magruder and General Jackson failed to move forward to attack the rear of the enemy as Lee had ordered. Magruder did not engage the enemy until after 5 p.m. and the fighting was nominal and non-conclusive. Lee scolded Magruder and said the attack upon those retreating must be vigorous in order to reap the fruit of victory—there was no time for delay. Jackson did not please Lee either because he delayed and did not cross the Chickahominy River until after 2:00 a.m. the following morning. He was supposed to join forces with Magruder the day before and post a unified attack.

Monday, June 30th brought lightning in the distance. Lee had an incredible opportunity fall in his lap that morning. While looking at a map of the area, Lee realized that McClellan's forces could be easily divided by a large attack at a choke point. All of the roads heading toward the James River converged on one little town called Glendale. This gave Lee an idea. *What if James Longstreet and A. P. Hill were to attack at Glendale before all of McClellan's forces passed through that point, while at the same time, Jackson was to attack McClellan's rear guard at White Oak Swamp north of Glendale?* Lee wondered. His mind began to see how coordinated attacks might be possible. Lee reasoned that if the attacks would occur simultaneously there could be drastic consequences for the Federals.

Unfortunately for Lee his plans did not go according to how he saw the maneuvers in his mind. He had assigned Major General Benjamin Huger to open an attack on Glendale because his division was the closest one to it. Huger, however, was too cautious and let the Union Army slip past him, through the swamp, through the town and on to Malvern Hill, a high piece of terrain being readied by the Yankees to be used for a strong defense. Jackson also came up short that day because he did not attack the tail of McClellan's Army with infantry when he fell upon them. Jackson found them at White Oak Bridge with a heavy defensive position. He chose to fight them only with artillery for hours and searched for another way through the swamp. This caused him considerable delay and allowed Glendale to be reinforced by the Federals. Lee was furious.

Finally, before the day's end, General Lee ordered Longstreet to hastily attack the Federal forces still passing through Glendale with everything he had. Longstreet obeyed and launched a total offensive attack at the retreating column of Federals. He could see them making their way down the Quaker Road to the fortified position at Malvern Hill and he tried to prevent this movement as fast as possible. Longstreet attacked the Union retreat at a two-mile arc that was both north and south of Glendale. The force in front of him was Brigadier General George H. McCall's men from Porter's Fifth Corps. McCall was flanked by Joseph Hooker to the south and several divisions led by Slocum, Kearney and Sedgewick to the north. The Union position, though still moving, had quite a bit of strength and depth. The point of Longstreet's spear included Brigadier General James Kemper, Colonel Micah Jenkins and Brigadier General Cadmus Wilcox with his Alabamans. These leaders led their men into a hell of a fight.

The Battle of Glendale was bloody and inconclusive. Every time the Confederates would break through the Union line, the gap was quickly filled with reserves from behind. At night the Union line was broken by a daring charge with bayonets. Hand to hand combat lasted for awhile in the woods until it became impossible to see who you were actually fighting. Men yelled like savages trying to spear each other to death in the dark. While the killers left their opponents to die, the forsaken wounded wept or screamed for help. These horrid memories would haunt the brave men for months. With the lull of enemy movement in the darkness, the Union Army pushed more men into their yawning hole made by the Rebel charge and closed off the gap. The ghoulish swamp-fight finally concluded. Confederates had over 630 dead and 2,800 wounded and the Union Army had 297 dead and 1,700 wounded.

The cries of the wounded for water and aid grew louder as the night matured. Troops on both sides scurried here and there with lamps trying to collect their wounded. It seemed there was pain, agony and death behind every dark tree. For the commanders of the Confederate infantry west of Glendale, it was a terribly sad night. They realized the wretched sounds in the woods were their men slowly dying. They realized their wonderful battle plans drawn in the morning brought them only emptiness and heartache that night.

113.

George McClellan was not at the Battle of Glendale on the sixth day of the war. He was five miles away on the James River on the gunboat Galena, having a meal with china and silverware. He told himself his men would appreciate why he couldn't be with them while they played catch-up to reach his headquarters (now located on the river at Haxall's Landing). They would understand his need of a little comfort after the terrible ordeal he suffered with the defeat at Gaines's Mill and the end of his Campaign. The men would understand he was where he needed to be.

As he sat there and drank a glass of wine, being careful not to spill any on the white tablecloth or his starched uniform, he thought of his wife, his political aspirations, and his legacy. Politics would have to be placed on hold a little while longer now that Richmond wasn't captured. Perhaps Lincoln would grant him once again the status of General-in-Chief of all the U.S. forces as he once had when he took over from Winfield Scott. Perhaps he could end this war diplomatically without firing another shot after he left the peninsula. McClellan made a mental note to write Lincoln about being supreme commander.

While enjoying his time on the Galena, McClellan composed a telegram to be sent to Washington.

"We have just finished another day of desperate fighting. Though hard-pressed by far superior numbers, we have performed admirably. I shall do my best to save the army but it will not be easy."

114.

The last and seventh day of the battle east of Richmond was on Tuesday, July 1st. The location was Malvern Hill. Malvern Hill was less than a mile from the James River and had a plateau at the top that looked from the naked eye not to be a plateau at all, but just a simple slight rise to the normally flat terrain. The field before it lacked the trees that the Gaines's Mill plateau had. Before the battle, General Robert E. Lee, Commander of the Army of Northern Virginia, met with his generals to consult about the war. The artillery started in the afternoon and then, because of some more delays which were all too common that week, the fighting of infantry did not begin until late afternoon. Lewis Addison Armistead, John Bankhead Magruder and D. H. Hill commanded the Confederate troops into battle against the heavily fortified Union stronghold. The entire Army of the Potomac of over 90,000 soldiers were solidly entrenched on that hill. The operation for the Confederates was doomed from the start. Lewis Armistead led the assault, but it was soon obvious there was absolutely no hope for success. The casualties quickly escalated until nightfall and the result for the Confederacy was 870 dead, 4,200 wounded and over 500 missing. Federal losses were a little over 300 killed, 1,900 wounded and over 800 missing.

Lee pondered the situation carefully at the close of the day. The Southern Army attacked against a fortified and entrenched army of vastly superior numbers. Plus, the Union men had nowhere to escape. They were desperate, like cornered animals. They had the James River to their back. Therefore they had to repulse the Confederate attack because there simply was not another option. Lee realized later he should have chosen a different strategy because the result was butchery.

D. H. Hill wrote later, "This was not war—it was murder."

115.

Kathryn Montgomery had a dream that night. She was driving in a buggy and Henry was in front sitting next to her and steering the team. In the back of the carriage was Molly and Jonesy. Their carriage was storming down a hill out of control. Kathryn and Molly were screaming. The two boys were scared. The buggy came to the bottom of the hill, left the road and went over a small cliff into a roaring river, horses and all. Kathryn was the first one to swim to the surface and look for the others while moving in the swift current. Molly surfaced downstream and then Jonesy gasping hard and trying to catch his breath. Kathryn was scared, afraid Henry had drowned. Finally, Henry came up out of the water and Kathryn was thankful. Then she awoke. There was a thunder and lightning storm outside and the wind was hitting the house furiously. She heard a loud clap of thunder and heard the cracking sound of a lightning bolt hitting a distant tree.

She knew her mind was playing tricks on her because Henry had left that day to return to the Confederate Army and fight with Jackson, Bruce and Jonesy. Also on her mind was that her father, Conrad, was taken prisoner and they had just heard the news the day before. She went back to bed but couldn't sleep because of the storm and worrying about Henry and her father. The next day after breakfast, Kathryn walked from town to her farm house and then hiked down the trail, back to her creek and the boy's stone wall. What she saw made her very sad. Two of the large willow trees inside the stone wall had been struck by lightning. They were cracked and broken apart. Shreds of wood were everywhere. With two of the seven weeping willow trees now gone only five trees remained within the stone wall.

116.

Debates and deliberations went on for two days at the Lee headquarters as to how far to pursue the Federals. McClellan had advanced southward, along the James River to Harrison's Landing and Berkeley Plantation, which was originally called Berkeley Hundred by its first English settlers. The troops were weary and bogged down in the mud as they tried to advance after the Union. The rain did not help. Jackson pleaded with Lee to relentlessly pursue McClellan in order to overtake and destroy him. Lee, Longstreet and President Jefferson Davis felt this was impractical because of the head start McClellan already possessed. The Confederate wounded also played on the minds of their leaders. For days the horrific smell of death and cries of agony were heard throughout the camp and lasted all night. For an entire week the casualties were transported back to Richmond in a continual stream. Finally, with McClellan having moved his army farther from Richmond and the Southern leaders hearing how he was quickly emplacing strong defenses out of fear of Lee's pursuit, the decision was made by Lee to return to Richmond and formulate a new strategy in which to try to conquer his foe.

The Peninsula Campaign came to an end. Lee's courageous attacks thwarted McClellan and won the battle for the South. But Lee wasn't happy with the results. McClellan's Army wasn't destroyed, only delayed, and the cost was high. During the seven days of battle 1,730 Union soldiers were killed, 8,060 were wounded and over 6,000 were missing. For the Confederate Army, 3,500 were killed, 15,750 were wounded and almost 1,000 were captured or missing. Over two hundred thousand men battled against each other that week and the scenery east of Richmond permanently changed. The South rejoiced because McClellan was driven away. The citizens of the Northern states were frustrated and bemoaned the outcome realizing the horrible war between the states would continue indefinitely.

117.

I can never forgive them, God. I will never! They have injured me and others too much. I cannot love them and turn the other cheek. They have taken my purity, they have taken my dreams. I am ruined. Where are you God? Molly's thoughts were frantic and racing. The house of her heart was burning down and there was no one there to put out the flames. She had just experienced another episode with Major Welch. Words couldn't describe how she now felt about him. She had long since passed feelings of despise for the man. There was pure evil in every move of his lips, his coarse fingers and the rest of his body. He was a blasphemer and a deceiver.

"The reprobate!" Molly exclaimed out loud in the darkness.

Molly had spent the last month as a prisoner at Harpers Ferry since Welch had brought her there following the battle at Winchester. Her clothes were rags and her bed was hard. She lived on the second story of an old home being used as a type of prison. She stayed in her own room, but there were other women in adjacent rooms she would see daily when she had to use the latrine or was given permission to be outside. She did not get to know any of them very well because Welch kept her, as his special prisoner, away from them in isolation and she was scolded when seen talking to one of them. She could see in their faces, however, the same shame and misfortune Molly was experiencing. She knew a few of the women voluntarily stayed at Harpers Ferry, but the ones in Molly's building were in custody against their will for supposed crimes against the government. Sometimes the faces would change when the charges were dropped or new ones were brought in, but the feelings of despair were constant. Molly was being detained on spy charges and her way of verbally handling her situation the first few days there only led to being physically abused and isolated by Welch and Tanner. Toad and the Children were there also, but Welch forbade them from touching her. She was *his* prize. It was unbearable but it was her life and she could do nothing to improve it.

This is an endless hell!

Like a deafening noise to the ears or a blinding light to the eyes, Molly's essence was being violated but there was no one there to hear her soul scream for justice.

118.

Bruce and Stonewall Jackson were allowed to retreat back toward Richmond for a time to regroup and give their men some much needed rest and inactivity. Nearly half of Jackson's command were either dead, sick or wounded. They needed to reconsolidate, rest and refocus. Robert E. Lee chose General James Longstreet and General Thomas Jackson as his principal lieutenants with whom to discuss strategy. They needed a few days to find out what the next Union strategy would be and decide how they should confront it.

Bruce was walking through the bivouac area with a biscuit in his hand and a banana in his coat pocket. The women of Richmond reminded him of the women back home in their generosity and support for the soldiers. The women had spent countless hours beside the bedsides of the wounded. And for the living they invited them into their homes and supplied them with fruit and other food, as much as they could indulge. Jackson had issued orders for men not to leave the campsite, but even the strict, former schoolmaster was loose in demanding it be severely obeyed. Bruce had gone into town on an errand and was now returning to check in with his boss.

When Bruce entered into Jackson's command tent (perched in the front yard of a large estate) it took him a moment to understand what was going on. Jackson was not inside but there were several people, mostly aides, standing around Jackson's field desk talking. They all turned as Bruce came in. One of them had extremely long hair, an unkempt beard and familiar eyes. Bruce saw the smiles on the other men's faces and then it hit him hard that standing before him was his brother Moss. Bruce stepped forward and embraced his brother who was now much lighter and was the owner of a sunken face. They grabbed each other with both hands on the shoulder as they had done many times before and stared into each other's eyes.

"Welcome back, brother," Bruce said with gusto.

Moss just nodded with a grin on his face.

Bruce hugged him and noticed another man next to Moss who had an unkempt beard and also looked undernourished.

"Who is this?" Bruce asked.

"This is Lewis Powell, he is a friend of mine from a Florida regiment," Moss shared.

Bruce looked at both men objectively for a moment, the elation subsiding in his heart. "Have you seen father yet?" he asked.

"No, that is my next stop. I have to talk to Jackson first," Moss said.

Things began to click together in Bruce's mind. He was keenly aware that Lewis was studying him intently. He wondered as to what circumstances these two weaklings could have escaped a Union prison camp.

"How did you get out of the prisoner of war camp?" Bruce asked gravely.

Moss grinned a little bit before saying anything and this struck Bruce as suspicious.

"I'm serious, Moss, I want to know. They don't just let their prisoners walk out of the camp. What happened?"

"It's a long story," Moss started to say.

"Tell it to me, now!" Bruce said.

"I'm transporting a message—"

"For who?"

"For Jackson," Moss answered.

"Why, what have you done?"

"Nothing, Bruce, calm down! It has to do with our government."

Bruce then acted instinctively. Afraid of allowing himself and his beloved commander from being betrayed, he overreacted. Bruce pushed Moss against a tent pole and held him against it. *His little brother Moss couldn't have executed a complex plan of escape!* "What did you two do? How could you escape? Did you make a deal with them? Have you become a spy for them?" With his last question Bruce was yelling. Moss wasn't making sense or answering his questions to his satisfaction.

"Bruce, I have a letter for Jackson and Lee from a businessman!" Moss pleaded with his older brother. Bruce had his fist cocked backward, seemingly about to batter Moss's hairy face with it.

"A businessman?" Bruce asked without letting down his guard.

Then Moss said the wrong thing. "It is about our leaders making a deal with a Northern businessman named Lefty….."

Lefty! Bruce lost control at that point, so disappointed and believing his brother had somehow sold out to the Union guards. He knew how they played mind tricks on prisoners and convinced them they would be doing their country a favor by helping the Union. He knew about the blackmailing, the lying and the torture tactics which could be used during war. Moss sounded confused and maybe delirious. He believed his brother was naïve and in a moment of weakness had agreed to a seemingly innocent task which would somehow help the Confederacy. His mind was reeling. Without fully understanding why, Bruce pushed his brother sideways, knocking him over a stool and Moss fell to the ground.

"How could you do it? You were only gone for a few months. How could you?" Bruce raised his boot back to kick him when Sandie Pendleton, Jedediah Hotchkiss and another of Jackson's aides grabbed the older Crawford to restrain him. Lewis Powell stood by, intrigued by the whole episode.

Moss was trying to speak but he could not get his words out. He began to choke. He was in pain. The entire tent was a flurry of activity as more people hearing the commotion from outside wandered inside to see what was going on. They were surprised to see Moss Crawford had returned and Bruce, one of Jackson's favorite lieutenants, was being restrained.

"What is going on?" someone asked. He was a captain and the senior ranking officer in the room. No one said anything.

Bruce had his head down in shame for his family. He was convinced Moss had become a traitor.

No one moved for a moment and Moss caught his breath.

"It's all my fault, sir," Moss said at last.

"What is your fault, son?"

"I have not explained myself well," Moss replied.

"What do you mean?" the captain asked.

"My friend and I were held captive as prisoners of war by the Federals at the old Capitol building in Washington the last four months. We made an arrangement with a businessman who helped us to escape if we would deliver a message to General Jackson and General Lee. We did not broker any deal with the Union but my hot-headed brother here believes I am now a spy."

"How did you have access to talk to a businessman, a seemingly honest broker, while in prison? You did not suspect it might have been a set up by the Union Army?" Bruce asked.

"No, I'm sure it wasn't," Moss answered curtly.

"How can you be so sure?" The two brothers were now talking as if nobody else was in the room.

"Because there was an innocent little boy involved named Wilfred who coordinated for his pa to talk to me through a fence during our outdoor breaks. Besides, in all of your negative speculations about my character did it ever occur to you the Union would have nothing to gain by me being allowed to go free because I was a spy? Why wouldn't I just leave their camp and re-join ours."

"Because, you would be hunted and hung without a trial if ever caught. They would search for you ruthlessly until they found you and then you would hang on the nearest tree."

"And how would that be different from what will happen when they find someone who has escaped from one of their prison camps?"

Silence.

Bruce choked a little and rubbed his eyes, for a moment wondering if he was in one of his vivid dreams. He asked Moss, "So you are telling us the straight and narrow truth? You have not bent your knee to the Yankee flag and brokered a deal to gain your freedom?"

Moss rose to his feet, turned around and then lifted up his shirt. All standing in the tent gasped. His back had a handful of bright pink scars in a circular shape along with some horizontal whipping scars.

Bruce rose to his feet and asked, "What is it, Moss?"

"This is what they do to prisoners who don't play nice and try to escape. The Union Army doesn't officially do it, but there are thugs who hang around the prison and receive a sanction to torture. A blind eye is turned on them as they do the secret will of the army."

"So, you tried to escape before?" Bruce asked unmoving.

"Yes. The night I arrived at our prison. I figured their guard would not be up yet and they would be as exhausted as we were. I tried to sneak down the stairs and out the front door, but they caught me and handed me over to some local thugs for punishment. The circles are from the end of a cigar." Moss then looked intently into Bruce's eyes. "I will never, ever serve the Union cause. You would know that if you knew me better. I will only bend my knee to Dixie, Jeff Davis, our new chief Bobby Lee, and of course, to Stonewall."

Compassion formed in Bruce's eyes as he rushed forward and embraced his brother. He held him tight and said he was sorry for doubting him.

As they stood there embracing, off to the side, Moss's friend Lewis fidgeted a little and said in his swamp accent, "I woulda' told you that your brother is as straight as an arrow but nobody asked me. You don't need to worry 'bout him. He is crazy for the South."

Bruce did not look at Lewis but he chuckled to himself, proud to have a brother faithful to the cause. "You tried to escape out the front door? That's idiotic."

Bruce also scolded himself at his own rashness and impatience by forming a verdict without all the facts. *Stonewall was right about me, I am too impatient and untested,* Bruce thought about himself.

"Come on," Bruce said to Moss. "I want to take you to see father."

119.

Yes we'll rally around the flag, boys, we'll rally once again
Shouting the battle cry of freedom,
We will rally from the hillside, we'll gather from the plain
Shouting the battle cry of freedom!

The Union forever! Hurrah, boys, hurrah!
Down with the traitor, up with the star,
While we rally around the flag, boys, rally once again,
Shouting the battle cry of freedom!

Secretary of War Edwin M. Stanton was running east on Pennsylvania Avenue heading for the Capitol building and he could hear the inspiring new war anthem called "The Battle Cry of Freedom" playing as he hurried. It was a special meeting on the Capitol steps and President Lincoln and his Cabinet were to be available to address the crowd on the growing unrest over the war. *Lincoln might say something about me,* thought Stanton. *Oh, how I want to be there.*

Edwin Stanton was running and nervous because unimaginably, in the three weeks since the battles by Richmond it was Stanton, not McClellan who became the scapegoat. With every great disaster there had to be a scapegoat, and the Peninsula Campaign was the greatest, most expensive blunder the American people could ever remember. They were bloodthirsty to tie the blame on someone's name, and despicably the name heard more often than not for the fault of the lost campaign was Edwin Stanton. General McClellan had done everything he could to accuse Stanton of denying him needed troops. He singled out Stanton both publicly and privately as the one agent who caused the disaster because when faced with a superior force McClellan was told to 'go at it with what you've already been given.'

We are springing to the call of our brothers gone before
Shouting the battle cry of Freedom!
And we'll fill our vacant ranks with a million freemen more
Shouting the battle cry of Freedom!

The Union forever! Hurrah, boys, hurrah!
Down with the traitor, up with the star,
While we rally around the flag, boys, rally once again,
Shouting the battle cry of freedom!

Oh, why did I have to be late today. I hope I don't miss it all, thought Stanton as he continued his way past mobs of people also heading to the Capitol. He liked the song he was hearing. It was upbeat, triumphant, and just the tonic the Union Army needed in order to prepare to go into battle again. Stanton couldn't help thinking about the vitriol of McClellan and how it was now directed at himself. The commander's stories were so passionate most members of Congress and the major newspapers not only sided with McClellan, but called repeatedly for Stanton's resignation. It did not help matters that nearly every day hundreds of wounded soldiers from the Peninsula Campaign would arrive by steamer to the Sixth Street Wharf and make their way to hospitals in Washington. This was a constant, visible reminder of the brutal setback for the country.

Stanton maneuvered through people standing in clumps and listening to the military band continue its selection. Most were under shade trees because it was a stifling hot day. What really hurt Stanton, besides the vociferous attacks in Congress, was that George McClellan had been a friend. Stanton alone was his ambassador to the President's Cabinet. Stanton didn't agree with everything the general did, but he stood behind him and supplied him with whatever he could because he knew that to cut down the head general would be to undermine the entire War Department. That's why it hurt when Stanton found out McClellan was comparing him with Judas and told others, "If Stanton had lived during the time of the Savior, Judas Iscariot would have remained a respected member of the fraternity of the Apostles."

Stanton had been called a traitor for repeatedly withholding necessary troops from McClellan. He had been called a scoundrel. He was now thought of as treacherous. *Do I really deserve this?*

We will welcome to our numbers the loyal, true and brave
Shouting the battle cry of Freedom!
And although he may be poor, not a man shall be called slave
Shouting the battle cry of Freedom!

The Union forever! Hurrah, boys, hurrah!
Down with the traitor, up with the star,
While we rally around the flag, boys, rally once again,
Shouting the battle cry of freedom!

Stanton was almost to the steps of the Capitol now. He pondered whether he should boldly march right up them and join the President and Secretary Chase already sitting there. He thought of President Lincoln and how he had responded these past few weeks. He had been splendid. Never blaming, never looking down on him or agreeing with the press. Never once suggesting he was looking for a new War Secretary. Honest Abe was so far sticking by him. Stanton did not know what was going to be said at the meeting today, but he hoped Lincoln would not change direction and make a big announcement about replacing the Secretary of War. Still, he would be justified if he did, thought Stanton.

The Cabinet had actually worked well together since the peninsula fiasco. They were closer now. Secretary Seward devised a plan to talk to the Union governors and ask them to initiate and appeal to Lincoln for the raising up of more troops so the government would not look as desperate. The plan worked and Lincoln was able to issue a call for the North to bring 300,000 more into the armed forces. And, at the behest of Seward, Stanton found a way to insure each new recruit was awarded an advance of twenty-five dollars. President Lincoln also named a new General-in-Chief a few days ago and it was not McClellan. It was Major General Henry W. Halleck, also known as "Old Brains." When Lincoln brought Halleck from the Western theater where he was serving with Ulysses Grant and gave him control of the Union Army in its entirety, the President censured McClellan, and not Stanton, because everyone knew this was a post the Young Napoleon was politicking to have again. Little Mac had actually given the President a written summary of how he thought the President should govern the nation and how the new General-in-Chief should lead if they truly wanted to win the war. Lincoln displayed little interest in McClellan's thoughts.

So we're springing to the call from the East and from the West
Shouting the battle cry of Freedom!
And we'll hurl the rebel crew from the land we love best
Shouting the battle cry of Freedom!

The Union forever! Hurrah, boys, hurrah!
Down with the traitor, up with the star,
While we rally around the flag, boys, rally once again,
Shouting the battle cry of freedom!

The band finished. A speaker addressed the crowd. Stanton hesitated and decided not to ascend the Capitol steps to join the President. People around him were starting to recognize him. Some were not happy, others were smiling. Stanton saw a small boy and his throat suddenly felt dry as a cracked desert creek bed. His one-year- old son, James, had passed away a few days ago and the funeral was still very much on his mind. James died by contracting smallpox from an inoculation. Stanton had cherished the boy and the weight of his death seemed almost too much to bear with so much going on at work. The President helped him through the week, having himself recently losing a son, and it seemed he knew what to say and what not to say. Stanton, though not a fan of Lincoln initially, was growing in admiration of the tall, thin storyteller from Illinois.

The people were applauding. The Treasury Registrar Lucius Chittenden was now speaking. Stanton used the paper in his right hand to fan himself. It was a little past one o'clock and with his jog on Pennsylvania Avenue Stanton was perspiring heavily. He realized part of it might be from nerves. *What was the man speaking about?* Stanton couldn't focus his thoughts. The Registrar sat down and the crowd grew quiet. All of a sudden Abraham Lincoln took to the podium and looked out over the crowd. Stanton knew the fate of his service to the United States of America was hanging in the balance. *What would Lincoln say? Would he address the Peninsula Campaign and the anger marshaled toward Stanton?* Stanton looked down at the step he stood on, wondered what laborer helped to construct it, and fretted until he heard the firm voice of his President.

"I believe there is no precedent for my appearing before you on this occasion, but it is also true there is no precedent for you being here yourselves." There was a ripple of laughter throughout the massive crowd sprawled out for over a hundred yards in all directions in front of the Capitol. Stanton smiled at Lincoln's jovial beginning. Stanton's mind wandered a moment, it seemed as Lincoln continued he was rambling but as usual he wasn't. He was dead on and brought everyone back with skilled precision to his next point. "Another person has been blamed by the press, the Congress, the citizenry and even some in our army for the failure of the campaign to seize the Confederate Capitol." Stanton perked up his ears and stared right into Lincoln's solemn face. "But let me make myself clear here and now, there is not a person on the face of this earth who deserves to be blamed for what I did myself!"

What did he just say?

The crowd was stone silent.

"Our hard-working Secretary of War, Edwin Stanton, did not hold back troops from General McClellan. Every possible soldier available had been given to the commander in order to accomplish his mission. The Secretary of War is not to blame for not giving when he had none to give. I believe he is a brave and able man, and I stand here as justice requires me to do, to take upon myself what has been charged on the Secretary of War. If you have to blame someone then blame me. I cannot imagine a finer individual to be leading our War Department during this war and I am resolute in my decision to stand by him."

Could he have really said what I thought he just said, Stanton wondered. A smile began to sweep his face as people cheered the President's words and applauded. *The people are cheering!* Stanton was encouraged. More than encouraged, he was jubilant. For the first time in a long time Stanton felt that he could breathe easier. A weight had been lifted off of him. *People were shouting and applauding what Lincoln has just said about me! He took all the blame! What a man the President is, what a man!*

120.

The Visitor knew he could only take one major risk with General McClellan. He had been supplying false reports and cautiously listening nearby the headquarters tent as often as possible to see what Young Napoleon was up to. It was a dangerous game he was playing of cat and mouse all through the Richmond battles back in June. Another spy was caught during the summer and they hanged him after a short trial. The Visitor almost thought of giving it up at that point, but he believed in his mission and felt he could still do some good. It was evident from the start of the war that technology and spying abilities lay unquestionably in favor of the Union. That is why the Confederacy desperately needed him. His job could not rely on reconnaissance balloons, photography and telegraph manipulation. He was also not an agent in a high-level government position. He was simply the eyes and ears of Bobby Lee that summer in the Union rear area.

It was his best performance of subtlety. The Visitor had carefully made out some sensitive-looking dispatches on weathered paper. It compiled numbers of troops and regimental numbers for the Southern military. The papers he created looked authentic. They explained how the Southern forces were pouring into Richmond to reinforce it. He identified a mid-level officer on the general's staff who was craving promotion and notoriety. He approached him and requested the officer do him a favor. Since the Visitor was supposedly in a rush to find his commander in the field and give reports to him from headquarters, he wondered if the person could look over the documents a member of his staff found on a Southern prisoner of war to see if they had any useful information in them. If so, he asked the officer to please pass them up his chain of command. The plan was that by the time the documents reached McClellan, the Visitor would be gone and the staff officer he handed them to would be eager to take credit for finding them himself. He knew this could only work once per commander, and this was his shot at McClellan.

The Visitor paid attention to every detail and his delivery to a Union captain was flawless. As he rushed away to find Torch he saw the captain out of the corner of his eye opening the handbag, quickly examine the documents and then run toward the command tent. The Visitor knew the documents alone would not be enough information to change McClellan's planning. However, it could supplement another report McClellan might have from the Pinkerton Agency or the press, and the general could creatively fill in the gaps. When an idea was conceived in George McClellan's mind it soon became gospel truth for him and his army. Robert Lee told the Visitor McClellan assumed there were always greater numbers of Confederate forces opposing him. Together they plotted how to capitalize on this weakness. The Visitor's papers would verify more Southern troops as fact and the rest was up to McClellan.

121.

General George McClellan learned of Abraham Lincoln's pick for General-in-Chief and he now knew Lincoln could not be a sincere man. He had seen Honest Abe recently and the President never said anything about the change. McClellan had also just received a telegraph from General Halleck, the new General-in-Chief, ordering him to bring his army north and unite it with the army of Major General John Pope. This was the last shoe to drop for McClellan's campaign. He picked up his pen to write a letter to his wife.

My Dearest Ellen,

Over five months ago, as you know, my army stepped foot onto the beaches of Fort Monroe with the express purpose of finding the enemy and destroying them along with his Capitol. You also know how the government thwarted me by changing their minds multiple times as far as who could fight with me and who couldn't. You already know how I feel about Stanton, that depraved hypocrite and villain. Now, the new general who Lincoln picked over me, Halleck, has just telegraphed me and ordered that I remove my army from the peninsula and join another man's army up north in order to engage the enemy. But the enemy is here! I desire to retake Malvern Hill and then proceed to Richmond. However, the Rebel forces have grown because of our government's delay and indecision. Halleck had promised me 20,000 extra men, but my scouts later told me soldiers have stormed into Richmond from the south and increased their army by 50,000. I had telegraphed Halleck telling him that I beseech him to allow me to stay and fight and if he would just send me the men from Newport News and the Atlantic coast and also 20,000 more men from the west, then I would have enough troop strength to go up against the newly reinforced Army of Northern Virginia. "Old Brains" evidently doesn't have any because he has refused giving the extra soldiers I requested and now has telegraphed me to hasten my leaving here so my forces could be of use to the other man. I do not want to blemish this letter with his name but know soon that man (who is a disgrace) will be badly whipped by Jackson. Oh, the treachery I feel on this lonely day in August! It is getting to where I cannot in good conscience serve our government any longer. Please let me have, my love, some encouragement when you have time to write.

Your Loving Husband,
George

122.

George McClellan disobeyed Halleck's order and sent 17,000 troops to Malvern Hill for the purpose of engaging General Lee and changing Halleck's mind. Upon encountering fierce resistance from Lee, however, McClellan changed his own mind and recalled the troops. They would leave Virginia the way they came. On ships. Young Napoleon's Peninsula Campaign had failed. And in doing so changed the momentum of the war. The Confederates were now moving north toward Washington to engage a new army the Union put together under General John Pope.

Before the Army of the Potomac would leave the field, Brigadier General Daniel Butterfield, a leader who fought heroically under Porter's Fifth Corps at the Battle of Gaines's Mill, composed a new song. While bivouacking on the fields of Berkeley Plantation, reflecting on their defeat and the number of deaths, Butterfield put together several notes for the bugle to be played at memorial services instead of the sounding of the volleys. The tune became known as "Taps" and was a fitting anthem by which to depart the Virginia soil and say goodbye to the campaign.

Day is done, gone the sun
From the lakes, from the hills, from the run
All is well, safely rest;
God is nigh.

Then goodnight, peaceful night;
Til the light of the dawn shineth bright
God is near, do not fear
Friend, goodnight.

PART VIII

A LOVE THAT WILL NOT LET ME GO

War makes thieves and peace hangs them.
GEORGE HERBERT

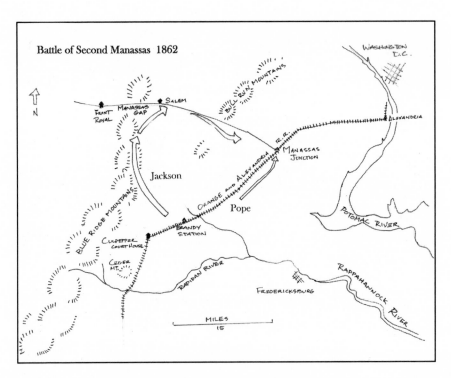

The Battle of Bull Run (Second Manassas)

123.

Abraham Lincoln completed his plan to free the slaves and called it the Emancipation Proclamation. However, he could not get anyone in his Cabinet to wholeheartedly agree to it. They liked it, but felt the timing was not right. The Union Army needed a win. People needed to see this war was going somewhere and it would be concluded with a Northern victory. Lincoln meditated on those cherished words, *'We hold these truths to be self-evident, that all men are created equal.'* He knew what he needed to do. He was beginning to change his course from when he was elected. Reuniting the nation was now just one of his goals as President. He also needed to forever end slavery in the United States. There were four million slaves in America who were not experiencing the dream of the founders. He wanted to allow the Declaration of Independence, America's founding document, to be realized in its fullest sense. It seemed to him he was inspired as he wrote the words of the proclamation. The country required a new birth of freedom. Though he felt stronger about this than any other plan of his, Lincoln decided to be patient and listen to his Cabinet. He was willing to wait to insure its success—but not indefinitely. Slavery would be abolished as soon as the military opened the door for him to do it.

124.

Bruce was lying in his cot thinking on a Sunday morning while waiting for his commander to return from church service. Over the weeks he seemed to have turned the page in his life that held Molly. Now he thought more about his military career and of the commander he served each day. Bruce felt as close as anyone could to Stonewall Jackson, besides the man's wife, but he still didn't feel like he really knew him. There were certain aspects of his personality that made Jackson appear aloof and distant from others, and it seemed as if he didn't care. He could stand in a shadow in the corner of a room during a meeting or social gathering and not say a word. When asked a question he would appear nervous and usually give a short response.

He was different with children, however. Jackson loved to talk and play with little children he encountered. Many adults familiar with Jackson's odd mannerisms were dumbfounded when they saw Jackson come alive and act spontaneous and foolish around their kids.

Jackson was a pious man yet Bruce knew this did not come from his attendance at church. Jackson couldn't learn much from the sermons he attended because as soon as the preacher began to preach Jackson would fall fast asleep. This occurred nearly every time he stepped foot into church regardless of the minister and the quality of the preaching. Jackson had the odd ability of sleeping while sitting in an upright position and from behind he appeared to be looking straight ahead. Though he missed most messages, Jackson knew a lot about Scripture and had memorized portions of the Bible. He thought it so important for people to learn Scripture he had started a black Sunday school class on Sunday afternoons while he lived in Lexington. The class was a success as it started with a few and grew to 100 people. Jackson took a personal interest in each of his students, knowing every one of their names. Some of the residents in town were not excited about slaves learning the Bible, they believed it would cause them to think more freely and perhaps rebel, but this did not deter Jackson in the least. He treated black people with the same dignity he afforded whites and he was wrenched inwardly by the fact society put the black race in bondage.

Bruce appreciated these aspects of Jackson's life and thought it would be wise to emulate such a man except for one area, Jackson's abiding faith in God. This kind of faith was alien to Bruce. He could see the benefits of attending church and even teaching Sunday School to negroes. But Jackson talked about God and his faith in Jesus Christ in a way that made Bruce feel uncomfortable. He could not understand some of the comments Jackson made after attending church or after spending time in the woods alone for prayer. Jackson didn't seem to mind Bruce's lack of interest and thankfully Jackson didn't ever try to persuade Bruce in that area. Bruce knew it would have been beneath his former professor to pressure him, and the theology Jackson prescribed to taught that eventually it would happen for others when God wanted it to happen. He believed people could not resist the love of God like they could from another person. Bruce didn't understand it completely but he knew Jackson was a Presbyterian. The only thing Bruce knew about Presbyterianism was that they believed God purposed everything and nothing in life escaped God's absolute power and control. He knew Jackson never doubted for a moment that God's fingerprint was on every human endeavor. Bruce had a hard time believing this, but he certainly couldn't disprove it so he kept his thoughts to himself.

While deep in thought Bruce suddenly heard footsteps outside of the command tent. The flap was pulled and in walked Stonewall with a large grin.

"Good morning Lieutenant Crawford," said Jackson.

Bruce jackknifed out of his bed and stood at attention while saying, "Good morning, sir. How was church service?"

"Excellent. Rev. Daniel Ewing preached a fine sermon," Jackson said while sitting at his wooden field desk.

Because of what others who regularly attended church services with Jackson had told him, Bruce knew Jackson slept soundly through even the most riveting messages. Therefore, Bruce decided he would pry a little bit to see what Jackson might say. "What was the message about, sir?" asked Bruce.

"He preached from First Corinthians chapter fifteen about the resurrection."

"What were his main points?" Bruce asked as seriously as he could, barely able to keep from laughing while he spoke.

Jackson shot Bruce a glance as if to see if he was indeed serious.

Bruce looked as sober as he could.

Jackson hesitated before answering, "Well, Lieutenant Crawford, if you are truly interested in what Rev. Ewing preached on then I would suggest you ask him to review his sermon with you later today."

Bruce was exuberant because he knew his question made Jackson uncomfortable and he was dodging the issue. "I guess I just wanted a short synopsis, not the entire message," Bruce offered.

Jackson looked straight at the tent wall as if in deep thought. Bruce figured he was trying desperately to remember some words from the sermon. Finally, Jackson responded. "Well, Rev. Ewing would be a good one to ask."

Bruce had to bite his lip to keep from laughing out loud at his ruse.

Jackson picked up the papers he needed for his next meeting, stood up and walked to the flap of the tent. But, before going outside, he turned to Bruce and said passionately, "For if, like some have said, the dead have not been raised, then Christ also has not been raised. Yet if Christ has not been raised then our faith is worthless and we are still in our sins, and those who have died before us have completely perished. And if we have only hoped in Christ in this life and he has not been raised then we are of all men the most to be pitied. But why, then, do we find ourselves in danger every hour, and fight with wild beasts, and are hunted mercilessly by the governing officials? Because Christ has been raised from the dead, the first fruits of everyone who is asleep," Jackson finished with a twinkle in his eyes. He gave an uncharacteristic slight wink to Bruce and departed the tent.

Bruce was left alone, speechless.

125.

August was hot the year of 1862. On the march, some of the animals died and men suffered from heatstroke. Jonesy was encouraged as Henry had rejoined the unit at Gordonsville. His leg was much better and he looked fattened up, no doubt due to the excellent cooking of Kathryn and Claire. The two discussed for hours each day the events that had taken place since the Battle of Winchester back in May. Henry was amazed at the success of the Confederate Army at the very doorstep of Richmond and proud of his friend for the obvious bravery he displayed during the battle at Gaines' Mill. Jonesy shared with Henry late one night his grief at seeing one man decapitated, and another soldier who had lost his entire face and screamed out for someone to shoot him in the head to end his suffering.

Henry shared with Jonesy about current events in Winchester and how after Stonewall departed town the Union supply teams re-entered the city and it became a rally point for infantry units traversing the area. Henry described how he had to be hidden when the Union scouts would come into town. Henry could have departed with the other wounded on wagons and head for Richmond, but with Colonel Neff's permission he stayed. And with Kathryn's help he survived not being captured. He had a harrowing experience once or twice and almost reinjured himself in the events, but he kept undetected. He told Jonesy that Scout had been a true supporter and friend through the ordeal and Jonesy smiled remembering the dog's nobility. In one instance Henry was in hiding near the stone wall for two days until Landon came to retrieve him and tell him the danger had passed. Another time he hid at the Grey Goose Tavern under some floorboards with the help of Culpepper. Kathryn was worried sick knowing how close her lover was to being apprehended and possibly executed in the process.

Henry also shared how horrified the Winchester citizens were to hear about Ashby and how excited they were to learn of the Confederate victory at Gaines' Mill. He described how they learned the news of McClellan's retreat to the James River on the day he departed Winchester and this news was going to make their Fourth of July celebrations all the sweeter. Henry also relayed to Jonesy the disturbing news of how the Federals had torn apart Senator James Mason's house plank by plank. Before Henry was engaged to Kathryn, he and Jonesy thought Ida Mason, the Senator's daughter, was one of Winchester's finest.

That week the two young men witnessed a firing squad assembled at headquarters to shoot deserters. They were friends with one of the soldiers who was executed. His excuse for abandoning Jackson's Army was to take care of a sick father. This excuse seemed reasonable to Henry and Jonesy, but Jackson would hear none of it. Wartime called for a strict adherence to duty and to obey orders, he said. It was excruciating for them to hear the crack of the single musket volley and then see a warrior they had fought alongside fall, killed by his own command. It seemed so needless but their leadership told them orders were orders.

Both the Winchester lads were also sickened at losing their brigade commander Charles Sidney Winder on August 9th. It was during the bloody battle at Cedar Mountain while fighting General Pope's Army. Henry had recently reunited with the 33rd Virginia after his leave of absence. The Corps Commander Nathaniel Banks was trying to atone for his defeat at Winchester and aggressively pounded the Confederates, causing them to retreat en mass. Winder was standing by a battery directing its fire when a Union shell exploded into his left side leaving him disfigured. He died within hours. Stonewall's 11,000 man army was up against a Federal strength of 50,000 and the day was nearly lost. The sheer brashness of Jackson during the battle and his unbridled courage might have singly rescued the army from defeat. When Jackson's left flank was imploding and regiment after regiment retreated from the field, Jackson went into action. He grabbed his sword still in the scabbard and raised it high above his head. He then grabbed the Confederate flag and lifted it up with his other hand while shouting at the men to rally them. Stonewall Jackson was seen riding forward, a solitary warrior moving toward the oncoming Union forces.

Jonesy and Henry believed it was the gutsiest thing they had ever seen anybody do. The soldiers within sight of Jackson were encouraged and began to turn around. Those running away stopped. Men regrouped. The

Confederates began to move forward again and soon, the tide went the other way—their way. Henry and Jonesy were right in the middle of the action and thankfully not injured. Over 200 Southern men were killed that day (compared to over 300 Northerners) and over 1,000 Southerners were wounded. But they had won, and forced the enemy to retreat from the field of battle.

126.

<u>Roads</u>

Nighttime comes but I'm not sleeping
The sound of war intense, I pray
Dangerous men at gates are keeping
Enemies of peace at bay

A long, long journey to my homeland
Roads that lead to where I know
Duty keeps me from my own land
Where the wind of peace does flow

Generals watch the war get violent
Politicians tell their lies
Cannons fire and friends fall silent
Soldiers weep and search the skies

A long, long journey to my homeland
Roads that lead to where I know
Death surrounds me in this new land
Where the wind of peace won't flow

Hans put down the fountain pen after finishing his poem and writing at the top of the paper the name he selected, "Roads."

"Would you blow out the lantern?" asked Ned.

"Hold your horses, Ned. I still have to write a letter to Chelsea. I haven't had a chance to write to her in awhile."

"Good grief! I barely get any sleep as it is. What the heck were you just doing?" Ned asked while he rolled over the other way.

"Writing a poem."

"A poem? A poem? Who has time to write a poem? And who's ever going to read it?"

"Ned, close your eyes. You'll be asleep and snoring in no time."

"No, I won't," said Ned.

"Yes, you will," replied Hans.

"I won't. And nobody's fool enough to read your poem."

"Quit your jawing, Ned!"

"Don't have to."

"Ned--!"

"Nuts!"

Riley lay awake smiling at the two. He put up with their bickering nearly every night and he grew fond of it.

Hans began his letter to Chelsea:

Dear Sweetheart,

I am alive and well and hope this letter finds you the same. We have arrived back into northern Virginia and I am thankful not to be down near the swamps any longer. I miss you sorely. I cannot keep my mind from wandering to your chestnut hair and beautiful smile. I wish there was a way that I could see you tonight though I know you're hundreds of miles away. As I lie here and think of you I cannot help but think that you are lying in your bed and thinking of me. If only you could be close right now. If only I could reach out my hand and touch your face. If only I could look into your brown eyes and see your beautiful smile. I am smiling now thinking of you and all that you are. You mean everything to me. Please keep yourself for me as I am keeping myself for you.

It was a horrific sight to see the lifeless bodies of my comrades lying all over the ground. I do not know if I can take much more of this war. It is startling and starting to disrupt my pure thoughts. I am a good soldier but I have seen the most awful things imaginable. We have so many in our ranks, so many good men who are wounded and have had to have a limb amputated. We have hundreds and hundreds who have left us because they are sick with the swamp flu and thousands because of wounds. Many have been taken prisoner and some have simply deserted. I do not blame the deserters. This war affects how you think and how you feel. I am not the same man I was when I left home. *I look the same, but I feel so different. I want to hold you for a month before I do anything else. And I need you to hold me.*

We move so slowly, even with our new commanding general. We are trying to hammer the Cornfeds, but they elude us and then attack us when we least expect. I will keep you posted. I have two true friends here named Riley and Ned with whom I spend every waking hour. Both of their families moved to Pittsburgh last year but they are originally from Winchester. Though Virginians, they love Lincoln and proudly fight for the North. Riley is my leader. He is the best corporal in the troop and an excellent horseman. I have a lot to learn from him about humility, service and leadership. Ned is another story. He's ornery and constantly complains. I don't think he has even fired his weapon yet or killed a man. He says he's a pacifist. Phooey. I can hear him snoring now.

In your last letter you asked me to search for Ruthie Evans' husband, Barker. I have not seen him and his unit knows not where he is. I suspect he either died near Richmond and was buried by the Cornfeds or he was taken captive by them. I am sorry I do not have any more information for you. Please give Mrs. Evans my condolences and tell her not to give up hope.

Well Dearie, I better go to sleep. I miss you. I look for your letters every day.

Love Hans

127.

Stonewall Jackson knew exactly what to do when given orders by Lee to slip behind enemy lines and destroy their supply channels. The target was Bristoe Station and the Orange and Alexander Railroad. The problem with this maneuver, besides the danger of Pope's Army, was that Jeb Stuart had completed a reconnaissance and found two of McClellan's Corps had arrived on the field after their return from the peninsula and were now somewhere near Fredericksburg. This put at least an extra 50,000 Union soldiers in the area, in addition to Pope's Army, providing them the opportunity to trap the Confederates embarking on any foolhardy plan. However, Robert E. Lee was audacious and loved to take risks. Jackson was just as daring and eager to cause damage to the Union. The two leaders worked incredibly well together for only having been merged for a few weeks. The coalition of Lee's daring and cunning tactics with Jackson's fierce, aggressive style of warfighting was an alliance that rallied the Confederates and put dread in the Northerners. The two men trusted each other and believed they saw in each other a common vein of thinking. They both hated this war and felt the more hastily they devastated the Union Army the quicker the war would conclude, lives could be saved and they could return home to their families.

There was something extra that distinguished the two from many of the generals from both the North and South; each were men who knew the living God and were not afraid of death. This formed an instant, permanent admiration of each man for the other that outsiders could not perceive at first glance. Jackson told someone once that if asked, he would be willing to follow Lee blindfolded.

With all of their similarities there was one glaring dissimilarity; the two men looked like opposites. Jackson appeared an unkempt, common laborer and Lee appeared as a stately gentleman. Both were West Point graduates, both distinguished themselves in the Mexican War, and both were cheered profusely whenever they would pass by a contingent of soldiers. The troops were not alone in their admiration and praise of Robert Lee and Stonewall Jackson, all Virginians and residents throughout the South adored them. But one looked like a backwoods farmer and the other a person of society. One had rough mannerisms and the other's actions spoke of grace.

Jackson's movements began before dawn on Wednesday, August 25th, 1862. His 23,000 men were in three divisions commanded by William Booth Taliaferro, Ambrose Powell Hill and Richard Stoddart Ewell. He was going to be moving around John Pope's force of over 50,000 fresh Union soldiers who were not sick from the swamps of Richmond or tired from the grueling battles.

General John Pope became known nation-wide as a braggart. He openly declared in his confrontations with Confederates so far in this war he had just seen the backs of them. He also told people that, contrary to McClellan's exhaustive planning of supply trails and massive rear headquarters areas, Pope would have his headquarters in his saddle because success and glory were ahead of him, not behind him. These comments did not earn him any favor with men in both armies. But, what caused fury on the Confederate side was when he announced he would show no quarter to Virginian civilians, they could be arrested and even executed at his whim.

Jackson, in his worn out kepi hat, rode Little Sorrel alongside the soldiers as they marched. Nobody knew where they were going except for Jackson and his local guide. The guide was out front, taking them mostly on back roads and sometimes through fields, across people's lawns, and over creeks. The citizens would cheer for them and some would march alongside their beloved troops. The order was given out not to cheer for Jackson for sound security, so when he would ride by, the troops would merely raise their hats and wave silently. The love and respect the men displayed for their commander every day was somewhat overwhelming for Jackson but deeply encouraging. His aides loved to belong to a leader who the men adored.

Henry Kyd Douglas, Dr. Hunter McGuire, Sandie Pendleton and Joseph G. Morrison all accompanied Jackson and Bruce on the march. But Rev. Robert Dabney, the esteemed Presbyterian minister who Jackson had as his chief-of-staff and Chaplain of the Shenandoah Valley Army, was no longer with them. He requested of Jackson a few days earlier to return to civilian life.

Bruce Crawford marveled at how well the soldiers marched that day. Twenty-six miles were marched in the heat and on many shoeless feet. Those who had shoes had worn out shoes. The men, however, did not complain. They knew they were on an important mission and they knew they were supposed to keep the noise down to avoid detection. Wells Joseph Hawks, Jackson's quartermaster, remained with the supply wagons in the rear of the column, but when possible he would send telegrams to the War Department requesting new shoes, hats, uniforms and other essential items for the soldiers.

When the march was over the men immediately fell to the ground to go to sleep because there were no rations. Some slept right in the road, most without blankets. The next day the exhausted soldiers were shaken up while it was still pitch black and told to start marching without breakfast. Even though this army of foot cavalry was used to long marches, these two days strained them, punishing their bodies and required great mental resiliency from every soldier. Jackson was very pleased with how the men were doing this Thursday, and hoped they could utterly surprise Pope's Army with their celerity.

The army made it to Bristoe Station, twenty miles away before the end of the day just as a locomotive with freight cars was arriving. When the train conductor saw the Confederates he sped ahead. Passengers began shooting out of the windows at the soldiers. The Confederates attempted to throw wooden rails on the track to stop it but it was no use. The train barreled forward with the information that a raid was taking place at Bristoe Station. Jackson would now have to act quickly. A moment later another train whistle was heard in the distance. This time, however, the Southerners had the minutes they needed to not only destroy part of the track, but to open the derailing switch. When the locomotive saw the gray coated men ahead standing by the station it attempted to speed up to rush by. As soon as it hit the switch it lurched to the right and derailed. The next train came moments later plowing into the back of the one derailed. There was now one long mass of deformed metal and wood and boxcars every which way. The next train saw the wrecks with enough time to put its engine in reverse and head backwards with the news to the south. Jackson decided to move forward with his plan.

Seven miles away was Manassas Junction where General John Pope held an enormous supply depot for his army. The problem was most of the men had fallen to the ground in great fatigue and many lay sleeping around their commander's feet. Just then, Brigadier General Isaac Ridgeway

Trimble (from Ewell's command) volunteered to take the 21st Georgia Regiment and the 21st North Carolina Regiment to go and secure the junction. Jackson consented. At midnight, the 550 men finally arrived at Manassas Junction to be greeted by artillery and musket fire from the Union defenders. Though brutally exhausted, the half-starving men from Georgia and North Carolina rallied, charged and took over the junction. What they found was a vast supply of stores in warehouses along with two batteries of cannon, 200 horses, 75 wagons and 100 railcars filled with supplies. They also captured over 300 prisoners, mountains of ammunition and hundreds of containers of much needed medicine.

Jackson's Army departed soon to join Trimble's contingent and when they arrived the thousands of weary troops were allowed to fall upon the supplies and eat to their hearts content. Some men ate delicacies they hadn't tasted in years like shellfish, but more useful to them were the new boots and clothing. Whatever could not be carried in their haversacks was to be left behind and burned so it could never be utilized by the North. Again Jackson quickly rallied his army and departed, much to the sadness of his troops. His great flanking movement had worked, penetrating the rear of Pope's Army and disrupting the nerve center of the Union Army's supply operations.

128.

John Nicolay, the President's Secretary, hated disturbing the Ancient during his rest, but this was an urgent message from the War Department. He found his boss asleep in a chair in his bedroom with a book in his lap. When unable to sleep Lincoln would often try to read to help calm his mind.

After touching his shoulder Nicolay said, "Sir, an urgent telegram was received at the War Department."

"Yes?" Lincoln sat straight up rubbing his eyes a little.

"I have a message from Mr. Stanton, may I read it to you?" Nicolay asked.

"Certainly, but let's step into the hall so we don't disturb Mother."

When they went into the hall and closed the door behind them Nicolay began reading the note from Edwin Stanton, "Sir, sorry to bother you with this news and so early in the morning but you asked me to keep you informed night and day. There was a Confederate Cavalry raid at Bristoe Station and another at Manassas Junction. They have ruined the railway, burned the bridge, taken over the supply depot and captured the Federal Guard there. We have sent General George Taylor to proceed there with his First New Jersey Brigade to deal with the situation and secure the junctions. We will keep you informed as events transpire."

When he finished reading Stanton's message Nicolay looked at the Ancient and remembered they had given him that nickname not just because he sometimes appeared as an old man, but appeared as a man from an ancient era like from the Old Testament or Aristotelian times. Lincoln indeed looked aged standing there in the large, dark White House hallway in the middle of the night. The President didn't move a muscle for the longest time. He looked up at his secretary and said, "Thank you John. I will now get dressed."

Before Lincoln retreated into his room they heard someone approaching them. It was John Hay, Lincoln's assistant secretary. He tepidly walked down the hallway toward them with a note in his hand.

"What is it, Hay?" asked Nicolay.

"I have a message from Mr. Stanton for the President," Hay said as he approached the other two.

Lincoln said, "Please read it to me, my eyes are not working well yet and it is too dark in this hallway."

Hay unfolded the paper and began to read, "Forgive me, sir, for another disturbance. It was not a Confederate Cavalry raid that attacked Bristoe Station and Manassas Junction. It was General Thomas Jackson and his army. Also, General Taylor's New Jersey Brigade has been wiped out and he was seriously wounded. This puts Jackson's Army between us and General Pope, less than thirty miles away. Pope is making every effort to interdict. Will keep you posted. One more item, hundreds of our boys taken prisoner and millions of dollars of our supplies destroyed."

Nicolay and Hay looked up into the President's somber face. Daylight began to penetrate its way into the White House windows.

Finally the Ancient replied, "So Jackson has struck again. He is between us and Pope and encroaches on the very doorstep of Washington. The mouse is now the cat and the cat is now the mouse."

"Sir?"

"Nothing, really, just seems like with this Jackson fellow there is more than meets the eye."

That was all that was said for the moment. Lincoln grabbed his bedroom door handle and bent his long frame over, resting his head on the wooden door.

Lincoln's assistants stood near their leader motionless.

Eventually he declared, "Gentlemen, I need to get dressed. It sounds like a major battle awaits us."

Robert E. Lee

Thomas "Stonewall" Jackson

George B. McClellan

President Abraham Lincoln

Lincoln and McClellan at Antietam

Burnside's Bridge

129.

Jonesy marched as fast as his legs would move him. He had already lost forty pounds since the war began yet he was still a good forty pounds more than Henry. Most didn't look on him and think he was obese, but he was massive and had a little chubbiness in his face and belly. His immense size unfortunately made him a perfect target for the enemy, but it also made him intimidating. When he would run toward the enemy with his bayonet fixed and screaming the Rebel yell like a madman, he was one of the most terrifying opponents you could come across on the battlefield. Henry told him if he was ever injured that he would have to stay where he had fallen because no man alive could carry him. Henry joked that if he left Jonesy to die he would have to tell Rachel he was sorry, but she fed her little boy too well.

Jonesy was never the smartest boy in his class but he had astonishing perception into things once he understood what was going on. He excelled as a follower. If you explained a task to him he would perform it remarkably well after a little practice. He was told to kill Yankees and Jonesy succeeded at this task. His sharpshooting skills made him the envy of his entire company. The life of a foot soldier suited him like a hand in a glove. He hated to go into a battle but once he was involved, it was the most thrilling experience he knew he could ever have. With unbridled energy flowing through him it would take him many hours to calm down after he participated in a firefight. He loved people so it tore at Jonesy when men around him were wounded and killed. Even the agonizing cries of the wounded Union soldiers wrenched his heart. Jonesy also loved animals, but this did not keep him from hunting as often as he could with his father to harvest game for Rachel's kitchen. He was all around about the best son and friend someone could have and that is why people enjoyed having him around. Henry said he liked having Jonesy around the most when they were caught in a driving rain storm because Henry would stand behind the Philistine giant and keep fairly dry. Jonesy didn't mind because he was going to get wet regardless.

The march continued. Jackson had his army march through part of the night. They finally halted and everyone dropped where they were, rubbed their sore feet and laid down in as soft a spot as they could find in a hurry. In a few hours they were marching again. The sun was coming up. Jonesy recognized the area from the summer before. His sore feet remembered the terrain and he knew in his bones this was where the war had begun for him. They were near the Warrenton Turnpike between Groveton and Centreville. Bull Run was just east of their position. Finally the order was given to halt and rest. Jonesy and Henry were excited not to have to keep marching. The men sat down and took another quick nap. Club came by and told all the men to be ready for quick movement but to remain at rest. Some of the men took out some food, others played cards. A game of throwing walnuts at each other started up by a few seventeen-year-olds. Some of the men took the opportunity to write a letter. It was the first time in several days the men were not marching, fighting or sleeping. Music from a harmonica filled the air. They enjoyed the eighty-five degrees weather and the breeze coming down from the hills nearby.

It was around five in the afternoon when the order was given out to prepare for an attack. The 33rd would form part of the main effort so they moved into ranks and took a strong battle position, desperately trying to listen for sounds of the enemy. The sun began to set when the first of the Union soldiers appeared over the slight rise, coming at them with bayonets attached.

Jonesy and Henry put a percussion cap on their loaded weapons and carefully sighted a target. Jonesy pulled his trigger first and down went a blue coat. Henry fired his musket and his shot ripped into a man's shoulder. Jonesy downed another one. There was smoke now from the nearby artillery and people shouting. Several Confederates were receiving injuries. A bullet grazed Henry's cheek. Jonesy picked out another target, an officer on a horse, aimed, and gently squeezed his trigger. *Crack!* The man on the horse fell. Other Confederates were firing with a vengeance. Tree limbs above the oncoming Union were being torn and twigs and branches were falling on top of them and all around them. The cannon roared. Henry was bleeding from his cheek but it wasn't a deep wound. The men looked at each other briefly and smiled, happy to be alive.

"Keep down," Henry shouted. "You don't want this to happen to you."

Jonesy nodded, tore open another pouch of gunpowder with his front two teeth. Used his ramrod. Grabbed a minie ball. Drove it down. Placed his percussion cap. Found a target and pulled the trigger. Another Union soldier was mortally wounded.

The order came. The 33rd Virginia was to move forward to attack the enemy's lines. Colonel John F. Neff led the charge for the regiment. Club led the charge for Delta Company. They moved in file toward an orchard where the Union line was furiously reorganizing and trying to form a solid line. The Confederate Cavalry had just sprinted through the orchard wreaking havoc.

The men did not fire as they marched forward until the order was given. As soon as the command was given the mighty crack of hundreds of rifled Enfields, Springfields, Harpers Ferry and Richmond Armory Muskets crumpled the Union line in front of them. Jonesy could see thousands of blue-coated men running into the orchard on the right. They reloaded and fired again. There was hardly any cover except some haystacks and a few trees. The sound of artillery was deafening. Jonesy thought of being home at his mother's table. Henry thought of Kathryn and the end of the war. More Union reinforcements. More noise and smoke filled the air. All of a sudden, a charge of Union infantry and cavalry shot forward and fired into the butternut uniformed men of Virginia. Jonesy saw his regimental commander who bravely led their charge fall off of his horse. Jonesy ran forward but was pulled back by others in his unit. The fighting was fierce, he would be shot down. The Confederates drew back. John Neff, their leader, lay motionless on the ground.

The fighting was intense for two more hours until it was too dark to see. Though the Union Army pushed the Southern troops back, more men from General Ewell's division continued to reinforce Taliaferro, the commander of the Stonewall Division. Taliaferro was wounded in several places yet kept leading. Jonesy heard that Ewell himself was badly wounded in the knee and had his left leg amputated. This was startling news for all the men to hear about Old Baldy. The rumor in camp was that both Ewell and Taliaferro would be out due to injuries for months, perhaps until the war was over. The crying of the wounded was hideous that evening and Club spent hours organizing small details of men to bury the dead and retrieve the casualties still on the battlefield. Jonesy looked around the terrain. He knew the Confederates had won the battle, but there were still about a thousand of them killed or wounded. Some very good men died that day and some of Jonesy's closest war buddies took injuries. He helped as best he could to comfort them and make sure they were taken to the field hospital in Sudley Springs.

The next morning after a brief march Jonesy and Henry found themselves and the rest of Jackson's command encamped all along a wide stretch of unfinished railroad which lay not too far from the hill at Henry House where they had waited in the woods the summer before. They were anxiously awaiting General Longstreet's troops to arrive to reinforce them because they could see they were up against a fortified Union position led by General Pope. Jonesy had never met John Pope but hated him as he hated Lincoln, Seward and McClellan because of the things he had heard Pope say and the stories he had heard about what Pope did to Virginian civilians.

Jonesy looked to the west and saw Kyd Douglas and Bruce Crawford ride slowly alongside the troops, apparently looking for the brigade commander. Jonesy did not see Bruce every day, usually just when Bruce made a special effort to locate his Winchester comrades.

The Rockbridge Artillery, the pride of General Jackson, began to retaliate when Union artillery opened up on the right of the line that morning. The barrage of canister shot echoed for miles around as smoke slowly filled the entire area. Jonesy and Henry believed the worst assault would be to their right where the Union was pelting with hundreds of mortars and cannonballs. However, the Union infantry assaults came mostly on the left side hitting units belonging to General Ambrose Powell Hill. His men held up admirably as wave after wave of zealous Union infantry hurled themselves against the musket fire of Hill's division. The fighting was so fierce Jonesy thought his unit would be redirected to support the gaps in Hill's line. The Union men broke through at several points and one time held significant ground, thus dividing the Confederate line. However, the Confederate men rallied at the cry of 'Let us die here, men, let us die here.' With stones they picked up and threw at the Federals when they ran out of ammunition, and sticks they used to club their opponents, somehow the Confederates regained their ground and closed up the holes. Jonesy's best friend that day was the bayonet. It had been the only thing between him and death in several encounters. Dried blood and dirt covered his face.

There were 2,000 casualties in a matter of a few hours with the heavy hand-to-hand combat. The men injured but left alive on the battlefield cried in anguish as the sun set over the once beautiful hills. Again, Jonesy was asked to help with the casualties who had fallen only on the Confederate side of the line. It was too risky for anyone to venture past the railroad cut where Pope's Union Army was entrenched in the fields beyond. There was no truce to gather the wounded so the men in between the lines would have to wait.

With the devastation of the day's battle surrounding them, several military chaplains called for a prayer service to help the men deal with the pain and grief and give them hope for the next day of battle in which more horrible bloodshed seemed inevitable. Jonesy and Henry knew the battle their army fought on that August 29th was a primer for what was to come but they were encouraged when it was reported throughout camp that General Lee had finally arrived with Longstreet and thousands of fresh troops for the fight. Tomorrow would bring about an interesting turn of events. *Maybe we will end this stalemate,* thought Jonesy.

130.

President Abraham Lincoln had been monitoring the battle ever since the raid at Bristoe Station. He was convinced General Pope was wrong about Thomas Jackson's intentions. Pope had been telegraphing the War Department he was going to prevent Jackson from a retreat and thus crush him. But Lincoln did not believe Jackson was in fact retreating. *This is the man who attacks opposing forces with less than half of their strength. This is the man who marches all through the night to appear at a battle with his army when he is supposed to be hundreds of miles away. This is the man who critics called a nervous and awkward schoolteacher who would fail if ever made a commander. But Jackson had yet to be soundly defeated on the battlefield! This is the man who with Turner Ashby was considered a ghost. No! If Pope knew Jackson like I do, and having to stomach the brunt of his every success, he would know Jackson would not be retreating but would be reinforcing to attempt an attack on the Capitol!* Lincoln thought.

Lincoln and Stanton spent the day at the War Department examining every message from Pope carefully. General-in-Chief Henry Halleck was with them, calmly reassuring them of his other forces nearby that would be of assistance. General George McClellan had returned from the peninsula that month and had two corps in Alexandria, Edwin Sumner's II Corps and William Franklin's VI Corps. Fitz John Porter's V Corps had already been attached to Pope's Army. It was obvious to Lincoln that Halleck was still furious with McClellan. Despite Halleck's repeated orders the General-in-Chief seemed unable to pry McClellan from the peninsula in a timely manner to support Pope. Lincoln needed Halleck to be the 'heavy' for him and he was not doing a very good job at it. If this battle at Manassas did not turn around quickly, Lincoln was considering firing Halleck for his lack of initiative and inability to lead his field commanders. He knew Halleck viewed the circumstances differently and that Halleck considered McClellan impossible to work with, but this would be another excuse and Lincoln was sick to death of excuses from his commanders that year. *Halleck might serve us better as a postal clerk,* thought Lincoln.

"Sir, we have just received another telegram from General Pope."

It was Secretary Stanton. Lincoln had stepped outside for a few moments in order to get some fresh air. It was hot and stuffy inside but there was a breeze out in the garden.

"Okay. What is going on now?" Lincoln responded. *I am positive this will not be good,* he thought.

General Pope was a friend of the Lincoln's and distantly related to them by marriage to Mary's second cousin. Lincoln knew Pope's father who was a judge for the state of Illinois. General Pope did not follow his father's footsteps and go into law, but entered the Military Academy and fought under Zachary Taylor in the Mexican War. For the first time since Pope had been leading troops during the Civil War Lincoln was second-guessing his ability as a commander. Things had gone so wrong today and Lincoln was never provided a good reason. Pope had over twice the strength of Jackson but could not make any progress against him. Pope had written earlier that he was seeking to stop Jackson's retreat but this, to Lincoln, sounded like madness. *Jackson retreat?*

Stanton cleared his voice before he read the telegraph from Pope,

"Ordered Porter to attack Jackson's left this afternoon but he refused and should be court marshaled. No progress made on the line. Will stop Jackson from retreating tomorrow."

"The man sounds confounded. Jackson is not trying to escape him. If he wanted to run away he would have accomplished that a day or two ago. No, Edwin, this is a trap and Jackson is the bait. My guess is that Lee is in the area and will attempt to trounce our army tomorrow. What has Halleck done about getting McClellan's men up there? Anything?" Lincoln asked.

"There is more bad news, sir. We have also just received a message from General McClellan. In it he states,

"Again, I will not be able to send Franklin or Sumner's Corps to support your new commander. I do not deem them ready for a fight. Perhaps the best course for you now would be to leave Pope to get out of this scrape and I will assist you in using all of my means to defend you and the Capitol."

"McClellan wants Pope to fail!" came a voice from around the bush. General Halleck approached the two men in the garden as Stanton finished reading the telegraph. "McClellan is hoping for the Union Army to be beaten so his own standing will be bettered."

"He surely cannot be so ruthless," said Stanton. "Can he?"

Lincoln looked down at the clay pieces of tile and stones making a walkway on the ground. There was no point in debating this. Precious lives were at stake and time was of the essence. "Telegraph McClellan and order him to advance Franklin's men immediately," Lincoln said to Halleck.

"I did that this morning, sir, and he sent them forward," Halleck said and paused to catch his breath.

"Well then what is this telegraph about?"

"After about six or seven miles of marching, General McClellan ordered Franklin to withdraw back to their base in Alexandria."

"What? He ordered them to withdraw?" Lincoln was appalled. "Why on earth would he do that?"

Stanton was near frantic, "We now have a calamity on our hands! General Halleck, have you no more control over your generals than to send orders by telegraph and have them subsequently revoked or not read at all?"

Old Brains remained quiet. For the first time that day he seemed to grasp what was at stake while standing outside in the quiet garden, miles away from where American men were being slaughtered. He had needed to clear his head with fresh air as well but he didn't realize it until now. "I will depart at once and attempt to reason with McClellan in person tonight," Halleck said.

Lincoln gravely smiled at the words 'reason' and 'McClellan' used in the same sentence.

Stanton mumbled, "Good luck, General," as Old Brains walked awkwardly away from them.

131.

My Dearest Ellen,

    I have heard that things for the new commander are not going well. Old Brains just left my tent, but before he departed he actually asked for a third time if I could supply two of my corps to support the battle at Manassas but I refused him. Such a villain as John Pope deserves to be thrashed and disposed of by Lee and Jackson, not glory in a victory. The nation will soon see that my leadership capabilities are not so easily replaced. I expect that the President will telegraph and ask if I can protect our nation's Capitol and once again lead all of the Federal armies in Virginia. I will reject the offer and it will be gratifying.

    Your Loving Husband,
    George

132.

The breaking of the dawn rendered a still and silent battlefield. It was Saturday, August 30th. Stonewall Jackson began his day with prayers and then met with Lee, Longstreet and Stuart. They were now in a holding pattern. Lee believed General Pope would have been heavily reinforced by McClellan during the night so he did not want to initiate an attack into a strong defensive position of superior forces. Stonewall was certain Pope would be pushing forward any minute with a grand assault. The men all along the line were ready and waiting as the hours passed slowly. Noon came and went with no major assault from either side. Then, three o'clock came and in the next moment a single cannon fired from the Union artillery. The battle began.

Stonewall Jackson rallied his men. After a crack of unified musket fire Jackson looked across the field toward the Union line. There, marching toward him was a long line of blue-coated Federals in a coordinated push to break his position. *There must be ten to fifteen thousand of them,* he thought.

He did not know what would happen if the Union Army were to advance all the way to the railroad cut where he had his men in a defensive position, but he was determined not to find out. He ordered the artillery to do what they do best and soon there were dozens of large guns blowing holes into the advancing blue hordes. Muskets or regimental flags would occasionally shoot up in the air. Bayonets were being busted and limbs were lopped off. The Union Army kept advancing. The artillery blasts were deafening and the smoke was pouring all around the lines. Jackson sent word to Longstreet and Lee on his far right to let them know what was happening in his sector. *Hold on men, hold on,* Jackson said quietly.

133.

General Robert E. Lee was surprised at how long the Union Army took to attack. When at mid-afternoon he heard the blasts of cannon to his left where Jackson was, he—like Jackson—knew exactly what was going to happen. As he rode his horse Traveller through some trees in order to get a better view, his aides cautioned him not to go too far to the front. When Lee broke through the trees and looked at the slanting fields he was startled at the mile long row of Union pouring toward Jackson's lines. *This must be what it looked like to the Union when we attacked them at Gaines' Mill,* he thought. There were slight rises to the ground making it look like repeated waves of men moving forward. Lee realized Jackson would not be able to repulse this strong attack alone. A few minutes later a messenger came to Lee with a request from Jackson for reinforcements.

"They must be penetrating his lines," Lee said to no one in particular. Then, he looked to his nearest aide and said, "Run to General Longstreet and tell him to immediately send a division to support General Jackson." The aide fled away with Lee's message and the Confederate Commander took another look at the swarming blue fields. He was proud of his chief lieutenants Jackson and Longstreet. Both were men of the Christian faith, both had served in the Mexican War, both served Lee without questioning his decisions, and both suffered tragedy and loss in their personal life. Three of Longstreet's four children died from scarlet fever seven months earlier. Jackson had also lost a wife and a son before the war, before Anna. Lee was confident God had prepared these men, peppered them with humility and was using them as special instruments. He couldn't be happier with the balance they each brought to the team. Longstreet was his old warhorse, steady, true and cautious yet always there when needed most. Jackson was the hammer, the audacious one who would agree to anything Lee presented no matter how foolish or daring. Jackson was fast, cunning and courageous. Longstreet, who Lee referred to privately as 'Old Pete,' was slow, methodical and precise. Both of these men were needed to give Lee balance. Lee leaned toward the aggressive nature which Jackson exhibited so he cherished the viewpoint of one so different like Longstreet. The most important thing to Lee, however, was they were both loyal to him. He never had to worry about them disobeying him or trying to politic behind his back. These two men respected the fact that Lee's word was final. His will was the law. They were men who knew what the word duty meant, the sweetest word in the English language to Lee.

Lee maneuvered to where he could see a larger portion of the terrain. Within minutes, Longstreet had emplaced his artillery and began showering canister and grapeshot at the left flank of the Union advance. The Federals were caught off guard at first but not deterred. They readjusted the fire of their artillery and began to answer to the threat of this new menace. Longstreet kept his barrage up for quite awhile shaking the hills and filling the air with drifting smoke. In a little while Lee noticed some confusion in the Union flank. Instead of nice, straight lines there were some gaps and some of the men were turning around. He wondered how things were with Jackson, if Longstreet's artillery had taken some of the pressure off the middle of Jackson's lines. Lee knew Jackson was using every available resource he could muster and had no reserves. If the Federals broke through him they would turn the Confederate left flank and sweep them all off the field.

Lee sent a message to Jackson to see how he was faring. The next moment Longstreet's men, already formed in perfect columns, began to move toward the Union's left side. Just the sight of this mass of men in cadet gray uniforms and either straw or kepi hats was inspiring to Lee. *There must be 25,000 of them,* he thought.

He soon received a note back from Jackson,

"Gen. L.'s flanking artillery has helped, we no longer need reinforcements."

Lee was happy. As he looked, he could now see Pope's second and third wave, capable of easily penetrating Jackson's thin lines, now dodging artillery fire and finding cover wherever they could. When the mass in blue saw the mass in butternut and gray viciously charging down the slope toward them on their exposed left side the men in blue panicked. Lee moved forward on Traveller a little more confidently. Longstreet's men rushed into the Federal left where men were hastily trying to put together a mass for a defense. There was no longer Union leadership on the field, just confusion. Lee watched as scores of men crumpled to the ground. He moved Traveller forward to have a better view.

Lee was now totally exposed but the threat around him had diminished. From his new vantage point he could see Jackson's line organizing and moving forward, pushing the Federals away from them. Lee knew for the first time that day there would soon be a massive retreat by the Union Army. Lee's forces now had the advantage; they had momentum, better ground, and excellent leadership on the battlefield. Lee could see a man who looked like Jackson on the left side wave his sword above his head and rally his troops to follow him. Lee could also see Longstreet right in the thickest part of the fighting on the right, willing to die with his men.

Lee was proud. This was a solid victory. The Confederates pushed forward moving over thousands of dead and wounded lying on the ground. They still pressed on. The two parts of Lee's Army were now moving in a giant "V" growing denser in the middle. The Union was in a complete rout and heading toward Henry House near Bull Run where they had fought Jackson the summer before. Lee sent a note to both his commanders to pursue the enemy to destroy them.

He did not have to worry. He knew they would do their best. Lee's only concern was the daylight left. As he saw the last of the blue men disappear out of sight he realized his forces only had about thirty minutes left before darkness in order to finish this great fight. He needed more time. He concluded it would not be the destruction of the Federal Army like he had wanted. Most of them would get away. Lee was still delighted at the day's events but stoic realizing the war might last much longer if Pope was able to retreat to Washington. Though there were horrific losses on both sides there would be no great shift in the balance of power. Pope would move to protect the Capitol and Lee would have to wait for another opportunity.

"Giddyup, Traveller. Let's go, boy," Lee said to his horse as he moved across the beautiful field of victory.

* * *

The final count at the Battle of Second Manassas was 16,000 wounded and over 3,000 dead. The Confederates spent days in the pouring rain caring for the wounded and burying their dead. Lee's horse, Traveller, was spooked and Lee fell breaking one wrist and spraining the other. He had to depart from Manassas in an ambulance, but he led his army for the first time onto Northern territory into Maryland. Lee hoped this move could bring reinforcements from Maryland residents who sympathized with the South. He anticipated filling up some of his decimated regiments with the new recruits from this border state. As they crossed the Potomac many of the soldiers sang the song "Maryland, My Maryland," to the tune of O'Tannenbaum.

The despot's heel is on thy shore,
Maryland! My Maryland!
His torch is at thy temple door,
Maryland! My Maryland!
Avenge the patriotic gore,
That flecked the streets of Baltimore,
And be the battle queen of yore,
Maryland, My Maryland!

Dear Mother burst the tyrant's chain,
Maryland! My Maryland!
Virginia should not call in vain,
Maryland! My Maryland!
She meets her sisters on the plain,
Sic simper tis the proud refrain,
That baffles minions back amain,
Maryland! My Maryland!

134.

Dear Landon,

How is my son doing today? I hope well. I have some things I want to write to you about in this letter. I know that you have had to be the man of the house while your father is away and I am proud of you. No boy should have to take care of his mother while his father is in prison. That is not how God designed the family to operate. You are a brave boy and having to endure much hardship as a result of this war. I am sorry you and mother and Kathryn are not allowed to live in our home. I am sorry I cannot be with you. I am sorry I am taken captive. I cannot wait to see you again and hunt with you in the fields and run our horses in the orchard by our place. Look at the stars in the evening and know that I am looking at the same ones and thinking of you and your ma. Please help mother with whatever she asks of you. Please do not complain and please mind like the good boy you always are. Soon this war will be over and I will be home again. Never take vengeance on a Union soldier. You must wait until you are old enough to fight. Mother has told me how some boys in town were fired at when they were found taking shots through a window at soldiers walking down the street. It is not worth the risk and that is not the way to fight against an opponent. A real man gives his opponent the opportunity to see him before a duel. You do not want innocent blood shed by your hands. Never fight merely for yourself or be outraged by a personal injury. Only fight and be moved to anger by an injustice done to others. Be the defender of the weak. Remember not to hit a woman. Never swear. Obey your mother. Trust in God. And always tell the truth. That's all for now—I miss you mightily and I am hoping one day to hear about a prisoner exchange.

Your Loving Father,
Conrad Montgomery

Written at Fort McHenry Prison, September 1862

135.

One evening Bruce walked into the headquarters tent and he encountered someone he would have never imagined being in the Confederate base camp. Standing next to the strange guest was Sandie Pendleton. Sandie said, "Bruce, thanks for coming so quickly. This individual said he knows you and has an important message for you."

It was Moses.

"Moses!" Bruce finally recovered from the shock and went over to his friend and grabbed his hand with his right hand and pulled him close to hug him with his left arm. Moses seemed a little tentative.

"Hello, Master Crawford. It is heartily good to see you," Moses said.

Sandie excused himself and departed from the tent.

Bruce grabbed Moses by the shoulder and said, "What on earth are you doing here, Moses? Are the Harrington's here as well?"

"No, suh. They don't knows that I have come."

"I am shocked to see you, I mean, you know that this is probably not the safest place for a free negro."

"I know, suh."

"Please, call me Bruce. We're boyhood friends."

"Okay, suh, I mean Bruce. I know it's not safe to be here, suh Bruce, but I was compelled to come. A family friend of ours needs yo hep."

"Molly? How is she? Where is she? Last I heard she was taken for questioning by some Union officers and nobody has heard from her since. My mother has written to me and told me that they had searched for her but couldn't find her. They think Daniel Tanner might be involved. Is that true?"

"It's worse, suh, she is actually being held prisoner at Harpers Ferry by the hands of not only Daniel Tanner, but the villain Major Welch."

"Major Welch? I've heard of him. He is the one who interrogated my mother a few months back. Some say he is not really in a unit in the Union Army but the Union tolerates him because he has a way with prisoners. On what grounds could they detain her as a prisoner?"

"Well, suh, she was taken against her will, dey said she was a spy and now's been held by dem for most of four months."

"Four months? Oh my God!"

"Please, suh, don't take the Lord's name in vain."

"I'm sorry, Moses, I forgot how sensitive you are to that. It's just unbelievable. How could she tolerate—how could they justify that?" Bruce asked.

"They says she done killed a man but it can't be true. You knows Miss Molly, she talks tough but she would never hurt nobody."

"What's going on, Moses? I mean, does her father know? Hasn't he been trying to help her."

"No, suh."

"Why?"

"Because he knows that she is in love with you and wants to marry you, and he could not stand it if his only daughter would marry a Confederate soldier."

"Wait a minute, Moses. You're talking foolishness now. What do you mean Molly wants to marry me? We haven't spoken for almost a year and a half and all my letters to her were returned. She hasn't written me once—how can you say that?"

"Because Moses knows. Dat's why. It's comes all over her face when your name is done spoken. Besides, she did get one letter from you that she treasured and took with her on her journey to Virginia, and that letter is how she got into trouble with Welch and Tanner and the other unsavory characters who are tormenting her."

Bruce walked around the tent at this point not saying anything.

"I've got to get some fresh air. Will you accompany me on a walk?"

"Yes, suh."

They walked outside where night was in full bloom with bright stars in the sky. They walked down a trail in the woods to an opening with a small lake. The stars and moon were beautiful as they reflected off the water.

Bruce looked up at his dark friend and said, "You mean to tell me that Old Man Harrington is so selfish about his views that he would keep his daughter locked up in a Union prison camp? I can't believe it, Moses."

"Well, dar is something going on, pehaps some arrangement been done worked up with the Union Army, but I does know Molly is being held against her will."

"Another question I have is about you. How do you know all of these things? Have you been spying on her?"

"No, no, Master Crawford, I's not spying. I would never spy on anybody!"

"I didn't mean in a bad way, Moses. The armies fighting each other, both sides, use spies and it is a legitimate way to gather information. Not if you're caught, however, because you would be hanged so you have to be good at it."

"That hanging part don't sound too legitmet to me," said Moses with wide eyes.

Bruce laughed.

"Anyway, Moses, how? How do you know this and why are you here now instead of three months ago?"

"I wanted to go looks for Miss Molly a long time ago and Mr. Harrington wouldn't let me. He told me he knew exactly where she was and it was none of my business."

"Then why are you here now?"

Moses smiled a big grin, "Because I don't listen to Mr. Harrington no mo."

Bruce smiled wanting Moses to continue.

"I left on the day after the Fourth of July to sees what happened to her. I gets down to Winchester at a bad time cause lots of Union and Fed'rates were going in and out of there. I's decided not to talk to yo mother or Mrs. Montgomery because on da outskirts of town I ran into some of my old friends who had slipped through the lines. They told me who to go talk to. There was an old blacksmith who worked for a general, I can't remember his name. He told me there were some young women held by a major and a mountain man at Harpers Ferry."

"Tanner!"

"Yes, suh. Tanner. I travelled over to Harpers Ferry and acted like a runaway and dey took me in and fed me and housed me. While I was there I discovered where Miss Harrington was. I's found her and we had a brief conversation. She sent me here, Master Crawford, and she has asked me to ask you to rescue her."

Bruce shook his head and thought, this doesn't make any sense. "What about Riley? Why wouldn't she ask for his help?"

"She's not thinkin bout dat young man!" Moses declared.

"Why, Moses? I'm not getting it. I'm not convinced."

Moses didn't say anything for awhile but looked down. Bruce knew he might have hurt Moses' feelings because he had basically called him a liar.

"Miss Harrington had conversations with Master McNair last Christmas when he was home on leave. They separated then and haven't talked since. If I can be so bold Master, I believe she really done fallen in love wit you."

"Moses, I want to believe you. I truly do. It would make my life if this was true, but I know Molly. You cannot read her mind or know her intentions or anything. Once you think you have her figured out then she turns completely around on you. Moses, I gave myself one more chance with her after being wounded in the heart and put off by her so many times. I decided to write several letters to her and share what was going on from a Confederate point of view. I went out on a limb, Moses, and it wasn't easy to do. I didn't know but maybe she was getting married to Riley or somebody else. But I never heard from her. It hurt me not to hear anything but I kept writing. I still had hope. But then her father sent back all of my letters and told me she was going to be married to somebody else. Since that time I have been over her. I have had peace, Moses, for the first time since I remember, I have had peace in regards to Molly because I resolved in my heart to let her go and that I would marry someone else."

"Master Harrington lied, suh."

"Lie? He doesn't lie, Moses. He is a pious man."

"I knows Master Harrington, suh."

"I know you do, Moses, and I don't mean anything by arguing with you. My mind is getting sucked back in and I don't want it to. There is pain in that journey and I have been hurt enough."

Bruce turned away from Moses and said, "I wish you had gone and spoke to Riley about this. He's on the right side, for crying out loud, and could have easily helped her out. I wish you hadn't come here!"

There was silence for awhile. Bruce could see that Moses looked dejected.

Bruce resumed the conversation, "You said she did get one letter from me?"

"Yes, suh. She told me about it the night she departed. She held onto it like it was gold."

Bruce raised his eyebrows at this and tried desperately to remember what he had written in it. "If that is true, and I am not doubting you, then why didn't she ever write back?"

"How could she, suh? Where was she to send it? Do you think the Union Army would deliver a letter to a Southern officer? Do you think it done be easy to get a message to dat General Jackson's aide? Do you know what they are saying 'bout dat man up north?"

"No, not really."

"They say he is a ghost, dat he is a phantom and he spooks all of the Union officers. When he done shows up to a battle then they know they will lose and they are putrified of him coming to Washington. They say he's ruthless and you is his right hand man. They also talk about dat General Lee."

"What do they say about him?" Bruce asked.

"Dat he's a fox."

Bruce smiled. "That's not such a bad name."

"You know who else was a fox?"

"Who?"

"King Herod. It's in the good book. Anyways, I knows der is no way for a Northern woman in Pennsylvania to gets a letter to a Southern officer without it being hand carried."

"Moses, if you don't mind me asking, why didn't she send a letter with you now if you're on an errand for her?" Bruce's eyes penetrated Moses' face as if trying to read his mind. Moses was apparently caught off guard with this question. He looked back at Bruce with utmost sincerity. He reached in his pocket and then reached out his hand to Bruce. Bruce put his hand under Moses' hand. Moses slowly opened his hand and something metal fell into Bruce's hand. When Moses moved his hand away Bruce saw an old metal bracelet made with copper fish hooks. Bruce stared at it in disbelief. He hadn't seen or even thought about that bracelet since they were children and he had given it to Molly on her front porch in Winchester one summer evening when he was only eight years old. Bruce now remembered the incident as if it was yesterday. He remembered the hard work building the wall with his best friends that summer. He remembered the heat and cooling off in Kathryn's stream. He remembered pushing Molly as hard as he could down to the ground and then feeling bad about it. And, he distinctly remembered how nervous he was to go to her house, stand on her porch and give her what he was now holding in his hand. He could not believe the flimsy gift still existed. He was proud when he saw it on Molly's wrist a few days later but then suddenly she stopped wearing it and he never saw it again.

At first his mind didn't want to believe this was happening and that it was really the same bracelet but there was no mistaking it. No one else could have made one so crude and Bruce recognized the hooks his pa and uncle used to make for him to fish in the Shenandoah. Bruce finally looked up into Moses' face and said sternly, "Moses, tell me truthfully how you got this."

"Miss Harrington gave it to me to give to you so you would know it was her, and, if you don't mind me saying, suh, to tell you she loves you. Her message to you now is—Come to me."

Bruce slowly sat down on the dewy earth by the lake completely stunned. He peered out over the water and thought about all of the times together as kids, all the fighting and all the dreams he had had of her. It sunk deep into him now and he should have seen it before this. Those two were made for each other. Both of them were stubborn. Both were leaders of their friends. Both were continually arguing with each other. Throughout all of their lives the two had been inexplicably drawn to each other, Bruce could see that now.

Learning this incredible revelation from Moses began to make Bruce think about other parts of his life. He looked up at the stars and the intensity and depth of them that evening. He always considered God as distant, someone who only came around in dire circumstances like helping Nathaniel Greene escape from Cornwallis during the Revolutionary War. Bruce always knew God couldn't have the time to know or care about every single person's situation. That seemed like a tremendous tale and a crutch religious folks relied on because they couldn't imagine a world where humans were ultimately in charge. Bruce had no proof one way or the other so he remained quietly skeptical. Even Jackson himself hadn't transformed his views. However, what happened that evening was shaking him. Maybe God did have a plan for him. Maybe Molly would one day be his. Bruce realized then that deep down he was sort of holding it against God for not allowing him to have Molly. It was easier not to believe in God than to believe in a God who didn't care about what ached in his heart.

Moses coming into his life that night changed more than his relationship with Molly, it blew away his concept of being on his own and fending for himself. As he sat there, Bruce put his head slowly down on his knees, and for reasons he could not explain a single tear slowly made its way down to the corner of his lip. He didn't cry in anguish, but two or three tears meandered the contours of his face. He had hoped for this night his whole life; confirmation that Molly loved him as deeply as he loved her. He also felt a strange warmness wash over him, almost like a blanket sweeping around his entire body inside and out. Bruce instantly thought it was God, however insane that thought was.

Bruce kept his face down on his knees for awhile. Suddenly the war seemed a little ridiculous. The new feeling spread from his heart to his mind and throughout his entire body. He really did love Molly with his whole heart. He couldn't deny it anymore. She was the woman for him; his one true love. But there was more going on inside of him. He was grieving the men killed and wounded he had fought alongside. He was grieving his own shortcomings. Bruce realized he wasn't just an observer of the war or a mere participant. He was complicit. He was the cause. His pride, strong will and feisty temper were roots in this conflict as much as slavery or pro-Union sentiment. He was guilty and he knew it. But he was also guilty of a greater rebellion. A rebellion to the king of the soul. Bruce had faced this war with his mind and will, but he knew now there was another way. There was a passage.

I love you God, thought Bruce for the first time. It felt good, but while thinking those words he realized the stronger feeling of God loving him.

Bruce thought of Christmas and the manger scene. He thought of the gift. Things started to click quickly for him and his mind began to race. *I'm tired of living on the outside and in rebellion. I'm sick to death of being king of my own castle. I give up. I repent of wickedness. I want to live in your kingdom. I want to follow you. I know there's more to life than this and it doesn't have to do with Molly.* Bruce thought of Good Friday and Easter. He thought of the cost. *Thank you for creating a path for me.* Without a church, without a minister, and even without a Bible, Bruce's heart and mind were renovated by conversing directly with God. He knew his life was different. He now had hope. And it came by way of Bethlehem.

* * *

Bruce wiped away the tear streaks with his hands and glanced up at Moses who was looking out across the lake trying to skip rocks. Bruce thought how odd it would seem if anybody were to happen to walk by them now, Jackson's aide tearin' up next to Moses. He used to pride himself in not letting his emotions get to him. *Well, so much for that.* Bruce stood up, adjusted his sword and walked toward the lake. Before he spoke he tried to regain his composure.

"Okay, Moses, I am going to have to get back to the command tent before I am missed. I guess the next question is what do we do now?"

"I have an idea. Would Master Crawford like to hear it?"

"Sure, Moses."

"I thought we could load up a wagon and you and I could make for Harpers Ferry tonight. They'd probably let me in again as a runaway slave. I could get you a Union uniform and secretly let you in. Then, you would have freedom to take Molly under lock and key sayin' you have orders to bring her to Washington or sumpin?"

"Sounds great, Moses, but I can't do that. I cannot leave my duties here. Jackson needs me every day and nearly every hour. He would never permit it and we have been forbidden to wear Union uniforms. Besides, do you think Welch would allow her to simply walk out of there with a stranger?"

Moses just stared at him. "What do you prose?"

"I don't propose anything except for me to get back to work," Bruce responded.

"So you will do nuthin to help Miss Molly?"

"I didn't say that."

Bruce stared at Moses trying to think about what he could possibly do without abandoning Jackson.

"Moses, you're going to have let me think about this tonight. Perhaps Jackson will give me a pass in the morning. He knows about my interest in Molly and he knows old man Harrington.

"What about me, suh?"

"You can bivouac with us tonight, Moses. I will tell folks you are a childhood friend and a free man. It shouldn't be a problem. Jackson has a special attendant, a former servant named Jim Lewis, you can bunk with him for the evening and if anybody asks tell them you are with me."

Bruce and Moses walked back to the bivouac area. After taking Moses to where he needed to go, Bruce checked with Sandie and then bunked down for the night. He tossed and turned unable to get the things Moses said to him about Molly off his mind. Eventually Bruce fell asleep and dreamed of a long, dark cave that emptied into a wide open area possessing an underground lake with an island at the center of it. Bruce found he could walk on the water across the lake and when he arrived there he found a campfire and Molly was there tending it. She embraced him and gave him a long hug. Bruce was about to kiss her but then he abruptly woke up. He was upset he could not finish the dream. He realized somebody else was in the room with him. He felt a hand on the top of his shoulder.

"Master Crawford?"

"Yes, what is it Moses?"

"I needs to go. I cannot leave Miss Harrington alone no mo."

Bruce was at a crossroads and he knew it. He couldn't let Moses depart and mess something up. He might never find Molly again and if he didn't he knew he would have failed her. Moses was also in danger and would have to pass through the Confederate lines without looking suspect of being a runaway.

Bruce sat up and looked into the darkness where all he could make out was Moses' eyes and said, "I have a plan, Moses, hold on."

136.

Molly sat on the tiny stool in the corner of the room thinking for the hundredth time about her possible options and the events that had happened the last few weeks. She would be a prisoner for only twenty-four more hours before they would come to get her. She had been tried and convicted of murder and she was to be hanged the next day at sunrise.

A few weeks earlier, after being apprehended by the Bullethead and Major Welch, along with the Mohican, Toad and the Children, Molly was taken to the Federal garrison of Harpers Ferry. She was put under house arrest in the second story, back room of a boarding house managed by Cornelia Stipes. Molly endured daily questioning by Welch and other officers. Thankfully, during that time she did not see Daniel Tanner much, but Toad and the Children were part of her daily life.

Toad was given the task of guarding the door to her room. When he was tired or needed a break he would have one of the Children cover for him. One of the Children, the one with only one hand, was from Martinsburg and Molly had developed a slight amount of trust with him through intermittent conversations. She could discern he was not thoroughly evil like the others, just greatly influenced. She took him on as a special project so whenever he was covering for Toad she would try to talk with him to develop a friendship. He would not allow her to say much at first because Bullethead and Toad had a sharp eye and would warn him repeatedly not to ever communicate with the prisoner when he was the guard. But Molly persisted.

She found out where he lived and who his parents were; where they went to church and what they did for a living. After many days Molly discovered that he began to open up a little more each time and began to trust her and enjoy her friendship. His name was Malcolm Carlisle and he was smart enough to not ever show any of his fondness for Molly to the others. In front of them he was consistently gruff and rude to her like everyone else. The others used to mock Malcolm and call him names like 'rodent.' They would also tease him about having a hand missing. Malcolm seemed not to mind, partly because he had nowhere else to go. Over the weeks, Molly had developed a deeper friendship with him out of daily familiarity and her desperate state. The feeling was mutual. She didn't mock him and he wasn't mean to her in private.

Malcolm had been instrumental in keeping Molly informed on what was happening to her on a day to day basis. It seemed Bullethead enjoyed the security of Harpers Ferry and decided to stay for awhile and use it as a headquarters. There were several thousand troops stationed there. It was so heavily fortified, the Union Army used it as an island amidst several counter-movements back and forth of the Union and Confederate Armies. Welch liked the proximity to Washington and the privacy he was afforded in a couple of old buildings which he used. He would send the Mohican, Tanner, out for errands and sometimes would wait anxiously for him for days until he returned. Tanner had a mind of his own and would sometimes disappear for weeks until he ran out of money or got bored. The Bullethead Welch would chew him out every time for not returning with his information immediately. Unfortunately for Welch, Tanner never made any corrections to his actions. He really didn't seem to care about what Welch wanted.

Through her relationship with Malcolm, Molly had sent a letter to her father asking for his help in her situation but she had no idea if the letter ever left the Ferry or was delivered to him. Things for Molly seemed to go from bad to worse. After several days of questioning and a preliminary trial with the accusation against her as a traitor, Molly was given a prison term of six weeks. This arbitrary trial and sentence gave Welch extra time to make unwanted advances toward her and try to win her heart. Molly refused every one of them while attempting not to insult him in the process. If provoked, Welch would hit her in her middle and in soft places which were covered with clothing, so that if she bruised, no one would ever know.

* * *

One evening in September old Bullethead came into her locked room after excusing Toad and Malcolm from the building. He had a different look in his eyes, a wild one which petrified Molly. She could smell that he had been drinking and his nose was unusually red. Molly sat on her stool against the wall and tried to press into the old wood and become one with it. Welch came close, grabbed her hand and looked into her eyes. He held out a new white dress he wanted her to put on.

Never, thought Molly.

Welch threatened and Molly was forced to change out of her old dress which now looked like rags and put on the new white one that looked somewhat like a wedding dress. Welch gave her no privacy. His eyes glowed as he watched Molly changing her clothes. He also gave her a white ribbon for her hair.

"You are a fine lady. I am very lucky you have come to me. God has given you to me as a gift."

"I wouldn't say that."

"Why not?"

"Because I am being held here against my will. With a gift there is joy. With love there is freedom."

"What do you know about love? What does any woman involved in this war know about love? The women I have met are treacherous and betray you."

Molly stared at him a moment calculating how far she could speak her mind. "When you speak of love you speak of meeting your needs. But love is more than animal lust. My legendary love will know this and I am waiting for him but he hasn't come for me yet."

"What the hell is a legendary love?"

"Ever since I was a little girl I dreamed of the man who would love me for who I am, not for what I could give him. One that would spend hours with me to try to understand me, and to try to help me understand myself and him."

"I have tried to do that, to talk to you, lady, but you never listen."

"The man of my legendary love will not be my prison guard. He will be one to whom I write love letters and poems. And one day when we are poor and have no money for food we will publish our love poems in a journal and make money by which to eat and travel away and see new lands."

"You're dreaming, deary. That'll never happen. Besides, what makes it legendary?"

"It is legendary because it comes once in a lifetime. Any other relationship is lesser."

"You are talking foolish, girl."

"Am I? Or am I finally telling you a little bit about the man who I will get to know and will be cherished by for the rest of my life." Molly was trying to drag on their conversation hoping he would decide to leave her out of tiredness or boredom.

"I am all you've got and you better get used to it. I am going to make you Mrs. Welch and we are going to live in the mountains and you are going to grow to love me by serving me."

"I cannot do that, Major Welch."

Welch moved a little closer to her and touched her hair, "You are getting older young lady, what are you waiting for? I can be your legendary love."

"I will never be in love with you."

Welch put his arm around her shoulders and drew her close, putting his nose in her hair and whispered to her, "I am all you've got. Everyone else has abandoned you. I think God is telling you that I am your long lost love. Your legendary love."

As his wicked breath ran down her neck Molly had a flash of chills and disgust. She turned away from him and declared again, "I will never be in love with you."

"Well, you are going to love me tonight!"

With that Welch yanked her hair downward and forced her from the stool onto the ground. Before she knew it he was on her and grabbing everything he could get his hands on. Molly dodged and tried to beat at him with her elbows and hands like she had done in the past but this time he was more persistent.

"Help! Help! Somebody, please help me!"

The attack was the worst Molly had experienced so far and Welch was having his greedy way with her and enjoying himself.

"Help me!" Molly screamed again, though it had never done any good in the past. "Malcolm!"

Malcolm, who Molly knew had developed an emotional attachment to her, hopefully wouldn't stand by and let this happen. Molly saw him enter the room.

"Excuse me, sir, I'll have to ask you to leave the ma'am alone," Malcolm sputtered out. His voice was calm compared to the violence in the room. He then walked up to Welch and tapped him on his back. Molly knew it had to take every ounce of courage for him to say anything. She looked up into his eyes with gratitude.

"Sir. Did you hear me? Leave her alone, please."

Welch turned venomously on his assistant and issued a command, "Get the hell out of this room or I will kill you, you one-handed rodent!"

Malcolm obeyed and disappeared out of the room.

Malcolm, don't leave now, I need you!

The attack continued for a moment when all of a sudden Welch's eyes enlarged, his mouth opened up and he bellowed a terrible grunt from his core. Molly heard footsteps leave the room while she pushed her assailant off her. She found there was a large knife handle sticking out of his back. Molly did not know what to do. She was exhilarated at the freedom and tried to catch her breath while Welch attempted fruitlessly to reach behind his back. A moment later she heard footsteps coming up the stairway. Molly wiped some blood off coming from a cut on her face and then fixed her torn, disheveled clothing. Welch was gasping for air. She looked at him in disbelief. He was slowly dying. *Could it be true?*

Toad, Malcolm and the other Child named Eric entered into the room. They stood just inside the door in disbelief. Welch was gasping and trying to speak. Molly was lying on the floor, battered and bruised and in near shock. Toad ran up to Welch and tried to speak to him but his eyes were bulging out. Whoever had stabbed him had used a Bowie knife with a wide, long blade and used a tremendous amount of force. The blade just barely penetrated Welch's chest on the opposite side of entrance wound.

Toad looked at Molly with disgust and said, "You've killed him. You've killed a military officer! You're going to hang, lady!"

Molly did not respond. She caught a glance from Malcolm who looked like he wanted to run by her side and help her up but he dared not move.

Eric ran out of the room telling everyone he was going to get a doctor. Welch took two more labored breaths and died. His lifeless body lay in one massive heap on the floor. His bullet-shaped head was beet red. His meaty arms lay still on the floor with his sweaty palms facing up.

Toad stood up, turned and kicked Molly in the ribs as hard as he could. She partially blocked his kick with her arm at her side but the pain was intense just the same. Toad then examined the knife protruding from Welch's back. He did not touch it but looked over it very carefully.

"I didn't kill him," Molly said softly.

"Shut up you dirty she-devil!" Toad yelled.

"Someone else was in the room," she spoke but it seemed to her the sound came from somewhere other than herself.

"You lying pig. Shut yer mouth!"

"Someone else must have killed him," pleaded Molly.

"That's impossible," said Toad. "I was just down the stairs and out front the whole time and nobody else came up here except Malcolm and he was the one who reported to me the major was stabbed. You were the only one in the room with him."

"It's not true, I didn't kill him. I didn't have a knife."

"Malcolm, gag her. I cannot stand to listen to this anymore."

As Toad examined the knife his eyes widened, "Hey, that's the same knife Tanner took from you when you were captured! What did you do, steal it back?"

Molly didn't answer so he kicked her again out of frustration.

"Um, please, I request that you not kick her sergeant," stuttered Malcolm.

"What'd you say to me?"

"Um, I'd ask that nobody would hurt her anymore."

"What are you saying rodent? Are you delirious? Shut yer stammering or I'll kick ya in yer face. Now help me get Welch up and take him downstairs. We can't leave him up here like this. Just look at him," said Toad.

They carefully moved Welch down the stairs, out of the building and into the house next door to be looked over by Army officials.

Malcolm was tasked with guarding her for the next few moments before some officers came to question her.

Molly locked eyes with Malcolm and asked him soberly, "Did you kill Major Welch for me?"

Malcolm didn't answer. He looked into her eyes for a moment. Molly could see he was terrified. He looked like a scared little boy who had just been caught doing something dirty.

"It's okay, Malcolm, you saved my life. It was a just thing to do."

Malcolm never responded. They heard people coming up the stairs. Malcolm finally smiled sheepishly and Molly reached out and quickly touched his cheek. Then he vanished from her life.

* * *

Molly was tried the next day and sentenced to death by hanging in two days at sunrise. The military tribunal used General Pope's command orders stating that any civilian causing harm to a Union soldier could be executed. What happened in Molly's room was an outright, cold-blooded killing and the board of inquiry had no sympathy for her. No one seemed to care about the vulnerable position she was in as he was attacking her, let alone consider that somebody else could have entered the room and stabbed the Major from behind. Molly did not rat out Malcolm but took the blame herself and kept silent.

Molly spent the first day after the trial weeping and feeling sorry for herself, wishing she could see her family and friends one more time. She also wished she could read all of her favorite literature again by Shakespeare, Dickens, Edwards and Swift. The next day she sat on her stool thinking about what she could tell Malcolm to convince him to try to rescue her that night. But, her hopes were dashed when Toad came into her room the next day and told her that Malcolm and Eric had departed and were no longer at the Ferry.

Toad explained he was personally responsible for guarding her until her execution the next morning and he had just drunk a pot of coffee so that he could keep awake. He then told her not to think about escaping because Daniel Tanner had arrived and he was guarding the area at the bottom of the stairs in case someone tried to rescue her. Molly was allowed one more bath and one more meal. She was refreshed by the cool water on her skin and the warm food in her stomach. She spent the last few hours thinking about her family and the Peacheys and Bruce's sweet letter. She hoped Tanner would not enter her room that evening, her last night to be alive.

137.

President Lincoln looked out onto Pennsylvania Avenue. He had been told thousands of residents were now fleeing their homes for fear of an attack on the Capitol. Beside them, the stragglers, deserters and wounded soldiers were in constant motion. When the second battle of Manassas concluded, the Union Army again poured into Washington in disarray and defeat, humiliated at the resounding thump General Lee and the Confederate Army had given them. Lincoln was weary. His heart ached for the men but he had no sympathy for their leaders. General Pope was denouncing General McClellan for not helping him in the battle. Pope was also processing a court-martial for Fitz John Porter because he failed to attack Jackson when ordered. George McClellan was irritable as ever and telling the press that the President, his Cabinet and his pick of Pope led to the catastrophe. And throughout it all the wounded continued to flood the city streets.

Washington was prepared to handle them this time, Lincoln thought while he watched. After the Peninsula Campaign, scores of buildings had been converted to hospital space for the wounded soldiers. Many schools, hotels, houses and churches were now filled with cots and medical supplies. Hundreds of women volunteered to become nurses to aid the dying and wounded. Lincoln's wife, Mary, spent hours that summer quietly visiting soldier after soldier and caring for them as a mother would a child. Lincoln found her newfound hobby a tonic for both of them as she would relay stories to him in the evenings of the young men she cared for each day. Lincoln loved her for this.

Thankfully, hundreds of the sick and wounded from the Richmond Battle had returned to their units before this last catastrophe. Some of the government buildings near the White House possessed rows of cots that had been emptied out in the weeks just prior to Manassas. Lincoln realized all of the space would be needed again. He turned around and walked back into his office. He could feel a depression darkening his countenance. He could tell his resiliency was being severely tested. His Proclamation was ready to be issued which would free millions of black men, women and children in slavery but his army could not secure a victory. *I hate officer rivalry,* he thought. The task at hand was what to do with Pope, McClellan, Halleck and Porter.

Lincoln reflected on the fact that Stanton wanted McClellan tried for treason for disobeying an order and not supporting Pope in his hour of need. Lincoln agreed with him that it seemed McClellan almost wanted Pope to lose, even though that thought was sheer madness. *Perhaps McClellan is mad,* thought Lincoln. He sensed something coming the day before when Stanton could not persuade Lincoln to censure McClellan. Lincoln thought that the War Secretary might retaliate by teaming up with Salmon Chase for a unified assault—and he was right. What Lincoln did not know until he met with them that day was those two had also enlisted Bates, Smith (Interior Secretary) and Welles and had written a document of protest suggesting most of his Cabinet would resign if McClellan was not fired. They said that Lincoln's entire administration would dissolve. Chase was too timid to bring Montgomery Blair into it, but the rest of the men obviously felt strongly that McClellan needed to be disposed of once and for all. Lincoln reflected on how many good people over the months had demanded Chase's resignation as well and he chuckled a little to himself about that. *What these men won't consider is the morale of the army. I am the one responsible for their leadership,* he thought. *I am the one who has the burden.*

When Lincoln sat at the meeting table he soon recognized his entire Cabinet was in a unanimous opinion for the first time. *This group has never agreed wholeheartedly to anything,* he thought. Usually a consensus had to be developed which wasn't unanimous. However, Lincoln always had the last say no matter how unpopular his decision might be. Whatever amount of political capitol he would lose, he always went with his natural instinct which, so far, had never let him down.

Salmon Chase pushed more than the others, "It is not that we don't value your opinion but we do not believe you are thinking clearly on this issue. Let us help you with this. In fact, we come just short of demanding we help you, sir. The future of our country depends on it. These are historical times and if the traitor McClellan is not abandoned we might actually lose this war."

As Chase concluded, Lincoln noticed Salmon looking at others while nodding to himself. *He can't even look me in the eye,* thought Lincoln.

"Salmon is right this time, Mr. President. We must make wise decisions with our next commander. John Pope is a good man and deserves another opportunity to excel."

Here we go. Now it's Bates' turn, thought Lincoln.

"Sir, the time is at hand to fire George Brinton McClellan! That is the short of it," said Edward Bates.

"Here, here," said Gideon Welles, Navy Secretary.

"McClellan ought to be shot, the traitor!" said Chase. "All of us here believe that except you," Chase snarled finally sneaking a glance at the President.

Lincoln noticed several of them squirm.

"That might be true, Salmon, but I wouldn't have put it in such harsh terms," said Bates.

"Sir, we have a signed document where we have all agreed on what should be done with General McClellan. Would you please respect it so we might move on toward victory?" asked Chase.

Lincoln cleared his throat to prepare to speak. He had never felt more fatigued as President.

Stanton, who had been fairly quiet so far decided this was his opportunity, since the others seemed to have had their say and were waiting for Lincoln to address the issue.

"Sir, you know how I feel about the issue wholeheartedly agreeing with my colleagues. You know if General McClellan had sufficiently aided Pope, Manassas could have been an outright victory and you could have issued your proclamation. He has had chance after chance and we simply cannot allow him to orchestrate another disaster for us. As humbly as I can say it, you must eliminate him as a commanding general. If not, sir, you will likely have several positions to fill in your Cabinet very soon," Stanton concluded soberly.

Lincoln glanced at Chase who was nodding vigorously. The others seemed somewhat surprised at Stanton's bluntness. Lincoln himself was a little shocked over their energy on this issue. Lincoln looked at them all, smiled and collected his thoughts a moment before speaking. Chase and Bates were sitting on the President's right. Lincoln noticed a missing button on Chase's jacket. At that moment, his assistant John Hay entered the room and sat down behind Welles next to the wall. Lincoln was glad to feel the presence of a supporter in the room. Hay looked at the Ancient and smiled. Lincoln would also have liked his friend Seward to be there but he was out of town. *That was convenient,* Lincoln thought stoically. The Ancient wondered what Seward would have to say on this issue, but then remembered that it didn't matter at that point—his mind was already made.

"Friends, I appreciate the bluntness by which you have purported your viewpoints as to how this war should be led. However, I am holding in my hand an acceptance letter from General McClellan to again lead the entire Potomac Army. I asked him this morning if he would accept this grave responsibility and help us regain some momentum." Lincoln looked around the table at the utter shock and despair. Salmon Chase put his head down on the table like an infant.

"I admit, McClellan acted as if to try to break General Pope and his plans—this is a shocking realization. So, this decision must appear to you as trying to cure the bite with the hair of the dog. But when you think about it objectively, no other general can strengthen our army like General McClellan. No other general could booster morale in a short time and get them back on their feet in order to wage this war. He is my pick and I would ask you to accept this. I, however, will not accept your resignations. We have more important tasks ahead of us and I need your help." Lincoln paused for a moment to let it all sink in.

Chase looked up but did not look directly at Lincoln. He stared at Stanton who was looking out of the window and had no color in his face.

"We must use what tools we have. There is no man in the army who can lick these troops of ours into shape half as well as he," said Lincoln unconvincingly.

"But he won't fight!" shrieked Chase in a high voice. His forehead was red and his lips terse.

"You may be right," responded Lincoln calmly. "But, as you noticed on your way here today, we have a panic on our hands. People are fleeing the Capitol. With McClellan in charge even a defensive posture would be better than what we have now," said Lincoln. "He excels in making others ready to fight. Would you like to hear his response?"

"Absolutely not!" said Chase looking rapidly at the others to echo him.

"You are going to anyway. One thing can be said for him, he is a consistent man in his strengths and his faults. He wrote back to me,

"So, I have been asked to save the country again. I will do so on one condition, that I have absolute authority over my troops and will not be asked to piecemeal them out to other commanders. This was risky and unnecessary. I will do what I can with the limited resources I have available to me and begin at once."

"So there it is," concluded Lincoln. He could see the pure anguish in the room and Lincoln sank to a new low. In fact, he felt a weight in his heart he had never experienced before. He knew in a moment his Cabinet would slink back to their offices stunned, hurt and betrayed. Lincoln was not happy about the decision either. He wondered who might tender their resignation by the end of the day. *Perhaps the best thing might be for me to be excused so I can go hang myself,* thought Lincoln as he stood up and concluded the meeting.

138.

Molly awoke from her slumber when a large artillery shell exploded near her building. More and more explosions sounded all around her and people were running to and fro in the street below. Molly did not know what was happening. She knew in a few hours she was to be hanged on the gallows in the courtyard. More noise from the cannon and more thunderous explosions as the shells broke through the rooftops and broke windows. Wooden steps and walls were being splintered, the earth shook and Molly moved to the interior corner of her room for a little more protection.

Toad came in and told her to stay where she was. He said any attempt of escaping would result in her being shot on the spot. For hours the shelling continued. Molly hoped for and thought it must be Stonewall Jackson and the Rockbridge Artillery. She was surprised he would attack such a fortified position as Harpers Ferry. The last she had heard was that Jackson was near Richmond helping Lee defend the Capitol.

The shelling ceased for a moment and Molly knew it was past her time to be executed. She waited. There was shouting and movement down on the street below her. The artillery began again, louder than ever as the shells began breaking into the buildings near her and exploding. Molly felt one penetrate the lower room of her own building and the floor shook violently. Part of the plaster from the ceiling fell down near her. She was startled by something in the doorway, and when the dust in the room cleared she saw a splendid man in a blue uniform and familiar eyes bounding toward her. Suddenly, an intense blast came from her left and everything went dark.

139.

The assault on Harpers Ferry was a highly dangerous mission for Thomas Jackson's troops. His task force had to be divided into three smaller columns which would separate for over twenty miles. This operation, engineered by both Jackson and Lee, was risky and had to be done with precision. Lee's plans were written up and called Special Orders No. 191. They contained in detail the execution for the Harpers Ferry attack. A large part of the risk lay in having to divide up their forces while in the enemy's backyard. Lee now had reports of General McClellan moving the Army of the Potomac toward him so Jackson had to move fast to achieve success or the entire Confederate Army would have to flee back into Virginia or be annihilated. Lee's total force was half the size of McClellan and Pope's consolidated command. Everything would depend on the celerity of Jackson's mission

Harpers Ferry was a strategic piece of land where the railroad travelled through. It was at the northernmost tip of the Shenandoah Valley. Heavily fortified by the Union since the war's inception, if Lee did not take control of the Ferry his pathway of escape to the rear would always be in danger. Plus, eliminating a threat behind him meant the Union manpower there could never be utilized for the North on a battlefield in Maryland.

Stonewall Jackson divided his command between McLaws, Walker and A. P. Hill. The three commands would sit like a triangle above Harpers Ferry on the heights surrounding it. The bulk of Jackson's force was with Ambrose Powell Hill who commanded Bolivar Heights. Hill, who Jackson was presently annoyed with, had asked if he could regain his command for this operation. Earlier Jackson had removed him from command and put him under arrest for insubordination. Since that time General A. P. Hill had marched in the rear of his column, in essence as a private, asking every day for Jackson to change his mind. When the Harpers Ferry operation unfolded Jackson relented and restored him to command because he needed a solid hand at the front. One good thing about A. P. Hill, he was never afraid to fight.

General A. P. Hill proudly sat on Bolivar heights with his forces skirmishing and intimidating the Union encampment just in front of them. His presence was keenly felt by the Federals who were pushed back to a small strip of land between the Potomac and the Shenandoah River.

General Lafayette McLaws battled for a day and won the top of Maryland Heights with his brigade commanders Joseph Kershaw and William Barksdale. Kershaw led a South Carolina unit and Barksdale a Mississippi brigade.

General John Walker took Loudon Heights with his North Carolina men. These forces formed a three-pronged offensive that started with showering down artillery rounds to devastate the morale of the men at Harpers Ferry. After two days with fifty guns raining death down from on high in a horrific cross-fire, the garrison stronghold had had enough and came out with a white flag.

The fruit of this quest for Jackson resulted on September 15th by gaining almost 13,000 prisoners of war, 12,500 weapons, 70 cannon, 200 wagons and over 1,000 mules. The cost of this adventure was just a handful of men killed and wounded. This now opened up General Lee's supply lines and ability to move back toward Virginia at any time without threat of a Federal force.

Jackson, Lee and Longstreet were pleased but did not know at the time of their victory that a Union corporal from Indiana had mysteriously found a copy of Special Orders No. 191 on a farm near Frederick, Maryland. The single piece of paper was wrapped around three cigars. As the man attempted to find a match for a relaxing smoke, some writing caught his eyes just before he crumpled up and discarded the paper. The order was addressed to Longstreet, Stuart, Jackson and D. H. Hill and was signed by the Robert E. Lee. The young man knew those names and feared them.

140.

Brigadier General Alpheus Williams was feeling pretty good after reviewing the secret orders an aide had just brought to him. As he read the copy he couldn't believe Lee had outlined precisely what he was going to do with his army for the next few days. Lee's forces would be divided and the Federals could crush them piecemeal if they acted quickly enough. Williams passed the order up to General McClellan and anticipated an immediate response regarding movement to locate and destroy the enemy. No order came. Williams sent a note to McClellan asking why they hadn't moved yet to capture an isolated Lee. No word returned. Williams went to visit him. McClellan outwardly seemed jubilant at finding out Lee's plans.

"What are you going to do?" asked Williams.

"Find Lee and destroy him," said McClellan.

"When?" asked Williams.

"As soon as we have enough troops," replied McClellan.

"When will that be?" asked Williams clearly annoyed.

"It will be when I say it is, General." McClellan turned away from him.

"Sir, if I can be so bold?"

McClellan shot Williams a warning glance.

"It has the routes Lee will take, the precise nature of their movements and the days of travel. For heaven's sake, it shows how we can defeat them while they are vulnerable. What more could we ask for?"

"We do not know the size of the Confederate strength. This could be a trap," stated McClellan.

"George, if you don't act immediately you will have made the gravest mistake of your life. In fact, you have already waited too long. I have heard the cannon fire from the Harpers Ferry area for almost two days."

"General Miles is at Harpers Ferry and he can hold his own. When we move to crush Bobby Lee, Miles will attack him from the rear and that will be that."

"So you are going to move and attack,"

"Yes, General, as soon as we're ready. Now leave before I put you under arrest for insubordination."

General Williams left with his heart as sick as it could be. Another great opportunity placed before them. Another great opportunity spoiled by high command.

141.

Bruce was finally able to rush into Harpers Ferry. While the prisoners were flooding the main road and filing out by two's and three's, he decided to have Moses stand guard at the top of the hill and watch for Molly while he dropped into the town. Bruce ran down the hill on the main road leading from Bolivar Heights and descended into the lower town area. He ran from house to house looking for a prison house and any sign of Molly's presence there. What he saw sickened him. Homes and stores were ripped to shreds and the devastation was everywhere. He found a dead woman in a reddish-colored dress who thankfully was not Molly. He found a small group of slaves hiding in a basement hoping not to be captured. Bruce didn't take the time to speak to them. He walked down the street calling Molly's name and hearing nothing but the wind. Lower Harpers Ferry was emptying out fast and Bruce was getting frantic. He found a gallows where hangings occur and he was scared he might be too late.

He had helped Jackson in making his decision about attacking and it didn't take much effort because his commander was already convinced it was the right thing to do. However, Bruce and Moses had to wait two extra days for their forces to get into position and the shelling to do its work. It was torture for Bruce, wondering of her well-being throughout every hour of delay.

As the new prisoners in blue stormed by him under a heavy guard, something caught Bruce's eye. It was a woman sitting on the edge of a front porch, dangling her legs over the side. Apparently she had nowhere special to go that day. She looked relieved it was all over. Bruce walked up to her and asked if she had known Molly or knew where she might be.

"There's quite a few women here mister, what'd she look like?"

Bruce described her to the woman in detail.

"I've seen her. She was carried out of the building just before her room crashed in."

"What do you mean carried out?" Bruce asked.

"A man in a Federal uniform scurried out with her. She didn't look well, looked sick or something."

"What do you mean?"

"Well, she looked asleep," the woman replied. "I was hiding under the stairs and saw the man walk out the door with her and I watched him take her into a building down the street from here."

"Where was that?" asked Bruce desperately.

"Just one block down that way and half a block up, across from the train depot. It's the narrow, gray building and it's next to the one caved in. There's hardly no paint left on it."

"Thank you, ma'am, thank you very much!"

As Bruce turned to leave the woman shouted after him, "You didn't tell me your name. Mine's Cornelia. Did you know you Southerners hit the commander here?"

Bruce didn't have time to make a new acquaintance though he was glad to hear about the commander. He raced down the street toward the building. He had walked by there earlier and searched the main floor and yelled to no avail. He thought she might be hiding but if she heard his voice she would say something. Now he knew he would have to search every corner of the house because she was hurt.

When he entered the house he first bounded down the basement stairs. He turned and saw the unmoving form of a woman laying on a military issue blanket. He rushed to her side and looked at her face.

Bruce had finally found Molly, but she was unconscious.

142.

Halleck was overjoyed to receive the telegram that evening and read it to the President.

"Something has fallen into my lap. Bobbie Lee has made a gross mistake. I will hand you the head of Stonewall Jackson on a platter by the end of the month."

Gen. George Brinton McClellan

143.

When Molly opened her eyes she expected to hear the loud explosions and to be in the same prison room but she was not. It was quiet. There was no one near her. She was lying amongst some blankets in a tent. She could hear birds outside. She wondered if she was dreaming. Perhaps she was dead. She laid still a moment and tried to feel if her body was hurt. There was pain in her left arm. She listened for activity outside and she heard nothing. She remembered nothing about leaving Harpers Ferry. She remembered the ceiling crashing in, the dust and a vision of someone. She did not know if the vision was real or a dream. She reached for her throat realizing she was thirsty.

Molly rose up and moved the blanket covering her. She was still in the white dress Welch had given to her and she had a thick bandage wrapped around her left arm. She crawled to the tent flap and looked outside. She could not see anyone. It was late morning by the cast of the sun. She stood up on the ground outside and looked around. The tent was on the edge of a large clover field aside a thick row trees. There were two men sitting in the dirt with their backs leaning against a massive oak tree and their hats over their faces. She recognized the form of one but not the other.

She cleared her dry throat slightly and noticed the noise did not disturb either man. She knew the man who was snoring. Molly winced a little because of her arm pain and slowly walked over to the one she did not recognize. She reached for the hat draped over his face and gently lifted the brim with her fingers. As she moved the hat slowly off of the bearded face she realized she had no idea who she might find there. The man did not awake and had the most sublime countenance on his lips, cheeks, nose and eyes. She studied the familiar face and realized all at once who this man was, the revelation almost knocking her over. Her heart stopped. Her throat dried up even more and she tried to swallow but she couldn't. There, just inches away from her, was the man she had thought about more than any other over the last few months. She did not expect to see him. And she did not expect to see him with Moses.

It was Bruce Crawford. She laid the hat gently back on his face and limped back to her tent. She crawled inside and laid on the mat and wondered at all that had happened the last twenty-four hours. She was supposed to be hanged. She could have been killed in that room with the onslaught of shelling. *How was it possible for Bruce to have found her?*

She thought of Moses. She spied a canteen next to her mat and took a long drink of water.

Soon, one of them stirred and walked over to the tent and peered in. It was Moses.

"Good mornin', Miss Molly," said Moses.

"Good morning, Moses. Is that Bruce Crawford out there with you?" she asked.

"Yes'm."

They heard the other man yawn and stretch and stand up.

"I have some questions for you Moses."

"Yes'm."

"Moses, is she awake?" The voice startled them both.

"Why, yes suh master Crawford, she's awake and awonderin what's goin on."

"Hello Molly, could you come out please?" asked Bruce politely while he walked toward them.

Molly exited the tent and stood up just two feet away from where Bruce was standing. She looked into his beautiful blue eyes. He stared back into hers. He had a half grin on his face.

Moses stepped back a little and Molly started to speak, "I," but didn't finish her sentence. "Thank you."

Bruce shook his head a little to tell her she did not have to thank him. Then he impulsively stepped forward and put his arms around her and hugged her tightly.

"It's good to see you," Bruce said.

"It's good to see you, too," said Molly. She gently hugged him back with her arm that didn't hurt.

Bruce let go and looked at her face, "It is?"

"Yes."

"Are you surprised?" Bruce asked.

"Yes, of course. I don't understand."

"What part?"

"Several parts." Molly looked behind her and saw a nice tree that had fallen over and was just at the right height for sitting. She sat down on it carefully while she talked and rested her left arm on her lap. "I don't understand what was happening at Harpers Ferry with all the explosions. I don't understand how I am here now instead of there. And, I don't understand why you are here with Moses instead of my father or Ned."

"Well, I can explain most of it to you," Bruce said, a little puzzled at her last question.

"Please do."

"Once I heard from Moses where you were, I spoke to General Jackson about the benefits of an attack on Harpers Ferry. He had already been thinking about it. He is a secretive man and does not like to discuss war plans so you have to say things in a round about way. He told me he had wanted to attack the Ferry for over a year, ever since Manassas. It made great strategic sense, especially since our forces are now in Maryland."

"Your forces are in Maryland?"

"Yes, they were until we crossed back over the Potomac to attack the Ferry. Anyway, General Lee also wanted to attack the Ferry, so plans were drawn up and orders were issued. Moses knew your approximate whereabouts in the town so we decided as soon as we attacked we would rush inside and locate your building and rescue you."

Molly was looking at Bruce in disbelief.

Bruce was looking at Molly in pure awe. This was the first time in their existence together she let him speak without interrupting him. *Molly has changed,* thought Bruce.

Bruce has changed, thought Molly, looking at the calm, mature warrior.

"Well, after the first day of shelling the Ferry I was a little nervous you might be injured in the onslaught. None of us had seen a better artillery attack, the scurrying men and buildings were like shooting ducks in a barrel. This worried us for your safety so early on the second day Moses and I scurried as close as we could to the main path leading down into Harpers Ferry. We had to wait for hours until they finally raised the white flag, but Moses and I were two of the first people into town after the surrender was negotiated and the infantry arrived to arrest all of the prisoners. We didn't want to miss you."

Bruce went on to explain how he couldn't find her at first, but then located her in the basement.

"I don't remember how I got down there," said Molly thoughtfully.

There was a moment of reflection before Molly asked her next question. "Where are we currently?"

"We're near a little town in Maryland called Sharpsburg. Antietam Creek is just down the hill through those trees. My unit is not too far from here."

"Maryland?"

"Yep. You've been out for quite a few hours. After we bombarded Harpers Ferry for two days they finally surrendered. It was the largest amount of prisoners we have ever captured, over ten thousand of them." Bruce walked over and sat down next to her on the tree.

Molly's thoughts suddenly raced to Welch, Toad, Tanner and the Children. She was thankful Welch was dead, but still mortified thinking of ever being found by one of the others. "So what happened to everyone who was at the Ferry?"

"All the soldiers?" asked Bruce.

"Everyone--"

"They were all taken as a prisoner of war."

"Are they secure, in a prison somewhere?"

"Not really. Actually, no."

"No?"

"Jackson couldn't take them all with him so most of them are in the process of being paroled."

"Paroled? You mean he is letting them go?"

"Eventually they will be. General A. P. Hill's unit is still at the Ferry dealing with all the logistics."

"I can't believe it."

"He had to. We couldn't possibly take them with us."

"So they are free out there somewhere and can show up at any minute?" Molly looked around the campsite as if trying to make sure none of the Federals were watching them.

Bruce started to say something about what will happen with the Union soldiers but then halted, noticing she looked petrified. "Are you okay, Molly?"

"Why did you bring me here, Bruce? Why to Maryland? Why not back home to Winchester?"

"I have to stay with the army. Jackson is a stickler for those who go absent without leave. We hang people all the time for that."

"Don't say the word hang around me ever again, please."

Bruce realized the old Molly was slowly coming back.

"Why not?" he asked, but then immediately regretted it. *She had been through enough. She didn't need to explain,* he thought.

"Because I was supposed to be hanged for murder the morning you began to fire at us."

No one spoke for a moment. *How could anyone imagine this woman as cultured as a Roman goddess ever lifting her hand to slay another man?*

Then Bruce remembered the fights they had been in as kids.

"That would have been a great tragedy for your family, for Winchester, and for me," Bruce said.

Molly startled at his last phrase. This was definitely a different Bruce than she remembered. *He would never have shared how he felt about me before,* she thought.

Molly looked into his eyes and asked her most pressing question, "Why are you and Moses together, Bruce? Why were *you* seeking to rescue me?"

Moses began to back away a little bit at this question. Turning around, he slowly slipped into the trees looking for a way to escape.

Bruce smiled and reached in his pocket and pulled out the old bracelet he had made for her. He opened his hand and proudly showed her his treasure, grinning like a Cheshire cat.

Molly gasped and stood up. "How did you get that? Have you been in my things?"

Bruce was confused, "No, Moses gave this to me from you."

"Moses? What are you talking about?"

They finally noticed how Moses had slowly drifted away, ever so quietly, into the trees and out of sight.

"Moses!" they both yelled at the same time.

Moses stopped moving and hid behind a large tree. They couldn't see him and he was not moving.

Bruce's mind was exploding. Molly hadn't given the bracelet to Moses to solicit Bruce's help. *Molly didn't need or want me after all,* he thought. *God, what is going on?*

Molly's mind was exploding. *Bruce knows now that she had kept that bracelet for all those years. Bruce must think I am desperate for him,* she thought.

They both looked at each other.

Bruce felt the fool.

"You mean you didn't talk to Moses about me to have him come and find me?"

"No Bruce. I haven't spoken to Moses for months."

More silence.

Awkward silence.

"I feel like a fool Molly, to have let Moses make me believe you had sent for me."

"No, don't," said Molly.

They both looked at each other a moment. Molly held out her right arm and said gently, "Will you take me on a walk?"

Bruce allowed Molly to wrap her arm through his as they stood up and walked in the direction opposite of where Moses went. They climbed a slight rise in the ground up to where some cedars were standing in a clump. They talked for almost an hour about all of their adventures, of their families, of their faith in God and in their feelings of the war. They spoke of everything except their feelings for each other until Molly decided to take a step of faith.

Molly glanced at Bruce and said, "I did not ask Moses to take my bracelet and give it to you for your help," she paused, "but I am glad he did."

They walked a little farther and found a trail descending for a few yards. Soon they were standing near the beautiful creek.

"I still feel foolish," said Bruce.

Molly decided it was time to end the status quo. She would share her heart with him. *What will be, will be.*

"Bruce, you have rescued me from tragedies that are too terrible for me to recollect and tell. You have become my knight in shining armor and I do not care why you came or if you feel slightly deceived or taken advantage of because I want you to know I couldn't be happier. Moses, bless his heart, knew all along how I felt about you, even if I wasn't quite sure myself. He probably knew for years that I kept your bracelet in my dresser drawer, and he found it and brought it with him when he came south looking for me. The important thing for me is that you came. You could have looked the other way but you came. You risked your life for me. You make me feel safe. This is a feeling I have not experienced for a long time. I have seen the dark part of humanity in the last few months and met some of the smallest people imaginable. I often thought I could never trust another man. Yet, I have also spent time with some wonderful people along the way who have made me rethink my views on having a husband and even on the war. I have been tortured by the Union Army, yet I find myself unimaginably thinking more like them than I ever used to. I've had to ask God for forgiveness for doubting him. He is bigger than my circumstances and has larger plans than I could ever imagine. And, in all of this there was one hope besides God keeping my sanity, one person I thought of which helped me believe everything would one day be okay."

"Riley?" Bruce asked.

"No, not Riley!" Molly said. She was surprised by Bruce's comment and hit him on the arm.

"You, Bruce Crawford! I have thought about you, well, not as a silly girl who speaks of her wedding and this and that before she ever has a fiancé, but as a hope that one day everything bad in this world, like my father dying when I was in grade school, would be recompensed with a gift from God, not only of his son Jesus, but of a friend to me in this life I could grow old with, and argue with and make meals for. That person is you, Bruce, and I could never truly admit this to myself until I saw your face under that dirty hat of yours when you were asleep sitting next to Moses."

"You saw my face?"

"Yes, I peeked at you when you were sound asleep and at that moment I knew for sure. I could admit to myself it was Bruce Crawford who was that man for me. What I am trying to say to you, Bruce, is that I don't want you to think about Moses and the bracelet and ever worry about my feelings for you again, because I--, I love you Bruce Crawford, with everything in my heart, and I want nothing more than to spend the rest of my life by your side." *There, I have said it all. It must have sounded like madness, but it was out and destiny will decide the rest for me,* Molly thought.

Bruce stopped walking for a moment and leaned against a tree. He was absolutely thrilled and shocked. He had never heard anything like this coming from Molly before in his life. He had never heard anyone speak so openly of their feelings for another like this, not even his parents! All the while she was talking to him he knew he would reciprocate with brutal honesty. He would be vulnerable and expose his soul fully to her.

Bruce took both of his hands and placed them on Molly's cheeks a moment before he spoke. He looked into her eyes and said, "Molly, this war has been hard on all of us and I know it has changed me. In many ways it has turned me into a man. I have learned about leadership and how to follow directions and orders, even when I do not like them and know they will fail. Jackson has made me think deeply about the love of God and doing the right thing and being a person of humility and character. I have been shot at, wounded, and almost captured once or twice. Through it all I have held on to the idea there is something better for me after the war and it is wrapped up into the person of Molly Harrington. I have thought about you and cherished you every day from afar. These last days, as I have come to understand the price and value of a relationship with God, I have prayed for you and asked him to help me find you. I have grown as a man, as a leader and now I want to be a husband because I have found in you the woman my heart has always longed for. I did not realize my love for you just today, but when we were eight years old and I pushed you to the ground. Ever since that night I first brought you the bracelet I have thought how wonderful it would be if I ever found myself by your side, as your man. This love, this belief in love, has never left my thoughts. From Kathryn's creek when we were young to this creek we are standing by now, Molly, I have loved you and I tell you now I love you from the depths," Bruce paused ever so slightly, "of all that I am. I want to be there for you in every experience you encounter, in every adventure life throws at us. Would you join me in this--?" Bruce didn't finish his sentence, but bent down onto one knee and asked, "Will you join me in this great adventure of life and marry me, Molly? It would make me the happiest man alive." Bruce held out his hand for her to accept.

Molly couldn't breathe. She looked down at Bruce in amazement. All filters were gone. They were speaking to each other as openly and honestly as anyone ever could and it felt invigorating.

"Yes!" and she dove into his arms knocking him over.

They wrestled on the ground and laughed for awhile and then Molly spoke first, "Well, we have just said some of our vows, now we need a minister."

Bruce smiled and said, "Isn't Moses a minister? Could we not have him take out his Bible and marry us right here by Antietam Creek?"

"We could if we could find him," Molly said laughing. "Moses? Moses?" Molly called for her lifelong friend.

"Moses!" Bruce yelled.

Soon, a very shamefaced Moses came out from behind some trees and walked toward them. He had been following them and knew that he was going to get some abuse for his actions.

"Moses, we need to talk to you," said Molly sternly, trying to scare him.

"I knows, I knows," Moses said sorrowfully. "I canst tell you how badly I feels for what I's done deceiving you folk."

Bruce cut him off, "Moses, be still. Don't worry about the past. It's okay. We forgive you.

"Truly?"

"Yes, silly," Molly answered giving him a quick hug. "We were wondering if you would marry us?"

Moses' eyes became as big as could be, "Marry you? Is you kidden old Moses?"

"No, we're not kidding," answered Bruce. "We have worked things out between us and said our vows to each other. We would like you as a minister of the word of God, to marry us right now. We would do it ourselves but we want it to be legitimate and have a witness."

"Yes indeed. I can marry you, I've performed many weddins. However, you want to do this now, here in dem dar trees, and by this old creek? What about in Winchester with the families?"

"We've both been close to death, Moses, and believe in seizing every moment as if it might be our last," Bruce said. "We are desperately in love and the time for this is now."

Moses turned toward Molly, looked deep into her eyes and received every confirmation he could have been given of her sincerity. He took out an ancient, yellowed Bible from his left breast coat pocket, grabbed both their hands and looked at them thoughtfully. Then Moses said, "You two's about to seal your lives to one t'another. Your weddin vows are da most sacred and solemn promise you can utter and must never be done rashly or irreverent-like. I can sees by the looks in yo eyes dat dees are not rash vows. And dat is good cause you will give count of dees vows to your creator who done made you. Marriage is institutionized by God and reg'lated by his commandments. Never forsake da Lord or dees vows made hea today. The Song of Solomon says, 'Place me as a seal over your heart, like a seal on your arm. For love is as strong as death, its jealousy as enduring as the grave. Many waters cannot quench love, nor can rivers drown it out 'cause the coals of love are the coals of the brightest fire.' Do you believe this?"

"We do," Bruce and Molly answered in unison.

"Okay, you'ons, please turn and face each other. Now, Master Crawford please repeat after me; I, Bruce Crawford, takes you Molly Harrington, to be my wedded wife, to have and to hold, from dis day forward, for better for worse, for richer or for poorer, in sickness and in health, to love and to cherish, 'til death do us part."

Bruce echoed Moses, phrase by phrase through to the end, staring at Molly's velvet complexion and tender eyes.

Moses looked at Molly and said, "Your turn Ms. Harrington. Please repeat after me; I, Molly Harrington, takes you Bruce Crawford, to be my wedded husband, to have and to hold, from dis day forward, for better for worse, for richer or for poorer, in sickness and in health, to love and to cherish, til death do us part."

Molly repeated Moses phrase by phrase smiling at Bruce and squeezing his hands.

"Do you have a token to give to Ms. Harrington?" Moses asked looking at Bruce.

Bruce pulled out the old bracelet he had given her years before and gently put it on her wrist for a second time. Moses smiled sheepishly at them, proudly taking credit for this part of their connection.

Bruce said, "This bracelet I give you as a constant reminder of my love."

Molly had a tear in her eye as she watched him place it around her wrist and say those words.

Moses said, "Please kneel here before me."

It was the first time that either one of them had kneeled before a black man. Moses scooped his hand down into the creek and poured out a bit of water onto their heads. He then laid his hands on their heads and prayed for them the most eloquent, beautiful prayer of dedication Bruce and Molly could ever remember hearing. It was from the heart; pure, godly and childlike. His phrases seemed to be caught up in the air and ascend directly to heaven in his blessings on them and his asking of God's protection. Finally, it was over and Moses helped them stand up and then concluded, "Inasmuch as I am a minister of the gospel of God's grace and 'cause of yo pledges to each other on dis 16th day of September, I now pronounce you husband and wife, Mr. and Mrs. Crawford. What God done joined together let no man separate. You may now kiss the bride."

Bruce and Molly had never kissed. They hesitated a moment and then Bruce leaned forward while Molly wrapped her arms around his neck and they kissed without abandon.

Moses beamed.

The couple walked hand in hand back up to the campsite and Molly asked Bruce how long he had. He said that he should return back to the bivouac site before dark.

"Well, that gives us the afternoon," Molly said with a squeeze to Bruce's hand. It was thrilling for her to hold the hand of her legendary lover.

Bruce and Molly enjoyed a light lunch with Moses of some ham, crackers, biscuits and oranges. As soon as they were finished, Moses excused himself to return to the headquarters area. He would report to Sandie Pendleton that Bruce would be there sometime in the evening. Bruce and Molly said goodbye to their dear friend and entered into the small tent and closed the flap.

They were now utterly alone.

Despite the simple wedding and their austere surroundings they believed they must have been the happiest couple alive. They were each deeply in love with the person holding them at that moment. The wondering was over but not the wonder. They did not hear the rain drifting through the elms, softly tapping on the clover below, and the supper hour came and went unnoticed.

Part IX

Antietam

All wars are civil wars, because all men are brothers.
FRANÇOIS FÉNELON

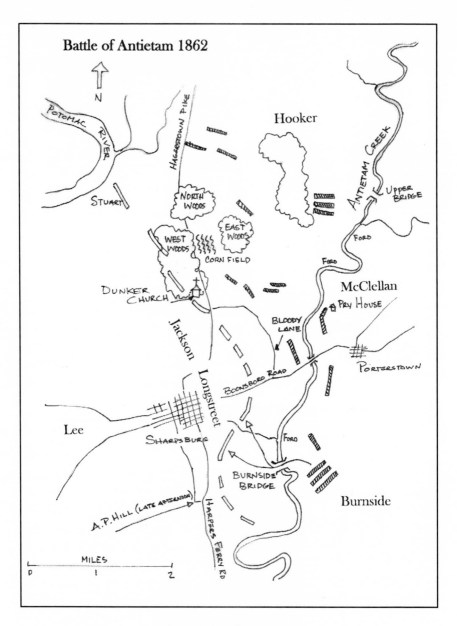

The Battle of Antietam

144.

The Visitor stood in McClellan's headquarters building near Frederick, Maryland. He was hearing for the first time that the Commander had in his possession a copy of Lee's orders and was going to trap the Rebel leader between two mountain passes. General McClellan would then be able to cut off and destroy the rest of Lee's forces who would be taken at unawares. The Visitor knew he had to depart the command area at once, yet couldn't make an immediate departure because the Young Napoleon was briefing and would be offended. The Visitor stood in the back of the room motionless except for an annoying twitch in his right eye that had been bothering him for the past three weeks. He did not like the twitch because it did not help him appear believable when he was relaying secret information from a 'reliable' source.

When the Visitor arrived at the Union bivouac site a few minutes before, he was surprised at the hustle and bustle and renewed excitement in the camp. He had ridden much of the night from the Confederate position on the Potomac River so he could see what McClellan was up to. When he arrived he was unusually fatigued, but even dog-tired he could tell there was something in the air. Wagons were being loaded, ammunition was being disbursed and columns of men were forming. He had never attempted it before but he knew the only way to find out what was truly happening was to enter the headquarters building. He saw other officers arriving there and flood into the building. Perhaps he could remain anonymous and save the Confederate Army from disaster. He believed it was worth the risk so he entered the command building and was soon thankful he did.

He stood in the very back of the room and as he listened to McClellan speak he realized the unthinkable had happened. By some mysterious twist of fate a corporal of the Union Army found the plans of the enemy and they were spelled out in full. General Lee and the Confederate Army would be ruined if they were not made aware of McClellan's good fortune.

McClellan finally dismissed the group and asked to meet with his corps commanders. This was the Visitor's chance. He slipped out the door and began walking over to where his horse was tied. He could see Torch and was just about to reach him when he heard a voice from behind that froze him in his tracks.

"You there, where are you going so fast?" The strong voice was of a commander who was in the briefing room. The Visitor knew of him but they had never spoken. He turned around and faced Brigadier General Alpheus Williams, the First Division Commander of XII Corps whose subordinate unit had found Lee's orders.

"Good morning, sir, I have got to prepare my men for movement."

"Which men are those?"

"My regiment, I'm in the 1st Cavalry Brigade with Colonel William Averell," the Visitor mumbled.

"Really? I know most of the officers in his brigade and I don't remember you. Bill Averell is a friend of mine. Do you mind if we go talk to him?"

"He's not here, sir, he is in Washington recovering from sickness."

"I'm aware of that. Which regiment do you lead?"

"I am the deputy commander for the 4th Pennsylvania."

"And where are they located right now?"

"Just north of here near Turner's Gap."

"What's your name?"

"James Smith."

"Really, Mr. Smith? Did you know there is a spy in our army who disguises himself as a lieutenant colonel?"

"No sir, I didn't know that."

"Are you that spy, Smith?"

"No sir, of course not."

"Then you wouldn't mind if we questioned you a little more, would you?" General William's aide approached him at this point.

"Sir, I told you that I am not the spy and you do not need to waste your time with me," the Visitor's eye was twitching and his forehead had beads of sweat on it.

"I don't believe you, sir."

The Visitor froze and tried to think fast. He knew he could jump on Torch and be off unless the men were to tackle him. This is precisely what he decided to do when he heard General Williams shout loudly.

"Arrest this man!"

The Visitor leapt for his horse. He mounted Torch but Williams' aide grabbed one of the reins from him before he could take off.

"Don't let them him go, Percy, this man is a spy!"

"Help! Quickly! Arrest this man, he is a traitor!" Williams shouted.

The Visitor kicked Torch in the ribs hoping the horse would run over the aide but it was no use. His beloved horse was soon surrounded by a mob of people. Someone grabbed him off of Torch and pushed his face down into the dirt while someone else tied up his arms. The Visitor had no idea that all of the Union commanders had been briefed about his existence just weeks before and they were watching closely who entered and departed McClellan's headquarters building. Williams took a careful eye at anyone he did not recognize, especially after an announcement that would be catastrophic for the Confederate Army. The Visitor had taken a fabulous risk and lost. He knew it would likely bring about his death.

General Alpheus Williams escorted 'James Smith' back into the command tent and conducted an inquiry which found the Visitor guilty of treason. He was soon sent to Washington under a heavy guard.

145.

September 16th, 1862 was clear and cool in the morning with light sprinkling in the afternoon. Riley, Ned, and Hans all camped with the 4th Pennsylvania Cavalry commanded by Colonel James Harvey Childs. Childs was recently given command of the 1st U.S. Cavalry Brigade because Colonel William Averell was still sick with malaria after the Peninsula Campaign. The three young friends reflected on their ride through Frederick, Maryland a few days before. They heard energetic cheers and enthusiasm from the people there. It made them proud and welcomed, encouraged to perform their best. Even Ned was appreciative of their time in Frederick though he was one of the most defeated souls in the Union Army that summer. He still had never fired his weapon at the enemy. Not wanting to be participating, but having no alternative, he slogged through the Chickahominy swamp near Richmond and returned to Washington with tired legs, sore feet and a bitter tongue.

Hans still alternately wrote to Chelsea and Mary each evening. The Union Army moved slowly and allowed for plenty of time in the evening for a good supper and to set up a comfortable camp. Hans used his free time to write poetry and letters. One poem he wrote was entitled "War Is No Longer Fun."

> *Little boys play with little boy's toys*
> *Soldiers, cannon and horses*
> *The soldiers fall wounded, the cannon destroys*
> *Until the battle worsens*

When all the toys have been knocked over
And little boys grow tired
They're collected up, stored in a box
Like nothing has transpired

Not so with me when I take hits
The fragile feel of life revealed
From dust to dust, slipped soul emits
No more the sword I'll wield

Riley still ached for Molly. He had written many letters to her but had not received any back. Ned's parents had written to Ned stating they had not heard from her and did not know where she was. Ned's mother asked him if he would take some leave and go to look for her, but Ned was refused when he asked his commander. Lucas Harrington wrote to Ned later and asked him not to take leave, stating he would be the one to look for Molly. Ned knew his parents didn't see eye to eye on how to deal with Molly, but Ned was unable to do anything about it now that he had enlisted. Lucas had also written to Riley telling him Molly would be his wife as soon as the war was over. Riley wished he could hear that from Molly instead of her father.

The three friends had mixed emotions when they heard General McClellan was to again be their commander. Hans cheered when he heard the news. Riley was encouraged but hoped McClellan would be more aggressive this time. It seemed to him both Lee and McClellan constantly defied the odds. Lee when the odds were against him, and McClellan when they were for him. Ned didn't really care, he just wanted the whole ordeal to be over.

The young men were not asked to do much of anything that day. They were part of the vanguard of the entire Union Army which numbered around 90,000 men. They had arrived at Antietam Creek the afternoon of the 15th, in time to set up a comfortable camp and eat a hearty meal before going to bed. They were assigned to the far left side of the formation almost two miles from McClellan's headquarters to the north. The rumor in camp was that they were about to hit General Lee's Army with one massive assault and destroy him. A piece of intelligence had been discovered which gave their side an advantage. Riley hoped General McClellan would get it right this time and be the victorious commander the country needed to end the war. Lee's entire army was said to have invaded Maryland and this gave the North a chance for a broad engagement.

Riley spent a moment reflecting on the fact that between him and the Potomac River a few miles away were his long-time friends from Winchester; Bruce, Henry, Jonesy and Moss. He might have to shoot at somebody he knew and he wondered if he could do that. He had written a letter to Molly the night before asking for her forgiveness if she were to hear about the situation occurring and he tried to explain to her again why he would raise up his hand against fellow countrymen. It was a little easier to enter into this upcoming battle knowing the South had invaded the North and still having the cheers of the citizens from Frederick echo in his mind. But he still wondered if he could do the right thing when the time came. Thinking about the forthcoming battle, he decided to write a quick note to Molly in case it was his last chance.

Dear Molly,

Greetings from Antietam Creek Maryland on September 16th. We have camped here just a few miles from the position of the Southern Army. It is likely today or tomorrow we will enter into a major engagement which could decide the war. Though I have not heard from you for a long time I am not discouraged regarding our friendship. My only concern is for your safety. Molly, if you need help in any way please allow me to assist you. As I reflect about our past friendship it is easy to think about how wonderful it would be to spend a life together after the war. I cannot imagine anyone who could exasperate you more than I. I know my writing is more forward than any of my words in person would be, but when a man knows not what the next twenty-four hours holds for him he acts almost desperate. I love you Molly Harrington and I would joyfully marry you if you would have me. I know that I could never again meet someone like you and I am thankful to God for allowing you to be born in Winchester and become a childhood friend, a schoolmate and hopefully a sweetheart.

Your friend,
Riley

The sun was setting as Riley folded up his letter and put it into his shirt pocket next to the one he wrote last night. He had nowhere to send them to. He wondered where she might be as he picked up a stone and threw it into the rippling waters of Antietam Creek.

146.

General George McClellan was encouraged at the recent developments. He had sent the I Corps, VI Corps and IX Corps into action toward Lee's position. These corps encountered fierce resistance as they tried to pass through several Virginian mountain gaps (Turner, Crampton and Fox) but their overwhelming numbers caused the Confederates to slip away and head back toward the Potomac. McClellan's troops cleared the passes and opened the avenue by which their commander could bring his behemoth army through. He was pretty sure he knew the outcome of the Harpers Ferry situation though he had not heard the final, official report from Colonel Miles. He decided to send a telegram to Washington anyway with all of the good news:

We've achieved a glorious victory. The enemy is retreating in a perfect panic. Harpers Ferry has been saved. Bobbie Lee has numbered his losses by the tens of thousands. The Confederates are scurrying back across the Potomac into Virginia.

G. McClellan

147.

President Lincoln was thrilled by McClellan's report and showed it to several members of his Cabinet. He was cautiously optimistic. He had gotten his hopes up too many times before, but this sounded like a genuine victory. He responded to McClellan by telegram saying:

God bless you and all with you. Destroy the Rebel Army, if possible.

Lincoln thought for a moment. Perhaps the time had come to issue the Emancipation Proclamation. Millions of suffering slaves couldn't wait any longer. Plus, he needed this to become law so England and France would no longer consider uniting with the South. England *must* side with the abolitionists, not the slave traders. Lincoln knew there were tremendous political and practical considerations wrapped into this decision. *Was the news from McClellan enough of a victory to make his announcement acceptable?* Lincoln reread the commander's telegram several more times and held it tightly in his hand throughout the day.

148.

The new husband, Bruce Crawford, found himself wildly in love with a person he could not be with. Bruce reluctantly said goodbye to his sweet bride and had Moses escort Molly westward, back over the Potomac. War was no place for a young woman and there was definitely going to be a fight. Though Bruce's mind was somewhat preoccupied with Molly he had to perform his duties as a staff officer. The night of September 16th when he returned to bivouac, he helped to emplace all of the brigade commanders where Jackson wanted them before the morning of the 17th.

The Confederate Army was prepared to stand and fight near the Dunker Church sitting to the east of the village of Sharpsburg. Bruce thought early on that all hope had been lost of fighting the Union Army in Maryland. But they had been blessed with more slowness from General McClellan providing Robert Lee's Army barely enough time to slip through the mountains and set up a strong defensive position along Antietam Creek. Bruce heard Lee was exuberant about the victory at Harpers Ferry. Without this good news the Confederate Army would have already been back in Virginia salvaging their supply lines and regrouping. Now, however, with Jackson's brilliant success at the Ferry, along with the hours McClellan gave Lee to gather all of his troops together, the Confederates had a fighting chance so they were going to take a stand and go to battle.

Bruce very clearly understood what the Southerners were up against. It was rumored that General McClellan had 100,000 men just on the other side of the creek from where Bruce was married. They were well fed, well-uniformed and well rested. The troops Bruce was surrounded with were filthy and stunk to high heavens. They had sores on their feet and they were thin, with gaunt faces from the months of marching in the summer heat. Everyone's head of hair and beards were completely disheveled.

No one looked healthy or rested, but this was the army that had put the Yankees on the run multiple times. Bruce often wondered what Jackson's Army could achieve if they had been outfitted, fed and rested as much as the Union Army. There was no doubt in his mind this war would have been over by now and the South would have been victorious. He also wondered about what would have happened if Bobby Lee would have accepted General Scott's offer to command the Union Army. What President Lincoln and the North constantly lacked were aggressive generals who were willing to go against the odds. *They will never win with McClellan in charge,* thought Bruce.

When he finished helping the brigade commanders with their positions, he stopped by John Bell Hood's Division which Lee had attached to Jackson's Command for this operation. Hood, originally from Kentucky, was a West Point graduate and one of the few men Jackson ever complimented as a "soldier." At Gaines' Mill, Hood's troops gave their everything. Not one of them left unscathed. All were dead or wounded. That evening Hood's men would eat for the first time in three days.

Later, Bruce walked over to the Stonewall Brigade where he would find the 33rd Virginia and his friends. Moss was already there speaking to Henry and Jonesy.

"Well, Bruce, nice of you to join us," said Henry.

Bruce noticed Jonesy giving him a wild eye.

"Do you have anything you want to tell us?" asked Jonesy.

"No, I see Moss has beaten me to it," Bruce replied. As soon as he spoke two things happened at once; Henry ran up to give Bruce a congratulatory hug and Jonesy lurched forward like a bull moose plowing right into Bruce's middle. In the process all three of them fell over. Moss dived onto the top of the pack and for a moment the four boys wrestled and laughed just as if they were back in Winchester.

"You crazy married man!" shouted Henry.

"I can't believe it," said Jonesy. "Who am I supposed to marry now? Molly had promised herself to me!"

"Yeah, right you big ox. You would accidentally crush her in your sleep the first night," Moss said.

"That's not polite," said Jonesy.

"Well, that leaves Julia for you and Moss to fight over," said Henry.

"Julia—she hasn't written me for a month!" exclaimed Jonesy.

"She writes to you also?" asked Moss.

"Of course," said Jonesy.

"I thought you were sparking that heavy Greek woman who used to work for Culpepper at the Grey Goose?"

"I don't like her and never have. Besides, I'm not looking for someone my size, they are not attractive to me."

"Well, what kind of women are you attracted to?" Moss asked laughing.

"Smart ones. Pretty ones. Julia will do just fine," Big Jonesy said.

"Get your thoughts off of her because she's mine," said Moss.

"You're just a kid, Moss, Julia needs a man," said Jonesy.

Moss flew at Jonesy and demanded he take it back.

"Hey, guys, keep it down. The Yanks are just beyond these woods here," said Bruce who knew more than the others where all of the troops were positioned and where the skirmishing had taken place that evening.

While the two unmarried men were wrestling, Henry took the time to shake Bruce's hand. "How in the world did you pull this one off? I thought Riley was slowly roping her in."

"I dunno. It's amazing really. When Moses came to recruit my help it truly changed my life. I suppose he could have gone and gotten Riley instead, but you know, I really believe now this was meant to be, ever since we were kids," Bruce said.

"What do you mean?"

"Well, as I look back on my life and on all of our lives I see how there was design and a plan in place. I think if Molly and I would have married sooner we would have fought heavily and it would have been a disastrous marriage. This war has changed both of us. This inconvenient war actually helped us both to become better people. I don't wish what Molly went through on anybody, but somehow God meant it for good for her."

"Was she pretty beaten up by Tanner and Welch?"

"Yeah, nearly every day, either emotional or physical abuse."

"Wow." Henry shook his head and thought for a moment He was sad his friend Molly had to endure that kind of awful, humiliating treatment. "It is amazing she could still love a man after that kind of abuse. Plus, having a father who wouldn't come to her rescue."

Bruce said, "It's a miracle, really, only God could have healed her heart."

Henry looked at Bruce and soaked in what he had said. "That Cretan Tanner also tried to hurt Kathryn in Winchester," said Henry. "And would have if Scout hadn't been nearby."

Moss and Jonesy had finished wrestling and heard the last couple of sentences. "If I ever see that scoundrel Tanner again I will crush him with my bare hands," said Jonesy.

"Nobody knows where he is," said Bruce.

"How's that?"

"They expected to find him at Harpers Ferry but he disappeared somehow and slipped away."

"That's a little cryptic. He vanished?"

"Moss told us Welch was killed with the same Bowie knife you had taken from Tanner at the Grey Goose. Is that true?" asked Henry.

"I don't know, it might have just looked like the same knife. It doesn't matter. People reap what they sow. Hopefully Tanner will be caught soon and justice will be served."

Moss said, "My first act after I return to Winchester is to find Tanner and kill him to avenge the honor of my sister-in-law. My second act will be to have Moses marry Julia and I down by the Shenandoah so he can sprinkle our heads with water, as well," Moss said playfully.

Bruce shot Moss an older brother look as if to say that that was privileged information.

"What was that about?" asked Henry.

"Moss, remind me never to tell you a secret again," Bruce said. Then looking at Henry and Jonesy he said, "You know, it was truly a remarkable time. It was part religious ceremony and part wedding. I took it as a baptism into a faith I finally believe in. Molly took it as a cleansing of her past experiences with men so she could be clean and pure for her new husband. Moses' actions seemed led by God and he was doing and saying things for us which seemed straight from heaven. The ceremony itself increased my faith."

"My big brother, a true believer?" asked Moss.

"A weak, immature one, but yes a believer," said Bruce. "I am looking forward to telling Jackson after the battle tomorrow."

Henry and Jonesy looked at the countenance on Bruce's face and marveled. "You seem different," Jonesy said.

"I feel different," replied Bruce.

No one said anything for a moment, all deep in thought.

"Men, I hate to break up a good thing but it is nearly midnight. Jackson wants us all up at three. It is time to get some rest," Bruce said, breaking their reflective moment.

"I'm the one who's going to marry Julia by the Shenandoah," said Jonesy defiantly.

"Where are Molly and Moses now?" asked Henry.

"They're in Shepherdstown with a wagon, waiting for word from us before they head home to Winchester. I told her that this battle might decide the fate of the country and she wanted to be nearby just in case."

"Hey, one more time before the battle tomorrow," said Jonesy as he held out his arm with his palm facing down.

"Un pour tous, tous pour un," said Henry putting his arm in.

"One for all, all for one," said Jonesy.

"I pledge my life," Moss said putting his arm in.

"I pledge my life," said Bruce joining the other three.

"I pledge my life," said Henry.

"I pledge my life!" concluded Jonesy.

"Duty! Strength! Courage!" They said in union as loudly as they could without disturbing those around them. The men said goodbye and departed for a three hour nap as it began to drizzle rain again.

149.

Lincoln was dumbfounded when Stanton brought him the telegraph from the War Department late that evening. It was clear and concise.

"Harpers Ferry lost. Commander Dixon Miles dead. Lee's Army in vicinity of Sharpsburg."

After a long while Lincoln looked up and said, "I don't understand how there can be such disparity between this message and the last one McClellan sent a few hours ago."

Stanton didn't say anything. He didn't have to. Lincoln could feel the anger emanating from the man. He also sensed an 'I told you so' about to be communicated. Lincoln asked, "How many were at the Ferry?"

"Around 10,000 troops along with their weapons and stores and stores of supplies."

"10,000?" asked Lincoln.

"Actually make that 13,000 if the men from Martinsburg retreated there because of Confederate movements in the area. They will all be prisoners of war."

Lincoln stood and faced Stanton, not moving and not speaking. He looked at the War Secretary seemingly waiting for him to say something positive.

"One more thing, sir," Stanton said matter-of-factly. "There must have been at least 500 runaway slaves there in hiding. They will all be sent back to their plantations now and severely disciplined."

Lincoln was despondent. His heart ached for the men at Harpers Ferry and for the slaves. He couldn't imagine what it would be like to run to a

United States garrison for protection and then be overtaken by the Rebel Army.

"Well, all of you were right," Lincoln said softly. "I must have made the wrong choice. Thank you, Secretary." Lincoln walked out of the room with his head low.

150.

General Robert E. Lee had hoped for a general engagement between the two armies. Due to thousands of stragglers along their journey and A.P. Hill's troops having been left to deal with parolees from Harpers Ferry, Lee found he was now in a precarious situation. He had one third of McClellan's troop strength, 25,000 facing 75,000. He had twenty-four brigades facing forty-four. He had 50 batteries of 200 guns opposing twice the amount. Plus, most of Lee's guns were smooth-bore and not as efficient for long-range fire as the rifled Parrots the Union had.

But it was not hopeless. If Hill eventually arrived Lee would have around 40,000 troops to fight with. Also, the Confederate Army was a war-proven fighting machine. Though they did not look pretty, needed a week's rest and several good meals and baths, they had courage and they would fight. They would fight for the South and fight for Lee, Jackson and Longstreet. Lastly, Lee knew McClellan. He knew how he thought and how he fought. Lee figured McClellan would believe he was facing a foe of 120,000. This would make him cautious. He would keep thousands in reserve. If Lee's troops allowed no serious exploits in their lines and waited for an opportunity, then perhaps what happened at Gaines' Mills and Manassas could come true here. The major difference was that for the first time in the war Lee found himself on the defensive and not on the offense. This was new and uncomfortable for the Gray Fox.

151.

That evening was the darkest, gloomiest night the soldiers had experienced. It had a certain heaviness to it and dreary feeling, shadowy and dream-like. It drizzled rain in the dark and dismal woods as the soldiers tried to sleep for a few minutes so they could be rested for the battle. They laid down on top of their muskets and wished they were somewhere else.

152.

On September 17, 1862 Union General Joseph Hooker, Commander of I Corps, began the battle of Antietam with early morning skirmishing followed by a barrage of artillery once there was adequate daylight. Hooker was a career military man who was eager for a victory and for distinction. His goal that morning was the little Dunker Church south of the cornfield and the eastern edge of the west woods. Hagerstown Pike ran from north to south and into Sharpsburg. Almost one mile north of Sharpsburg was a Dunker Church on the west side of the Pike which backed into some woods and a ridge. A half mile north of the church was a thirty acre cornfield on the east side of the road with the east woods surrounding it. Hooker was located one mile north of the cornfield and began movement early. He knew the enemy had fortified the cornfield area as their northern left flank. If he could penetrate and fold in their lines at the cornfield, the church and the ridge behind it, the Rebels would have an untenable position and be forced from Sharpsburg. He knew Lee's troops ran from north to south between the Federals on their east and Sharpsburg to their west. What he did not know was that it was Stonewall Jackson and his soldiers who were located in the area he was attacking.

Hooker's men advanced with raw courage, firing and reloading, firing and reloading. The shiny bayonets reflected the sun as the men moved down both sides of the Hagerstown Pike heading south. They soon ran into a fury of Rebel soldiers who were just as determined to return the fight and not give up their ground. The result was that the cornfield became a wicked arena of death and destruction, both sides not backing down and falling at a tremendous rate. Still, Hooker's 10,000 soldier assault advanced and made some costly progress. Though hundreds lay dead all around them from both sides, their next stop was the Dunker Church per their commander's intentions.

The minutes seemed like hours as regiment after Northern regiment attacked the Confederates. Brigadier General George G. Meade, Brigadier General James B. Ricketts and Brigadier General Truman Seymour moved their men admirably with all the skills of a trained infantry commander being put into play. However, regiment after Southern regiment repelled the attack. The 12th Massachusetts lost 224 of their 330 men in those moments. Harry Hays' 7th Louisiana 'Tigers' Brigade lost 323 of their 500 men.

The savage butchering was awesome and the artillery laid a continuous barrage of shell and canister on both sides of the enemy lines, chopping corn stocks and men at an alarming rate. *This is desperate, this is madness, this is war,* thought Hooker. *The artillery is blasting my men to hell!*

Moments later, General Joseph Hooker was shot in the foot and taken out of the battle. At the time, Brigadier General Abner Doubleday was stealthily advancing south on the western side of the turnpike hoping to catch the Confederates at unawares and change the momentum to favor the North. John Gibbon's 'Iron Brigade' also looked like they might penetrate the line when their commander was evacuated.

Joe Hooker departed, hopeful he would soon hear the report of victory.

153.

Jonesy, in his butternut and gray uniform and kepi hat, was more nervous that morning than he had ever been causing his left hand to involuntarily shake a little bit. The 33rd Virginia Regiment was to the left of the Hagerstown Pike in the West Woods. They waited while hearing the fighting and devastation take place just a few hundred yards away on the eastern side of their woods. Jonesy and Henry knew it would be their time to fight very soon. Some men were having the chaplain pray for them, others were reading a small Bible, others were writing one more note to home and handing it to a buddy for safekeeping. Jonesy and Henry sat and stared at each other, wincing every time a shell would explode nearby. They could smell the smoke of the cannon, they could sense the fear in the ranks, they could hear the cries of the wounded already from the brigades fighting across the road.

The chaplain stopped by, stooped and prayed for them to be brave and courageous and to trust in the Lord because he would be their strong tower that day. He moved on to talk to others. Jonesy stared at Henry. They both knew, as it was talked about by others, this battle could change the entire war. If either side had a solid win it might be thoroughly decided because both armies were using everything they had. Jonesy knew if they somehow won this battle Washington would be their next stop. McClellan's Army of the Potomac was the last line of defense for Lincoln.

One of the former leaders of their regiment was now leading the Stonewall Division, Brigadier General John R. Jones. Both Jonesy and Henry liked Jones, a VMI graduate, and thought he might do okay as a leader. Their brigade commander was now Andrew J. Grigsby who used to command the 27th Virginia. He replaced Charles Sidney Winder after he died at the battle of Cedar Mountain in August. Their new regimental commander was Colonel Edwin Gray Lee, who possessed a Washington College law degree. Club Jones, now the head company sergeant, was rallying the troops, getting them ready to fight. As he walked by the Winchester lads Club glanced at Jonesy and gave him a knowing nod. Jonesy knew his pa was worried about him, but Club also knew Jonesy was a crack shot and would do fine in a pinch. Jonesy was proud of his skills with the musket and proud of his father who had taught him everything he knew about hunting and soldiering. For Jonesy, his father was his most complete man.

The fighting continued to be heard to the northeast of their position in a cornfield. But all of a sudden, directly to the north of them, not in the direction of the cornfield, men started yelling of a Federal attack. The 33rd Virginia took position and steadied their guns. They heard a loud crack from the first wave of Federal muskets but Jonesy couldn't see anything yet. He and Henry laid two old logs on top of each other and kneeled down behind them watching their fields of fire. They heard one of the other regiments running and shouting and firing their weapons. Jonesy saw General Jones shouting at his division and moving forward. Club was yelling now. Jonesy looked at Henry and saw him nod. It was time to go.

Jonesy and Henry jumped over their logs and pushed forward. Jonesy shot his musket at what looked like a blue-uniformed officer standing in some smoke ahead of him. The soldier fell over. Shells were exploding around them. Henry shouted at Jonesy to stay close. They were still in the trees and it was hard to see the enemy. They could see wave after wave of gray coats swarming to their right. More were moving forward and engaging the oncoming enemy. They were not quite to the edge of the woods but they could see the trees opening up a bit now. The field beyond was filled with blue-uniformed soldiers. Jonesy could not take a shot yet because there were gray-coated men just ahead of him. The folks in front were falling fast.

Club ran over to them and shouted that General Jones had gone down and now General Starke was in command. A few moments later someone shouted out that Starke was killed. Jonesy and Henry took position behind two large trees and began to shoot and reload as fast as possible. The battle lines were becoming confused. Some Yanks had gotten past them on the left. They kept shooting straight ahead. Their brigade commander Grigsby was now put in charge of the entire division.

More fighting. More loudness. More fallen Confederate soldiers. There started to be an exodus of Virginia men who were ahead of Jonesy and

Henry. The Southerners were beginning to be dangerously cut off. They kept firing.

"Move back, move back!" Club shouted as he ran past them back toward their camping area.

They had not been able to repel the invaders. The blue-uniformed soldiers were all around them now overwhelming their position and the men in gray were either falling down or running backward. Henry grabbed Jonesy who was firing one last shot. They both turned and ran as fast as they could. Jonesy was a lumbering giant jumping over logs and dead men in his hurry to get back to safety. They saw a few Confederates stop and try to form a defense, but the Winchester boys kept running knowing it was futile. The noise was horrific as men were shouting, muskets were cracking and shells were exploding, along with the sound of the movement of hundreds of people through the splintering woods.

They saw Bruce who was on his horse trying to rally the men who were fleeing backward.

"Wait, wait, General Hood's men are coming!" Bruce tried to shout over the din of the battle to the petrified men.

Henry and Jonesy got closer to Bruce who was turning his horse Copper Jake around. Bruce eventually recognized them and yelled out, "Why are you running? Move forward, Hood's men are being sent up!"

"We were told to by our command. There was no one left but us," Henry replied to Bruce while Jonesy turned around and took another shot at some Federals to the far right.

The tree limbs cracked and then a thump!

When Jonesy looked back up at Bruce, who was sitting on his scared horse, he had already missed it. As if in slow motion Bruce crumpled over and fell to the ground. Henry and Jonesy ran to his side. There was a large wound between his left arm and where his heart should be and a chunk of flesh was missing. Two ribs were exposed and his left arm looked as if it was only dangling by a few tendons coming down from the shoulder.

Bruce gasped several times. Copper Jake darted off. Henry looked around them and saw more blue coats drifting forward from where they had just run. Jonesy kneeled down and gently placed Bruce's head in his big lap.

"No, Bruce, no!" Jonesy screamed.

Henry put his hand on Bruce's chest that was heaving and struggling as if to try to calm it down. They both knew he was mortally wounded by an artillery shell and probably had only a few breaths left. No one could survive a blow like the one he had—he would bleed out in just a moment. There was nothing they could do.

Bruce was still alive, gasping for air, and he looked up into Jonesy's face. Jonesy noticed that Bruce was also bleeding from a cut on his head. Henry turned to the north and took a shot at an advancing Yankee. Bruce's body began shaking as he looked intently into the eyes of Jonesy. It seemed he wanted to say something. Jonesy was in torment and tried to give a smile to his cherished friend.

"Rest, brother, rest," Jonesy said softly. "You've done well, just rest."

Bruce struggled with one last attempt to breathe and his eyes closed for the final time. Jonesy wished he could breathe his own life into him. He held Bruce a moment longer and tried to grasp what was happening around them. He knew he didn't have time for mourning because of the danger.

Henry glanced back and saw Bruce was gone. "Let's go before we're killed, we are sitting ducks and it's almost too late," Henry said.

Jonesy looked down again at the pure, now-gentle face of his childhood friend, the leader of the gang. "I'm taking him with me," Jonesy said.

"But they are almost upon us!" cried out Henry nervously looking around. Minie balls whizzed past both of them, one hitting the ground next to Bruce's body.

Jonesy stood up with Bruce's crumpled remains in his arms. He and Henry looked quickly around the area for anything they might have dropped. Suddenly, both men recoiled because of a flash behind them.

What they witnessed was astounding. A storm of fresh Confederate soldiers swarmed all throughout the trees bellowing out the Rebel yell and rushing at the enemy. Jonesy and Henry looked at them and couldn't help but smile and shout with them.

"It's Hood's men!" said Henry.

The thousands of Confederate soldiers just entering the fight moved forward and attacked with ferocity. They had finally eaten a meal and it restored their wrath. All the Union soldiers were destroyed. Hood's men moved through the area and eventually were out of sight. The danger in the woods was gone. The Federals were pushed back.

"Let's go," said Henry.

"Yes, let's bring him home," said Jonesy.

Jonesy carried Bruce while Henry carried Jonesy's Springfield. They headed for Jackson's headquarters which was behind the woods of the Dunker Church on Hauser's Ridge. When they cleared the woods a group of Confederate cavalrymen were riding by in front of them. One of them slowed down and asked Jonesy who he was carrying.

"Bruce Crawford," said Jonesy.

"Crawford, huh. Does his brother know yet?" asked the soldier.

"No, just happened," said Henry.

"I'll let him know for you," said the rider.

"Thank you," Jonesy replied as he continued his walk toward the ridge.

The Winchester men found Sandie Pendleton and placed Bruce down on the ground near several other dead soldiers.

"I'm sorry," said Sandie because he knew how close the three were.

Nothing else was said for a long while.

The men stood there looking down at Bruce's body, once so lively and energetic. Bruce was spirited and always getting the boys to try some new idea he had. Now he was gone. Bruce was the first to bring them together and now he was the first of them to depart.

Henry and Jonesy sat down for a moment and Sandie walked off. They could hear the battle raging behind them, but it seemed like another world to Jonesy. They could see from where they were that some homes in Sharpsburg were on fire due to the shelling and it made for an ominous sight.

Henry put his hand on Jonesy's shoulder. "I'm proud of you, Jonesy."

"What for?"

"That was a brave thing you did back there."

"Didn't do anything."

"You were about to carry Bruce out knowing we would be killed or taken prisoner."

"You were there with me."

"Yeah, but it was your idea."

The boys sat for awhile longer as aides rode to and from the headquarters area delivering messages from their commanders. Hood's men had saved the day and repelled a major surprise attack of the Union from the north. The morning wasn't over yet, but the Confederates had done remarkably well against all odds.

Jonesy saw a rider galloping toward them in the distance and knew at once it must be Moss.

Soon the cavalryman approached the two and dismounted. Tears streaked his face from his emotions and the wind hitting his eyes while riding furiously.

"Is it true?" Moss asked as he looked past the two at the lifeless form of his brother Bruce.

Jonesy stood up and put his mighty arm around Moss's shoulders. "It's true."

154.

General John Bell Hood's 2,300 man division swept through the west woods and pushed up the turnpike. With heavy casualties, they entered the cornfield where barely a stalk was unharmed and cleared through the field bayonet against bayonet. Body for body. The effect of the carnage was a psychological slap to both sides.

Jonesy and Henry left Moss and Bruce and had joined up with Jubal Early's soldiers and 200 others from the Stonewall Division who had rallied to fight again. They were able to come at Hooker's troops from the west while Hood cleared the cornfield and moved against Hooker from the south. General McClellan had summoned his XII Corps Commander, Joseph K. F. Mansfield to the fight to help Hooker. With this thrust they were able to rejuvenate their offense and abruptly stopped Hood and Early. Hood's men fought viciously and died as a result. As he maneuvered back toward the rear, an aide asked Hood where his division was located. His cold response was, "Dead, on the field of battle!"

II Corps Commander Edwin Sumner had committed Sedgewick's division not knowing General Lee had just shifted the divisions of Lafayette McLaws and John Walker from Longstreet's command farther south to help Jackson in the north. Sedgewick's Union forces soon found they were surrounded and suffered near annihilation receiving 2,200 casualties in twenty minutes and Sedgewick himself was hit thrice and removed from the field. Yet, more of Mansfield's XII Corps men under George S. Green's Division pushed the reinforced Rebels backwards almost to the Dunker Church which was being used as a hospital for Southerners. Before the church was overtaken by the Federals, however, their push suddenly halted. Mansfield fell mortally wounded and there was confusion in the chain of command.

General Thomas Jackson with 5,500 men had repulsed more than two Union Corps in a little over three hours of fighting. Though nearly half of Jackson's men were now dead or wounded, he had held the line and lived up to the nickname 'Stonewall' he received the summer before at Manassas. He made sure his sector was secure, mended his lines and reinforced the men with ammunition and artillery support. The fighting had now switched closer to Sharpsburg where Longstreet's troops were defending a sunken road.

155.

Moses and Molly arrived in Sharpsburg by mid-morning. They had heard the loud cannon blasts roar for two hours when Molly decided they should re-cross the Potomac and be of use in the war effort. They went to work in several of the buildings in town that began to accumulate wounded Confederate soldiers. They brought water to them and fresh bandages to the physicians working diligently and as fast as possible. Molly spoke kind, soft words of hope and faith to the critical ones the surgeons had separated out and left to die.

* * *

Around noon Molly was seen by Henry and Jonesy out in the fields around the Dunker Church bringing water to those who were crying out. The battle had stopped in this region and several women were trying to attend the needs to the severely wounded because there were not enough soldiers to keep up with the task.

Henry noticed her familiar shape from a distant and pointed her out to Jonesy.

"Oh, my gosh," exclaimed Jonesy. "She is helping out wounded soldiers and she doesn't know about her own bridegroom. How horrible, one of us needs to tell her."

"She knows," said Henry studying her intently.

"What?"

"I saw her stop by Jackson's headquarters earlier and spend some time by Bruce's side."

"So she already knows and she—" Jonesy couldn't finish his sentence seeing the beauty of the moment he was partaking in.

The two men watched their childhood friend for a few minutes going from one wounded warrior to another dipping a ladle in a bucket of cold water and raising it to their lips. She spoke seriously to one and then even laughed with another, all while holding close the terrible reality concerning her Love.

Henry and Jonesy walked over to the supply area. They filled up their canteens, received more ammunition and percussion caps and then marched back to their positions. They were ordered to be prepared for a counter-attack.

156.

Robert E. Lee was trying to keep the middle of his line from being overrun. Now that the left flank was becoming quiet the center part of his line was receiving all of the action. Lee knew that if McClellan was smart he would put all he had into the middle and then chase the Confederates to the Potomac River. Lee had D. H. Hill in the center with his men lying down in a road. Over the years of wagon use, the road had fallen several feet from the rest of the surrounding ground. This sunken road was now a strong defensive position for Hill to use but he did not have enough men. If McClellan moved in an entire corps Lee knew they would be overrun. He decided to move Major General Richard H. Anderson to support Hill in the sunken road. Lee now had no units in reserve.

For hours the bloody contest continued. Union regiments from Sumner's Corps would charge forward while Confederate guns would knock them down. Occasional breaks in the line occurred but nothing permanent happened until the early afternoon.

While other units tried their hand at peeling the Johnny Rebs from the sunken road, the Irish Brigade, led by Brigadier General Thomas F. Meager, was waiting their turn with trepidation. Unbeknownst to Lee at the time, Father William Corby walked up and down the Irish line ministering to the soldiers standing beneath their emerald green regimental flags. Finally their time came and they rushed into battle. Devastation followed. The Confederates were in too good of a position and 540 of the Irish Brigade were wounded in the first few minutes. They were quickly ordered to withdraw.

However, Confederate General Richard Anderson was wounded along with several other key leaders on the Southern side. When the next blue wave of men came into sight, Lee's defensive line bent and bowed and finally broke. The carnage in the road was wicked. Some wounded Confederates were smothering in their own pools of blood. The sunken road was now called the 'Bloody Lane' because of the death in and surrounding it. The 61st and 64th New York Regiment made the difference for the Union line by seizing a small knoll whereby they could fire directly down into the road. The New Yorkers pummeled the massed Confederates with musket fire which couldn't miss. A heavy moment of butchering followed before the Rebels decided to take some action. The Southerners still alive who could see their line was turned, left the ditch and flew back toward Sharpsburg. Soon, the Confederate position was totally abandoned and the Federals pursued them as fast as they could. General Longstreet ordered his artillery to defend the retreat and soon the armies entered into another stalemate, just on different terrain.

The Confederates were solidly whipped. Lee knew it. He had no reserves and his line was in shreds. Thankfully for Lee, General McClellan failed to capitalize on this advantage.

157.

George McClellan remained in his headquarters miles to the rear monitoring events with the messages of his corps commanders. Just behind the 'Bloody Lane,' McClellan had two other corps he kept in reserve just in case Lee used his superior numbers to attack and overwhelm them. William Franklin's VI Corps had 12,000 men itching to advance and join the battle and Fitz John Porter's V Corps had another 10,000 men who were in the rear protecting McClellan. William Franklin pleaded with McClellan to enter into the fight and attack the weakened Rebel lines but McClellan refused.

"What if we were to lose? The Republic would be lost. Lee's broken lines will have to remain as they are—it might be a trap," McClellan told the junior commander.

158.

The only thing left to do that day was what had already been decided by the commander-in-charge the night before. Major General Ambrose Burnside was to use his IX Corps to attack on the southern left portion to provide a diversion to Hooker's attack on the right. However, Burnside waited and did not attack while Hooker's men paid a heavy price. Burnside had four divisions with over 12,000 soldiers to utilize in his position just southeast of Sharpsburg. What he and McClellan did not know was that Lee had just four weakened brigades of roughly 3,000 total to oppose him in that sector. Because the Union attacks were not synchronized Lee was able to maneuver men from the south to help the fighting in the north. Though given orders from McClellan at 10 a.m. to begin his attack, Burnside spent precious hours trying to cross a stone bridge over Antietam Creek which was heavily defended.

The bridge was 120 feet long and spanned a section of Antietam Creek that was 50 feet wide and waist deep. On the west side of the bridge towards Sharpsburg there was a 100 foot high wooded ridge with massive boulders which offered protective fire for the Southerners who defended it. The road the Union Army needed to get to the bridge paralleled the creek and the ridge behind it. It was totally exposed and offered easy targets for any unit daring to come into sight. For some reason, instead of simply fording the creek wherever they could, Burnside believed he needed the limestone bridge and wasted hours trying to conquer it. The 11th Connecticut received 140 casualties from trying to attack and cross over the bridge. Their commander was mortally wounded and the unit had to stop the engagement. The 2nd New Hampshire and 6th Maryland also tried to gain the bridge to no avail.

At noon McClellan ordered Burnside, "Even if 10,000 soldiers are killed in taking the bridge, take it!"

Ambrose Burnside was frustrated. The man had characteristic facial hair which led to the nickname of men having 'sideburns.' He was a West Point graduate and had performed admirably in the military so far. He did not want to be seen as a coward. At 12:30 p.m. Burnside ordered the 51st New York and the 51st Pennsylvanians to attack the bridge. They charged downhill and took up a position on the east side of the bridge. They used the terrain to send howitzer shells over and into the troops defending the bridge. Finally the Confederates retreated some. The New Yorkers and Pennsylvania men saved the day for Burnside and eventually took the bridge. The problem was that the few Georgians who defended it had delayed an entire corps for almost four hours.

At length, Burnside maneuvered 8,000 men to the other side of the bridge and he hoped this final assault against Lee's battered army near Sharpsburg would seal a victory for the Union. He had heard about the failures of Hooker, Mansfield, and Sumner and was thankful he would be the one to carry the day for McClellan. Besides, he had nothing to lose. General McClellan earlier offered him the use of reserves if he got into pinch. *If that time comes he better deliver,* thought Burnside.

159.

Robert E. Lee needed some good news but it failed to come. He was proud of his commanders and their soldiers' heroic deeds throughout the battle against unbelievable odds. The fact that the Federals had not completely destroyed the entire Southern cause this day was somewhat mystifying to Lee except for one thing; what he knew about his warrior's courage and heart. Yet, even now, Lee knew how weak and fragile their lines were. They were in an untenable position which was alarming to him. To see now all of Burnside's soldiers massing to the east of Sharpsburg between him and Antietam Creek was most demoralizing. Lee did not know what to do. All of his other units were receiving pressure on their lines from the Dunker church south to where Burnside's troops were ready to assault. Jackson and Longstreet were already thoroughly engaged. General Lee could not launch a flanking attack to the right or to the left. He was thinned, about to be broken and had to wait it out. He figured he had an hour at best before the Union Army capitalized on their advantage.

160.

Riley, Ned and Hans were utilized as messengers and orderlies, carrying Union wounded back to the rear where the hospitals were. They were literally all over the battlefield that day helping in any way they could. They brought up ammunition from the rear, they delivered messages to McClellan, and they worked hard at helping the medical people deal with the thousands of casualties whose numbers kept growing. The cavalry commanders were frustrated with General McClellan that morning because he would not use them for what they should have been used for—an offensive weapon that could go up against Rebel units in battle. McClellan felt the U.S. Cavalry was not trained and ready to be in the battle yet, so he assigned them piecemeal to infantry units to be used as their commanders saw fit.

Finally, around three o'clock in the afternoon, when General Burnside had crossed the bridge and was massing his troops on the other side in their battle lines, the order was given for the 4th Pennsylvania. They were to be on the far left side of the line to withstand a flanking unit by the Rebel cavalry if attempted. The sight was awesome, three of the four IX Corps divisions were on the field and ready to move toward Sharpsburg. Colonel James Childs led his cavalry units bravely across Burnside's stone bridge and provided support to the regiments in defense of the severe left flank.

Riley, Hans and Ned were all with Colonel Childs, racing to and fro between units, helping as needed while Longstreet's artillery rained down on them. Musket snipers were hitting them from buildings on the outskirts of town but their fire wasn't very accurate. Riley was told to keep his little unit on the Harpers Ferry Road and watch for any movement from south of town.

161.

Moss Crawford was incensed at the death of his older brother. He spent the next few hours with his friend Lewis Powell and General Jeb Stuart attempting to maneuver around the Union right to the north of the cornfield. With several skirmishes and provocations in the area Stuart finally gave up the idea. They returned to Jackson's headquarters hearing news of the attack unfolding on the Union left to the south. Burnside's men were two hundred yards from Sharpsburg and Lee's defenses had all but given up. Stuart asked for volunteers to form a task force for the dangerous mission of defending the line south of Sharpsburg. Moss was the first to volunteer and couldn't wait to engage the advancing enemy. Within a few minutes, one hundred and twenty gray-clad horsemen, in the spirit of Turner Ashby, approached the line of battle and could see how outnumbered they were. Moss and his squadron took out their thirty-six caliber, six shot revolvers and kicked their horses to keep moving. Their first target was a small contingent of Union cavalry near the Harpers Ferry road.

162.

General Lee was about to move to higher ground and abandon the Maryland Campaign. The 9th New York Zouaves, with their open-fronted jackets and baggy red trousers, had pushed Confederate General David Jones' division almost to Sharpsburg where military members had clogged the streets trying to escape or find care. Only a few determined men from Robert Toombs' brigade stood in the way of the oncoming Federals. As soon as the thin line broke Lee knew there would be a catastrophic conclusion to the battle. His aides were prompting him to move away and depart the region before chaos ensued. Lee hesitated. He wanted to savor one last moment.

Out of the corner of his eye to the right Lee saw some movement far away down the Harpers Ferry road. Lee asked a nearby lieutenant to look in his telescope and see who was coming up the road. "Whose troops are those?" asked Lee.

The lieutenant looked and answered, "They are flying the United States flag."

Lee's heart sank. He thought of A. P. Hill's 3,000 strong Confederate unit that had been left at Harpers Ferry to complete the surrender and process the paroles while the rest of Jackson's forces moved to the aid of Lee there at Sharpsburg. Lee received a message from Hill they had left that morning for Sharpsburg, but it was a seventeen mile hike and the men would still be exhausted from their recent missions.

Earlier Lee held hope against hope that somehow Hill's troops might defy what was humanly possible and show up before the battle was lost. *But it would not be that day and that battle,* he thought. Lee looked again at his crumbling lines and knew he had better not tarry, his moment was over. He needed to issue contingency plans to his two chief commanders Jackson and Longstreet immediately. Lee's wrists throbbed with pain from his injury last month. He began to turn his horse to leave. *This day could go no worse.*

"Wait a minute, sir. There is another column coming." The lieutenant had looked again. "Oh my, General Lee, there is a unit coming that is flying the Virginia and Confederate flags!"

Lee did not move a muscle and said unflinchingly, "That is Ambrose Powell Hill coming from Harpers Ferry. He is going to save the day for us."

163.

As Hill's gray masses began the Rebel yell and started to run into the side of the Union left, several things happened at once. Chaos ensued in the ranks of Riley's cavalry unit. Colonel Childs was struck by a cannonball in his left hip passing directly through his body. Riley, Hans and Ned stared at their fearless leader who was mortally wounded. Childs encouraged his men to fight heartily and be courageous. He gave a family friend a message to give his oldest son to 'be true to his country.' With that he died and his men decided to rally in his honor and go against the wave of attackers now crossing into their sector.

"Let's kill these Cornfed's and stop short their advance," yelled Hans.

The three friends grabbed their swords and began to run their horses through the oncoming Rebels hitting as many as they could without falling off of their mounts. Red-haired Ned showed a half-hearted attempt and then turned and fled quickly toward the rear, over the bridge and into the sunset.

164.

Seeing the salvation of the army by Hill's troops was exhilarating to Moss but it did not slow him down. He, Lewis and a few others bolted across the Harpers Ferry Road just as the first wave of attackers were flying into Burnside's corps. His goal was the small band of cavalry seemingly re-energized with the surprise of more Southern troops.

Moss moved forward toward two men who were using their sabers to hurt the infantry around them. Moss got within range of one of them and shot his Colt revolver at him and missed. He turned around his horse, now a black stud named Mercutio, and tried again. He fired at the courageous young man who found himself in a sea of wild, enemy infantrymen. This time his shot found its mark in the belly of the rider.

"Hans! Hans! Are you hit?" someone shouted.

Moss perked his ears up at the familiar voice who cried after his wounded friend. He could see that the first rider whom he had wounded was now being pulled off his horse by one of Hill's men while others cheered at his prize.

Moss could see the other rider focusing on him and Moss stared back, took out his revolver, aimed and fired. As he pulled the trigger the rider sprang his horse forward and the shot missed. He rushed close enough to Moss to yell at him and said, "Put your weapon away Crawford, and fight me like a real man." Both horses turned and sped off only to slow down again. *I know that voice!* thought Moss. More soldiers were moving past them. Just beyond their location the blue infantry troops were moving away and forsaking their advance toward Sharpsburg. Moss knew his opponent in blue was being abandoned. He took one more shot at the rider's side while he turned his horse around again. This time the shot whizzed next to the man's head. There was no longer any doubt who this person was; a childhood acquaintance, his brother's best friend from school, and a traitor to his native state in her hour of need. His opponent was Riley McNair.

Both men were isolated now as the other gray riders were caught up ahead of the assault toward the exposed side of the Union line. They would soon realize Moss wasn't with them anymore.

Moss had some business to attend to. Something personal. He took one more shot at Riley. This shot hit his lower left leg a few inches above the ankle. Moss threw his gun to the ground and drew his sword out of its scabbard.

Riley moved within earshot again and yelled, "Moss Crawford run away, because I will kill you if you don't."

Moss laughed out loud and said, "Look around Riley, you're surrounded. You aren't going anywhere even if you did kill me."

"That may be true, Moss, but you are my concern right now. I ask you again, please do not make me kill you," Riley shouted at his opponent.

"Bruce is dead! Your stinkin' new Yankee friends killed him earlier this morning. I hope that makes you feel good—traitor!"

The two men squared off about forty five yards apart, stopped their horses and stared each other down. Off in the distance Private Thomas Hans Draeger was asking for some water. He was holding his bleeding stomach and lying on his back.

"I'm so thirsty," he said over and over, yet no one was listening. No one was by his side. He was left alone to die.

Behind the mounted adversaries the Confederate Army was sweeping the Union Army from the field. Though A. P. Hill's men had marched all day without a break and without rations they struck their opponent with ferocity and brutality. Burnside's lines crumpled and then melted away, fleeing in desperation back across the bridge to safety.

The two old friends faced each other like mounted warriors from an ancient era. Two knights. Both commissioned by their king to destroy their opponent. Two gladiators. Ready to fight until death. Only one would remain standing. The other would fall.

Moss realized he was not thinking clearly, some strange spell of revenge and anger had been cast on him since Bruce's death. He hoped it would not hurt his judgment. All his senses were alive. He felt the wind, he smelled the earth and wildflowers, he heard the commotion of battle and he saw only the solitary figure of his enemy.

165.

Riley was furious to be in this situation. He did not want to kill Moss, but he knew he had no choice. He had seen Moss before when his anger had been riled. It did not matter if he was fighting a Goliath, he would attack, though he knew he would lose. Moss would be out of his mind, his anger would take over and he would develop a blind rage with a dangerous tunnel vision. Riley could see that look in his eyes now, even from a distance.

It pained Riley to hear Bruce was dead. However, it hurt him even more to know that Hans was dying and he could not do anything about it until he dealt with Moss. Hans was a true American patriot. Bruce, Moss, Henry and Jonesy had made their choice and they must bear the consequences. They gave their allegiance to an entity that raised its ugly head against the United States of America. They even invaded the North as if to make a statement! There is a price to pay for every bad decision made. They had chosen poorly. They had chosen wrong. *It is not my fault they are in this situation now,* thought Riley.

Riley winced because of the pain in his lower calf muscle where Moss had shot him. He could tell it wasn't too serious, but it hurt like the dickens. Riley was about to charge but a thought flashed in his mind of the Crawford family; of Lawrence and Sarah and fourteen year old Lucy. *What would Lucy do without her older brothers? What would the Crawfords do without their boys? This damn war. This damn civil war.*

As very slight tears began to form at the corners of his eyes for what he had to do, Riley lowered his head and kicked his trusted steed. He was off, charging, and he raised his sword with his right hand. Moss was now coming at him with his sword raised, as well. The two men slashed as they passed each other and after their first parry, Moss somehow struck at

Riley's back cutting into him as they rode by. They turned and again raced toward each other. This time Riley gained the advantage because after their clash the swords fell down into Moss's lap and slashed the top of his right leg. Moss cried out in anguish as Riley turned his horse around and came at him again. This time Riley stabbed him under the shoulder just above his heart which knocked Moss forcefully from his horse.

Riley decided he would not be the one to determine if Moss should live or die so he turned his horse and headed toward the bridge General Burnside had taken earlier, zigzagging his way through infantry from both sides. He heard some minie balls whiz by him as he rode to find some help for his wounded leg.

Ouch! One ball glanced the side of his head just above his right ear and nipped his right eye socket. Riley was in pain but kept moving. Riley did not realize that Moss had remounted his horse and was charging in his direction until he looked backward. Riley rushed to the bridge, not in fear but in pain. Blood flowed into his eye and down his cheek. He needed help. He could only see out of his left eye now and he slowed and looked behind him while his horse, Danny, clip-clopped over the Antietam Creek Bridge. He saw how Moss was storming toward him. Riley stopped completely and turned his horse.

Soon, the two men faced each other on the bridge. *Why God? Why are you testing me like this?*

Moss was seething in rage and looked unsteady. Neither one moved for a moment. Riley watched Moss dismount and walk slowly toward him with his sword waving back and forth. Moss was wounded and clearly needed help. Riley noticed that the front of his uniform was soaked dark with blood. Riley knew it was mere pride that led his opponent toward him. He thought of turning his horse and running away but a mass of soldiers in blue were pushing across the bridge behind him blocking his path. *Moss is doomed. He has to see that.*

Yet he still walked toward Riley. Riley dismounted his horse and landed on his wounded leg which nearly knocked him over. He held onto the side of the bridge with his left hand to regain his balance and looked at his opponent.

"What now, Riley?" Moss shouted.

Riley did not respond. The Federal forces behind him were drawing near, yet Moss persistently walked with his sword held out to fight. A sudden series of cracks emitted from behind Riley toward Moss. Riley looked into Moss's eyes and knew instantly the shots mortally wounded him. Moss fell onto the hard bridge deck.

Riley limped over to the pool of blood surrounding the gray clad body. He stood over his boyhood friend as he took his last breath. The macabre deed was over. Moss was dead.

Riley turned to find Danny and then everything went black. The Confederate Army swept the Union soldiers off of the bridge.

166.

Major General Ambrose Burnside requested reinforcements as soon as he saw the thundering herd of fresh Confederates pouring in off of the Harpers Ferry road. His messenger left immediately and came back in a relatively short amount of time.

"We are far too outnumbered to win this contest. I have decided to refrain from pouring more troops in today, but do try to hold the ground we have gained so to attack again tomorrow."

Burnside held the message in his hands in disbelief. He had heard from friends of his who worked for McClellan that the commander thought there was close to double the Confederates as compared to the Union Army, but Burnside knew this was downright impossible. *If they had so many men then where were they?*

Burnside had a choice to make. Though the left side of his corps was turning in terribly, he still had strength on the right side. He could try to bring his reserves from the other side of the creek into the fight to turn back the tide. He sent a message to the Kanawha Division for a counterattack to reclaim the bridge and then penetrate the Confederate forces and reach Sharpsburg. Burnside commanded the rest of his reserve forces to mass around the Antietam Creek Bridge and hold it at all costs.

Once the Kanawha Division's attack failed and Burnside had reconsolidated his forces, he again sent word to his commander only to receive McClellan's reply,

"I can do nothing more for you."

Ambrose Burnside fumed because he knew the battle was lost unnecessarily. *All of the work and lives spent to gain the bridge today was for naught!*

167.

The next day saw little fighting, but a lot of death and agony. Over 24,000 men had been either killed, captured or wounded within twelve hours of daylight. Nearly four thousand Union and Confederate soldiers perished that September 17th. The North had a little over 2,100 killed, 10,000 wounded and 1,100 captured. The South had approximately 1,700 killed, 8,500 wounded, and 1,000 captured. The artillery hell fired from both sides crippled and maimed thousands catapulting the casualty rate far beyond anyone's worse fears.

Jonesy and Henry removed Moss from the battlefield and laid him next to his brother, Bruce, to be transported home. They also found out Riley McNair had been wounded by musket-fire and late in the day taken captive by some of Hill's men. They did not go to visit him. They couldn't bear to look at him.

The sights and sounds from that solitary day of fighting would be remembered by every man alive until their final breath. Bodies were strewn around the field in every twist imaginable. Some were piled up in certain places and used as a defensive wall. Acres of men wounded and calling out for help imprinted on the survivor's conscience. Haversacks, muskets, canteens, clothing, boots, cartridge boxes, broken wagons, tin cups, spades, bedrolls, bayonets and ramrods were strewn all over the ground along with dead bodies, dead horses and shattered tree limbs on red-soaked clay. In the cornfield north of the Dunker Church where the fighting had been the heaviest during the early daylight hours, there was a sight straight from the pits of hell. There lay dead body next to dead body next to dead body. Though one never would, out of respect for the fallen, one could have walked the whole width and length of the field without having to step on the ground.

Robert E. Lee stayed throughout the 18th boldly and defiantly with his army just inches away from McClellan's hordes, as if daring the man to come and try to attack him again. McClellan never moved. When the sun descended Lee made his decision that he could not attack the Union Army in their entrenched position at this location. They would have to leave Maryland and perhaps re-enter it at a future day to take up the offensive again. If McClellan would delay in his pursuit, Lee thought he could buy some time to refit his army and give it the rest they needed for another assault on Washington. Perhaps this time from the north through Pennsylvania. The Gray Fox retreated his men under the cover of darkness and slipped them across the Potomac River to an area near Martinsburg. On this march there was no singing.

168.

Lincoln received the telegram with mixed emotions. Henry Halleck brought the President the message from General McClellan and read it to him,

"Our victory was complete. The enemy is driven back into Virginia."

"What am I to make of this, General?"

"Well sir, I would be proud at what the army has accomplished."

"I was hoping for some more details about Lee's Army of Northern Virginia being ruined," Lincoln said trying to hide his disappointment.

Halleck didn't say anything.

"Are we to assume General McClellan is pursuing the Confederate Army?"

"I cannot comment on that, Mr. President," Halleck replied.

Lincoln rubbed his whiskered jaw as he re-read the telegraph. "Make a reply and tell the general, 'Find and destroy the Rebel Army, if possible.'"

"Is that all, sir?" asked Old Brains.

"That is all," answered the Ancient.

PART X

A CANDLE IN THE WIND

Only the dead have seen the end of war.

PLATO

169.

The day after the battle, Molly worked hard at nursing the wounded soldiers the entire morning. Moses and Molly were to depart in a rickety wagon to take them back to Winchester. The two horses pulling them were Mercutio and Copper Jake. In the back of the wagon were the bodies of Bruce and Moss by special permission of General Stonewall Jackson. The commander agreed to let Molly take them home to be properly buried by their family. Molly was also given a condolence letter written by General Jackson to Lawrence and Sarah Crawford, along with a few personal belongings Moss and Bruce possessed at their bivouac site.

Before she left, Molly visited the prisoner of war camp and found Riley. He was sound asleep and wounded. He had been shot near his right eye, yet the projectile did not go into his head but glanced off of his skull. He was lucky to be alive and had bandages wrapped diagonally around his wound and eye. Molly could tell he had a terrible gash in the head. His leg was also bandaged.

Molly sat by Riley for awhile thinking about the twists of life and love. She thought of what Moses said two days earlier that love is as strong as death and the coals of love are the coals of the brightest fire. The other prisoners milling around were jealous because the fair lady in their presence was so preoccupied with her thoughts she didn't notice anyone else.

Molly did not want to wake Riley. She slipped her hand in his and held it for a moment. *Oh Riley,* she said to herself. *You and I were so close once. I thought you might be the one. I need to tell you I fell in love with Bruce and married him. He is the love of my life now. We can be friends but I will never be in love with you. You are brave. You are a kind man and a gentleman. You deserve a good woman to be with. I forgive you for fighting Moss. I know it must have been a very bitter task for you to do. Hopefully the next time I see you this war will be over and we will both be residing in our beautiful Winchester. Goodbye Riley.* Molly slipped her hand out of his, quietly departed the cantonment area and climbed into the wagon to travel home with Moses.

170.

Molly's brother Ned, found Hans' body the next day and reached in his dead friend's coat pocket. He discovered two letters, one for each of his girlfriends in the event of his death. Ned put those in his own pocket for delivery later. Ned knew Hans had written them the night before. The red-haired Winchester boy with the long neck did not open the letters, but opened up an envelope stuffed with papers. Ned saw they were poems. The one on top was dated the 16th of September. Ned remembered Hans was writing something as Ned drifted off to sleep the night before last. *A Hans original!* Ned chuckled to himself thinking about Hans trying to be a great poet. He decided to read the poem out loud to see if it made any sense.

I Cannot Sleep Tonight by Hans Draeger

Children sleep in a sleep so deep
The glow of peace their light
They care not why they slumber so
They sleep deep through the night

To death we all must soon embrace
It's death, our one last foe
Our footsteps can never be replaced
We touch and then we go

Children sleep in a sleep so deep
The glow of peace their light
They care not why they slumber so
Yet I fear death tonight

\To death we all must soon embrace
It's death, our one last foe
Our steps can never be erased
We have to reap what's sown

Ned looked down at the poem and shook his head. *Good grief. Poetry is much more than just rhyming words,* thought Ned. *I'll bet he never took any poetry classes. Everyone wants to be a poet or a great writer. No one wants to work at it. Everyone thinks it's so easy. The meter in this is all messed up!* Ned shook his head again as he picked up Hans' lifeless, heavy body and placed him on the wagon that was being utilized to carry off the Union dead. He then prayed a short prayer for Hans and his family and placed the packet of poems inside his friend's coat.

171.

General McClellan was annoyed to receive the President's message. "Where is the praise? Where is the congratulations?" McClellan asked his staff. He wrote back to Washington and declared,

"I feel some little pride in having taken a beaten down and demoralized army and defeated General Bobby Lee so utterly and have saved the North so completely. My only hope is that one day in the future, history students will show me justice and give me the recognition I deserve."

172.

Moses and Molly crossed the Potomac, drove through Shepherdstown and took the road toward Martinsburg. It was a quiet trip and neither Molly nor Moses spoke more than a sentence or two the entire morning.

The wagon trip between Sharpsburg and Winchester would be a two day trip because they did not leave until early afternoon on the 18th. Molly reflected on the last few days while Moses steered the team.

Moses glanced at Molly now and again but seeing the look in her face he dared not disturb her.

Most of the afternoon Molly thought over and over again of the hours she spent with Bruce on their wedding day. She thought of how he must have suffered during those final seconds Jonesy held him in his lap. A tear escaped Molly's eye. She thought of his forlorn look as he lay in a heap next to the others. Molly sat by Bruce's side for an hour in disbelief that the love of her life was actually gone. She was afforded little time to celebrate and plan their future life together and she felt a horrible hollowness seeing him dead after a single day. She had saved her love for one great man and now he was gone.

Molly was thankful she had given herself to Bruce without restraint, and he had equally given himself to her. Bruce and Molly shared an intimate afternoon together caring little about anything else but their love and pleasure. It was the one small piece of utopia they would share together in this lifetime. Being vulnerable and fully exposed was as alien to them as living without fear or shame, but the two had adapted well.

The travelers rode to Martinsburg and spent the night with a family friend of the Harringtons who was thrilled to see Molly again and learn eyewitness accounts of the gruesome battle which was so far the bloodiest single day of the war. As they visited on the front porch that evening they did not realize they were being watched by a stranger in town.

173.

That evening Henry was asked by Sandie Pendleton to bring a message to General Lee's headquarters for General Jackson. Sandie was busily preparing for their expected retreat and needed Jackson to know some vital information while he conferred with the other leaders. Henry walked to Lee's headquarters in Sharpsburg enjoying the change of scenery from the fields of blood and death where he had been working the entire day.

When he arrived at the door the guard asked him what he was doing and then let him slip into an open room where other aides and messengers had assembled. Henry stood in the room wondering what was being said in the next room where the commanding generals were meeting. All of a sudden, a man walked in from the outside and Henry looked at him as if studying a ghost. The man was in a Union uniform and had a straggling beard and long hair. No one seemed to mind to have a Union officer in their headquarters building but this is not what bothered Henry. What flabbergasted the young man was that the man in the blue uniform was Daniel Tanner.

Instinctively Henry shot forward and tackled Tanner. The man was unprepared and fell backward into a lamp table and crashed onto the floor. Henry began beating at him with his fists before others grabbed him and pulled him off.

Joseph Turnham, an aide to Robert E. Lee, stormed into the room from the general's conference yelling, "What the devil is going on here?"

Henry shouted, "That man is Daniel Tanner! He is a traitor, a thief and a liar! He tried to kill my wife!"

Tanner stood up and straightened his uniform while Joseph Turnham tried to calm Henry down. "Hey, hold on boy. There is a mistaken identity here. This is not Daniel Tanner."

"It sure is!" shot Henry. "I'll bet my life on it. No one has beady eyes like his."

Turnham got right in Henry's face and said clearly, "Look, this is not Daniel Tanner from the Winchester area. This is William Tanner, his identical twin. He is one of our spies. His twin brother Daniel is working with the Union, but William here is one of our best men—one of our very best spies."

Henry was befuddled and did not want to believe it. He wanted to strangle Tanner and reason with everyone later. He stood there and glared with his fists clinched, his face red and his veins exploding.

William Tanner walked cautiously toward him with his hand out ready to shake Henry's but Henry did not move.

Joseph Turnham said, "You're going to have to trust my judgment on this one, son."

Tanner said, "I can see my twin brother has caused your family harm. I am sorry for that. My entire life I have fought against the comparison of one so unlike myself. We separated while young teenagers when our parents died and we have had no contact with each other since. In fact, I think he has disowned me and vowed never to speak to me again. However, one who has met Daniel has a hard time believing I am not him and vice versa. Because of biology I will bear his perfect image the rest of my days. I am not Daniel Tanner and I, William, have pledged myself fully to the cause of The Confederate States of America and have worked with General Lee and Jefferson Davis these past eighteen months. My brother cannot decide which side to support so he plays the middle."

Henry still did not move, still could not accept the impossible, that there was another man in the exact likeness of his nemesis.

"Will you shake my hand in friendship for the cause we are in?" asked Tanner.

All the eyes in the room were on Henry and he was starting to feel very warm. Finally, Henry raised up his right hand and the two hands touched and clasped.

Joseph Turnham said, "There now, no more disturbances or I will put you both under arrest. William, General Lee will see you now and if any of you in here have messages for the commanders I will take them to deliver them at once."

Henry brought his hand back to his side, took out the message from Sandie and handed it to Turnham to give to Jackson. He then took one more look at Tanner as the man walked into the commander's meeting area. Henry left the house with his mind racing. He had seen a ghost. The ghost of Daniel Tanner.

174.

The Visitor boarded the ship with the other prisoners. He had a black cotton sack over his head so he could not see the port they were leaving from, nor see the exterior of the ship. He did not understand why they were keeping things so secret unless they were trying to keep it secret from their own allies, from the United States Government itself. The Visitor had a bad feeling about this and wondered whether he would ever leave the ship alive.

When they had been brought through the hatch and down the ladder into the hold, they were all shackled to the floor. An announcement was made as their heads were uncovered.

"Welcome Rebels. You will most likely never leave this ship and your remains will be fed to the sharks. We will be going out to sea far enough so if you escape this vessel you will drown and never reach land. In fact, we will go out so far that you cannot even see which direction land is. Therefore, it will be your best interest to pay attention to all of the rules and to speak to us freely and openly about everything you may know about the Confederate Army and their plans. The more you speak to us, the better chance you have of departing this ship and returning to where you belong. We give you no guarantees of food or fair treatment and some of you will stubbornly refuse us and not speak to us. You will be beaten, starved and dealt with severely until the day you choose to speak freely to us about the enemy. Now then, this is Muldoon." The speaker pointed to a large burly man wearing baggy pants and no shirt. His skin was bronze from the sun and he wore silver bracelets on his arms. The muscles in his arms were oversized and tight. The man had a beard but had shaved off his sideburns and some of the facial hair on the cheeks leaving hair only around his mouth and chin. He held a whip in his hands and he did not look happy.

"Every day you will have the opportunity to spend time with Muldoon in the punishment room. When you decide you do not want to spend time with Muldoon anymore then you come and see me. You may call me Mr. Nice. I will listen to you and help you with options about how to leave this ship."

The man entitled Mr. Nice stopped talking for a moment and looked around at the forty men who would be his prisoners for awhile.

"Who would like to speak to me tonight and forego this whole awful ordeal?"

The Visitor noticed that instantly six hands went up followed by two more.

"Fine, fine. I will speak to you one at a time. Muldoon, as soon as the captain sets out to sea you may begin taking men one at a time into the punishment room."

The Visitor watched as Mr. Nice returned to the main deck with the eight men who had raised their hands. He put his head down and thought to himself that he would have to be killed before agreeing to be one of their spies or assassins. *Hey, why is the ship still heading out to sea if men are saying they will confess and cooperate?* The Visitor wondered.

175.

"Why does he not follow Lee and attack him?" asked President Lincoln to his wife Mary.

She just smiled and did not respond. They were sitting on the bed removing their shoes after a long day. Mary had raised money for the wounded soldiers flooding Washington after the battle in Maryland. She had spent the day buying fruit and flowers and delivering the items to some local hospitals. She also had written many letters home for those men who could no longer write.

"The man astounds me, Mother," Lincoln said, clearly annoyed.

"I know Mr. Lincoln, I know. Things will work for the good, you'll see."

"I know you're right. I just cannot figure out what goes on in the minds of these commanders. If they want glory and fame then they could have it easily—if they would just attack!"

Lincoln finally calmed down and crawled into bed. *Perhaps we'll hear good news in the morning,* he hoped.

176.

While General Lee and his army poured across the Potomac and fled back into Virginia early on the 19th, Molly and Moses again climbed into their wagon and headed south to Winchester. They just had a few miles left to travel before they would be home and would have to speak to the Crawfords about their sons.

They rode down the valley turnpike with thoughts of what to say to the Crawfords when they finally arrived at the front of their house with two bodies in the back of the wagon. It would not be an easy task. *Thankfully Sarah and Lawrence, if he was home, were gracious people, but who could bear this tragic news?* thought Molly.

As Copper Jake and Mercutio led the way and saw them toward their destination, Molly and Moses spoke some about the events of the last month and Moses' daring adventure into slave territory by which he sought to rescue Molly. Molly told him how thankful she was of him and how truly appreciative she was of all that he had done for her. As they rode on they could make out in the distance the gently rolling hills to the north of their home. Molly was thrilled to be back in her land again, despite the circumstances and the darkness in her heart about losing Bruce.

Suddenly there was some activity to the left of the wagon. When Molly realized what was going on she saw two horsemen who she recognized and dreaded. One was Daniel Tanner, the villain, and the other was his accomplice, Toad. Molly was mortified and Moses was trying to giddy up the team to no avail. Toad grabbed the reigns of one of the horses and slowed him down while Tanner stayed right at Moses' side next to the wagon.

When the team was completely stopped, Tanner grabbed a hold of Moses' shirt wrenching him down out of the wagon making him tumble to the ground. Toad and Tanner then dismounted and Toad came over to Moses and kicked him in the ribs. Tanner took the reins of the wagon and climbed up and sat next to Molly who tried to jump out the other side. Tanner caught her by the neck and maneuvered her back around.

Toad began to mercilessly kick and beat Moses while repeatedly calling him a nigger and a black Lucifer. Tanner watched the scene with delight and laughed. They told him they were going to take him down and sell him to a plantation owner and tell them he was a runaway. The venom of Toad and Tanner was in full strength. When they glanced at the cargo in the back of the wagon they hooted and laughed in scoffing derision.

While the focus was on Moses, Molly slipped her right hand into a burlap bag laying next to her on the bench. She slowly removed the heavy metal object while pulling back its trigger. She brought her hand around and stuck the nose of a LeMat revolver right into the side of Tanner's hairy neck just underneath his jawbone.

Tanner froze.

"Give me a chance! Ain't you a lady?" he asked while shifting his eyes, thinking of his next move.

Molly thought about his words for half a second and then squeezed hard on the trigger.

Crack!

Daniel Tanner shot sideways into the back of the wagon and crumpled over next to Bruce and Moss. He was now just as lifeless as them.

Toad startled, raised his hands and fearfully looked at Molly who was aiming the gun in his direction.

"What did you say you were going to do to my friend Moses, who helped save me from you and your miscreant pals?"

"Nothing, ma'am, please don't shoot. It was Mister Tanner's idea all along. I don't want no trouble," Toad was now stammering worse than Malcolm ever had.

Molly wanted to pull the trigger so she would never have to wonder in fear if this tormenter would show up again. She knew she would have dreams about him and wonder at every odd noise outside. But something stayed her hand. Moses was slowly standing up behind Toad and brushing himself off. Molly thought about Toad being a reprobate and if she killed him now he would certainly go straight to hell. She did not want that on her conscience. Killing Tanner was self-defense, but killing Toad could not be justified. She wanted to give Toad a chance to make right with God, even though she had nothing in her heart for the man by way of compassion. While still thinking through the moral implications of her situation, she was just about to lower the pistol when Toad did something to provoke her. Toad took to the offense and grabbed Moses around the neck with one arm and pulled a knife out of his pocket with his other hand.

"If you so much as flinch, lady, I'm going to kill your friend," Toad growled.

Molly held up the pistol and aimed at Toad's head. The moral implications were resolved. The last thing she remembered before pulling the trigger again was the look of fear and surprise in Toad's eyes.

Crack!

One loud shot and the situation changed. Moses was shaking and highly troubled. His red lips and white eyes were wide open in disbelief. Toad had fallen backward and had a wide, bleeding gash in his neck. He slowly raised up, put his hand on his neck to stop the bleeding and ran off as fast as he could with a loud yowl. Moses stood frozen, not knowing what to do.

"Ma'am?" Moses tried to speak and ask a question but he couldn't. He looked at Tanner dead in the wagon and at Toad scurrying away through the trees. He shook his head with wide-eyed astonishment. Molly did not try to take another shot at the scared little rabbit as he disappeared from their sight.

Finally Moses was able to ask Molly where she had gotten the pistol.

"Bruce gave it to me on our wedding day, before he left me alone. He said to carry it with me for protection." Moses nodded with wide eyes.

It took a little while for Moses to settle down. He was hurting from his beating and still in shock that Molly had shot someone so close to him. Molly stepped down from the wagon and gave Moses a hug telling him how sorry she was to have to scare him like that. Finally, when he had calmed down, Moses asked if he should take Tanner out of the wagon and bury him behind the large oak tree. It would not be an uncommon sight in those days for a traveler to see a dead man buried by the side of the road.

Molly thought for a moment and then decided not to move Tanner. "Let's take him with us. Perhaps some good might come of it," she said. Molly was rejuvenated with the thought that Daniel Tanner and Major Welch were no longer alive. The two friends climbed back into the wagon, cleaned Tanner's blood off the old wooden bench they sat on and continued on their way to Winchester.

* * *

When the wagon pulled up to a stop at the Crawford house Molly became more nervous than ever. Her right leg shook a little. She had rehearsed a line or two of what she would say, but as she and Moses walked up the front steps she couldn't remember a word of it. When the door opened something happened she did not expect. Sarah, seeing her, immediately stepped forward and gave Molly a mighty hug.

"Oh dear, oh my dear daughter! My daughter Molly - you've come home with my boys. Thank you Molly!" Tear-stricken Sarah did not release Molly from her grasp for a long time. Lucy moved past the adults and slipped down the front porch steps and looked into the back of the wagon.

Sarah released Molly for a moment and looked into her eyes. Both of them were crying. Molly realized that Sarah had heard the news already and was just waiting for them to finally arrive. They hugged some more and then Sarah flew down the steps to look at the faces of her sons.

After peering into their still, final expressions Sarah said, "Bless you Moses. Bless you Molly, for bringing them to me. It was hard enough to hear the news, but to think of them being left out in the weather or buried in a shallow, anonymous grave would have been too much for my heart to bear. Bless Jackson for allowing you to come."

"How did you hear the news?" asked Molly.

"We received a bereavement telegram from President Jefferson Davis himself," replied Sarah as she stepped up onto the wagon and hugged her boys and wept. Molly expected to see Sarah mourning. She was not alarmed by the intensity of Sarah's moans and crying. *My how she loved them,* thought Molly.

Molly noticed that Lucy was sitting on the porch steps with a dazed look in her eyes but not crying. Molly walked over and sat next to her.

"Are you okay, Lucy?"

No response.

"It's all right. You don't need to talk. It sounds like you heard the news about Bruce and I getting married. If you ever need to talk I am here for you." Molly put her arm around Lucy and the young girl broke down and cried as Molly pulled her close and held her.

Grandmother Elizabeth Crawford then stepped outside the front door and looked at the sight before her. Moses was still up on the porch watching everything unfold.

Grandma Crawford turned sideways, looked up at Moses and said, "And what do *you* have to say for yourself, young man?"

"I has nuttin to say, ma'am," Moses glanced away nervously trying to find somewhere else to look with his eyes.

"Eliza, come down here now and look at your grandsons. Molly and Moses brought them home for us so we can pay our last respects and bury them properly," said Sarah to her mother-in-law.

Grandma Crawford gave a faint nod of understanding and grabbed Moses' hand with both of hers. Moses stood there startled. She said thank you silently with her mouth. Moses then helped Grandma Crawford down the steps so she could join Sarah in saying her goodbye.

177.

President Abraham Lincoln met with his Cabinet on September 22nd, five days after the battle of Antietam. William Seward, Portland Chase, Postmaster-General Montgomery Blair, Edwin Stanton, Navy Secretary Gideon Welles and Edward Bates were all present. Lincoln began the meeting reading some parts from a humorous book he had just received. His closest associates Seward and Blair enjoyed the brief respite from business matters, but stolid Chase and fiery Stanton seemed somewhat perturbed at the delay.

Lincoln concluded the reading and began with some introductory remarks, "You know, I had hoped, and had actually thought for awhile that General McClellan had given us a resounding victory which had crushed the rebellion. As more telegraphs came to me on the 17th and 18th I realized he actually let a great victory slip away from him. And, he still hasn't pursued Lee's Army as I would have liked. However, saying that, McClellan did deliver to us, though not a stunning blow, a powerful stop to the momentum of the Rebels. If you have been reading the newspapers they are singing his praises and writing as if this was the greatest victory of the war. Perhaps it was and we don't know it yet. What matters is that the citizens in our country are somewhat encouraged with the military and what it is able to achieve.

"I believe it is now time to issue my Emancipation Proclamation. We have discussed it before and I need to tell you I have already decided to issue the order now and I am not soliciting your advice about the timing. I would like to hear if you have anything to say about the wording or any other minor changes. Before you comment I would like to tell you the timing of this was a decision I made awhile ago and having submitted the plans to my Maker, he has allowed everything to work and I am resolute in seeing this through."

Lincoln's language was more vague than he had anticipated. He could tell by their faces that they were all a little confused at the last sentence or two. He was trying to tell them that he had prayed to God that if and when the Southerners were expelled from Maryland he would issue the Proclamation, and he felt bound almost by an oath to the Almighty to move forward and make this a reality. *They all know I am not a religious man*, thought Lincoln. *That is why when I speak of higher matters they wonder where I am going with it. So be it, I have spoken my piece.*

Lincoln then decided to read part of it to them; "That on the first day of January, in the year of our Lord one thousand eight hundred and sixty-three, all persons held as slaves within any State or designated part of a State, the people whereof shall then be in rebellion against the United States, shall be then, thenceforward, and forever free; and the Executive Government of the United States, including the military and naval authority thereof, will recognize the freedom of such persons, and will do no act or acts to repress such persons, or any of them, in any efforts they may make for their actual freedom.......... And by virtue of the power, and for the purpose aforesaid, I do order and declare that all persons held as slaves within said designated States, and parts of States, are, and henceforward shall be free; and that the Executive government of the United States, including the military and naval authorities thereof, will recognize the freedom of said persons."

With this order all the slaves in the rebellion states would be made free. This did not include the border states of Kentucky, Maryland, Missouri, Delaware and several counties from northwestern Virginia. Only Arkansas, Texas, Louisiana, Mississippi, Alabama, Florida, Georgia, South Carolina, North Carolina and Virginia would have to abide by this order. Seward offered a suggestion to change the wording from just 'recognize the freedom' to 'recognize and maintain the freedom."

Lincoln explained that he had thought of this change but assumed the more forceful approach might be harder to achieve. In the end he sided with Seward and wrote in 'will recognize and maintain the freedom of such persons.'

Edwin Stanton said he liked the document just how it was written and would stand behind it.

Chase laboriously communicated that it is not what he would have written had he been President of the United States. However, he would stand behind it as if it were his own. Lincoln asked him what they could do differently and Chase responded that the Proclamation would not make slavery illegal everywhere at once.

Lincoln agreed and said, "We would actually need an amendment to do this the way Secretary Chase is suggesting." *We've been over and over this,* thought Lincoln.

"It is a start and I believe an important one that begins to free the millions of slaves that are in bondage now. Sure, only 20,000 to 30,000 slaves would be freed when this Proclamation goes into effect on New Year's Day, but it provides the legal framework so that when the war concludes, all of the slaves living in the South will be freed. Plus, as states are won over by our army they will become free states," said Lincoln.

Bates and Welles were somewhat quiet but passively agreeable to the measure.

It was Lincoln's ally Montgomery Blair who was the only dissenter. He did not disagree with the document as much as he was saddened that issuing it would hurt the fall elections. Lincoln smiled inwardly knowing that his colleague was a premier politician through and through. One who could keep an eye on re-election even when looking at a document which could change the course of human history. He liked Blair's political savvy but he wished he could see the larger picture. Lincoln spoke to Blair and told him he had considered his objections but found them unfounded.

Seward cut to the chase and summarized saying, "This represents a shift in the war objectives of the North. Reuniting the nation is no longer the only goal. This is an important document and an important time in history for our entire nation. Mr. President, you have our support."

With that, Lincoln handed over his draft to the Secretary of State to certify and make official, and the order was issued later that day.

178.

My Dearest Ellen,

Now that I have saved the country twice they owe me a small favor and I will press the P. on this or resign. Edwin Stanton must be replaced and Old Brains must relinquish his supreme command of all the military to me. I have proven that I can command the largest army on the globe and achieve victory when in a situation where I am outnumbered. They must see it. They have to see it or I will resign. As far as this new 'Emancipation Proclamation,' it is an immoral document that will lead slaves in the South to revolt and insurrect. I will protest this to Lincoln when I demand he restore me to my rightful position. Have you heard what the press is saying about me, my love? Believe me when I tell you it is nothing compared to how the troops feel. I frequently hear comments of praise and support, begging that I never leave as commander again. You should hear them, Ellen. It would make you proud of me. I believe I should run for President in '64. How could I lose?

Your Doting Husband,
George

179.

A day after the Federal prisoners from Antietam Creek were marched into Winchester, Riley received a visit. Some of the ladies from town had actually baked goods for the men who fought against their husbands, sons and brothers. Sarah Crawford asked Claire Montgomery to walk with her to where the prisoners were. Not all of the Sharpsburg prisoners passed through Winchester, only the ones en route to Richmond. The officers would go to Libby Prison and the enlisted to Belle Isle on the James River. Riley was one of those brought through the city while leaving the Northern Shenandoah Valley.

For days after the Battle of Antietam Creek the Confederate wounded wandered into town looking for care. Many were shoeless, most had bloodstained clothing, ripped in order to give surgeons access to their wounds. The Winchester women cared for these forlorn men and gave them the attention they needed, feeding and giving them a roof for the night. Now their hearts went out to the prisoners, some of whom were also the walking wounded like Riley.

Along their stroll to the church, now utilized as a makeshift prison, Claire and Sarah ran into Rachel Jones who was also walking to find the prisoners with some food she had prepared for them. When the three women arrived to the old building downtown where they were being kept, they found many of the prisoners were sitting outside on a curb, ready to march away that afternoon.

Rachel gave Claire and Sarah her potato salad and waited on the street corner while they went inside to search for Riley. The prisoners looked pitiful and were under a heavy guard. The two friends found Riley just inside the doorway of the church, sitting on the floor. He had a patch covering his right eye and a black wound on his head beside the patch. He was startled to see the ladies, especially Sarah Crawford who he dreaded ever seeing again.

The McNair boy tried to stand up, but the women made him stay down and they themselves found two old stools and sat by him. Riley looked down, began to shake his head and say over and over again, "I'm sorry. I'm so sorry for what I did." He felt a hand on his shoulder and glanced up. Sarah Crawford was looking sweetly into his eyes.

"Riley, I want you to know something before you leave Winchester today. When I heard you had killed my Moss I wanted to kill you. I wished it was you who had died in your duel against my youngest boy. It was even more grievous to me that Bruce had also died that day and I heard from Moss' friend, Lewis, how you knew about Bruce before you fought with my youngest." Sarah paused for a moment to collect her thoughts while Riley remained breathless, wondering what she was about to say.

"However, Riley, I want you to know something. I forgive you. I forgive you for killing my boy Moss. And I forgive you for fighting in the Union Army."

"Are you sure?" Riley asked pessimistically.

"With all of my heart I forgive you, son!" Sarah exclaimed with glistening eyes, embracing him.

Riley was speechless. This was unexpected. The story of how he would meet Mrs. Crawford again never concluded this way in his imagination. He had gone over and over the final encounter with Moss and wished Moss had killed him or that he had somehow avoided the angry young man altogether. He thought about how disastrous it would be to speak to Mrs. Crawford, and now it was over and she had been unjustly kind.

Riley looked back at Sarah and choked out, "Thank you, Mrs. Crawford."

A moment later Claire also chimed in, "Riley, never feel awkward around us because of the choices you have made. You, Ned, Henry and Jonesy are just kids caught up in something much larger than yourselves and it has ramifications out of your control. Look, we brought you a gift of some biscuits, Rachel Jones' potato salad, some ham and even a few cookies Kathryn made. I doubt you'll find such good cooking for a long time."

"Have you lost sight in your eye, Riley?" asked Sarah.

"Yes, ma'am. But the doctor said I'm lucky to be alive."

"You are blessed. We are all blessed because of a loving God who spontaneously rewards and forgives," said Claire smiling at him.

"I believe that," said Riley.

Both women gave him a quick hug and departed. Riley was greatly encouraged to see them but the feeling did not last long. Soon after he ate their food he became sick, as did everyone who ate the potato salad. Riley McNair was dead by nightfall.

180.

The older warrior concluded his visit with President Jefferson Davis and they shook hands. Afterwards Davis made the necessary communications which enacted a prisoner exchange. The capture of so many high ranking officers at Harpers Ferry allowed the Southern President some leverage in speaking to the Federal officials about prisoner swaps. The North would be more than happy to regain some of their senior officers.

Davis was dismayed at this most recent report of suffering, however. The prisoners on board this 'ship of torture' were enduring more than most he had heard about. The man who just left his office was obviously beaten and bruised over a long period of time. Hopefully it would not be too late to exchange their imprisoned leaders for the Visitor and for Conrad Montgomery who was being held in Maryland.

181.

The spectral figure walked the back streets of Winchester after dark, alone and mysterious. He was harvesting food that would sustain him for the next twenty-four hours. The rumor in town was that he was the ghost of Daniel Tanner. The lone specter didn't mind. It would keep people inside and away from him while he gathered things to eat from their gardens and storage cellars. His enemies were the dogs sprinkled around town that alerted their residents with his arrival. He had to move fast and get back to his hiding place each evening before getting caught.

182.

Muldoon told the Visitor it was his lucky day as the ship made for the nation's Capitol. A prisoner exchange had been agreed upon and the Visitor was to be released as soon as possible. The Visitor knew the older gentleman must have made it safely out and let someone important know he was there.

The first stop for the Visitor after the ship docked was at the War Department. Secretary Stanton wanted to speak to the man before he left for Virginia.

While conversing briefly about the war an announcement was made in the room that the President of the United States had just entered the building and would be there momentarily. The Visitor stood up along with Mr. Stanton.

Soon, in walked President Abraham Lincoln. Lincoln walked over to the Visitor and stared at him for a moment. Both men sized up the other.

Lincoln started the conversation, "You know, you have caused us quite a few problems over this last year?"

The Visitor merely nodded a reply, communicating that he understood.

"I am not happy about giving you up, but in your physical condition I do not think you can cause us much harm for a long while. Tell me something, why did you fight for the Confederate States of America?"

"For my family. For my state. For the men who fight alongside of me. For a belief that the founding values of our free nation were violated when you raised an army and invaded the South."

"I have strong beliefs about our founding values, as well," said Lincoln wearily.

Neither man said anything for almost a full minute while the President paced the room a little. Then Lincoln turned to the Visitor and asked, "Are you a person of strong Christian faith?"

"Not really."

"Neither am I. I do not believe in an afterlife. I believe that our actions on earth, our words, our memories in people's minds are our afterlife and our only legacy. Are you happy with your legacy?"

"Yes, sir, I am," the Visitor said confidently.

Lincoln smiled, thought, *very fine soldier.*

The President looked into his face and asked with a twinkle in his eye, "One more question. You know Jackson. What do you think makes him tick, makes him such an aggressive commander?"

The Visitor did not hesitate in his response, "I believe it is his strong Christian faith. He never brings attention to himself and does nothing for his own praise or promotion. He seems to tackle tasks with an inward compulsion and he does not worry about the afterlife. He embraces death, says God knows exactly when that will be and he has no need to be concerned with it—this makes him all the more aggressive and fierce."

"And dangerous," added Lincoln.

"Yes, the troops love it."

Everyone in the room took a moment to absorb the words.

"In a small way I envy that," stated Lincoln and then he turned and walked away from the Visitor toward the door. "Farewell."

The meeting was over.

183.

President Lincoln decided to visit McClellan's headquarters to see the troops and hopefully to inspire his commanding general to attack and engage Lee. McClellan had done nothing since the battle at Antietam Creek and it was now October. The President and George McClellan had a cordial meeting and Lincoln gained renewed hope that an offensive plan was formulating. Soon the Union Army would return to Virginia. Lincoln was now sure of it.

While climbing a small rise away from camp with a friend they looked back at the Army of the Potomac. It was an awesome sight to behold and Lincoln shook his head to think of it remaining in bivouac. The corps and divisions encircled themselves as far as the eyes could see around the McClellan Headquarters, almost as if to protect the commander himself.

Before he left the battlefield they asked Lincoln to sit by Antietam Creek and hear from the Army Band and men's choir. It was one of the most sacred moments Lincoln experienced knowing that parts of the ground were still moist with the blood of the fallen. The effort, the sacrifice, the number of dead and wounded were all astonishing realizations. The anointed ground contained red stains still easily seen in the areas where heavy fighting occurred such as the cornfield, the bloody lane and beside Burnside's bridge. The choir decided to sing a song recently written by Julia Ward Howe called, "The Battle Hymn of the Republic."

Mine eyes have seen the glory
of the coming of the Lord,
He is trampling out the vintage
where the grapes of wrath are stored,
He has loosed the fateful lightning of his
terrible swift sword:
His truth is marching on.

Glory! Glory Hallelujah!
Glory! Glory Hallelujah!
Glory! Glory Hallelujah!
His truth is marching on.

I have seen him in the watch-fires
of a hundred circling camps,
They have builded him an altar
in the evening dews and damps,
I can read his righteous sentence
by the dim and flaring lamps:
His day is marching on.

Glory! Glory Hallelujah!
Glory! Glory Hallelujah!
Glory! Glory Hallelujah!
His truth is marching on.

He has sounded forth the trumpet
that shall never call retreat,
He is sifting out the hearts of men
before his judgment seat,
Oh be swift my soul to answer him
be jubilant my feet:
Our God is marching on.

Glory! Glory Hallelujah!
Glory! Glory Hallelujah!
Glory! Glory Hallelujah!
His truth is marching on.

At this point in the song the President stood, clearly moved by the lyrics Howe had put to an older tune. He couldn't sing with them because of the sudden dryness in his throat so he moved his lips while the song continued.

In the beauty of the lilies
Christ was born across the sea,
With a glory in his bosom
that transfigures you and me,
As he died to make men holy
Let us die to make men free:
While God is marching on.

Glory! Glory Hallelujah!
Glory! Glory Hallelujah!
Glory! Glory Hallelujah!
His truth is marching on.

184.

As the last days in October were crossed off of the calendar, Lincoln grew more and more impatient. He told Seward and Blair one evening, "McClellan will surely strike by November. He will have given Lee a six week head start, but I am confident he will surely strike by November." Seward wasn't so sure.

The first of November came and went. The 1862 elections came and went. Because of the disastrous battles in the war so far, an inactive Union Army and the unpopularity of Lincoln's Emancipation Proclamation among Democrats, the Republicans lost quite a bit of influence.

The Republicans had 22 seats vanish and the Democrats picked up 28 seats. The Unionist party also lost seats. Thankfully for Lincoln the Republican Party still held control of the House of Representatives because of their alliance with the Unionist Party. But, this news was little consolation. The Democratic Party, already upset about the Emancipation Proclamation, were vehemently against Lincoln's decision to suspend habeas corpus on September 24th. They spread the word he was trying to make himself a dictator. They further claimed he had made the war a strictly abolitionist endeavor.

Lincoln, as he always did when bad things happened, took full responsibility for the losses. He hoped McClellan would have moved forward and attacked, possibly before the elections, to remind the country the nation is still at war. Instead, McClellan delayed.

He wouldn't do this on purpose just to hurt me would he? wondered Lincoln to himself. *No, that would be preposterous. I think I know McClellan's character enough to know he wouldn't hesitate to purposely thwart the political process.*

Yet, the more he thought about it, the more he wasn't sure and the more it bothered him.

The President then received a telegram from General McClellan stating the Army of the Potomac could not cross the Potomac and pursue the Confederate Army because the cavalry horses were too broken down from fatigue.

"Is this a joke?" asked Lincoln of General Halleck. "Surely this is not a serious telegram?" Lincoln inquired, looking at his top military advisor.

Old Brains merely scratched the bottom of his elbows and then his cheek, not knowing what to say. He had a curious look in his face but he gave no reply to the President.

Lincoln told Halleck to respond to McClellan's telegram with a question, "Fatigue from what?"

185.

After his visit with the President and a visit with the Confederate President in Richmond, the Visitor was helped by Conrad Montgomery down the familiar street to his house. It had been a long time. The Visitor spoke to Conrad on their journey home about how he had slipped into Harpers Ferry prior to the attack by Jackson and was able to help Molly. He described how he found her and picked her out of the rubble just before her entire prison room imploded. The Visitor was overjoyed to learn from Conrad that Molly had been found by Lieutenant Bruce Crawford and taken safely into Confederate custody.

The Visitor was not able to make it up his own front porch steps without help from the long-time friend beside him. He was still recuperating from wounds received from Muldoon in the punishment room. When Conrad knocked loudly on the front door of the Visitor's house they could hear a flurry of activity inside. The door was opened and everyone inside looked out, stunned at the pitiful sight of one of the gentleman.

Molly looked at his face and grasped for the first time who had rescued her out of her prison chamber.

The initial hugs and greetings were completed and then the Visitor whispered to his new daughter-in-law the words she longed to hear since she was a little girl. While enduring his torment, the Visitor learned of the survival of an old friend of his. This extraordinary news would change Molly's life forever.

The arrival of the two men made for a treasured day in Winchester. Lawrence Crawford and Conrad Montgomery were home to stay.

186.

Mid-November found Jonesy and Henry in the Blue Ridge Mountains with tattered blankets and no shoes. The two young men had cut strips of fresh cowhide and wrapped them around their feet and ankles to survive the snow and ice. They were not only suffering physically but emotionally. It was a powerful blow to their morale when at Sharpsburg they lost their two closest friends from Winchester. They recently heard from home that Riley was dead, as well. Jonesy especially took this news hard. Riley's death was another reminder of their innocence being lost by the war.

The way Jonesy mentally made it each day was through his thoughts of home, his ma's cooking and the close friendships he had made growing up. Since he was an only child, the Crawford boys, Riley, Henry and the Winchester girls essentially became his brothers and sisters. Jonesy looked forward to re-entering this family life when the war concluded. These thoughts were what propelled him from battle to battle and even night to night—that he might experience once again the fullness of his favorite people in his favorite setting. That each battle brought him closer to home was a fact as true to him as the trees he slept between and the frigid river he bathed in. The death of those he was closest to eroded part of Jonesy's will to fight, and Henry was beside himself as to how to fix him. Their conversations were no longer lighthearted and joyful. Jonesy wasn't being Jonesy and Henry had no idea what strategy to use in order to bring his old friend back.

However, two events happened that seemed to help Jonesy get back in step emotionally. One morning the two had just awoken after the bugle call and were heading to their unit formation when they had an unexpected encounter. General Stonewall Jackson rode by the two Winchester youth, stopped his horse and stared at them. He had a peculiar look on his face and it indicated to the boys that Jackson noticed these were the best friends of his long lost aide Bruce Crawford. The general took off his hat, bowed his head to them and proceeded on. The boys took it as a salute to the life of Bruce Crawford and an encouragement to them to persevere despite their loss. It was almost as if in that moment he perceived their pain and told them thank you for their service. The boys saluted sharply until he rode out of sight amidst cheers from other soldiers who saw the leader heading their way. This personal touch from their beloved commander was appreciated immensely by the two warriors.

The second event occurred a few days later when the unit was directed to march through the town of Winchester on their way out of the valley. The citizens lined the street and cheered to encouraged their ragged warriors. Some of the folks in town were discouraged to see such a tattered, dilapidated-looking bunch of men. Down from the sky flew sleet and rain while many of the soldiers marched barefoot and jacketless. Despite the rain it was excellent tonic for the men who were from there because many were able to receive gifts along the way. Jonesy himself received a new pair of shoes, a coat and a blanket from his mother, Rachel. Henry was thrilled to embrace Kathryn, if only for a few moments. After their march through Winchester Henry noticed the spark in Jonesy was back. Though not cured completely, he became more like his old self and smiled broadly once again.

187.

On the holiday morning, Molly told Kathryn she had something she needed to do before she enjoyed the day with her friends. She dressed warmly and walked up the road to her old home which was boarded up. No one had utilized it since the Harrington's left the year before. She walked to the back and found a loose plank of wood against an open cellar window. After working her way inside the window she walked up two flights of stairs to the bedroom which had the access to the attic.

Molly stood there alone but shouted out, "Ned! Ned! I know you are up there! It is Molly! Please come down so I can talk to you!"

She heard nothing.

"Ned, it's important. I have heard some news about father."

For a moment there was silence, and then she heard a response.

"I really don't care to hear anything about the man. I despise him."

She could hear Ned blow his nose and sniffle while he talked.

"No, I'm not talking about Harrington. I mean Father!"

Again there was silence. Then lanky Ned replied, "He was left for dead on some battlefield. What more is there to know?"

"I think he is still alive, Ned. Would you come down now so we can talk face to face?"

"I can't go back to the war, Molly. I cannot bear it any longer. It is changing me. It is--."

"I won't make you. But I need your help to find father."

Molly began to hear him move across the attic floor toward the opening. He slid down the crude attic steps and stood before her. Ned was always thin but to Molly that day he looked emaciated. His eyes were sunk deep into their sockets with dark rings around them. His neck and limbs looked like wires.

"Happy Thanksgiving, Ned," Molly said as she gave her older brother a hug. "Let's leave here and go get something warm to eat."

As they walked to the Crawford's home they discussed all of the events of the last days and caught each other up. Molly shared how her new father-in-law met a strange man on a ship who told him a remarkable tale of how Cotton Matthews escaped from a Mexican prison camp a few years after the war. They now had a lead by which to try to find their long lost father. This was the only good news Ned had heard for months.

Ned quoted to her some poetry he had written while in hiding.

"What do you think?" he asked.

"It's awful," replied Molly. "I like the poems of a dead Union soldier named Hans Draeger."

"How in the world did you hear about him?" asked Ned.

"Some of his poems were found on the battlefield near Sharpsburg and a newspaper man printed them."

Befuddled Ned shook his head in disbelief, "Nuts!"

188.

The stout man told his fellow generals he just received a letter from the President and must be excused a moment to look at it in private. No doubt the President was congratulating him again. He walked into his office as he unfolded the note and to his surprise it was not a very long message. When he read its contents he couldn't believe his eyes. The country he saved had betrayed him. The long-legged baboon had back-stabbed him. The seven words on the paper stung like no words he had seen before. All of his hopes. All of his plans. All of his dreams were extinguished that instant like a candle in the wind.

He will pay, thought the man. *No matter how I spend the rest of my life, I will get even. You are wrong, Mr. President, and you have no right to do this. I'm the commander-in-chief. I'm the nation's beloved general. They want me to lead them and not you. The troops love me. My subordinate commanders love me. My family and friends love me. Only a deranged woman loves you. You are a disgrace and you have gone too far. Watch your back, Mr. President. You're going to fail and I'm going to win!*

George Brinton McClellan stood up and kicked his field desk over in a rage, spraying its contents all over the floor. As other officers came into the room, McClellan opened up the crumpled telegram in his hand and read the words one more time.

"Effective immediately you are relieved from command."

189.

Stonewall Jackson wrote a letter to his beloved wife Anna, who was expecting the birth of their first child. After updating her on where his army was encamped, he concluded the letter with these words,

"I hope to be able to join you in a prayer for peace and trust that all Christian people will do the same. However, peace should not be the chief object of prayer in our country. It should aim more especially to implore God's forgiveness of our sins and praying that he will make our people a holy people. If we are but his, all things shall work together for the good of our country and no good thing will he withhold from it."

Jackson placed the stylus on his desk, bowed his head, and prayed for the safety of his wife, his troops and the Confederate States of America.

190.

As the sun set beyond the valley that Thanksgiving Day, Scout laid across the raised, broken earth in front of the four markers. He gently placed his long, soft nose on top of his front paws. Scout and Molly had walked to the grassy patch underneath the five remaining willow trees near the half-circle stone wall by Kathryn's stream. The man Molly shot and killed had no one who would claim him or care about his death. Molly asked her friend's parents if she could bury her worst enemy alongside her husband and two childhood friends inside the wall. She was not denied.

This was not an easy decision for her but she decided to honor the despised man in his death by placing him near those she valued most. While her friends fought in their war and died, she fought her war and found forgiveness.

A merchant in town engraved on a stone marker a verse Molly authored. It now suspended a few inches over where her bridegroom laid his head.

> *"If given but a day to live,*
> *Just a day and then life's over,*
> *I'd choose the day you made of me*
> *Your wife in fields of clover."*

Molly sat on the stone wall and wept for those who she loved so deeply. Scout looked up when, in the distance, a whippoorwill sounded its sorrowful call. Scout whined a little, closed his mournful brown eyes and dreamed of happier times.

EPILOGUE

At the end of 1862, the Southern Army was ready to shift into a corps command like the Northern Army. President Davis asked General Lee who he would recommend to be the new corps commanders and receive the rank of lieutenant general. Longstreet was chosen because of Old Pete's longstanding service to the Confederacy. For the other corps commander Robert E. Lee chose Thomas Jackson because he was 'true, honest, brave and spares no exertion to accomplish his object.' In the period of eighteen months, Jackson went from being a major and an instructor at VMI, to being a lieutenant general and in charge of half the Confederate Army. Almost 100 regiments were now under his command. Jackson never let this go to his head, however, and his Christian influence echoed across every barnyard and battlefield throughout Virginia.

The Northern Army was also in transition. After relieving George McClellan, President Lincoln appointed Ambrose Burnside to lead the army. The men in blue slowly trickled into Virginia and eventually met the Confederate Army on the hills behind Fredericksburg. There they suffered a humiliating and costly defeat incurring almost 13,000 casualties to the South's 5,500. Burnside was relieved of command and Joseph Hooker was appointed to lead the Army of the Potomac. This failure of the Union Army that December brought President Lincoln to his lowest point emotionally and politically.

The U. S. Senate met to decide what to do about his disastrous leadership. They listened to a man on Lincoln's Cabinet who fed them one-sided information, not understanding their informant was a backbiting gossip with an unending thirst for influence. It was Salmon P. Chase. Chase wanted to hurt Lincoln who held the position the Secretary of

Treasury thought he himself had earned. Instead of retaliating against Lincoln directly, Chase sought to remove his next greatest opponent on the Cabinet and targeted William Seward. His influence in the Senate did not go unnoticed, and Chase garnered significant support. Dejected, Seward submitted his resignation to Lincoln which his courageous leader refused to accept.

With Lincoln's greatest act of political diplomacy and tact, he avoided a coup and performed magnificently to save his Cabinet from Senate interference. In the process, Chase was exposed to his friends and enemies throughout Washington as a disingenuous, power-hungry child. Chase resented the President's actions but there was nothing he could do about them but to own his wrong. He begrudgingly submitted his own resignation to Lincoln which the President gleefully took from him. After letting the man sweat a few moments, the President tore up the letter explaining that he liked the balance of power on his team. When the crises passed, Seward extended an olive branch to Chase and invited him and his two daughters over for a Christmas Eve meal. Chase declined. He was pale and ill and in no condition for a social visit. Lincoln's dexterity in office salvaged his Cabinet, strengthened his presidency and moved the nation closer to victory.

George McClellan ran against Lincoln in the 1864 Presidential election. Democrat McClellan lost the Electoral College vote 21 to 212.

Despite McClellan's slowness and pride, the Union Army established for Lincoln at Antietam Creek enough political equity in September to announce his order against slavery. On January 1, 1863 the Emancipation Proclamation was enacted and immediately freed tens of thousands of slaves. As the months went on it provided the pathway to free millions. No longer would a man be able to own another man as a piece of property in the United States of America.

Appendix A

THE MAJOR BATTLES AND THE COMMANDERS
WHO FOUGHT IN THEM

Manassas (July 21, 1861)

Union

BG Irvin McDowell (Commander, Army of Northeastern Virginia)
BG Daniel Tyler (1st Division Commander)
COL Erasmus Keyes (1st Brigade Commander)
BG Robert Schenck (2nd Brigade Commander)
COL William T. Sherman (3rd Brigade Commander)
COL Israel Richardson (4th Brigade Commander)
COL Andrew Porter (2nd Division Commander)
COL Samuel P. Heintzelman (3rd Division Commander)

Confederate

BG G.T. Beauregard (Commander, Army of the Potomac)
BG Joseph Johnston (Commander, Army of the Shenandoah)
BG Thomas Jackson (1st Brigade Commander)
BG F. S. Bartow (2nd Brigade Commander)
BG Barnard E. Bee (3rd Brigade Commander)
COL Arnold Elzey (4th Brigade Commander)

Kernstown (March 23, 1862)

Union

BG James Shields (Division Commander under MG Nathaniel Banks)
COL Nathan Kimball (1st Brigade)
COL Jeremiah C. Sullivan (2nd Brigade)
COL Erastus B. Tyler (3rd Brigade)
COL Thornton F. Brodhead (Cavalry Brigade)

Confederate

MG Thomas Jackson (Commander, Army of the Shenandoah)
BG Richard Garnett (1st Brigade)
COL Jesse Burks (2nd Brigade)
COL Samuel Fulkerson (3rd Brigade)
COL Turner Ashby (Cavalry Brigade)

Winchester (May 25, 1862)

Union

MG Nathaniel P. Banks (Commander, Division of the Valley)
COL Dudley Donnelly (1st Brigade)
COL George H. Gordon (3rd Brigade)
BG John P. Hatch (Cavalry Brigade)

Confederate

MG Thomas Jackson (Commander, Army of the Shenandoah)
BG Charles Winder (First "Stonewall" Brigade)
COL John Campbell (2nd Brigade)
BG William Taliaferro (3rd Brigade)
COL Stapleton Crutchfield (Artillery Brigade)
COL Thomas Flournoy & BG Turner Ashby (Cavalry Brigade)
MG Richard Ewell (Second Division Commander)
BG Arnold Elzey (4th Brigade)
BG Isaac Trimble (7th Brigade)
BG Richard Taylor (8th Brigade)

Seven Days Battles (June 25 – July 1, 1862)

Union

MG George B. McClellan (Commander, Army of the Potomac)
BG Edwin Sumner (II Corps)
BG Israel B. Richardson (Division Commander)
BG John Sedgewick (Division Commander)
BG Samuel P. Heintzelman (III Corps)
BG Joseph Hooker (Division Commander)
BG Philip Kearney (Division Commander)
BG Erasmus D. Keyes (IV Corps)
BG Darius N. Couch (Division Commander)
BG John J. Peck (Division Commander)
BG Fitz John Porter (V Corps)
BG George W. Morell (Division Commander)
BG George Sykes (Division Commander)
BG George A. McCall (Division Commander)
BG William B. Franklin (VI Corps)
BG Henry W. Slocum (Division Commander)
BG William F. Smith (Division Commander)

Confederate

General Robert E. Lee (Commander, Army of Northern Virginia)
MG Thomas J. Jackson (Jackson's Command)
BG Charles S. Winder (Division Commander)
MG Richard S. Ewell (Division Commander)
BG W. H. C. Whiting (Division Commander)
MG D. H. Hill (Division Commander)
MG A. P. Hill (Separate Division Commander)
MG James Longstreet (Separate Division Commander)
MG John B. Magruder (Magruder's Command)
MG Lafayette McLaws (Division Commander)
BG David R. Jones (Division Commander)
MG Benjamin Huger (Division Commander)
MG Theophilus H. Holmes (Division Commander)

Second Manassas (Bull Run) (August 28-30, 1862)

Union

MG John Pope (Commander, Army of Virginia)
MG Franz Sigel (I Corps)
MG Nathaniel P. Banks (II Corps)
MG Irvin McDowell (III Corps)
MG Fitz John Porter (V Corps)
MG Ambrose Burnside (IX Corps)

Confederate

General Robert E. Lee (Commander, Army of Northern Virginia)
MG Thomas J. Jackson (Left Wing Commander)
MG James Longstreet (Right Wing Commander)
BG J. E. B. Stuart (Cavalry Commander)

Antietam (September 17, 1862)

Union

MG George B. McClellan (Commander, Army of the Potomac)
MG Joseph Hooker (I Corps Commander)
MG Edwin V. Sumner (II Corps)
MG Fitz John Porter (V Corps)
MG William B. Franklin (VI Corps)
MG Ambrose Burnside (IX Corps)
MG Joseph K. Mansfield (XII Corps)
(These Corps contained 19 Divisions)

Confederate

General Robert E. Lee (Commander, Army of Northern Virginia)
MG James Longstreet (I Corps Commander)
MG Lafayette McLaws (Division Commander)
MG Richard H. Anderson (Division Commander)
BG David R. Jones (Division Commander)
BG John G. Walker (Division Commander)
BG John Bell Hood (Division Commander)
MG Thomas J. Jackson (II Corps Commander)
MG D. H. Hill (Division Commander)
MG A. P. Hill (Division Commander)
BG Alexander R. Lawton (Division Commander)
BG John R. Jones (Division Commander)
BG J. E. B. Stuart (Cavalry Commander)

APPENDIX B

THE VIRGINIA & KENTUCKY RESOLUTIONS

by Thomas Jefferson & James Madison, 1798

OCTOBER, 1798

1. Resolved, That the several States composing the United States of America; are not united on the principle of unlimited submission to their General Government; but that, by a compact under the style and title of a Constitution for the United States, and of amendments thereto, they constituted a General Government for special purposes, -- delegated to that government certain definite powers, reserving, each State to itself, the residuary mass of right to their own self-government; and that whensoever the General Government assumes undelegated powers, its acts are unauthoritative, void, and of no force: that to this compact each State acceded as a State, and is an integral party, its co-States forming, as to itself, the other party: that the government created by this compact was not made the exclusive or final judge of the extent of the powers delegated to itself; since that would have made its discretion, and not the Constitution, the measure of its powers; but that, as in all other cases of compact among powers having no common judge, each party has an equal right to judge for itself, as well of infractions as of the mode and measure of redress.

2. Resolved, That the Constitution of the United States, having delegated to Congress a power to punish treason, counterfeiting the securities and current coin of the United States, piracies, and felonies committed on the high seas, and offences against the law of nations, and no other crimes whatsoever; and it being true as a general principle, and one of the amendments to the Constitution having also declared, that "the powers not delegated to the United States by the Constitution, nor prohibited by it to the States, are reserved to the States respectively, or to the people," therefore the act of Congress, passed on the 14th day of June, 1798, and intituled "An Act for the punishment of certain crimes against the United States," as also the act passed by them on the -- day of June, 1798, intitled "An Act to punish frauds committed on the bank of the United States," (and all their other acts which assume to create, define, and punish such other crimes is reserved, and, of right, appertains solely and exclusively to the respective States, each within its own territory.

3. Resolved, That it is true as a general principle, and is also expressly declared by one of the amendments to the Constitution, that "the powers not delegated to the United States by the Constitution, nor prohibited to it by the States, are reserved to the States respectively, or to the people;" and that no power over the freedom of religion, freedom of speech, or freedom of the press being delegated to the United States by the Constitution, not prohibited by it to the States, all lawful powers respecting the same did of right remain, and were reserved to the States or the people: that thus was manifested their determination to retain to themselves the right of judging how far the licentiousness of speech and of the press may be abridged without lessening their useful freedom, and how far these abuses which cannot be separated from their use should be tolerated, rather than the use be destroyed. And thus also they guarded against all abridgment by the United States of the freedom of religious opinions and exercises, and retained to themselves the right of protecting the same, as this State, by a law passed on the general demand of its citizens, had already protected them from human restraint or interference. And that in addition to this general principle and express declaration, another and more special provision has been made by one of the amendments to the Constitution, which expressly declares, that "Congress shall make no law respecting an establishment of religion, or prohibiting the free exercise thereof, or abridging the freedom of speech or of the press:" thereby guarding in the same sentence, and under the same words, the freedom of religion, of speech, and of the press: insomuch, that whatever violated either, throws down the sanctuary which covers the others, and that libels, falsehood and defamation, equally with heresy and false religion, are withheld from the cognizance of federal tribunals. That, therefore, the act of Congress of the United States, passed on the 14th day July, 1798, intituled An Act for the punishment of certain crimes against the United States," which does abridge the freedom of the press, is not law, but is altogether void, and of no force.

4. Resolved, That alien friends are under the jurisdiction and protection of the laws of the State wherein they are: that no power over them has been delegated to the United States, nor prohibited to the individual States, distinct from their power over citizens. And it being true as a general principle, and one of the amendments to the Constitution having also declared, that "the powers not delegated to the United States by the Constitution, nor prohibited by it to the States, are reserved to the States respectively, or to the people," the act of Congress of the United States, passed on the -- day of July, 1798, intituled "An Act concerning aliens," which assumes powers over alien friends, not delegated by the Constitution, is not law, but is altogether void, and of no force.

5. Resolved, That in addition to the general principle, as well as the express declaration, that powers not delegated are reserved, another and more special provision, inserted in the Constitution from abundant caution, has declared that "the migration of importation of such persons as any of the States now existing shall think proper to admit, shall not be prohibited by the Congress prior to the year 1808;" that this commonwealth does admit the migration of alien friends, described as the subject of the said act concerning aliens: that a provision against prohibiting their migration, is a provision against all acts equivalent thereto, or it would be nugatory: that to remove them when migrated, is equivalent to a prohibition of their migration, and is, therefore, contrary to the said provision of the Constitution, and void.

6. Resolved, That the imprisonment of a person under the protection of the laws of this commonwealth, on his failure to obey the simple order of the President to depart out of the United States, as is undertaken by said act intituled "An Act concerning aliens," is contrary to the Constitution, one amendment to which has provided that "no person shall be deprived of liberty without due process of law;" and that another having provided that "in all criminal prosecutions the accused shall enjoy the right to public trial by an impartial jury, to be informed of the nature and cause of the accusation, to be confronted with the witnesses against him, to have compulsory process for obtaining witnesses in his favor, and to have the assistance of counsel for his defence," the same act, undertaking to authorize the President to remove a person out of the United States, who is under the protection of the law, on his own suspicion, without accusation, without jury, without public trial, without confrontation of the witnesses against him, without hearing witnesses in his favor, without defence, without counsel, is contrary to the provision also of the Constitution, is therefore not law, but utterly void, and of no force: that transferring the power of judging any person, who is under the protection of the laws, from the courts to the President of the United States, as is undertaken by the same act concerning aliens, is against the article of the Constitution which provides that "the judicial power of the United States shall be vested in courts, the judges of which shall hold their offices during good behavior;" and that the said act is void for that reason also. And it is further to be noted, that this transfer of judiciary power is to that magistrate of the General Government who already possesses all the Executive, and a negative on all legislative powers.

7. **Resolved**, That the construction applied by the General Government (as is evidenced by sundry of their proceedings) to those parts of the Constitution of the United States which delegate to Congress a power "to lay and collect taxes, duties, imports, and excises, to pay the debts, and provide for the common defence and general welfare of the United States," and "to make all laws which shall be necessary and proper for carrying into execution the powers vested by the Constitution in the government of the United States, or in any department or officer thereof," goes to the destruction of all limits prescribed to their power by the Constitution: that words meant by the instrument to be subsidiary only to the execution of limited powers, ought not to be so construed as themselves to give unlimited powers, nor a part to be so taken as to destroy the whole residue of that instrument: that the proceeds of the General Government under color of these articles will be a fit and necessary subject of revisal and correction, at a time of greater tranquillity, while those specified in the preceding resolutions call for immediate redress.

8. **Resolved**, That a committee of conference and correspondence be appointed, who shall have in charge to communicate the preceding resolutions to the legislatures of the several States; to assure them that this commonwealth continues in the same esteem of their friendship and union which it has manifested from that moment at which a common danger first

suggested a common union: that it considers union, for specified national purposes, and particularly to those specified in their late federal compact, to be friendly to the peace, happiness and prosperity of all the States: that faithful to that compact, according to the plain intent and meaning in which it was understood and acceded to by the several parties, it is sincerely anxious for its preservation: that it does also believe, that to take from the States all the powers of self-government and without regard to the special delegations and reservations solemnly agreed to in that compact, is not for the peace, happiness or prosperity of these States; and that therefore this commonwealth is determined, and consequently unlimited powers in no man, or body of men on earth: that in cases of an abuse of the delegated powers, the members of the General government, being chosen by the people, a change by the people would be the constitutional remedy; but, where powers are assumed which have not been delegated, a nullification of the act is the rightful remedy: that every State has a natural right in cases not within the compact, (casus non foederis,) to nullify of their own authority all assumptions of power by others within their limits: that without this right, they would be under the domination, absolute and unlimited, of whosoever might exercise this right of judgment for them: that nevertheless, this commonwealth, from motives of regard and respect for its co-States, has wished to communicate with them on the subject: that with them alone it is proper to communicate, they alone being parties to the compact, and solely authorized to judge in the last resort of the powers exercised under it, Congress being not a party, but merely the creature of the compact, and subject as to its assumptions of power to the final judgment of those by whom, and for whose use itself and its powers were all created and modified: that if the acts before specified should stand, these conclusions would flow from them: that the General government may place any act they think proper on the list of crimes, and punish it themselves whether enumerated or not enumerated by the Constitution as cognizable by them: that they may transfer its cognizance to the President, or any other person, who may himself be the accuser, counsel, judge and jury, whose suspicions may be the evidence, his order the sentence, his officer the executioner, and his breast the sole record of the transaction: that a very numerous and valuable description of the inhabitants of these States being, by this precedent, reduced, as outlaws, to the absolute dominion of one man, and the barrier of the Constitution thus swept away from us all, no rampart now remains against the passions and the powers of a majority in Congress to protect from a like exportation, or other more grievous punishment, the minority of the same body, the legislatures, judges, governors, and counselors of the States, nor their other peaceable inhabitants, who may venture to reclaim the constitutional rights and liberties of the States and people, or who for other causes, good or bad, may be obnoxious to the views, or marked by the suspicions of the President, or be thought dangerous to his or their election, or other interests, public or personal: that the friendless alien has indeed been selected as the safest subject of a first experiment; but the citizen will soon follow, or rather, has already followed, for already has a sedition act marked him as its prey: that these and successive acts of the same character, unless arrested at the threshold, necessarily drive these States into revolution and blood, and will furnish new calumnies against republican government, and new pretexts for those who wish it to be believed that man cannot be governed but by a rod of iron: that it would be a dangerous delusion were a confidence in the men of our choice to silence our fears for the safety of our rights: that confidence is everywhere the parent of despotism -- free government is founded in jealousy, and not in confidence; it is jealousy and not confidence which prescribes limited constitutions, to bind down those whom we are obliged to trust with power: that our Constitution has accordingly fixed the limits to which, and no further, our confidence may go; and let the honest advocate of confidence read the alien and sedition acts, and say if the Constitution has not been wise in fixing limits to the government it created, and whether we should be wise in destroying those limits. Let him say what the government is, if it be not a tyranny, which the men of our choice have conferred on our President, and the President of our choice has assented to, and accepted over the friendly strangers to whom the mild spirit of our country and its laws have pledged hospitality and protection: that the men of our choice have more respected the bare suspicions of the President, than the solid right of innocence, the claims of justification, the sacred force of truth, and the forms and substance of law and justice. In questions of power, then, let no more be heard of confidence in man, but bind him down from mischief by the chains of the Constitution. That this commonwealth does therefore call on its co-States for an expression of their sentiments on the acts concerning aliens, and for the punishment of certain crimes herein before specified, plainly declaring whether these acts are or are not authorized by the federal compact. And it doubts not that their sense will be so announced as to prove their attachment unaltered to limited government, whether general or particular. And that the rights and liberties of their co-States will be exposed to no dangers by remaining embarked in a common bottom with their own. That they will concur with this commonwealth in considering the said acts as so palpably against the Constitution as to amount to an undisguised declaration that that compact is not meant to be the measure of the powers of the General Government, but that it will proceed in the exercise over these States, of all powers whatsoever: that they will view this as seizing the rights of the States, and consolidating them in the hands of the General Government, with a power assumed to bind the States, (not merely as the cases made federal, (casus foederis,) but in all cases whatsoever, by laws made, not with their consent, but by others against their consent: that this would be to surrender the form of government we have chosen, and live under one deriving its powers from its own will, and not from our authority; and that the co-States, recurring to their natural right in cases not made federal, will concur in declaring these acts void, and of no force, and will each take measures of its own for providing that neither these acts, nor any others of the General Government not plainly and intentionally authorized by the Constitution, shall be exercised within their respective territories.

9. Resolved, That the said committee be authorized to communicate by writing or personal conferences, at any times or places whatever, with any person or persons who may be appointed by any one or more co-States to correspond or confer with them; and that they lay their proceedings before the next session of Assembly.

Appendix C

BOOK CLUB QUESTIONS

1. Why does Virginia secede from the Union?

2. In Part Two, do Conrad Montgomery and Lawrence Crawford have good arguments why the North should not have invaded the South? Why or why not?

3. Why did the Battle of Manassas end in such a disaster?

4. In Part Four, who do you think had the stronger argument, Mrs. Claire Montgomery or Union General Alpheus Williams? Why?

5. Should Stonewall Jackson have invaded Kernstown? Why or why not?

6. Why did the Peacheys say they did not participate in government? Is this view still held by a lot of people today? What do you think of this view?

7. Does the author give a fair representation of both the Union and the Confederate positions?

8. Why does Molly run away from home? Why do you think her family didn't do more to rescue her?

9. Which side won the Battle of Antietam? Why, after the conclusion of the battle, were leaders on both sides frustrated?

10. What is true about the main characters in Chapter One "Innocence" that remains true throughout the book when they are adults?

11. Should Lincoln have disciplined General George McClellan after the Battle of Second Manassas?

12. Who is the greatest hero or heroine of the book? Who makes you the most mad?

13. How does what happens to Riley at the end of the book make you feel?

14. Have you ever met anyone like Rachel Jones or like George McClellan? Please describe.

15. Overall, who was your favorite character and why?

16. What are some things you learned about the Civil War that you didn't know before you read *In Danger Every Hour*?

17. What do you hope happens if there is a sequel?

SPECIAL THANKS

To my wife Lauri, who helped me from start to finish. To Nickolas, Madison, Hannah and Isaiah who were patient while I wrote. To Lori Shaw, for all of her fine tuning. Also, to Pam Baker, Jenny Ferson, Rebecca Lara, Jimmy Shaw, Ellen Vinzant and Vicki Zimmer for their willingness to donate hours helping with this project. Lastly, to my dad, a retired Army chaplain, who taught me the value of serving the Master.